Wild Card

An Amber Farrell Novel
Book 3 of the
Bite Back series

by
Mark Henwick

Published by *Marque*

Series schedule, reviews & news on
www.athanate.com

Bite Back 3 : Wild Card
ISBN: 978-1-912499-15-1

First published in December 2014 by Marque

Mark Henwick asserts the right to be identified as the author of this work.

Cover design: CreativeEdge, Andrew Dobell
Cover model: Maria Askew

Author's note:

Asian names:
Throughout this series, I use the Western sequence (First, Middle, Last Name) to depict names, so as to match with the majority of characters in the books. Most Asian societies would put the Last Name first.

AMZ240916

Chapter 1

MONDAY

She walked bravely for a woman who was going to her death.

She was dressed simply, with a warm ski jacket, and jeans tucked into flat-heeled boots. Her platinum blonde hair was caught up in a pony tail, which swung jauntily, jarringly at odds with her situation.

It took tremendous courage or bewildering stupidity to do what she was doing.

It was 3 a.m., the streets were empty and this was not one of Denver's thriving areas. Some of the streetlights still worked, edging everything in baleful, sodium yellow. Small businesses lined the street, bolted and locked down, steel shutters like indifferent eyes closed against the night. Telephone wires, draped from pole to pole across the road, swung idly in the wind. Dark alleys sighed with fetid smells, trash spilling out into the hard light. Only two cars had passed in the last ten minutes, and no one else was on the streets.

Not a place for a woman to walk on her own.

But she knew she wasn't alone, of course. She'd been instructed to walk without looking back; she would know someone was behind her. And she knew who it had to be. She knew she was being stalked by a monster.

What could she possibly want that was worth the risk?

Or was this another trap?

If it wasn't, I would listen. I had promised; I would listen first. My nails dug into my hands. My boot heels clicked on the sidewalk.

And if it was a trap, I'd take them to hell with me.

Meanwhile, I listened to the voices whispering in my head. Just sounds, I said to myself, not people, not anyone who might end up dead on my watch. Between the hissing came street names, junctions, all within a block, keeping pace with us.

Enough. It was time.

"Call it," I whispered, and my voices answered.

"Clear on your two."

"Clear four."

A pause. My adrenaline surged, but eventually the report came. "Clear on your six and two in place."

"Clear eight," followed immediately.

"Clear ten."

"Clear twelve." Even through the comms, the last voice was smooth and deep, like rocks in a river rolling together. I could banish the images of everyone else, but Victor Gayle's voice was too demanding. It didn't bring to mind the image of him now, somewhere out in front of me, ghosting through the night and seeking out the trap I feared must be there. It forced me to see the image of him earlier, sweat and tears glistening on his dark skin, comforting the families of Reynolds and Zimmerman while the sheriff's people argued with the FBI over jurisdiction of the bodies. Two of his men who'd died trying to protect Jennifer Kingslund, when Frank Hoben and his gang broke into Manassah. Two whose deaths I might have prevented.

After that, I felt sick over asking him to provide people tonight, but not only did he do it, he insisted on coming as well.

"We good to go?" he asked me.

"Go," I said. I called the woman's cell, watched her reach into the pocket of her ski jacket, hold it to her ear. My voice thickened until I had to force the words out. "A van will pull up. Get in the back. Do what they say."

The van rolled past me, glossy midnight blue, its powerful engine muted, quieter than the rumble of the tires. A block ahead, it slowed alongside her.

The door opened. For a second, she held off, as if she'd started to have doubts. It was way too late for that. Arms snapped out, catching her, and she vanished inside. The van accelerated away just as a Dodge pulled alongside me.

"Call it," I said again as I got into the Dodge, and the voices whispered the even stations of the clock, still all clear.

Then a final, "Tango secure. Comms and tracking clear," from the van. Target secured—restrained in the back of the van. No suspicious activity on comms channels. Apart from ours, of course. No tracking devices found on the target.

She was clean and we were clear.

"Team Sierra, go home," I said, and felt the pressure lighten as the outriding scouts disconnected and went away.

We stopped to let Victor swap with the Dodge's driver, who walked off briskly without looking back. There was no sign of a trap yet, but regardless, that was one more safe. One less to worry about, I hoped.

"Hey," Victor said quietly as we pulled away.

I reached over and squeezed his thick forearm. I said into the comms, "Phase one, complete. Phase two, green." First part of the mission successful, target secured and scouts away, phase two commencing. I took a deep breath and picked a number. "Mike Papa three, in five. Out."

I watched silently as Victor hauled the car around.

Just before the Platte River bridge, we pulled off into a side road lined with commercial properties. My randomly selected meeting place, the third of four possibilities I had set up. We turned in at a fading 'For Rent' sign and parked around the back. Two minutes later, the van pulled in alongside us.

Hillary Clinton and George Bush came out the side door and helped the driver swap the plates.

We got out; they tossed their masks and the old plates into the Dodge's trunk. Victor gave them a nod as they took our places. We watched them drive away.

The van sat there, engine turning over. It looked crouched over its wheels, squat and dark, pointing down a path I hadn't wanted to take. My heart rate was already climbing. I rubbed my hands together, feeling as if I needed another shower.

"You sure?" Victor said. His hand rested on my shoulder—the right shoulder, fortunately. The left shoulder was still recovering from Hoben's bullet at the factory in Longmont. At least the Kevlar vest had absorbed most of the damage.

Victor was frowning at me. I could feel all the questions building behind the concern, and I could do nothing about it. Not now; maybe not ever.

My stomach was churning, but I nodded. "Platte River Road," I said. "Up and down. Nice and slow."

River on one side, industry on the other. No one to hear. No one to see. No one to know.

I slid the panel door open and stepped inside, slamming it closed behind me. It was pitch black and she was effectively blind. Even the Athanate would have difficulty seeing in here, but I wasn't just Athanate. I was becoming Were as well, and werewolf abilities were bleeding into me. I could see a little into the infrared spectrum. Certainly I could see well enough to know she wasn't struggling as she lay there, trussed up like a chicken. It wasn't that she was calm. She was scared, as she should be—her breath shallow around the gag and her heart racing—but she knew struggling wasn't going to achieve anything, and Ops 4-10 kept no dummies.

The van rocked on its stiff suspension as Victor drove us out, back onto the road.

I sat facing her, cross-legged on the floor, waves of anger flowing through me.

My old covert army unit, Ops 4-10, had come after me. The same unit I'd given heart and soul to for ten years. They'd sent a team with Keith, my ex-boyfriend of all people, to snatch me off the streets last Friday and take me back to their scientific group, Obs. As far as Obs were concerned, once I'd been bitten by what they still called a vampire, I'd become a freak, an object to study, and I didn't need basic human considerations.

They'd have my old cell ready for me—a bleak, windowless cubicle, where I'd never see the sun again. I'd sworn I wouldn't go back, and when Keith's team tried to catch me, I'd called in the FBI. They had a team investigating military units where the Defense Department had lost oversight, and Ops 4-10 had become exactly that. Or worse.

Keith and the rest of his team had been rounded up and were guests of the FBI.

And now this. Another member of Ops 4-10, trying to draw me out.

The wolf had become very strong in me. Last week I'd felt the first ripples of the potential to change form when I'd been attacked in an alley. Now? Now, it felt like there were claws scratching at me from the inside. I wanted to growl; I wanted to seize her by the throat, bite hard and taste her life blood.

I was fighting myself to hold it together, to push the wolf back down.

After a long couple of minutes, I felt stable enough to reach out and remove her gag.

I took a breath, forcing my voice to stay calm and even. I still sounded like a complete stranger.

"Hello, Julie," I said.

Chapter 2

"Amber?" she said hoarsely. I could see her eyes straining to make me out.

I didn't reply. The van turned and Victor drove slowly onto the riverside road.

She tried again. "Is he all right?"

Now that was an interesting start. Of course I knew who she meant.

"Keith is fine. Your husband's in a nice, comfortable cell. In the morning he'll probably have a nice, comfortable chat with a state-appointed lawyer. Hey, maybe read a book, catch up on some TV. That'll go on till the army claims him and explains what the hell he was doing, or he gets sentenced for attempted kidnapping." Talking eased my throat a little, but it tightened up again as I went on. "Not exactly the cushy confinement I would have been enjoying, if his little trap had been successful."

"You said you'd listen to me," she said. Voice steady; keeping the discussion on track. Top—our training sergeant—would have been proud of her.

"You've got cast-iron balls, Julie, unless you don't know what happened for some reason."

"I know what really happened," she said. "Are you ready to hear the truth? Or would you rather rant a while longer?"

I had to give her props for that. It was a calculated insult, designed to defuse any righteous emotion I was building up and guide me back to what she wanted to talk about. Even knowing the tactics she was using, I couldn't let it pass unchallenged.

"I already know a hell of a lot," I snapped. "I know Keith was on an official 4-10 operation to pull me in and chuck me back into the cells for Obs to run tests on. I know he called me to the trap. I know he used bait that guaranteed I'd turn up. I know he was in charge. Seems to me, I know enough."

I could have put the light on, let her sit up. I could have made it easier for her. But I didn't want to. I couldn't say I was enjoying this, but it felt as if this was something I needed. Julie was standing in for all the army people who'd betrayed me. She was Ops 4-10. The least she deserved was to damn well squirm a bit. The most? Well, I hadn't gotten that far. Yet.

"You know the facts, but you don't understand anything," she said. "It wasn't—"

"I don't understand?" I grabbed her hair and pulled her head up in the darkness. "You're right, I don't understand. When I last saw Keith, he said none of my buddies in 4-10 would ever come after me. Didn't matter who was running the unit. Didn't matter what they said. None of them. And you know what?" I shook her. "I believed him."

"It wasn't 4-10," she said.

That stopped me. As she intended.

"Then who the—"

"4-16."

Unbelievable. I let the silence stretch. My senses told me she was calmer now that she'd gotten that out. And my gut said she wasn't lying. The problem was, I wasn't sure where old human instincts about someone lying ended, and Athanate senses took over.

I'd gone through both sides of interrogation training under that son-of-a-bitch instructor, Ben-Haim. Trouble was, so had Julie.

What if my Athanate senses weren't working yet? We both knew how to fake it in the short term with a human interrogator.

Whatever they say in books and movies, no one fakes it in the long term.

If Julie was faking it, did that mean she expected to be rescued? Victor's team had professional scanners that said she was clean, and anyway, this truck was shielded. No one was following any electronic beeps from Julie. So had she miscalculated?

Or were we simply being visually tracked from a silent nightflier? The Ops group had them.

This was like playing chess in three dimensions. And I didn't have time. Especially if Ops 4-16 were after me.

She'd called them 4-16, their official name. We almost never called them that. To us they were the Nagas, the headhunters. If you passed the physical training, but didn't make it into Ops 4-10, you got looked over by the Nagas. As a sergeant responsible for washing out some of those recruits, I was dismayed to see the ones that the Nagas took on. They didn't take anyone with any physical or skill problems, but they sure as hell had taken recruits I'd regarded as mentally or morally unfit. But as much as we were separate from the regular army, the Nagas were separate from us. I didn't know what they did or how they did it. But would I want to be captured by them?

Hell, no.

I had to know what I faced and be absolutely sure that the information I had was true. How to do it? Torture wouldn't work in the time I had, and I wasn't ready to become that person.

But there were other techniques both Julie and I knew.

I'm in restraints, electrodes taped all over me, fighting to keep calm. Ben-Haim's face is inches from mine. His eyes are clear, rested. There's beer on his breath. Utter silence in the darkened room. He is showing me deliberately that he is fed, relaxed and in control, and that I am alone.

"Everyone has a weak point. Everyone."

He waits a whole minute. Behind me, a tap drips monotonously.

"We're going to talk about the time before you joined the army. We will step back. Little steps. A day. A week..."

I shook the vision from my head and jerked Julie closer.

"Let's talk about Keith's decision process that ended with him leading a team to kidnap me, Julie. Does he feel responsible for me being out here? Because that's one explanation for the cute little toy that my friends in the feds tell me was in his pocket. You know the one I mean. You are married to him, after all. What is it he calls it...oh, yeah, the Insurance Policy." I shook her so her teeth rattled. "Ruger .22 snub, with soft nose bullets."

I threw her back on the floor, so angry I felt sick to my stomach, just as I had felt when Ingram called me and laconically read through the list of equipment.

The Ruger wasn't standard issue. It was a tiny polymer revolver that Keith carried for backup on certain types of operations. A girl's gun, I'd teased him in different times, long ago. Back when we'd been an item.

He'd used it twice to my knowledge. Both times in crowds, both times without even drawing it, fired through his jacket. No one had noticed anything. Except the targets. Briefly.

I counted backwards, concentrated on my breathing. I was losing this, and I'd keep losing it until I controlled myself.

Julie could tell I was off balance. "Of course I knew he took it," she came back scornfully. "And he would have used it, if you'd been stupid enough to fall into the trap. Or damaged enough."

Damaged? She was trying to divert me, to take control again.

"Great. We've covered Keith," I snarled at her. "Now, explain why you're here in Denver and asking to meet me. And Julie," I yanked her head up again, "just in case you've forgotten, I'm not human anymore. I can tell when you're lying."

That got a reaction. I could smell the sweat, sense her heartbeat going up a notch. Good.

"No lies, Amber."

I let her wriggle around to sit up against the bulkhead.

I didn't help her and I left the light off.

She took a slow breath, and began. "Colonel Petersen used to run 4-16. Now he runs both units. He categorized you as a code red security breach and formed a team from the Nagas to snatch you. But he had to come to 4-10 to find a volunteer who knew you to run the team. Keith took it. He got everyone else to stand down, so Petersen had to go with him."

This is supposed to make me feel better?

"There wasn't any way to get a message to you in time. We both tried calling. You weren't picking up," she said.

"What the hell are you trying to say?"

"Amber, you're good. You were one of the best. But do you honestly believe you'd stand a chance if a team of us really came for you?"

Point.

"Are you telling me he deliberately messed it up?"

"Of course he did." Her voice was steady. Only her heartbeat betrayed her. She didn't realize it, but I could almost hear the blood pounding in her veins; I could see the way her eyes strained to try and see me in the dark.

The van's tires rumbled noisily over some broken pavement before settling down to a steady hum again.

Keith *had* sounded odd when he'd called me. He'd mentioned Colonel Laine, and maybe he'd guessed that Laine had already been in contact with me. Was that a warning?

Then the trap was set up next to the Convention Center, with a hundred ways for me to approach unseen and become suspicious.

He'd been wired for sound, so he couldn't have warned me by speaking.

And what about the look on his face? Had it been relief when the FBI sprang my trap?

Maybe, maybe, maybe. How much did I want it to be true? Backtrack, trip her up.

"That doesn't explain the gun," I said.

"No." Her heart rate soared. "That was for real. If you walked into the trap. He thought it was what you'd want, given the alternative. If you understood what the alternative was."

The 'alternative'. A cell beneath the Obs laboratory. But surely Keith and Julie didn't know about that. Why would they think I'd rather be shot than taken back? And what had she meant, before, by 'damaged'?

Was she just distracting me again?

I had skills I had to use. Even if my Athanate senses weren't functioning properly, I could hear her pulse, and no one can control all their automatic responses. I could smell lies. I just had to put the right stress on her. I moved silently across the van.

"Tell me," I hissed close to her ear, making her jump. "Tell me what you think the alternative was. What you think would happen if I was taken."

"They'd take you back into Obs." She stopped. Was that the limit of her knowledge, or was she reluctant to go on?

"That's my personal nightmare, all right," I said. "But it's worse than that. Kidnap me or shoot me—either way, you'd have practically declared war on the Athanate."

She didn't know the word. Colonel Laine must have kept my briefings secret. I liked that. I felt it gave me an edge, and everything about her was clearer now I was up close. I could taste her puzzlement. I crouched over her, inhaling every stray molecule that escaped from her. I could smell her shampoo, the soap she'd used in her last shower, the detergent she'd used for her clothes. I could read the smallest changes in her. I had complete control.

"Athanate, Julie. Not vampires, Athanate. Living people. People who feel emotions just like humans." I let my breath touch her neck and felt her shy away. "People who drink blood. People who can tell if you're lying. People like me."

What the hell was I doing?

I could feel my jaw loosening and my fangs getting ready to appear. I'd pushed the wolf down only for the Athanate to take over.

Threatening Julie was teasing my own Athanate thirst. Diana and Skylur had warned me against biting. My unstable hybrid mix of paranormal was dangerous enough for me—they thought I still might go rogue. But I'd had time to adjust; I stood a chance of being able to pull through. It would be far worse for someone I infused—and I didn't yet know how to bite someone without the risk of infusing them. I *had* to restrain myself until Diana could mentor me to control my instinct to infuse, and test the outcome. I had to.

That was the future. But right now, I had to know if Julie was on the level.

"Are you lying to me, Julie?" I murmured.

"No." With me so close—biting distance—she was walking the ragged edge of fear. I reached out and snapped the light on. A fluorescent tube fixed to the ceiling flooded the van with harsh light and deep shadows.

The sight of me looming over her didn't make her any less afraid, but she managed to keep still. Her breath came quickly, but her eyes were steady. One tough woman.

Why was I doing this? Truthfully, I was afraid it was because I didn't want to believe her. I didn't want to make her separate from all the shit that had been thrown at me. I wanted someone to hurt the way I hurt. And I wanted to feel that pain coursing through her, to breathe it in. To taste it.

I gripped her hair and stared into her eyes. She was still trying to force her heart rate down. Failing. I pulled her head back, exposing her throat. A shiver slid through her, quickly suppressed. A growing awareness. She'd made a judgment call on a person called Amber Farrell, a person she'd known in Ops 4-10. A judgment call that she'd be safe with that person.

She was now grasping at an instinctive level what she'd known only as words before. I *wasn't* fully human any more. I wasn't the Amber she'd known.

Her hindbrain was kicking and twisting to escape, but she fought to keep control. Impressive.

I could hear her Blood coursing through her neck, just inches away. I could smell it, I could feel it, I could almost taste it. My teeth pulsed with eagerness.

I reached with my other hand, sliding it down her left arm to where her wrists were bound behind her.

"Amber. Please don't," she said. Not so controlled now.

My fingers rippled over the bindings, brushed the back of her hand.

"Are you here for Petersen? Is this some kind of a trap?" I whispered.

"No." Her head shook once, abruptly.

My fangs manifested, grazing her skin sensuously, and I felt my jaws go loose and heavy with anticipation. The lightest pressure and her skin would part.

A wordless cry built up inside me, leaked through my control. The pulse in her neck thudded against my fangs.

She lost it, over the edge into the abyss. Panicked, she twisted beneath me, arching away. Terror billowed out of her and caressed me like silk. It was sweet as warm syrup on my dry lips, perfume to my nose. There was fear, sweat, soap, even the aroma of fajitas she'd eaten for dinner six hours ago. But no hint of lies. I swallowed painfully, tried to close my mouth.

I threw my weight on her, my hands moving snakelike to her bound hands. My fingers found hers. Third finger. Ring. Rings, two of them. She wasn't on a 4-10 mission. Standard Ops 4-10 operating procedure: no identifying marks, no jewelry, no ID. Or they'd gotten a whole lot smarter about it all.

No. No. She wasn't lying. She hadn't lied about anything.

Enough, for God's sake, Amber! Stop it!

I wrenched myself away, twisting around and curling up on the floor with my face hidden in my hands. What the hell had I been thinking? The taste of sweetness changed to cloying, tongue-curling foul and I fought to stop myself from throwing up.

Victor turned the van around and began to drive back the way we'd come.

It was very quiet in the back. Eventually my gut stopped heaving, and I was left feeling drained and shaky.

I pulled myself upright, leaned back. Sweat cooled my skin.

Julie, too, was gathering herself. "Are you all right?" she asked finally.

I laughed bitterly. "I should be asking you. I'm sorry. Kinda ran away with me there."

There was a pause. "Is it that hard, to not..."

"Is it that hard to not bite? Sometimes." But that wasn't the problem. I shut up. I couldn't explain to her without going into a whole load of things that weren't relevant and which she would have trouble understanding. And which I didn't want to admit to, because they scared the hell out of me. I couldn't explain that my wolf and my Athanate seemed to be spurring each other on, and that I'd just started to feed on her fear.

Like a Basilikos Athanate.

I'd sworn I wouldn't go that route. I was becoming Athanate and the road split right before me, right now. Go down the Basilikos path and I might convince myself it was all right to prey on humans and feed on fear. Which was why I'd made Diana swear to kill me if I did.

Just how close would she allow me to get?

I grabbed the cutters from the tool compartment, fumbling them, my hands shaking with reaction. "Turn around," I said.

She studied me for a moment, eyes narrowed, before turning her back to me. Brave woman. I clumsily cut the cable ties binding her hands and feet.

Then I retreated and sat against the side of the van, deliberately not looking at her.

I didn't need this, whatever it was that Julie wanted to dump on me.

More problems just sprang up every which way I turned. No one, me included, could work out what the hell I was. Athanate, Were and Adept all mixed together. Each type had its dangers, and everyone warned me the influence of the others would make the dangers worse. I was scared to let any paranormal persona take over and even more scared I wouldn't be able to prevent it.

I had just seen an example of the threat—Were struggling with Athanate—and the worst possible result. What if next time, it wasn't Julie, but Alex or Jen I wanted to bite? Could I hold off?

My gut wrenched at the thought of Alex and Jen, afraid of what I might do to them. And wrenched again at the thought of losing them because of that.

I really couldn't afford to get messed up with whatever problems Julie had thought she'd bring to me, not even something as 'simple' as springing Keith. But I'd said I'd listen.

I concentrated on slow breathing, hunting for at least a bit of calm, if serenity was completely out of the question.

"You didn't finish on Obs," I said finally. "And you didn't finish explaining the reason for that Ruger either."

Julie cleared her throat. Her heart rate spiked back up.

"I don't suppose you'd let me tie you up first?" she said.

I almost smiled. "Don't get smart." For a moment, the last couple of years fell away, and we were just two soldiers doing a difficult job and sharing a bit of dark humor. I'd missed the easy camaraderie. But then again, I'd also missed some bad times for 4-10 as well, from the sound of it.

"Not much of a joke, really." She stirred, unconsciously easing herself away from me. "I don't know what effect this is going to have on you."

I frowned at her.

"You've got to understand first what's gone wrong with 4-10," she said. "Not with the people on the ground, with the command structure. People like Petersen." She paused. "When this operation came up, it was the last straw. We were afraid the whole command had gone over to the dark side. So Keith and I went looking for information."

"You think I'm going to be upset because you've been bucking the chain of command? What did you do? Break into his office?"

"It wasn't that," she snapped. So they had broken into his office. Must have been ultra-careful.

"It was what we found," she went on, more quietly. "You don't remember much for a while after they got you back from South America, do you?"

"Some." I was about to go on and say that it was only to be expected, an aftereffect of being bitten. But then I realized that no one from Altau had ever said anything to me about memory lapses after being infused. The Altau might purposely screw with your memory, but that was something else entirely.

How much had I forgotten?

Julie watched me as my mouth opened and closed a couple of times.

It was like trying to see something in your blind spot. You know it's there. You can't quite catch it.

I could remember Petersen making me sign an agreement, and Colonel Laine coming in later, telling me he'd taken over Obs. I could remember after that point. Before that? Flickers. Jumbled sounds and smells and tastes and images, without a thread to connect them. And my mind sliding away as I tried.

Who had been running Obs before Colonel Laine arrived? Petersen? My skin crawled.

Why hadn't I thought about it? Why was it so difficult to think about it?

What had Judicator Remy said at the Assembly? He'd said he detected evidence of mental blocks in my head. Remy's conclusions about me were false, forced on him by Basilikos, but that didn't mean he'd made up his evidence. I hadn't dismissed his talk of blocks, but I'd thought maybe there were things I had done to myself. Strong places in my head for memories I wanted locked away. A stomach-sickening lurch accompanied that thought and I stamped down on it.

"They screwed with your head, Amber," Julie whispered carefully. "When Colonel Laine was about to take over Obs, they closed it all up, sure they'd get their hands on you again soon."

Now my heart was racing. When Keith had yelled out something like that to me as he was arrested, I'd gone and gotten drunk. Why? What was there? What made me not want to confront it?

"But Laine put a new team into Obs and sent you out here to Denver," Julie went on remorselessly. "He became suspicious of what they'd done. They knew he was on to them, but they have support he doesn't. That's why he's running now."

Things clicked into place. The feeling that the colonel was always giving me extra leeway. In truth, he was doing whatever he could to keep me away from the base and Petersen while he figured out what had been done to me.

"But it's been too long. Whatever they did to hide what was done to you was supposed to be a temporary fix. They think it might be about to fail. They don't know what'll happen." She paused. "And the catch is, my telling you about it might speed that up."

"And what were they trying to do?" I asked. I felt cold and remote. My wrist itched where my bracelet sat. The bracelet was a gift from the Adepts. It was intended to warn me of danger, but it'd gotten a little freaky over the last couple of days.

The van stopped and I tensed up. Victor knocked on the door panel.

I moved across and knelt by the door. "Yeah?"

"Things movin'," he said. "Gotta make time to talk."

Julie put out a hand to take my arm, then stopped without touching me.

"One minute," I said to Victor, and turned to listen to her.

"Amber, I don't like doing this, but I'm desperate. Keith and I can't go back. That's fine, we can handle that. But Keith's where he is now because of what he tried to do for you. You get him out, and we'll tell you everything we know."

I blinked. I hadn't expected that, but I could understand her position. I just nodded and opened the sliding door.

Victor was standing outside, with his cell dwarfed in his hand. He glanced behind me, into the back of the van, and hid his sigh of relief.

"It's Trey," he said, handing the cell over.

Trey was the one I'd assigned to watch Julie's motel.

"Talk to me," I said.

"Good thing Ms. Alverson is clear of here." He was talking low, as if he wanted to whisper. "Team of three freaking ninjas just went in her room. Slick as anything. Four came out, so I figure someone else went in through the back too. Black clothing, ski masks, MP5s with silencers. Got in a truck, but not moving yet. Took some stuff from the room."

"Shit. Trey, get away. Now."

"They haven't made me."

"Don't risk it. Move. Keep the cell on, keep talking."

Julie's motel was on East Colfax as it headed out from Aurora. I'd told Trey to watch from across the road, in the RV park. Four lanes and a median strip on top of the forty yards to Julie's room. He should be safe, but if I was running the op, I'd have had a couple of people on roofs scanning the area with nightscopes.

"Your motel just had a visit from the Nagas," I said to Julie as she came out of the van to join us.

"Sweet Jesus, that was quick." She looked uncomfortable. "I thought I'd have a day clear."

"Keith arrested, you AWOL. Petersen knew you'd be here. What cover are you using?"

"My private backup."

"We have to assume he's cracked that. You need to disappear. You have anything valuable in the room? Security problem?"

"No." Her eyes flicked to Victor and back. "Some proof of the things I was telling you about. You, the command structure, the whole mess."

I shrugged. I wasn't interested in the proof about me. Julie had convinced me. As for the rest of it, I'd trust the FBI to crack open every file, and then some, if Agent Ingram was running the show.

"I'm clear," Trey said. "They're still parked. No, wait, I can see their truck. They've pulled out behind me."

Trey sounded a lot less confident suddenly.

"Vic, we may need backup in a hurry," I said, and Victor started dialing on his cell.

But I had Trey turn onto the interstate and they didn't follow him there. After a couple of minutes without pursuit, I told him to get off the interstate, swap the plates on his car and then go home.

Another cell chirped. It was my cell's ringtone, so I reached for my pocket, but I'd given it to Victor to hold.

He fumbled it out, muttering about charging for being a telephone exchange.

I chuckled, but that stopped as soon as I heard the voice on the cell.

"Amber, it's Pia. We need you here, now. Jen's coming around."

Chapter 3

"You're with me," I said to Julie as Victor drove us to where my car was parked.

"I can take care of myself," she said.

"What did you say to me not fifteen minutes ago? You think you can handle it if a team comes looking for you?"

She didn't have an answer to that.

I wasn't going to let her go. She didn't know Denver, didn't have any contacts except me and there were a hundred ways the Nagas would be able to find her. And I needed to hear the rest of what she had to say.

"You're with me," I repeated. "In fact..." I hesitated. This was really flying by the seat of my pants. "In fact, I have a job for you while we wait to spring Keith."

"I'm not a..." she said, her face closed. I was pretty sure she'd been going to say 'blood donor', but we were in the cab with Victor and she knew I was keeping the paranormal side away from him.

I snorted. "Not that sort of job. You were on that oil company gig in Nigeria, back in '07, weren't you? Close protection is your specialty."

"I have *all* my little Ops 4-10 badges," she snapped back. "And I wasn't *on* that gig, I *led* it."

Victor wiped a hand over his chin, hiding a smile.

I needed to protect Jen and I needed to do a hundred other things. Unfortunately, none of my warring paranormal abilities seemed to include cloning myself. Having Julie available was incredible luck. Victor's people were good, but I wouldn't put them up against the Nagas. And Julie already knew that there were paranormal threats. I couldn't start briefing Victor's people for a possible attack by Basilikos. At least Julie was only a single breach in the confidentiality rules. I'd have to figure out how I squared that with House Altau when the time came. And I'd need to argue for Altau to give me David and Pia back, to work with Julie on the protection detail.

"You're hired," I said, and didn't give her time to argue. "Part of the deal for Keith. You too, Victor. I know Jen's going to want to be back at Manassah. I've got other tasks, so I need Julie coordinating the protection, because she understands the threats. But I'll need you to provide rotating crew for 24/7 security."

He nodded, his lips pursed. "Long as Ms. Kingslund wants us there."

Jen had fretted at the security before, but after her kidnapping, I doubted she'd be complaining. And if he was worried that his men had failed in their job, I thought Jen would focus more on that they'd died trying against unequal odds. Jen had argued to keep the security detail smaller, and she'd be hurting because of that. I was confident that she'd want Victor's team.

Victor dropped us off at my car.

"You take care," he rumbled, speaking so quietly I felt his voice as much as heard it.

I thanked him for everything he'd done. "Check on Trey," I added as he was leaving, and he was calling as he pulled away.

We climbed in my car. As I drove I pulled the blindfold we'd used in the van from my pocket and handed it to Julie.

"Sorry. This location is confidential."

She rolled her eyes, but put the blindfold on.

"At least I won't have to watch you driving," she said, tilting the seat back and stretching out. "Nice car, by the way. Being a PI pays better than I thought."

I laughed. "I wish. Payment in lieu. But I do like it."

And I did. I'd been unable to drive it the previous week, with Matlal teams who knew the car actively searching for me. There were still Matlal Athanate out there in Denver, of course, but since the Assembly and Basilikos' defeat, they had a lot more on their minds than hunting for me.

∞ ∞ ∞ ∞ ∞

Haven was lit up like a Disney castle.

Julie, good soldier that she was, had slept the whole way, but the change in speed alerted her and she sat back up as we drove along Bear Ridge.

"There are guards. You'll probably be frisked," I said.

"Again," she replied. They'd been thorough when they'd snatched her in the van.

I was right. Haven was on alert after the attacks over the weekend, and security had been tightened all the way around.

I was fine. My hand scan and their noses confirmed who I was easily enough.

They weren't happy with Julie.

"Who is she, House Farrell?" said the senior guard.

"A former colleague of mine, Julie Alverson. She's been employed by my House for security purposes."

"House, this whole site is secret. You can't just bring her in."

"The location's still secret; she doesn't know where the hell we are. And as for knowing about Athanate, all this," I waved at the bustle, "isn't telling her anything she and a whole battalion of army people don't know."

The guards still weren't happy. They couldn't raise Bian from a crisis meeting to clear it. Time was wasting; I needed to get in to be there for Jen.

"Julie's House Farrell," I tried. "She's my responsibility."

Tension rose in everyone at the gate. Julie because she didn't know what I was claiming, and the guards because their Athanate senses disagreed with my words.

"She's unbitten," the senior guard said. "I'd guess unbound."

I'd probably fallen foul of yet another Athanate rule I hadn't had time to learn, but I couldn't back down.

"I'm House Farrell. I'll dictate who's in my House."

The guard blinked at that. He motioned the others back and stood close.

"House," he muttered, "it's your call. But understand, there are responsibilities that go with it. Absolute responsibilities. Remember that."

I swallowed and nodded.

Pia was producing a handbook of what being House Farrell entailed for me, and I desperately needed time to study that. If only everything else would stop for a minute.

The guard stepped back and the gates swung open.

I drove through and a traffic marshal guided us to parking. It'd been getting full as I left earlier, but things had escalated while I was out.

House Altau and all the Panethus Athanate were gearing up for the changes brought about in the aftermath of the Assembly. The Theokos subgroup had left Basilikos; crossed the floor to join Panethus. An avalanche of security procedures were being exchanged between teams. The Canadian Houses had elected to leave the Midnight Empire and join Panethus. More avalanches. All Altau's scattered American sub-Houses had to be integrated into the new Panethus systems. Technology was capable of fantastic things, but for this monumental and complex a task, nothing beat having people right in front of you.

And Panethus itself was changing. The defining focus for the creed had shifted from their philosophy of benevolent, consensual personal interaction with humans to a goal of integrating with human society as a whole—Emergence. In that apparently simple switch, a vast array of allegiances had shifted. An Athanate could be a staunch advocate of positive, symbiotic relationships with human kin and fiercely opposed to making the Athanate visible to the world at large.

Old allies suddenly felt uncomfortable. The finest graduations of trust needed to be recalibrated. For that, Athanate needed to meet, to scent and sense the meanings behind words, face to face.

All of which meant Haven's lawns being churned to mud as a hundred or more cars and SUVs parked across them and meetings spilled out from the house itself over the lawns.

Guiding Julie, still wearing her blindfold, I barely registered it all.

We hurried down the stairs; I was too impatient to wait for overused elevators.

Through the double doors to the suite where Jen had been recovering. I tugged Julie's blindfold off.

Pia and David were standing outside the door, Pia clearly upset.

"Thank God," she said.

"This is Julie; she's joining us." I brushed past them, and opened the doors to the sound of Jen and Alex shouting.

Chapter 4

"Amber!"

Both of them said it at the same time, both of them moved toward me, and then both suddenly stopped as they realized what the other was doing. Tense and awkward barely covered it.

Alex held up his hands.

"You guys have to talk," he said and walked out.

I wanted him back, but maybe it would be easier to talk to Jen alone for the moment. Alex knew more than Jen about everything that had gone on.

His departure got Jen and me moving again, and we met in the middle of the room.

I held her tightly to me, trying to squeeze the trembling from her body.

"What the hell happened to me?" she said, her voice muffled against me. "Why is Deauville here? In fact, where *is* here? Why wouldn't he answer any of my questions?"

"Slow down. There's a lot for you to take in." There were some chairs and a sofa set around a coffee table on one side of the room. "Come on, let's sit." I snagged a blanket off the bed as we walked, and draped it over her shoulders, which got me a tentative smile. She'd still be in shock, and that wasn't going to change in a hurry. I needed her to keep warm.

She was pale and shaky. We'd cleaned the blood and filth off her yesterday and tied her golden hair back in a knot, but it only seemed to accentuate her pallor.

We sat stiffly on the sofa, almost as if we were strangers. I gave myself a mental kick. This wasn't about how uncomfortable I felt, it was about getting Jen through the confusion and trauma of her abduction, and what I'd had to do to heal her. I tried to relax.

"Before I start," I said, "I told you last week, I'd never refuse to answer your questions again. That applies—"

"Only last week? But...how long has it been? I remember..." She touched her face, lifted her arms and looked at the unmarred skin, then her hand reached quickly for her side, where she'd been shot. There was nothing there—no wound, no scar. "It was all a dream?"

"No." I grabbed her left hand and trapped it between mine. "It's Monday today. Sometime early Saturday, you were kidnapped by Frank Hoben."

"You warned me," she muttered, frowning. "Why's it all so blurred? It's like I read about it happening to someone else."

"I think that's partly shock," I said. She didn't ask about the rest of it. I was relieved and worried at the same time.

"Reynolds!" Her head jerked back up. "Zimmerman. They were…"

"They're dead, Jen."

She looked down at our hands in silence. I could hear the murmur of voices outside, the feel of bustle throughout the building, but Jen looked oblivious to it.

Her voice had dropped to a whisper when she spoke again. "It was all my fault, wasn't it? I shouldn't have gone back home to get those files. Hoben shot them." She blinked, wrestling with her memories. "They were lying there wounded, but he killed them because I'd killed one of his men. He just shot them as they lay there." Tears eased out of her eyes and slid down her cheeks. I wanted to brush them away, but I didn't dare move. I let her pick her way through her recollections of what had happened at Manassah and afterwards.

"I killed him," she said, surprising me by leaping forward to the last thing she would be able to recall before the rescue. "Hoben. I shot the bastard. I remember picking up your gun. I did kill him, didn't I?"

"You killed him."

"Good." She shuddered. "But he shot me. I remember that, too."

"He did."

She looked up at me. Her free hand moved the blanket and sweatshirt from her side again. There was no mark on her skin.

"Right there," I said.

There was a quiet knock on the door, and Pia came in with a tray of coffee.

Jen focused on her as she knelt gracefully to put the tray down.

"I know you," Jen said hesitantly.

Pia smiled at her and put out her hand. "You weren't fully conscious when we met. I'm Pia."

As they shook, I could see Jen framing another question, but Pia cut her off.

"I look forward to talking with you when Amber's brought you up to speed," Pia said.

Jen grimaced as she watched Pia leave, her face a picture of her struggle to remember. I wondered how much she would remember of Pia urging us to come together when Jen had woken briefly on that first night. Could she recognize Pia from her aura?

"I can't promise it will all become clear," I said. "But I have to start somewhere."

I poured the coffee to gain a bit more time. Jen's blue eyes came back to me, and now there was a hint of something besides the confusion in them. Maybe even a little fear.

"You did say you realized we weren't in Kansas anymore, Toto." I said. What if I'd messed with more of her memory than I intended?

"Oh yeah. I remember that okay. Thursday. We were getting ready to go off and sign the deal on the racetrack." She gave a little laugh. "You got all evasive about being a werewolf." I could feel a tremor pass through her hand. "You're not a werewolf?"

"No." I hesitated. Not completely true, but I was thinking of the Athanate side of things. It was one thing for Jen to say last week that she had figured out I had to be paranormal and she was okay with it, and another thing entirely to tell her I was going to want to drink her Blood. "Not exactly."

"Vampire?" she whispered.

I took a deep breath, trying to overcome the feeling of my lungs being squeezed. "Vampires don't exist. But the myths come from something real, a people called the Athanate. When I met you, I was becoming Athanate."

I felt another shiver pass through her.

"And now?" she said.

I huffed. "Now it's just gotten weirder."

She gave another short laugh, almost a bark. "I always said weird for you has a different meaning than the rest of us."

"No one knows exactly what I am. I'm a mix of Athanate, Were and Adept—what people generally think of as vampire, werewolf and witch."

"And I'm an...Athanate now too?" Her face was pale and her nose pinched. "I must have died, right? You brought me back from the dead?"

"No. That's a vampire myth. Athanate are living. Dead is dead."

"But you did something. I can almost remember..."

"You were certainly dying from the shot and, well, everything else that happened to you." Everything that animal Hoben and his men had done to her. "One of the abilities Athanate have is to heal. I healed you."

We looked silently at each other. Jen's face slowly lost a little of its pallor. Apparently, healing was better than being revived as a vampire, even if she didn't understand how the healing took place.

"Deauville was looking after me too," she said. "I remember, I woke up a couple of times."

"Yes." How could I broach the subject of what Alex was and what he meant to me? I hedged. "Alex used to be a doctor. He—"

"He's another vamp—I mean Athanate?"

"No." Not so far, anyway, but who knew how that was going to turn out. Gods, this was complicated. "He's a werewolf."

She paused a minute to let that sink in. Then, predictably, her mind went to her corporation, and she frowned. "He's one of the wolves who were making trouble for me out at the resort property, scaring the workers away from Silver Hills, wasn't he? I knew it. I knew there was something weird—"

"It was a mistake, Jen. The pack—"

"Hell yeah, it was a mistake, all right. I'll sue the bastards."

Not the way I wanted the conversation to go. At least the color had come back to her cheeks. "In which court?" I said.

She blinked. "I see what you mean."

Amazingly, we actually managed to laugh, but Jen stopped suddenly.

"Oh God, my company. What does everyone think happened?"

"They'll know you were kidnapped. The police will still be at Manassah now. But it's only Monday, remember. As soon as we organize a cover story, you can contact your company and anyone else who needs to know. I guess nothing will have happened other than crisis meetings."

Jen thought about that and nodded. At least I wasn't having to explain everything, step by step, to her. She would understand the need for paranormals to avoid exposure. She'd become accustomed to my being evasive. Only now I'd have to explain to her why she was regarded as no longer a security risk. Because she was kin.

"Is that going to be difficult?" she said. "The cover story?"

I hadn't thought about it too much, what with everything else going on, but it was a problem. "We blew the factory up and killed everyone inside. Yup, that's difficult. On the other hand, they have a team here whose job is to clear up this sort of thing."

"A team here? So, this is a place for Athanate?" She waved to encompass the whole building.

"This is Haven, the home of House Altau." I needed to set things up for her. "There are two types of Athanate, and Altau are the leaders of the good guys, the Panethus. I guess because they haven't worked out what the hell I am, Altau have set me up as a subsidiary House—House Farrell."

"House?" She could hear the emphasis.

"Like a family, a group." A group comprising Athanate and kin. How to explain?

"And Pia?" she said.

"Pia is a member of House Farrell. So is David. You remember meeting him?"

She nodded.

"And Alex. And maybe a couple of others." Julie, I'd just claimed, but I didn't know if that was valid. Would that mean Keith as well? Oh, God.

"Deauville," she said, ignoring the rest. Her tone made it clear that news was unwelcome.

Before she could question me any more about that, the door swished open and Bian came in, wearing a trim burgundy pantsuit, the leopard-spot tattoos that covered her upper body just showing above her shirt collar. She was followed by an assistant who was juggling phones and clipboards.

"Ms. Trang?" Jen said faintly. "What on earth are you doing here?"

"Ah," I answered for her. "Bian is the head of security here, Jen. You two have met?"

Bian laughed. "I'm the signatory for the consortium that owned the land for the new racetrack. One of my overt jobs." She came and sat on one of the chairs in front of us. "I couldn't make the official signing ceremony. Shame. It would have been fun."

"So you're Athanate, too?" Jen said, looking pale again. Too many things to take in at once.

"Yes. I see Amber's briefing you." She straightened and pressed her hands together, bowing her head slightly to Jen. She spoke in Athanate and followed it in English. "Honor to you, Jennifer kin-Farrell, and twice welcome."

"Kin?" Jen said, looking at me. I glared at Bian. I wanted to run this at my own pace, and here she was, steamrolling through it all.

Bian looked blithely unconcerned, listening briefly on a phone held by her assistant and then scrawling something on one of his clipboards. She waved at him to leave.

"I was just getting to that," I said. Bian's grin was unnerving, but it was nothing to the pressure I felt from Jen's look of inquiry. She must realize, even though I'd said Athanate are different than vampires...

"The myth of the vampire is right in one aspect. We need Blood."

When she didn't flinch, it felt like the steel strips that had been wound around my chest had unexpectedly loosened.

"I mean, I will need Blood. No one is sure exactly when." I watched as Jen dipped her head, her eyes steady. I let myself hope a little more. "And the types of Athanate I mentioned—the good guys, Panethus? We don't just need Blood, we need emotion as well."

"She means love," Bian said, topping up our coffee. "Panethus Athanate and their kin are bound by love."

I was watching Jen's eyes. I saw every feature of her face with a hard-edged clarity. Her pupils grew and a tiny sigh escaped her. My heart kicked and I felt the now-familiar looseness in my jaw. I clenched my teeth. Fangs had to come later, when she had a chance to get used to the idea, but my Athanate was purring at her reaction. *Oh, yes.*

Jen smiled, as if she could sense what I was going through, although that was impossible of course. For the first time in this room, I started to relax and smile back.

And the door opened again. It was Alex.

Bian turned to him, repeating the gestures and the Athanate greeting. I tried to stop her but she was already giving the translation. "Honor to you also, Alexander kin-Farrell, and twice welcome."

Jen gasped as the implications sank in.

Chapter 5

"Oh," Bian said. "You didn't get to that part yet. Sorry."

I could have strangled her, even if she had the grace to look concerned.

The temperature in the room plummeted. Jen shifted away on the sofa and sat stiffly, not meeting my eyes. Alex looked sympathetic, but he realized there was nothing he could do that would make it any better at the moment.

"Uh, right. Sorry for interrupting," he said. "But a message came in from Larimer." The alpha of the Denver pack. "He wants Amber and me at a meeting as soon as possible."

Bian sat back in her chair. "He might have the right to order you around, Alex, but not Amber. And you're going to have to come to a decision about your primary allegiance sometime soon."

Alex shrugged it off. "This came in through the comms center here. Skylur passed it on as agreed. I'm not asking your permission, I'm just informing you as a courtesy."

Bian's eyes narrowed. "And why the rush, little wolf?"

"We'll find out, but I guess it'll be to do with the promise Amber made."

"What promise?" Bian said.

"I don't have authority to discuss—"

"They have a problem with a rogue," I interrupted Alex. I was sick of the secrecy and distrust between Were and Athanate. In my unique position, as part of both, it felt completely wrong to me. "I agreed to investigate the situation for them in return for the pack's help with Jen's situation." Jen bit her lip and flushed slightly. I could see she didn't like being the cause of this argument, however indirectly. I touched her hand briefly. "Worth the price," I said quietly.

Alex frowned and turned away.

"Not only that," I said, "but an FBI special team has taken an interest in the case. They think it's animal killings, but the anomalies haven't escaped them. If they dig until they find the Were, do you think the Athanate will be far behind? Better if this is dealt with quickly, by us."

Bian also frowned. "The Were are better at sniffing out strangers. Why would they need you? In fact, I'm about to ask *them* for help."

"I think we've done enough for you, unless you're suggesting a quid pro quo," Alex cut in before I could say anything.

"The pair of you, stop it," I said.

There was a moment's blessed silence.

I wanted time with Jen, alone. I wanted time with Alex and Bian, to try and get everything straight in my head. But what I had was this mess and I had to deal with it now.

"Bian, I'm walking a tightrope here," I said. "I'm part Were, but I'm not part of the Denver pack. That's causing as many issues in their community as my being an unaffiliated Athanate caused in yours. If I'd stomped in here a few weeks ago, demanding that the Athanate do this and do that, you would have squashed me like a bug. I'm not going to piss off Larimer and jeopardize any hope of a peaceful resolution with the Were just because you and Skylur can't ask nicely for what you want. Now. What *request* would you like me to take to Larimer?"

She ran her hands up and down the arms of her chair, then sat back again. "That they help us track down the remainder of the Matlal Athanate in Denver."

"But we—" Alex started.

"Enough." I held a hand up to stop him. To my surprise, he did. I didn't want him to argue the pack's side against Bian, either. I hadn't worked out all the reasoning yet, but I was going with my gut feeling. "I'll put the request to Larimer. Now, is there anything else we need to discuss before we go?"

"You're not leaving me here," Jen said.

"Yes, they are. It's not safe for you anywhere else." Bian dismissed the idea of her leaving. "And your being out there would be a hindrance to Amber."

"I am *not* staying."

I felt like a firefighter leaping between fires. Every time I thought one had been put out, another came back. "She'll be safe. I have some additional arrangements in place. If you're concerned, you can give me David and Pia back."

It was Bian's turn to frown again. "What arrangements?"

"I have a friend outside who's from the same army unit I was. She's good and she's a specialist in close protection. If I have David and Pia to brief her on the threats, and Victor's team as well, then Jen's going to be as safe back at home as she is here."

I could see Jen's face tighten at the mention of extra security, but she sure as hell couldn't argue against it now. She was pale again, looking tired and upset. She needed this to be finished.

Bian hadn't come up with an immediate objection and she was distracted when her assistant came back in with some more documents for her to sign off on.

She quickly sent the assistant on his way again. "You have to be back here on Wednesday anyway," she said. "All of you, *together*." She paused. "There's a reception for all the Panethus Houses before they return to their countries. I need to present House Farrell," her eyes flicked back and forth between all of us, "*and* kin to them. It's vital they have the opportunity to meet you."

"Why?"

"They don't entirely believe the problem with your Blood. Oh, they sort of accept it mentally, but they need to know it in their gut. When they get a sniff of you, they'll really understand that whatever benefit it may have to ease crusis comes with Were cross-infusion. Without that to cool them off, Skylur's under too much pressure from people trying to bargain for a taste of you."

I could sense she wasn't telling me everything, but there wasn't much hope I'd get her to be more forthcoming in front of the others.

"It's a formal occasion," she went on, eyeing my clothes. I'd borrowed sweats rather than walk around in the blood-soaked clothes I'd been wearing at the Assembly, but I was a still a scruffy mess. "Dress up pretty. Please."

"If we're going back to Manassah…" Alex cleared his throat. "What are we going to tell the police and everyone else?"

Jen looked up.

"You were kidnapped Friday night, people were killed, police were all over your house," Alex said. "Then we're going to return you unharmed on Monday. Meanwhile, a whole factory has exploded and there are bodies all over it."

Bian nodded to acknowledge his point. "The cleanup team was at work on the factory site almost as soon as we left. The bodies outside were cleared away. They had to leave the ones inside, but the explosion and fire were…thorough." Her eyes passed over me. Tullah, my assistant and an emerging Adept, and her dragon spirit Kaothos had been responsible for the explosion. Mostly Kaothos. Bian had to suspect Tullah was a very powerful Adept, and she'd made her thoughts on the matter plain: either I took Tullah into House Farrell, or Bian would be after her for House Altau.

Best of luck getting past her mother. Mary was not a woman to cross, even discounting her Adept powers, and she thought Athanate and Adepts should stay far away from one another.

"It's not ideal," Bian continued, "but we can get away with another gangland battle. The last members of ZK kidnap Jennifer, a group from a Mexican drug cartel try and snatch her. In the confusion, Amber gets Jennifer out of the building. The explosion is caused by a stockpile of weapons that ZK had."

Alex scratched his head. "Jen got knocked on the head, suffered a concussion, which is why she can't give much detail. She didn't want to go to a hospital, but I insisted she stay in bed before letting her return home. We decided not to talk to anyone until she was well enough to answer questions."

Jen looked coolly at him.

"Are we saying I did it alone," I said, "or should we keep closer to the truth and say Alex helped?"

I wanted Jen to understand that Alex had been there to rescue her as well as treat her afterwards.

"We could say Alex drove the car you used," Bian suggested. "Not quite the same image as him shape-shifting on the stairs and biting people's heads off, but it'll have to do." A smile lurked at the edges of Bian's mouth, as if she knew what I was doing.

Jen nodded, hiding a shudder and looking around her. She was surrounded by monsters.

Bian pulled a comms device out and spoke rapidly in Athanate.

"You're being brought another change of clothes and a scrub to remove any gunshot residue or other evidence. After you've all cleaned up, you can head off. I'll communicate back to Larimer and explain the delay. He'll understand." She got up. "Amber, I need a word with you separately."

She led me out, ignoring my protest. Outside, she waved all the others into the room to join Jen and Alex, and closed the door behind them.

"I'm sorry," she said immediately, taking the wind out of my sails. "I didn't handle that well. It's a serious matter to have issues between your kin."

"Alex knew, Jen didn't," I said. "That probably makes it even worse for her."

"I know. But it'll work out," Bian said. "She *is* kin. Adept Emerson confirmed it, and even I can tell."

I shook my head. That wasn't the point.

"You didn't want to talk to me about that," I said.

"Well, not that alone. First off, I'll need you to report back tomorrow on how it goes with our furry friend Larimer."

"I can predict that right now. Not well."

"Then it's going to be up to you to do something to change that, Amber. You're going to be in a unique position here. You'll have to take over the role of being a liaison with the Were. And this hunting down their rogue is a godsend. Skylur wants them obligated."

"I'll be a liaison, fine. But I won't try and force them to do things. And since I'm not hunting down the rogue for them on behalf of the Athanate, there's no obligation involved."

"But your primary allegiance—"

"Is to what's right for all of us, not Altau getting the Denver pack to work for them."

We had a staring contest, but no one beats me at those.

"Amber, I already knew things would be interesting around you, but you've got to understand, we're on a war footing here. We don't have time to debate, we don't have time to wonder who we can trust."

"And when have I given you reason to distrust me?"

"It's not what you've done or not done, it's where you are. In your head."

Someone arrived with a bundle of clothes and gels. Bian opened the door for them and we moved further away.

"What do you mean?"

"The reaction you've just had! You'd take sides with the pack against Altau." She overrode me as I tried to argue. "Right or wrong isn't the point. It's your instinct for a human-centric view of what's fair and right. You make decisions without any idea of what they entail." She grabbed me. "This is important. Like what happened with David. You want that again? Am I getting through to you?"

David had nearly died because of decisions I'd made without realizing the consequences. Yeah, she was getting through to me.

"Okay. But I didn't ask for this and no one told me the rules. In fact, since you say I'm unique, I'd say there are no rules. I'm caught between you and the pack, and I won't act against either of you."

"Wonderful, but there's no time to explain everything, and there won't be while this crisis is running. You need to trust us. You *have* to trust us." She banged a hand against the wall in frustration.

"I *do* trust you, on the big issues. But I gave my word to Larimer, and even if I hadn't, the Were and Athanate need to work together. That's *not* the same as Skylur telling the pack what to do. Or vice versa."

Bian huffed.

"And your army friend, what's the situation with her?" She waved at the room.

"Julie? What do you mean?"

"You've claimed her as part of your House, but she isn't bound."

"I trust her."

"Yeah, and we have to trust you. If she leaves, she's going to have to have memories erased. You aren't trained to do that. With Diana away, I'd be the one that has to take over that responsibility. Of course I'll do it, but I warn you, I'm not as skilled as Diana. It's not a pleasant experience."

My stomach tensed.

What had I done to Jen?

"You still don't know where Diana is or when she'll be back?" I asked.

"No."

I looked sideways at her. "You say you're on a war footing. Diana's second in command here and you simply don't know where she is?"

"Uh huh. Skylur, as president of the Assembly, is always going to have to be able to answer questions with Adepts listening and checking he's telling the truth. Diana must be doing something that she wants Skylur to be able to deny at the moment. It isn't the first time."

I suspected she was more worried than she sounded. And she picked up on the reason my thoughts had gone straight from Jen to Diana.

She leaned closer, using exactly the same technique as I'd used on Julie, and getting the same reaction from me.

"It's important for Diana to be back for Jen, isn't it?"

"You know?"

She looked aside, her face hardening. "Amber, I know what happened to Jen. I saw the way she'd been beaten and raped by Hoben and his gang. Your healing her was extraordinary. Your link to her must be very strong." She paused. "But, there's something wrong. She knows what happened, but she's acting as if it were nothing. You did something to her memories, and you're afraid you've damaged her."

My throat was tight. I nodded. "I didn't know what I was supposed to do. You were just telling me to heal her. Alex was yelling that her heart was failing." I shivered, reliving the blind panic of the moment. "Jen and I, we'd had this strange sensation before, like I could feel her heart beating, I could sense what she was feeling. Something to do with auras, I guess."

"Not aura. *Eukori*," Bian said. "The space and reach of the mind. The home of the soul."

"Huh?"

"Our Athanate telergy acts through the eukori. You can think of it as a sort of aura if you must, but instead of just shining out around you, it's a path into your body and mind." Her voice dropped. "With the closest of kin and lovers, they say it's the place where the souls touch."

She was staring at me, her eyes glittering as if she was thirsting for Blood, but her fangs remained hidden.

I cleared my throat. "Well, I was using it to keep her heart beating and to feel where she needed healing…" I stopped. How to explain it?

"And?"

"I could feel what she felt, everything, that day. All the awful things." I shuddered. "And everything that happened to her was because of me."

Bian's eyes darkened. "So you took it. You reached through the eukori and you took the emotions away from her. Into yourself. Left her with nothing but the dry knowledge."

I nodded, my stomach churning with a nightmare of unconnected sensation and emotion, called up by Bian's questions. I forced it back down, suddenly aware that I was trembling.

Get a grip!

She watched me and waited.

"I have a place for this stuff."

A jumble of images. Dad, sitting beside me, explaining that our cat had been run over.

That my friend's Dad had been posted to another state and I wouldn't see her again.

And then, Dad lying in the bed, surrounded by all the medical equipment that wasn't keeping him alive, telling me that I would have to move on, that I would have to pack this up in the strongbox in my mind and be there for Mom and Kath.

I had done it. It had worked for a couple of years…

And a last image. The ground at the bottom of the clock tower at South High, calling to me, promising sweet oblivion as I struggled to close the strongbox.

I slammed the strongbox shut.

Bian was still watching.

"I just need to be sure that I haven't hurt Jen."

"You're going to have to wait for Diana to come back. Or maybe ask Skylur." She sighed and moved away from me. "You have an absolute talent for complicating things, Round-eye. Even when it's not your fault and you're right, like Vega Martine."

I'd almost forgotten Vega Martine, which was dangerously stupid. From everything that happened at the Assembly, I was convinced that she was the real driving force behind Basilikos, not Matlal. He had been nothing but a front for her. A good one, to get away with it so long. Even now, days later, my skin still prickled with the slithery sensation I'd felt when she'd tried to talk me out of allying with Altau.

I shivered. Another thing to worry about.

"What's happened about her?"

"Nothing much, but it's sure got everyone's panties in a twist." Bian turned abruptly, taking my hand and pulling me back toward the door.

"She simply walked out, right through the Lyssae. That shouldn't be possible. They should have known she wasn't Altau and torn her apart."

"Are you sure they didn't?" I remembered Anubis' bloody jackal snout and wondered what evidence he would leave behind when he finished with someone.

Bian snorted. "Yes. The good news is that it's got Basilikos as worried as us. She's definitely not some scheme they were running." She reached for the door handle and stopped. "I keep forgetting how much you don't know. At the Assembly, everyone in Panethus, me included, was spooked by the thought that Basilikos had found a way of compelling people that we couldn't detect. Scary, but not the end of the world."

"How so?"

"Adepts sense beyond the depths Athanate can. If we'd known we had a traitor, we'd have got Adepts in. They don't like working with us, but some will." She licked her lips. "There are benefits."

"Emerson and her partner worked with the Warders. Like that?"

Bian nodded, a little smile rippling across her face. More secrets for me to dig out of her.

"But what Vega Martine pulled off, that's got everyone worried. The one thing we can't fake is the marque. That mental presence, and that scent, they're essential components of who we are—it's how we identify ourselves and each other. An Athanate who can change her marque at will is the stuff of real nightmares."

I could think of at least one other way of getting out of Haven besides walking out past the Lyssae, but I'd let Bian puzzle a bit, and swap some of my secrets for hers.

We were interrupted again. An assistant came in and handed Bian an odd-looking cell phone.

"Ah. Yours." Bian gave it to me. "New secure comms if you need to talk to me or anyone here. Replaces the cell Skylur gave you last week."

"Is it a burn phone?"

"No. An encrypting phone, with a dummy conversation in clear transmitted over the top."

"How smart's that dummy conversation?"

"Oh, y'know, sorta like really full of random things people say. Almost indistinguishable from the real thing." She grinned. "Not perfect, and the encryption's not unbreakable, but it cycles through different methods. Basilikos might have their claws into the federal apparatus, but not to the extent they'd spot this, let alone have time to crack it."

"Maybe. They'll still be looking for me, I guess."

"As soon as they get themselves organized again. Unless, of course, we find a way to persuade them otherwise. Now," she said, turning back to the door, "if I've timed it right, I'll get to catch Jen in the shower."

"Over my dead body, Pussycat."

Chapter 6

Freshly scrubbed of any evidence from the fight at the factory, and wearing new borrowed sweats and running shoes, we all crowded into my Audi. I still didn't feel clean. Maybe something in the soap they'd given us didn't agree with me.

Alex wrestled the keys off me. Even though I wasn't driving, I still insisted that Jen take the front passenger seat. There was more room and I could tilt the seat back to let her rest. She didn't spontaneously explode at being put next to Alex—not quite.

David and Pia squeezed together happily in the back. Julie and I less so, but I knew I would need her on the phone once we were well clear of Haven.

I left the blindfolds off. This was my House.

Yes, and problems will be your responsibility, said Tara. My dead twin sister, comforting as always.

Thanks, sis.

I called FBI Agent Ingram on my standard cell as soon as we got onto I-70.

"Ms. Farrell," he drawled. "You're ahead of schedule if you've got news for me." I could almost see him leaning back and putting his feet up on the desk. "You comin' in to talk?" he asked.

"Better than that, Ingram. You got a recorder on this?"

He chuckled.

"Yeah, stupid question," I said. I handed the cell to Julie. "Say your piece."

She looked tense for a second, her tongue touching her dry upper lip, before she spoke. "Message for Keith Alverson. I'm with Amber. I'm safe at the moment, but I have Nagas trying to track me." She paused, her eyes gleaming while she stared right through me. "You were right. Ops 4-10 command is completely gone. Petersen can't be trusted. I know I said we shouldn't do it this way…that we should try other things, but I was wrong, I'm sorry. It's too late. Talk to Agent Ingram. Amber vouches for him. Codes: Treble. Usable. Tango. Thunder. Island… Endit." Her eyes closed and she sighed. "I love you, hon. Be safe."

I took the cell back.

"You there, Ingram?"

"I am, and I have to say, I'm more ears than a barn full of donkeys, here."

I managed a smile. "Play that to Sergeant Alverson," I said. "He'll give you the full detail on Ops 4-10, the unit we were in. We were a covert Special Forces battalion tasked to carry out operations where the US had to have plausible deniability. I swear we were legitimate. But you were right about the lack of oversight. Something's gone seriously wrong in the command structure. No one seems to know about it."

"You don't say. But interesting timing, your call."

"How's that?"

"Well, y'see, someone just stuck their head up and claimed these boys."

I felt a chill creep up my spine. Julie's eyes widened and we bent our heads around the cell.

"Who?"

"Some woo-woo folks called the...hold it..." I heard papers shuffling. "The Joint Forces Committee for Strategic Planning Research and Operational Evaluation. Jeez, what a name, JF-CoStPROE. Anyway, these guys, well, the Director of National Intelligence knows about them. I've got a request to release my prisoners to them, and the DNI's office has given the nod. A van's on its way."

Julie shook her head urgently.

"Ingram," I said, "I'm working on gut reaction here, but this committee may be where the problem is. Can you hold Alverson? Just for a while. Please?"

"Ms. Farrell, I have my orders, so that wouldn't be possible." He coughed. "Outside of a medical emergency, say. But come to think on it, I do believe he had a rash this morning."

"It's highly contagious. Life-threatening."

"I'll seek medical confirmation of that." He hesitated. "We are talking here about the guy who was running that team? The one with the Ruger?"

"Yes," I said quietly. "Hard choices, Agent Ingram, hard choices."

"Lordy, when you guys play hardball, you mean it."

"We do."

"And who was that speaking earlier?"

I looked at Julie, and she nodded.

"Julie Alverson, also Sergeant, also formerly of Ops 4-10," I said.

"Huh. I'll have to meet your Sergeant Alverson, after I've spoken to my Sergeant Alverson, assuming the doctor says he's okay to talk."

"We'll meet in good time. And as a thanks, I'll throw in the former Ops 4-10 commanding officer, Colonel Laine."

"Now you're spoiling me, Ms. Farrell. But then, I think we have lots to talk about besides this here covert battalion."

"That in good time too. One impossible thing at a time."

I ended the call.

"Will he do it? He sounded as if he was hedging."

"That's just the way he talks." I wiped my hands on my sweats. I didn't want to think about the alternatives. Time to change the subject. "What was that about not agreeing with Keith? You didn't want him to come?"

"No, I didn't." Julie refused to drop her eyes. "I argued that we should get a group together and make a formal complaint up the chain. I was wrong."

My Athanate senses or my human instincts said she was telling the truth.

"Keith said we'd all let you down, after you'd been bitten," she went on. "He said we owed you."

I huffed, uncomfortable at the thought. "Any debts are paid."

Did I let them down? Why had I just blindly followed the rules I'd been given? If I hadn't been bitten, would Colonel Laine still be in command of Ops 4-10?

We'd arrived at Alex's house. There would be police still at Manassah. Alex and I didn't have time to talk to them now. We were going to split up here, with Alex driving me to the meeting with Larimer and David driving the rest back to Manassah in my car.

I handed my guns over to Julie for the time being. I didn't want to go to Larimer's armed, and Julie would need weapons to provide Jen's protection. I added getting more weapons to my to-do list.

Jen got out and gave Alex's house a casual once over, before turning away. Of course, it wasn't a patch on Manassah. I could feel Alex's fur ruffle. He made a big thing out of calling Larimer to update him.

Jen pulled me aside.

"I didn't say thank you," she said.

"It's noth—"

She pressed a finger to my lips, stopping me. "Don't you dare say that."

"Yes, ma'am."

Her lips twitched, but her face went serious again. "Amber, when you healed me, you did something to my head," she said uncertainly. "To my memory?"

Crap.

"Ah. Yeah. I tried something. Didn't work the way I thought."

"It doesn't feel right. Crazy, huh?" She shook her head. "Like I would want that shit back? But I can remember you kneeling there, all that paint on your face." Her fingers traced the contours of the war paint I'd worn. Her eyes held mine and her voice dropped to a whisper. "You came for me. And I can remember what it must have felt like, but I can't feel it any more. I have to have that feeling back. I have to."

I bit my lip. Light as a breeze, I sensed the tentative touches of our bond through the eukori. "I don't know how. We'll need an expert. And I don't know if you can pick and choose pieces of it."

"I'll take all the rest for that one moment." She shook her head again, leaned into me. "I know we have some issues." Her eyes flicked over to Alex. "But I don't give up that easy."

Alex ended his call. "Got to go," he said, thumbing his car keys. His garage door started to rattle up.

"Will I see you later?" asked Jen, not moving an inch.

The world didn't owe me time to fix my personal problems. At some stage, some wonderful stage when I knew what was going on in the paranormal community, and could judge the importance of what I did and didn't do—at that stage, I'd pull a timeout. But I couldn't yet.

"I don't know," I said. "I'll try. It'll depend on what comes up." I pulled away reluctantly, and she let me go.

Chapter 7

Alex had a Ford.

Actually, not *a* Ford, *the* Ford. The '69 Boss in Black Jade. The king of muscle cars.

We could have gone in his SUV, which was parked on the street, but I guess he was making a statement.

I wasn't going to argue. The rising thunder of the V-8 tickled me all the way down to my toes as we swung out onto I-25 and headed south. I put everything else aside for a moment and wriggled happily in the contours of the Corbeau racing seat.

Alex smiled a little for the first time that day. My heart skipped a beat. I wished we could just have a simple, uncomplicated few minutes where I could watch his face, his hands on the steering wheel, and think about where else I'd rather be with him.

Shame to spoil it, but...

"How deep is the shit I'm in?" I said. I left it open who I was in trouble with: Alex, for binding him, or Larimer and the pack, for getting him to help rescue Jen from Hoben. And for binding him.

Alex grunted and sighed. *"We're* in deep."

My stomach did a happy flip.

He went on. "You need to be in the pack, for the sake of the part of you that's Were. It's not that there are no werewolves that run solo, but think about it. Your Athanate side's still in crusis and you need to stay in Denver for Altau to keep an eye on you. That means in the Denver pack's territory. Even without the Athanate issues, it'd be hard for a werewolf to live in another pack's territory. A werewolf who's just becoming a werewolf? No way."

"Okay, I get that."

He frowned, as if he felt I hadn't really understood.

"You can't be half in the pack. If you're in, you can't ignore Felix's orders. He can't let the pack structure crumble just because of you. The pack wouldn't let you do that either."

"Well, like I said to him, why can't he deal with it like Altau? Make me a sort of associated pack."

"It's not that easy. That's an Athanate thing. It'd make Felix look weak." Alex hesitated over saying something else, then just finished off: "He can't afford that."

It wasn't the time to make the point, given he was driving, but we'd need to be clear on every aspect of this, however difficult it was to put it all in words. We couldn't have things unsaid between us.

The big V8 howled as we overtook another car like it was stopped. Alex tucked the front end expertly into the next corner and then powered us out of it.

"On the positive side," he said, "he's got your promise to help track down the rogue. That's more important than you think."

"Well, good. But you said we're both in it." I looked at him, unhappy at the thought of messing him up with the pack, and struggling with the Athanate side of me that just wanted to say he was mine and to hell with them.

He snorted. "Yeah. Well, I got involved in the fighting at Longmont. He'll have an issue with that."

"Hmm. He explicitly told you not to. And your response will be?" My binding him didn't seem to be at the top of his mind. One knot of worry eased, but only making the others feel worse.

Alex stared at the road for a while without answering. I could feel the wolf stirring unhappily in him. It was my fault, putting him in this position with his pack. I sensed he would fight, if it came to it. At the moment, challenging him on that wasn't going to help. I'd have to handle this carefully, or do something spectacular in the meeting to distract them. The pack was part of Alex at a deep level. I didn't want to break that.

"I'm going to claim pack obligation," he said finally. "Felix has to acknowledge that."

"But I'm not a pack member yet."

"You are for me." He grimaced. "And that's playing lawyer, which doesn't go down well in the pack. But it changes the argument from disobeying him to whether or not you're in. As long as we can obey him in the future, and that we're going to have to do, to be in the pack."

"There're all sorts of arguments, Alex. Are you changing to hybrid like me?"

"Hey, we've changed our marques. You're part Were. There's nothing that tells me I'm part Athanate. I haven't grown a different set of fangs or wanted to start drinking blood. I don't feel any different."

Early times yet.

"Well, I wonder what Larimer's take is on that."

"Felix," Alex said with emphasis.

"Felix," I allowed. "How is he going to feel about that?"

"He won't be too happy. It's part of the role of an alpha to be suspicious about things like that and Felix is a damn good alpha. The thought that I might challenge him because you're compelling me, and it's all an Altau plot, that's just feeding the normal alpha paranoia with nitroglycerine."

I sighed. It said something that I could actually understand Felix's paranoia better than I could understand Alex on this. I was reluctant to come straight out and talk about the binding. It felt too intimate. But I was going to have to deal with it, one way or another.

"I can see his point. This is not a complaint, okay? Don't you think we've rushed into this? I mean our relationship. Look, Alex, I can understand it looks odd to others. It must look very suspicious to Larim— to Felix."

"Not having second thoughts again?"

"No! But what if Felix is right, and I've been using some Athanate voodoo on you all along? Without knowing. I mean, I didn't have a clue what I was doing for Jen in the van and I ended up healing her." I took a breath and rushed on. "And now we're bound together, all three of us. I'm not complaining. Hell, it feels great. But I don't know what it means for us, I don't even know how I did it, and I...ahh...didn't have your permission."

Alex grunted. "Yeah, well it was a shock, all right." He shifted in his seat and concentrated on slinging us around a sharp corner. "But I'm not complaining either. Look at it this way: I didn't have your permission to infuse you."

That was a point. But two wrongs made a right? Two crazy things neither of us intended made it even?

"But what if I've compelled you, so you only think it's okay? What if I'm still compelling you without you realizing it?"

"Same as you've done for Kingslund?"

"No!" I rubbed my face. "I don't know."

Had I? Had I made Jen fall for me, so I could have her as kin?

"Jeez, you're getting all messed up in the head, Amber."

A tentative smile tugged the corners of his mouth.

"I'm serious," I said. "Neither of us really knows what's happening. Am I doing something to you? Even, y'know, sex, for example. As an Athanate, I can make you want it, and then I can make you like it. And if I do that, I might as well be Basilikos."

"That isn't anything like Basilikos and you didn't compel me. Werewolves haven't got powers like the Athanate, but I could tell if you were trying to make me do something. And, sure as hell, I could tell if you tried juicing me with that enviric stuff you Athanate have."

"Really? You've come across it before?"

Alex shrugged and kept his eyes firmly on the road.

Hmmm.

"Bian?"

He flushed and his knuckles went pale on the steering wheel.

"Oh."

We drove on a while. Deep down, I'd known it really. She used to be the Were liaison for Altau, so she'd presumably spent some time with the pack. And Alex.

"Am I allowed to be jealous?" I said.

"No!" The corners of his mouth turned back up. "It's history anyway."

I laughed, glad to release the tension for a moment. "Okay, not this time." And I'd draw a discreet veil over Bian's leopard-stalking of me as well.

"I guess, until we work out what it means for us, we don't say anything about binding." Alex hunched a little.

I felt uncomfortable too. "I don't want to start like that with the pack — lying."

He dipped his head briefly. "Don't lie. If Felix asks us, we tell him. In fact, I think it'd be dangerous for any of us to try and lie to each other."

"Alpha thing?"

"Dominance thing. It's very difficult to lie to a more dominant wolf and impossible to your alpha."

But maybe not impossible for the alpha to lie to me. And what about while I wasn't in the pack? Could I lie to him now? Or not tell the whole truth? I grimaced. Alex was right; I'd need to be very careful.

"Okay, we can't lie," I said, trying to form a plan as I spoke. "We can't help provoking him—we're a provocation just by existing. We can't back him into a corner. We've got to get him into a position where the obvious way forward is a good outcome all around."

Yeah, I thought. Maneuver a werewolf alpha who's probably seen this kind of political manipulation for a hundred years before we came along. But I didn't say it.

"We should be able to get him to agree you're part of the pack through me," Alex said. "You realize that means you'll lose some leeway to act on your own. You can't defy the alpha. It would make him look weak. We're not Athanate, we're werewolves—we need a strong leader to be a strong, healthy pack."

"Enough," I muttered.

Again, I had the idea there were things unsaid. I kept quiet while he took another tight turn, but he didn't continue where he'd left off.

Instead, he glanced at his watch. "We'll be at Coykuti in five."

"The ranch is called Coykuti? Something to do with coyotes?"

He shook his head. "It's from Arapaho. It means to set free. When Felix first set up, this was where the pack used to run."

"Now they go to Bitter Hooks. Why the change?"

"Coykuti's not big enough, even with the whole mountain behind it. People have got places all along the edges now; they've cut back on the trees. That's why it was so easy for Tucker to persuade us to scare off the builders at Bitter Hooks. Kingslund's Silver Hills resort would have sat bang in the middle of our range."

"Jen, not Kingslund," I insisted quietly. I didn't add, *and Jen's land, not the pack's.* Must have been that tact thing I kept hearing about.

We turned again, onto the last snaky road that led to Larimer's ranch.

"Jen," Alex muttered eventually.

"She never intended to build it, you know."

"So you said. And now?"

"Why would she change her mind now?"

He didn't answer.

I tried to clear my head and calm myself. I needed so much from this meeting. Diana had warned me, but what had she actually said? That if I joined a pack and left, I could go rogue. And if I didn't have the influence of an alpha while I was in transition, I could go rogue. She'd avoided directly telling me, but the implication was there—for my sanity I should join Alex's pack.

I didn't want an alpha. My House was enough pack for me. But the way my wolf and Athanate fed on each other, it felt like I was juggling flares at a fuel dump. Echoes of the sick fascination of feeding on Julie's fear still oozed out of dark corners of my mind. Lurking inside me was a weakness that might pull me to the Basilikos side, or drive my wolf rogue.

If Felix refused to allow me to join the pack, would I survive? What if he made a condition: pack or House? Surely he wouldn't do that.

The trouble was, I didn't know how Felix would act. I didn't understand the Were enough. I simply hadn't had the time to find out. And I was in the same position as I was with the Athanate and the Adepts; a little information was probably more dangerous than none.

Once I understood all the fractured parts, *if* I could get to that situation, I had a hope of fusing it all together.

I'm an optimist like that.

We pulled in through the Coykuti gates and parked by the ranch house, next to a long, black Volvo and a Dodge Ram colored like a fire truck.

I got out and looked up, over the house's maroon roof, to the slopes behind. The dark wave of pines seemed to be reaching down the mountain and stopped no more than fifty yards from the back door of the house. A narrow dirt track wound upwards through the woods and disappeared. I could feel the coolness from the shadows beneath the trees, and an eerie silence hung over everything. I shivered. This whole place had the same sense of watchful waiting as Bitter Hooks.

The ranch itself was old-style: timber and stone, long and low, with signs that bits had been added or changed as the need had arisen. The roof tiles were fired clay. I suspected they'd been made here, from the earth beneath our feet. I had to say it looked good; it looked like it was part of the mountain.

Where we'd stopped, in front of the house, the screen of cottonwood and maple all but obscured the road we'd come in on. And beyond the work yard to our left, the rickety, ancient barn where I'd last met with the pack stood in the meadow.

"Not the barn, this time?" I asked.

"Only for big pack meets," Alex said. "This is more of a closed session, by the sound of it."

"Like a trial," I muttered, as we stepped up on the wraparound porch, the boards creaking loudly under our feet.

Chapter 8

I'd half expected Larimer to have a special room for an audience, like Skylur in his underground lair, but we met casually in his living room. We were ushered in by a woman who didn't speak and left immediately. I sensed more of the pack in and around the house, but they stayed out of sight.

The living room was a huge, sprawling space, with enormous leather sofas and chairs scattered around a set of coffee tables, all handmade from railroad ties. A working loom and spinning wheel sat in one corner, half obscured by a rank of spikey-leaved Madagascan dragon trees in pots. An old saloon mirror dominated one wall, across from an eight-foot-long painting of plains buffalo which stretched over the fireplace. There were water jugs and glasses on the tables. Bowls of fruit and nuts. Almost a welcome.

We sat opposite Felix. To our right sat Ricky, the big blond Viking I remembered from my visit to the barn, though he was wearing clothes today. He was big enough, he made the oversized chair look normal.

To our left was a small man, very neat and formally dressed in a suit and tie, with a goatee and dark brown hair brushed straight back. He sat with his legs crossed, looking lost in his chair compared to Ricky and Felix. I recognized him as one of Alex's friends from the charity ball. He smiled briefly back at me and returned to jotting on a pad in his lap.

"Finally," said Felix, by way of starting. "We don't have much time."

Alex glared at him and the small guy stirred on his seat. Felix relented and introduced me, pointing at the others. "You've met Ricky. And this is Dr. Noble."

"We almost met," I said to Noble. "You helped me escape the charity ball."

"I tripped the doorman," he replied, pursing his lips. "That's hardly help. But I'm pleased to meet you at last."

I laughed.

Felix got up and started to pace like an animal in a cage.

That felt uncomfortable, but not as much as seeing the effect it was having on the others. Ricky and Alex tracked his movement as if mesmerized. Even Noble's scribbling in his notebook went on hold for a minute.

Felix stopped abruptly and turned to face me.

"We had an agreement, didn't we?" he said.

"Yes," I replied.

"Tell me what it was."

I'd kinda expected this. It was the standard disciplinary setup, getting me to admit I knew exactly what I was supposed to be doing first, and then going through where I'd failed. Like screwing Alex in his office and not making any progress on tracking the rogue down.

"There's a temporary arrangement in place, which I guess means I'm a sort of honorary werewolf and honorary member of the pack. While that's the case, I'm on call for you. I'm supposed to leave Alex alone and work on tracking down the rogue."

"Succinctly put. What about my instructions for Alexander himself?"

"No contact. And he wasn't supposed to get involved in fighting between Athanate."

Failed again. Both counts. I'd visited him at his office and Alex had helped storm the factory at Longmont where Jen had been held.

I could explain each step and give reasons for it, but I didn't want to go down that route. That felt like admitting this was like a trial, and besides, I wasn't sure Felix would listen anyway. I kept quiet and waited.

Felix was looking at me. To see if I was going to justify our actions?

I thought I'd made the right decision to shut up for the moment.

"I've set a precedent for your status and given clear requirements for your behavior which you have not followed. You visited him at his work."

I throttled my demon. I had a lot I could have said. Alex hadn't been working when I'd visited him in his office; he hadn't been able to work. Felix had had him running as a wolf during the nights, trying to strengthen the pack bond and weaken his bond to me. Too much time as a wolf had been pushing him to the edge. He'd been so close to wolf, Olivia had to keep people away from him. And I'd brought him back.

Felix wasn't finished. "Then you persuade him to join you in attacking the Basilikos Athanate at Longmont."

I hadn't. He'd insisted.

Alex stirred, but neither of us interrupted Felix. Alex seemed to be able to take the spin Felix was putting on this much more easily than I was, or he was better at hiding his emotions.

"Remember, you came to me to petition to be part of the pack. Your immediate actions so far show that you can't be. The pack can't operate in anarchy. Not only do you disobey my instructions, but you also persuade Alexander to do the same. He has a senior and responsible role."

He started pacing again.

"This is not how a pack works."

Why wasn't Alex arguing back? Should I take his silence as a message to me to keep quiet?

It was a fine balance between letting Felix blow off steam at me and letting him get up momentum toward a decision to throw me out. I didn't want that. It would put Alex in an impossible situation. And I needed the support that the pack offered, for my own sanity, while my wolf and Athanate worked out a compromise.

I gave up trying to guess what I should be doing and tried what I thought was a perfectly valid counter. "Well, half the problem is that I don't know how a pack works."

Felix stopped and stood in front of the fireplace, leaning back against the mantle with his arms spread out.

"A pack works by every member of the pack contributing positively," he said. "It's not something we set down in rulebooks. It's something you have to feel. To experience. It puts roots down into your soul. You gain. The pack gains. My problem is, you just don't seem to feel it."

I was feeling more and more worried by the angle he was taking. It was as if he was saying I should just instinctively know everything I needed, and by not knowing it, I'd proved I couldn't be a pack member.

Was this some kind of test? Was he deliberately provoking me to see how much I'd take?

"How can I if I'm not a member of the pack?" However much I needed the pack, I couldn't let him go off in that direction. "And why can't I just be affiliated? It's not as if I'm a threat by being in your territory."

"You aren't qualified to judge that." His voice lashed out. "Maybe that's the way things work for the Athanate, but it's not how we do things in the pack. We don't share territory. Every werewolf that gets infused within our boundaries is accepted into the pack, but the pack and the member need to be willing and the member needs to accept their role and responsibilities. That means you need to accept me as alpha and do what I tell you to. If the pack's not willing, or the member's not willing, then they have to leave. Or die."

He'd crossed a boundary there and I felt rather than heard a subliminal growl from Alex and an immediate, instinctive response from Ricky.

Shit. Exactly what we were trying to avoid. Had Felix deliberately manipulated us to this point? Why?

Noble cleared his throat.

Felix glanced at him and nodded.

"I want to check that we're clear about the basic constraints of pack dynamics, and then I think it's in everybody's interests to state clearly what they want."

Yeah. Leave the possible consequences out of it for now.

Thank you, Doc.

Felix returned to his seat and took a sip of water while the emotional edge simmered down.

Noble tapped his pen on his pad a couple of times. "It's not an issue of any one person laying down pack law about territory or hierarchy, not even Felix. The pack doesn't want to share territory. The pack doesn't want members disobeying the alpha. Your point about not understanding the pack is valid. With Felix's permission, I'll try and help there."

Felix nodded again. "Fine. Alexander?" he said.

"Amber in the pack," Alex said simply.

Felix's face remained blank and he turned to me.

"I need whatever it is that a pack and alpha provide to help me through the transition, and I want to be with Alex," I said. That sounded selfish, but to say I wanted to be part of the pack with this sort of thing hanging over me wouldn't have been truthful. Even so, I had to add a qualifier that was going to piss Felix off. "Without conflicting with the other parts of me."

"That's the problem," Ricky said.

"It sounds like you want the benefits of the pack without submitting to me," Felix said. "What kind of a signal do you think this sends to the rest of the pack? You see my problem?"

I'd give him that he hadn't gotten as heated as he had been before. I'd even give him that he'd selected this small group of trusted advisors rather than a pack meeting so that he could, in his eyes, go easy on me.

"So, here we are. First choice, you're Were, you're accepted into the pack and all that goes with it. You are subject to pack laws and you obey me. Second choice, you're Athanate. You don't have a pack. You stay in Denver. You have no rights to call on the pack and you owe me no obedience."

There were other choices, like leaving Denver or being killed, but we were keeping quiet about those.

"But I'm a hybrid," I said, trying to feel some flexibility.

"For the pack, it comes down to Were on one side and everything else on the other."

"What about Alex?" I could feel the tension soar again. Felix didn't want to explore this. Alex and Ricky were friends and senior pack members. If Alex came down on my side, Ricky would be pack-bound to oppose him. It dawned on me that Felix had to be thinking that however this turned out, it weakened the pack. "Hold on," I said, before he could respond. "First things first. We were supposed to say what we wanted. What is it you want, Felix?"

He stirred in his seat. "Of course, no alpha wants any member of the pack to leave, and that goes double for someone like Alexander, at a time like this."

"His marque's changed and it doesn't seem like it's going back."

I could see I was displaying a real talent for picking the topics Felix didn't want to talk about.

"That's the reason for my orders to stay apart. Whether or not you're conscious of doing it, you're having an effect on Alexander. His marque and his mental state."

"But if we're mated…" Alex said.

"Then you're both pack," Ricky replied before Felix could say anything.

But that could just mean we were a pack together, without necessarily being part of the Denver pack.

"Alex is kin," I said. "Does that count?"

"If it counts, then you're still subject to pack law," Felix said. "Alexander can't mate outside the pack. Splitting a pack is an attack on the whole pack, and I would treat it as such. Exerting Athanate control over Alexander would come under that as well. Another reason for you to stay apart until I'm sure that's not the case."

Athanate and kin can't split like that. I might be a very young Athanate, but I knew that already. And I felt it too; it'd be like ripping my arm off.

As for the exerting control, I'd freaking bound him. Yeah, that would probably be classed as influencing him. And however right it felt to me, if Felix realized it, did that mean I'd signed my own death sentence?

I shook my head. We were at a dead end here. Figuratively, I hoped.

But underlying all the arguments was the sick sensation deep down inside that this just didn't feel right. I'd called him alpha in the barn when I'd first met him, but Felix as the alpha of my pack didn't sit well with me at all. I had no idea what my relationship with my alpha should be, but I was damn sure it shouldn't feel like this. Something very fundamental was going on inside me, and it didn't want Felix. It felt like he had no right to give me orders, and my wolf was driving me to disobey him in a game of dominance.

My surface attitude; that I could change. I'd spent a long time in the army where sometimes I'd just saluted the uniform and carried out the orders.

Couldn't I manage that here? If my life depended on it?

But underneath. Had this sudden surge against him been triggered by his behavior toward me, or did it just mean he should be my alpha and this feeling showed I was already on the road to turning rogue?

"Are you claiming to be part Athanate, Alex?" Noble asked, breaking my chain of thought. "Your change of marque has all of us concerned."

"No. I have no feeling of affiliation with Altau," Alex said, and a little of the tension reduced when Felix nodded in satisfaction. That was a huge point for them. I could understand that. The thought of a senior, trusted member of the pack actually loyal to Altau rather than the pack would have had my paranoia fired up too.

"We should put the Athanate issue aside," Alex said, "and concentrate on the pack."

Noble nodded.

Felix folded his arms. "You're implying that you remain a loyal member of the pack," he said, "and yet you're disobeying my orders. *You* know that doesn't work for us."

"It's not about loyalty or obedience. The question comes down to whether Amber is pack or not. If she's pack, then she has a right to call on the pack." He paused, and I could feel him searching out the best path. No one else spoke. "When we mate, our mates are pack, whether they change or not. And she's acknowledged you as alpha. For me, she's pack."

"We're not animals. I don't get confused between mating and sex," Felix replied. "And as for acknowledging me, she immediately put a limitation on it. She said she wouldn't go against Altau interests."

"I've said the same to Altau about the pack interests," I pointed out.

"But then the Athanate comes back into the discussion. You can't be half in the pack—"

"Altau say the same, but they're willing to say I'm an affiliate."

"And even if I agree to that, Alexander didn't go running into the building at Longmont where *you* were being held, he went to help rescue your kin. How far are you going to stretch the pack obligation? Your kin? Your whole damn House? Altau?"

He had a point. I swallowed. More seat of the pants stuff here. "My House isn't separate from me."

"That's Athanate talk."

"Well, fine, I'm part Athanate. But I'm part Were, too."

I wanted to say that my pack wouldn't be separate from me either, but I couldn't yet.

Noble stopped his jotting and heads turned. It intrigued me how much quiet influence he seemed to have. What kind of a werewolf was he? He didn't fit in the obvious enforcer category that Ricky did. But at least he seemed to be on the side of finding a rational way through this.

"I'm not willing to come to a final decision right now," Felix said.

Ricky grunted an agreement. "Long-term solutions are probably better reached after some time for contemplation," he said.

Uh! Enough with the dumb stereotypes, Amber. He's not just an enforcer.

"Which leaves some interim requirements," Felix said, "before we get on with the purpose of this meeting, which was to talk about the rogue."

He stared at Alex and me. "Alexander will be accompanied by a senior pack member at all times," he said. "Ricky, that'll be you, Ursula or Silas. He stays at your house. I'll review the situation when we're rid of our current problems."

"We can't really spare—" Ricky started.

Alex tried to say something as well, but Felix cut them both off. "I'm not saying you stop hunting the Matlal pack, just that Alexander is never alone with Amber without supervision. I need a second set of eyes and ears to convince me he isn't having his mind affected. We *cannot*," he stressed the word and glared around the room, "we cannot have the pack disrupted at this juncture. That includes getting involved in Athanate politics or getting distracted from the challenges that face us. That's final."

But he's already bound to me, and I'm bound to him.

Shut up and salute.

Neither Ricky nor Alex were happy, but Alex had picked up on something that Felix said. "There are more from the Matlal pack? I thought we'd dealt with them."

Ricky shook his head.

Noble was unreadable, his eyes hooded as he watched the three of us.

I cleared my throat. Felix turned and stared.

"I just wanted to suggest I get involved in the hunt for the Matlal Were, as well."

"Why?" Felix said, but beneath the rough response, I thought I'd actually said something right.

"A couple of reasons," I said. "Firstly, they're Were and they've been in Denver for a few months. It just might be they've got an idea about the rogue. Maybe they've come across him. Or her."

Ricky nodded.

Felix just grunted, his eyes narrowed and calculating, so I continued: "Secondly, they're part of Matlal's House, directly or as affiliates. They might know where the Matlal Athanate are hiding." I wasn't going to get a better opportunity, so I plowed on. "Also, Altau are requesting your assistance in this. They're too stretched—"

"With their own preoccupations and they want us to fix their problems and track down the Matlal Athanate. No."

"But—"

"No. Since you offered it, we'll take your help with the Matlal Were, but we're not putting effort into helping Altau again." He waved his hand as if he were swatting away flies. "If we come across them, we'll inform Altau. Nothing more. We deal with the Were, Altau deals with the Athanate. That seems fair to me."

"We could at least try and ensure she has some of the Were to question," Ricky said. "They might not know about the Matlal Athanate, but they must have some idea where the other Matlal Were are, and, as she said, they might know something about the rogue."

"Good point. Agreed."

"What will happen to them afterwards?" I said, afraid I knew the answer already.

Felix's flat stare confirmed it.

"Can't you try to assimilate them somehow?" My skin crawled at the thought of interrogating prisoners who were going to be killed.

"They're not the assimilating types," Noble said quietly. "It's not that kind of situation."

"If you're with us, you'll see," Alex said obscurely.

"What's Altau's position on the Matlal Athanate?" Felix asked. "Or any Basilikos in Denver? Are they going to adopt them?" He knew the answer to that. Any Athanate House would kill Athanate from the opposing creed who ventured into their area without specific permission. I could hardly say the Denver pack were being unreasonable.

I shifted in my seat. I wasn't going to progress in that direction. Time to change tack. There was so much I didn't understand about what was going on. "Why are they staying?" I asked. "Matlal's out of power; his House has been effectively disowned. There's nothing for them. It's a death sentence to stay in Denver. Why don't they just run?"

Ricky froze. Noble stopped scribbling on his pad. It looked like I'd just stumbled on some secret that they'd not wanted to tell me.

I put on my best polite, attentive face and waited.

"They made a decision as soon as Matlal lost his position, didn't they?" Alex said.

Felix silenced Alex with a look. I could see him weighing up whether to allow this to be explained to me. In the end, he waved Alex on. He was staring at me as if he wanted to gauge my reaction to what Alex told me.

"We don't know where Matlal brought them in from, but we're sure they didn't have their own territory, or we'd know about it. We're not like the Athanate, but we do communicate." Alex reached forward and poured us a glass of water each from a pitcher on the table. "Anywhere else they go, they have nothing. But they do have something here, if they can hold it."

"You're saying they have a chance to take this territory from you? Damn! How many of them are there left?"

Ricky sniffed. "There might be a couple of dozen left."

"Then how could they take Denver?"

"With help," Alex said. "I said we're not like the Athanate, but there *is* an association of werewolves. It's called the Central Mountain Confederation."

I felt the overtones in his voice and prickled with unease on behalf of my maybe-pack.

"They stretch from around Calgary all the way down to Cheyenne," Ricky said. "Colorado is the first piece of Rocky Mountain real estate in the south that's not part of the confederation."

"They've requested we join them. We refused. Three times so far." Alex took a sip of water. "The Matlal Were will know that. If they can claim to be a pack in residence, and they're willing to join the Confederation, we'll have real trouble. The Confederation will come in on their side."

I was surprised by the anger that caused in me. How could the Confederation dare to do this?

"There's no way you want to join the Confederation?"

Felix shook his head angrily.

Parts of the whole picture suddenly crystallized in my head. Felix was walking a tightrope here, with the Altau on one side and the Confederation on the other. What if some of the pack didn't agree with his stance? No wonder he was so prickly about the solidity of the pack.

On this I was with him completely. I'd picked up Alex's reaction to the Confederation and that had just become my position. I didn't want them here.

"What about other packs who don't want to join?" I said. "Could we form an association purely to *not* be in the Confederation?"

"There's nothing as powerful as them, and there's no sufficient reason we could use to persuade others to get involved."

"They're just going to bury their heads in the sand until it's their turn?" I asked, even angrier.

Silence greeted my question. I couldn't say Felix looked happier at my outburst, but he looked less unhappy.

"So, you can see," Ricky said. "Our priorities are split. If the rogue goes on killing he *may* be caught, but he's gotten away with it so long, what are the odds on that? On the other hand, if we don't clear out the Matlal Were within days, we *will* be fighting for our lives against the Confederation."

"No! The rogue hasn't been caught because no one put the clues together. No one has been thinking it's one person. Well, they are now, and it's not just a detective in the PD, it's the frigging FBI. With a project team that's looking at all sorts of anomalies and which has landed right here in Denver. If they aren't already suspecting there's a paranormal community, they will soon, and the rogue could be what triggers that."

"Yes, but what Ricky says is right, too," Felix said. "We need the Matlal cleared out in a matter of days. If we end up fighting for our lives against the Confederation, that's an even bigger signpost to us than the rogue."

"A true dilemma," Noble agreed. "I advise, again, discussing with Altau the possibility of assistance against the Matlal Were..."

"No!" Felix made a chopping motion with his hand. "The Confederation and Altau both want to take away from us the very individuality that makes us a pack. The only difference is the speed of it."

"I disagree, but anyway, they wouldn't be able to help much at the moment," I said, and heads turned back to me. "The residual effect of Matlal."

"Athanate politics," sneered Felix. He glanced at his watch. "We've overrun." He pointed at me. "You have to be well away from here."

Noble got up and exchanged looks with Felix. There was a silent communication between them.

I tried to catch Alex's eye as Noble herded me toward the door, but his head was down.

I was hating it, but Alex's way of acceptance was better. There wasn't an alternative at the moment. If I needed the pack, I had to accept the pack rules. So much for manipulating Felix into a position. Instead, I'd had the stark choices laid out: insanity, death or obedience. Felix had been so careful not to repeat that explicitly in front of Alex. Again, I got a sense of the whole picture facing Felix and a grudging admiration for his handling it. If he'd openly threatened me again, Alex would have responded. This way, he'd made progress toward keeping both Alex and me in check.

And exactly what major business was coming up that would be important enough to close this conversation? Was Alex being held back to split him from me, or was he involved in whatever happened next?

"Meet us later," Ricky called to me. "8 p.m. at the Sten Tallrik restaurant in SoCo. We'll brief you on the rogue and the hunt for Matlal's pack."

As we reached the front door, Felix came out of the living room and held up a warning finger. "You can be briefed on the hunt for the Matlal pack, you can assist in planning, but you will not get involved in any fighting. That's an order. Now, go."

Salute the uniform.

Noble pushed me outside, before my inclination to snap back could get me into more trouble.

He led me to his Volvo and opened the door, but only to reach inside.

He handed me a business card. No address, but his first name was Theodore and his cell was listed.

"When can you make time to talk on Wednesday?" he said.

"But I'm already being briefed tonight—"

"This is not about the rogue and the rival pack. It's about you and what you need to do to become Were. It's about your being able to function efficiently while you do that, so think of it as every bit as important as Felix's tasks."

Hell. Someone willing to help me. I mentally picked myself up off the floor.

"Lunch," I said. "1 p.m. Where will you be?"

"At the Psychiatric Center in Centennial. Let's meet at the seafood restaurant at Peoria and Arapahoe."

"Done."

The woman who'd shown us in earlier appeared around the side of the house, driving a rusty Chevy pickup that must have been forty years old. Noble opened the passenger door for me and I slid in onto the scuffed leather bench seat.

Noble walked back to the house.

"Where?" the woman asked. Not going to be a chatty drive, apparently, but on the upside she wouldn't be asking me to go shopping with her either.

"Aurora," I said.

If I was going to have to wait till tonight for a briefing on the rogue and Matlal's pack, I had interests of my own to look out for.

Chapter 9

"Rom! That your skinny ass hanging out the truck?"

Aurora's best garage was hidden away off the main drag, and its best mechanic was reaching behind the engine of a long Buick. It looked as if the car was trying to eat him.

"Funny woman." Rom backed out from under the hood and we grabbed forearms, slapped hands and bumped fists. Either he changed it every time, or I always got it wrong. He laughed.

"What I got that you after today? Not my ass."

There was nothing wrong with his ass at all, but I had my hands full. Theoretically.

"Jofranka here?"

He shook his head, and gave a wave. That probably meant his niece was back at home, cleaning, cooking for her brothers, and trying to keep her father from drinking. Rom did what he could, and Jofranka spent any free time here, or down the Liu Leung Kwan, helping out.

"Is her bike here?"

He nodded. She left any valuable possessions here rather than at home. The bicycle was only a cheap Chinese import, but it'd fetch the price of a bottle of rotgut.

"You think she'd be okay if I borrowed it for an hour?"

"She'd be fine. Don' want my Harley?"

"Thanks, but nothing that can be traced," I said and left it at that. One of the things I loved about Rom was he just accepted I knew what I was doing. And his curiosity never reached his mouth.

The bike was hanging from a hook inside Rom's apartment, and her helmet with it.

Perfect. I wound my hair up, loosening the helmet grip and fitting everything inside.

"Borrow your shades too?"

He handed over the insect eye glasses he used for riding his Harley, and my disguise was complete. I'd have preferred to be disguised in Lycra, but the sweats would do. No one was going to recognize me cycling past.

∞ ∞ ∞ ∞ ∞

It was as easy to get around Aurora on the bike as it was in a car. Ten minutes after I left Rom's, I was cycling past my old landlady's house.

I'd had to leave when Hoben found out I lived there. I'd brought danger to the Desiartos' lives. Mrs. Desiarto had liked me, but after a booby trap of Hoben's almost killed her, she hadn't been sorry to see me go.

There was a dark green SUV parked at the end of the street. Not too close, but close enough for a guy lurking behind those tinted windows to see anyone going in and out.

I took the next left and in another ten minutes I passed Mom's.

This one was a panel van, in industrial blue. I gritted my teeth and concentrated on cycling away at a steady pace. A right turn and a glance down the next street showed another van. Front and back under surveillance.

These weren't amateurs. Ops 4-16 was in town and they were trained to the same standard as Ops 4-10.

I had gone by too quick to check, but they'd probably drilled a small hole in the side of the van. They'd be filming through that hole, and a cyclist going back for a second pass might catch someone's attention. For that matter, they might have video feeds from both sites and someone smart enough to put it together.

I didn't dare attack the watchers. I had no weapons and there'd be live comms between sites. There'd be backup close at hand. Even if I did get away with it, any attack would only serve to focus attention on Mom or Mrs. Desiarto.

I couldn't *not* do something either. At some point, Petersen would escalate. It'd be the easiest thing in the world for him to take Mom and force me out of hiding.

If I'd put this operation together—hunting down a woman in Denver—there wouldn't be much hope for my target, if she was alone.

Good thing I wasn't alone.

Before I escalated this, I wanted to check for Nagas watching my office, but that needed to be done on foot. I headed back to drop off the bike and bum a lift from Rom.

∞ ∞ ∞ ∞ ∞

"Well, now, Ms. Farrell, like your former colleague, you surely are full of the most fascinating information."

I was talking Agent Ingram through the Naga stake-outs over the phone.

"I'm glad you're finding it interesting, but I'm kinda hoping for some action here." The demon that lives in my throat—and too often gets me in trouble—tried to double up the short syllables to match his drawl.

My army training had focused on the tactical. The problem in front of me was Nagas staking out my friends, family and business, with a threat to innocent bystanders. My army training wanted to go in like a steam hammer and flatten the threat.

But the real strategic problem was the whole structure that had allowed Nagas to exist, and then allowed Petersen to take over Ops 4-10. And to fight that, I'd gone to the people with the power to deliver a solution.

Now I had to finesse Ingram into wrapping up my tactical problem at the same time as he fixed the strategic one. It would be all fine to close down the Ops 4 group, but the Nagas were here on the ground.

"I hear you," he said. The sound blurred as his hand covered the phone, but I could make out background noises of teams being prepared for deployment.

Ingram might seem ponderous, but he moved like an angry rattler when he needed to.

"Your teams are aware of the type of people they're after?" I said when he came back on.

"They're loaded for bear." He didn't sound pleased. Something wasn't going right.

"What's up?"

"What's up, Ms. Farrell, is the law of unintended consequences."

"Is that like Murphy's?"

"They're related." There was more heated background chatter before he came back on. "What we have here is a classic victim of success scenario. We can't cover all the bases."

He wouldn't give me operational details over the cell, but I could guess what he was saying. The stakeouts at Mom's and Mrs. Desiarto's could be swiftly and efficiently isolated. My office was at the junction of Evans and Colorado. Too many bystanders, too many escape avenues. I'd worked my way around carefully and spotted at least two suspicious vans here.

"I'm reading it that I'm on my own here?"

"And I'm making a request to you to stand down. As I understand it, you're there with no weapons, no backup, no vehicle. As soon as we take the others out, the guys you're watching are going to get a message. They'll assume they're next and hightail it out of there. We'll see what they do on traffic cameras and we're going to try and get eyes aloft."

"They won't go straight back to wherever their command center is."

"Likely not. But that's the plan."

"Okay." Time for me to pull back a bit. "I'm with it. And thanks."

"Yeah." More sounds in the background. He was getting into a vehicle and joining the operation. "These unintended consequences," he said after the noise of car doors closing, "they play on the whole project too. I've got too much to do to cover the rest of all the things I'm thinking you're busting to tell me."

"I can wait." I couldn't say I was busting to tell him, but I believed that he might provide as good a path for Diana to prepare for Emergence as the colonel would have.

"People can wait, but the FBI cannot." He paused. "This project just got a whole lot bigger."

I frowned. There were things he was carefully not telling me here, aware that he could be overheard on his end. The 'project' was Project Anthracite, the secret FBI team set up to investigate 'anomalies'. That wide-ranging brief covered problems in the US Army like the Ops 4 group, but it also covered investigations of clusters of unexplained criminal incidences. Like the number of unsolved deaths in Denver which appeared to have an element of animal attack involved.

He was telling me that the FBI were putting more teams onto this.

Why?

I had to get him alone and find out.

Meantime, the Denver pack—meaning me—was under even more pressure to catch the rogue. I didn't want to think about what would happen to Alex, Ricky, and the rest of the pack if the FBI found out about them. The thought of them caged in a place like Obs, or under arrest for murder, made me feel sick. These rogue attacks had to be stopped before the whole paranormal community risked the kind of exposure they'd been dodging for millennia—being hunted as monsters.

What were the FBI expecting to find? And what could I do to prevent them from stumbling onto the Were while I caught the rogue?

But all I could say was: "I hear you, Agent Ingram. I'll call later. Good hunting."

"I thank you, and good day to you, Ms. Farrell."

∞ ∞ ∞ ∞ ∞

Much later, I trotted away and down onto the Cherry Creek Trail that'd lead me back up toward Manassah. I knew the exact moment when the FBI had struck. It was the moment when the two vans I'd been watching had driven off hurriedly in different directions. I texted Ingram the license plates, but I already knew that was a waste of time. I hoped the FBI had been able to put up a helicopter to watch where the Nagas went, but even if they did, I expected the Nagas to abandon the vans and disappear.

The run was good. I needed the exercise and the time to think.

With his surveillance busted, what would Petersen's next step be?

What if he figured out I was staying at Manassah?

I'd need to cut off contacts with anyone I cared about and couldn't protect.

And how was I going to explain this to Mom?

Chapter 10

When I drove out that evening, I was scrubbed and changed and unhappy.

I'd made a promise to Jen never to refuse to answer a question from her, and that I'd never lie. She hadn't been happy that I was going straight back out, and she'd been even less happy that I was seeing Alex. Outlining the job I had to do for the Denver pack might have made it clearer, but it didn't make things better.

The worst thing was she didn't say anything after I'd finished telling her. Somehow, I'd have preferred being yelled at.

I had to go.

Julie was being briefed by Pia and David. Victor's guards were outside. I left it as smooth and secure as I could under the circumstances.

And Jen had passed on a request from the Denver PD to give a statement about Longmont at my earliest convenience. Sufficient to the day; I'd talk to them tomorrow.

∞ ∞ ∞ ∞ ∞

The Sten Tallrik Restaurant turned out to be low and deep, squeezed between a sports shop and realtor down in SoCo, the area bounded by Capitol Hill and Speer Boulevard. It'd been part of my beat when I'd been in the police, but below my radar—not a place I'd had to visit.

Alex and Ricky were already sitting at table, waiting for me. I was surprised to see a third person there, with her back to me. From the spiky shock of red hair it had to be another of the Denver pack—Alex's secretary, Olivia.

Alex got a kiss, Ricky got a handshake. I was unsure how to greet Olivia. When I'd promised I would do everything I could to find a way to overcome her inability to change into wolf form, I'd been overdoing it on the vamp pheromones and practically seduced her. I guessed I had to stop claiming I was straight, given I'd taken Jen as my kin, but I didn't want to mess Olivia around.

She bypassed all that wondering by jumping up and kissing me on the cheek. Friendly without overtones, if I read it right. Good. I didn't need any more complications.

They'd got us one of the best tables, tucked away in an alcove. Between the music and the murmur of other diners, it was fine for our discussion.

There was a pitcher of beer on the table and Alex had apparently ordered for me. I'd have to whisper something in his ear next time I was nibbling it. I order my own food.

The prickly feeling I'd had earlier in the day had returned, which didn't help my mood. But brushing that aside, I opened up the conversation on the rogue, telling them what Agent Ingram had said about the FBI's special interest, and laying my cards on the table.

"Here's the great news. I have no idea how to proceed, guys." That got a chuckle from Alex and Olivia. "The thing that's good about that is I have no preconceptions. We start from nearly nothing and work out how to do it right. Everything, every little scrap of information, every wacky idea, could make the difference."

"Yeah. We've got to do this right, first time and in record time," Ricky said. He wasn't overjoyed at this, but I settled for him not being hostile, and being motivated to keep us ahead of the FBI.

"I don't have much. Let me start. Challenge if you disagree. We'll see where that gets us."

They nodded.

I took a swallow of beer and waited while some appetizers were laid out. Little artichokes wrapped in bacon, speared with a cocktail stick. Great finger food.

"The rogue is a large werewolf. Based on paw size and jaw strength, I'd say equal in size to the largest of the pack." More nods. "They've been in Denver at least six years, quickly escalating from a couple of non-fatal attacks to murder."

"The bodies have all been found within a couple of hours' drive of downtown. The locations seem to be random. The people were killed elsewhere. There's no obvious race or gender bias in the victims. The oldest body was of a man estimated to be forty years old, the youngest about twenty. Of those identified, there was no pattern in their histories from the brief search I was able to do, although I guess the unidentified bodies would constitute a disproportionate group."

"Ages twenty to forty. Are you suggesting there's an age bias?" Ricky asked.

"Uh huh." He'd been listening. "No teenagers or children. They would tend to attract much more notice from the police."

"So he deliberately avoids kids as a precaution?" Olivia said.

"Possibly."

"What about the top age?"

"I'm speculating here. The largest number of bodies look like they're drifters. There's an age profile for that, which I'm guessing matches our list."

I let them think about that for a minute. Then I said, "You said 'he', Olivia. You have a reason?"

She frowned. "This is like a serial killer, isn't it? They're all male."

"Is it like that?" I looked around the table. This is where all my previous experience went out the window—I needed their specialized knowledge. "Is a rogue like a serial killer? Could a female werewolf go rogue?"

"Rogues can be male or female," Ricky said.

"Serial killers and rogues are completely different," Alex said. "A psychopath behaves in specific ways, probably from childhood. A rogue becomes a rogue at a point in time and the wolf side goes first. The trigger may be the human side, but there might not be any evidence, on the human side, for some time."

Or the trigger might be the Athanate side in my case.

"Some Were say you wouldn't even be aware that your wolf was rogue for a while," Ricky said.

"Not this long, surely?" I asked, and he conceded the point.

"Anyway, we don't even know for sure that it's not a pack of them," Alex pointed out. "We can say 'he' to keep it simple, but we should keep our minds open."

We thought about that while our main course was brought out. I forgave Alex for ordering for me. We all had steaks, raw, and cut into strips. We cooked them ourselves on hot, flat stones that the wait staff brought to the table on an iron tray, along with potatoes and salad.

"This rogue is behaving like a serial killer in what he does when he's in human form," Alex said, while the steaks sizzled. "He plans, he selects, he even has a secure procedure for dumping the bodies afterwards, given how long it's taken to find some of them."

I'd come to that conclusion, but it was reassuring to hear someone else reach it. "That probably means there are more bodies out there."

"And he must have a place he uses for killing," Ricky said.

"A vehicle to take the bodies out to the dumping area? Some disguise so he wouldn't attract attention?" Olivia said.

We kept throwing in suggestions while we ate the steaks and I made mental notes.

All of the things they came up with were good investigation points, but I needed more help on the paranormal side of the case.

"Is there a connection between the size and strength of the wolf and the human?" I said.

Ricky stirred.

"Yeah," Alex said. "Changing is not a fixed rule, but this person is big and strong."

"Give me an idea of how big a person you think the rogue is in human form."

"At minimum, Alex's size," Ricky said. "And the biggest I've seen is Silas. He's about six-ten."

Ricky himself was about six-six, and Alex six-two. Neither of them were people who disappeared in a crowd.

"Bigger human, bigger wolf," Ricky said. "Although there's some variation. Two guys exactly the same size might end up different-sized wolves."

"What makes the difference?"

"Ego," Olivia said, and laughed. Ricky scowled at her, but she went on. "An alpha ends up bigger than a beta who was the same size as a human."

"Dominance?" I said, and Alex waggled his hand—he didn't think it was that straightforward. Anyway, it made no difference to what I needed, which was a basic description of a human form of the rogue. Big and strong. Very basic, but a start.

"Okay," I said when it was obvious the suggestions had dried up. "I'll be at the police station tomorrow to give a statement about Hoben kidnapping Jen. I'll visit Morales and see if there's anything more. CSI may think some things are unrelated when they're not."

"We'll need a base," said Alex. "Somewhere we can meet and store evidence. I've got a small meeting room at the office we don't use, and Olivia can coordinate for us."

"Felix won't like that," Ricky said. His eyes flicked to me.

"Where then?" Alex asked.

"I think Jen would allow us to use a room at Manassah," I said.

Ricky nodded, but Alex growled.

I ignored the subtext. "You have any experience in this kind of work?" I asked Olivia.

"Not police work, but I did work in a lab once. I reckon I can handle basic forensics."

I was happy for the offer of help, but I didn't think experience in a lab made her capable of a forensics investigation. I had already gotten used to working with the Athanate, who seemed to have experts on tap in any field that was needed. Obviously, the Weres' resources were a bit more limited. It was going to take some adjusting.

"One last thing I want to say. We need to keep this investigation close. This rogue has been careful and clever to get away with this for so long, right under the noses of the pack and the police. It's a slim advantage, but he doesn't know we're hunting him. He doesn't even know we're aware of him. If he does find out, he might disappear or hide his tracks even better."

"A rogue's dangerous and unpredictable," Alex said. "If he finds out we're hunting him, his reaction may be to eliminate the threat. Or attack any point of weakness."

Whether Alex meant it that way or not, it meant Jen was a vulnerability for me. Alex could take care of himself. Pia and David were tougher than they appeared, but Jen's battles had all been fought in boardrooms. Julie's role as close protection was becoming more vital to my sense of balance. I'd have to keep her briefed on this hunt as well as what was happening with Matlal remnants and Nagas.

I wanted to help her get Keith back, but how would I hold on to her after that?

And what about Mom and Kath?

I finished my main course lost in thought, while the others talked, but when my plate was cleared away, the only conclusion I had reached was that getting the rogue off the street needed to be done faster.

The staff were trying to tempt me with the dessert menu when Alex and Ricky politely excused themselves: Alex stepped outside to return a business call, Ricky to wander around to the other tables, talking to the customers.

"It's his place," said Olivia, when I asked. "That's where the nickname Ricky comes from, the name of the place—y'know, Tallrik, tall Ricky. Sten Tallrik actually means Stone Plate; it's the signature dish. The pack loves coming here."

Even while she was talking to me, her eyes were following Ricky. I smiled.

"You two an item?"

"What? Oh, no. I don't think he wants to."

I snorted. I'd seen the furtive looks when he thought no one would notice. "He wants to."

"Ah." Olivia sat back and went all thoughtful, teasing a spike of her hair down the middle of her forehead.

Since we'd been abandoned, and only because of that, I ordered a chocolate fudge cake dessert with ice cream. Olivia asked for a second spoon.

"Sex on a plate," she groaned, and I had to spoon-fight to keep her out of my portion. "Which is the only place I'm getting it at the moment."

"Hey, take the initiative. I would."

"Hussy. Is that what you did with Alex?"

"I would have, if I'd had a chance."

She giggled, and then went quiet for second before shocking me. "Well, what if I asked you to kiss me?" She blushed.

Crap. I thought I'd gotten the pheromones under better control.

"No, not for real," she said when I frowned. "Screen kiss."

"Why?"

"It works for Alex. I bet it'll work for Ricky."

I felt as if I'd missed a vital sentence and lost the thread of the conversation.

"What?"

She leaned in. "They were talking earlier, when I got here. Ricky's teasing Alex about your other kin."

"Jen?"

"Yeah. Alex is getting so hot and bothered about the thought of you and her. Girl, you are *not* safe when he's around."

I laughed. "Bring it on. What'd Ricky think?"

Olivia looked away and played with her drink. I let her mull it over, and when she turned back she edged closer and dropped her voice.

"I'm not in the pack, but I get to meet all of them. I think they're kinda on Alex's side. I know Ricky is."

"Interesting." I smiled at Ricky across the length of the restaurant, which I figured would be almost as effective as kissing Olivia. Nothing like girls talking boys to turn a man's head. "So why is Felix being so difficult? Is it the Athanate thing?"

"Smelling like vamps doesn't help, but it's the pair of you getting together that has him rattled."

I'd already figured that out. Just not the reason. "But why?"

"Doh! You're alphas."

"What?"

"For God's sake, Amber." She rolled her eyes. "Alex on his own is as dominant as Felix. There's barely a girl in the pack who doesn't want to get her belly on the floor and ass in the air when he's around. You can turn it on, when you want. The pair of you together would be like werewolf crack. Real alpha pairs make strong packs."

"Shit." That explained a lot about Felix's stress level. "Just what the pack doesn't need at the moment."

She leaned in. "Listen, the guys don't like to talk about dominance, and you didn't hear this from me. Here's how it goes. With Alex supporting Felix, it's like Felix gets all Alex's dominance added in to his. The pack loves it, and it plays well opposite the Confederation."

"Okay."

"Now, if Alex goes, Felix loses his support. Not terrible, but not good either. The Confederation might try and exploit it. But if you stay, the pair of you could challenge. Whatever happens, the pack would be weaker, even if only for a while, and the Confederation would come in like vultures to exploit that."

I hated the thought of the Confederation coming in. "What if we both support Felix?"

She shrugged. "I don't know if you can. But obviously, that's the best result for Felix. It would make his status even higher."

"Yeah, but—"

Ricky was trotting back toward us, waving at Alex, who'd just come back in.

Hell, all the girl talk worked!

Then I saw the cell in his hand and the look on his face.

"Got a call," he said. "Silas spotted a group of Matlal. Move."

Chapter 11

"Leave your car," Ricky said. "We'll go in mine." His shiny Dodge Ram truck had the extra row of seats, enough space for all of us. Girls in the back, of course. He was making the tires squeal before we even got the doors closed.

"Where were they spotted?" Alex asked.

"Swansea, out by Commerce City. A diner called the Oaxaca, near 56th."

Swansea was an untidy strip, bordered by the South Platte River and Interstates 70 and 270. It was flat, dusty and poor, sandwiched between storage depots and processing plants. The interstates ran by on viaducts and embankments, lifted up as if they were afraid to get their skirts dirty. Railroads ran through, as well as a couple of big roads, the unending Colorado Boulevard for one. It was an easy place to get out of, an easy place to watch. A pretty new Dodge like Ricky's would stand out.

I tried to bite my tongue. Felix didn't want me involved in this hunt at all. He definitely wouldn't want me telling his people what to do.

Never get involved in someone else's command. I'd had that ground into me in the army.

"How many?" Olivia said.

"Not sure," Ricky replied. "Silas is there on his own. There's a guy outside the diner that he thinks is a lookout. He doesn't want to get any closer."

"Have we got enough people to stop them from getting away or to isolate them somewhere?" I asked. Damn. The tongue biting had stopped working.

"Depends on how much time we have and how open we want to be," Ricky grunted. "We're spread all over tonight."

"You've got trackers on their cars, right?" I just couldn't seem to stop myself.

"No." Ricky hunched his shoulders and turned onto Colfax. Great. Now I'd put him on the defensive.

He'd be taking Colorado Boulevard and that meant our ETA was fifteen minutes.

Alex talked briefly on his cell to another team, down near the University. They'd take the interstates and come into Swansea from the north, closing off the escape there, but it was going to take them half an hour to get in position.

Maybe too long, unless we delayed the Matlal Weres. "Well, you've disabled their cars, then?"

"We don't know which cars are theirs," Alex said.

"Guys, let the air out of some tires." I sat forward, gripping Alex's headrest. My hand sneaked around out of Ricky's sight and rested against Alex's shoulder. "If it makes you feel bad, you can always pump them back up afterwards."

Alex and Ricky glanced at each other.

"We're not sure we want to take them down there," Alex said. "It might be better to follow them back to wherever they're hiding."

"If you had trackers, I'd agree." I stopped. They'd survived this long without me—there was no reason to think they'd mess it up if I didn't take charge.

Try and think constructively. What did I have to help? Oh, yeah.

"There's a place not far from there they might have a bolt hole," I said. "Old auto auction house on 64th and Jackson, just across the interstate. It's one of Hoben's, so they might know about it. It's hidden behind a store selling farming machinery. There wasn't any power usage when we were checking for Hoben last week, but they might go there."

Ricky raised a brow. Alex hit a speed button on his cell.

"Ursula? Got a spare person?"

Ursula had something to say about that, and Alex held the cell away from his ear.

"Yeah, okay, okay. If you get there in time and can spare a person, have them look over the auto auction house on 64th and Jackson. It's behind the...hello?"

He looked at the cell. "I guess she heard enough."

"I like her already," I said, and Ricky snorted as we turned north on Colorado.

"Are you guys carrying?" I asked. Alex and Ricky nodded. Olivia shook her head. "Remind me why you're here?" I said to her.

"I don't have the marque," she replied, turning away to look out the window. "That might come in handy."

"Like walking into the diner and counting how many there are?"

Her head dipped. "If it's what the pack needs."

Brave woman.

Not having the marque didn't mean she couldn't be identified as Were. She still had Were scents all over her. Maybe she could disguise that a bit, if we needed her to do something totally crazy.

"And of course," Olivia said, "you're here only as an observer."

Crap. The scent of adrenaline was making me twitchy. She could see it.

Past Park Hill, and we were suddenly on the wrong side of the tracks. Malls and houses gave way to long, low industrial buildings as we crossed I-70. Colorado Boulevard merged into Vasquez. Streetlights became wider spaced. Off the road, tall security lights appeared in the night, shining down on acres of truck parks and depots. Sites were separated by stretches of chain link fencing, which trapped wind-borne litter. Plastic bags flapped like little white flags in the dark.

Alex nodded to the left. "Diner's over there."

He called Silas again. "We're coming off on 56th," he said.

"Don't come in too close. Don't do a drive-by." Silas' voice was tinny. "It's a dead end."

"So what ways can they get out?"

"If you stay up that end of the spur, that's the only way for a car. There's all sorts of paths, rail tracks and short cuts heading everywhere. We've only got a couple of people in position so far."

"They picked this place deliberately," I said. "There'll be a lookout. How do you know he hasn't made you already?"

As if in answer to my comment, Silas swore. "They're moving. They must've spotted us. Shit! About a dozen. They're going in all directions."

"How many cars?" Ricky shouted.

"None. None." I could hear Silas sprinting across gravel. "Shit," he said again. "This is a cluster-fuck. Do what you can."

Ricky skidded us onto the roadside, pebbles spitting out beneath the wheels. He and Alex were out of the truck like they were spring loaded. A group of four men from the diner were running down an open rail track, heading toward the I-270 underpass.

"Olivia, drive around to Commerce," Ricky shouted back over his shoulder, jabbing his finger to point to the other side of the interstate's embankment.

I didn't like this at all. It wasn't my idea of an efficient operation, but worse, we were just reacting, running blindly into an area we barely knew.

Olivia slid into the driver's seat and dialed on her cell as she turned the truck around. "Ursula, four guys heading your way, Alex and Ricky behind them."

She'd turned the Dodge slowly, which gave me enough time to see movement in the waste ground that Alex and Ricky had passed through.

Two figures followed them.

"It's a trap!" I yelled and jumped out.

I heard Olivia cursing behind me, but I focused on the path ahead. I'd back Alex and Ricky against the four they were chasing. A couple more coming up behind and maybe more lying in wait? That changed the odds.

They had a head start and they were all werewolves. Even in human form, they ran quickly. I couldn't be sure of overtaking them and I didn't dare fire at the ones I'd seen chasing Alex and Ricky; it was too dark and all of them were lined up along the track. I didn't want to risk hitting my pack.

I pulled the HK and fired a shot into the ground off to my right.

One pursuer turned his head at the noise and the flash, and shouted something to his friend. I hoped Ricky or Alex looked behind them as well, or Olivia had managed to call them as they ran.

I was running alongside a processing plant with huge, white silos looming out of the night. The fencing shook. One pursuer had had enough and raced off into the jumble of metal gantries and storage containers. The other redoubled his efforts. I could hear him yelling, but I couldn't make out what he said. The Matlal Were had a comms system. We had a bunch of cell phones.

Frigging perfect.

The figures ahead of me split.

We were coming up to the bridge over Sand Creek. There was a running track along the creek that I had used before. There were now three directions they were escaping in: straight ahead towards the interstate underpass, left and right onto the track. There were only three of us chasing, and I didn't want us to follow all of them. If this wasn't a trap, it was at least a well-prepared escape route and they probably had some nasty surprises lying in wait.

At the bridge I paused, panting.

I could make out figures ahead, and others moving in both directions on the running track. My wolf eyes let me see that much, but I couldn't see who was who. Where was Alex?

Breathe. Close your eyes and breathe.

Hana?

Speaks-to-Wolves, my great-grandmother, had appeared to me in a dream vision and told me that my wolf spirit, Hana, would talk with me. Well, I'd had one word from her so far, and not even directed to me.

Breathe.

Of course I was breathing! I closed my eyes and let the night air slide through my nose. It was full, rich. Amazing! I'd never noticed how full before. Folded layer on layer, till it had all the substance of a river of molasses.

The night had a thousand tales to tell, but I was only interested in one.

Alex had run across the bridge. I followed him, holstering the gun and using my arms to pump for more speed. There was no way I was going to let him be suckered by someone coming up behind him. Ricky and Silas and the rest had to get on with their own battles. And Felix—either he understood I had to act, or he could go straight to hell.

I gained. I hit the underpass, and the streetlights showed me the action breaking up again. The first group was down to two and they'd split left and right. Alex had gone after the one running right, which was a good move. Left was probably going to end up at the auction house and whatever welcome Ursula had set up for him there. Behind Alex was one of the guys who'd tried to set up the ambush, now realizing he was the one caught between opponents. His friend out in front didn't look as if he was going to stop to help him out.

My body had settled down to the rhythm of the chase. I felt I had plenty of reserves. I didn't care whether that was from my Athanate or Were. My eyes focused on the hot shapes of bodies running in front of me, and my ears were alert to the possibility of being suckered myself, with someone trailing me. I kept expecting the Matlal chaser to break off, but he must've come to the conclusion this was the best odds for him. Did that mean they expected help up ahead?

We were cutting across sites. Like runners on some obstacle course, we vaulted and climbed fences, sprinted across yards and ducked between trucks and buildings.

A couple of yells followed us, but night watchmen were there to keep people out. By the time they knew we were around, we were leaving.

We came out on 60th Avenue and the lead Matlal charged across the junction with Vasquez, veering to the left towards an empty mall. Horns blared as a Mac truck bore down on Alex, making my chest squeeze, and then he was past. The second Matlal followed and I followed him, more convinced than ever that there was something ahead of us that they were aiming for.

A Dodge Ram came alongside, pacing me.

Olivia saw the Matlal Were ahead and gunned the engine. He snatched a glance over his shoulder, saw the Dodge. His steps faltered.

I still couldn't use the gun, even if he headed away from the others. We were back in areas with people living nearby. People running after each other was one thing; firing guns was completely different. This had to be kept quiet.

Hunt!

Not a word. A feeling. My body was like a bell that had been struck with this hammer of a word. My vision clamped down on the werewolf turning in front of me, but my head was full of presence. Alex, others, even a distant Ricky and an unsure Olivia.

Pack!

A second strike rang through me. He was turning, turning.

Threat!

And I was on him, with human form and wolf brain. He was struggling to raise a gun, as slow as if he were drowning in mud. All caution thrown away to save his life.

I smashed his arm away. His gun dropped and skidded on the sidewalk as I lowered my shoulder and took him square in the chest.

He rolled.

Submit!

His tumble brought him upright, crouched with his feet under him. No pup, this one.

Submit!

His eyes told me he wouldn't. He leaped for his gun, hand outstretched, touching it as I landed on his back, breaking ribs.

Submit!

His fingers closed over the gun and he started to twist around.

I wrenched and snapped his neck. Clean, quick.

There was danger ahead for Alex. I didn't spare the body a glance. Olivia would have to deal with it. I sprinted after Alex's scent. I'd lost sight of him at the next turn. The night around us felt full of unseen dangers. The thought I would be too late clawed at my guts, drove my legs harder and harder. My wolf scrabbled inside, wanting to be released, to *run*, to *hunt*, but I needed hands to shoot with, if it came to that.

I was on 62nd, pounding eastwards. I could see them again, a block ahead, their bodies trailing heat to my wolf eyes. It looked like smoke curling behind them.

There were gates; the Matlal werewolf turned and my sense of danger shot up. I called out to Alex, my voice weak from effort, but he turned too.

A minute later I reached the gates. It was a cemetery. The streetlights barely reached inside. I ran in, every sense straining to penetrate the gloom.

It was a trap all right. They'd used their comms to call in someone to wait in the cemetery. It was our good fortune that their backups were spread too wide and only two had made it here.

Still...*Pack! Threat!* It was like a huge wave, lifting me up and hurling me forward. I grabbed one of the Matlal Were and threw him into another, tangling them both.

I felt rather than heard Alex's killing blow to my left and a cold joy flashed through my gut.

"Submit," I growled.

No use. The nearer one leaped at me, snarling, with a knife held stiffly out in front of him. He was a foot taller than me, probably twice my weight. That knife would go through me like a lance if I let it. I deflected his wild strike, crouching enough to get below his center of balance and as he fell over me, I surged back up. He flipped and tried to spin around, but I had a grip on his arm, dragging it down. Unable to control his arc, he crashed into a headstone and slumped at its base.

I turned.

The last one was backpedaling rapidly into the night.

The shadows seemed to grow solid and monstrous behind him. He thudded into something immovable that grew arms and reached and twisted. There was a sound like wooden sticks breaking. The Matlal werewolf fell to his knees. Blood spurted from his mouth and he collapsed into an untidy pile.

Oh, shit.

I drew the HK. What the hell was this?

"Amber, stop! It's okay." Alex called. "It's okay."

I held the gun in front of me, panting and shivery with adrenaline. I let the barrel rise to point at the sky.

Whatever it was snarled.

Alex was suddenly there, one hand held up to me and the other in front of him.

"Ursula," he said, "this is Amber."

There was no response. We were all panting: Alex, me and the smoky bulk that was Ursula.

"Back up, Amber."

I carefully stepped back, making sure I didn't go ass-over on a grave.

Ursula followed. She stooped over the body of the Were I'd fought, checked the neck pulse. There would be nothing.

By the time she stood straight again, my wolfy senses were piecing her together. I could smell Denver pack, and I holstered the HK.

When he was sure Ursula and I weren't going to go head to head, Alex pulled out his cell and dialed.

"Cleanup crew," he said without preamble. "Rose Hill Cemetery, Commerce City. Three bodies here." There was a pause. "Well, find him, damn it. You know standing orders at the moment."

He turned to me. "What about the other guy who was chasing me?"

"Dead. Left him for Olivia."

"Good." Alex snorted. "Ricky's going to be pissed, though. Brand new Dodge and it'll need the treatment already." He turned around to Ursula. "Any more?"

"The guy who gave me this." She held up a comms set. "Underpass, 64th and Vasquez."

Clever, to use their comms to track them.

"You heard them setting the trap here?" Alex asked after he'd passed the location to the cleanup crew.

"Uh huh. Came in the other entrance. Seems I wasn't needed."

She stood a hand width taller than Alex and just as broad.

I couldn't see her eyes, but I got the feeling she was watching me, and she didn't like what she saw.

"Ricky?" she asked Alex.

"On the trail next to the creek." Alex was already calling him on the cell. "Silas?"

"We didn't see him," I said. "They split all ways from the diner. He must have followed a different group. What about the car auction place? Any Matlal survivors?"

She shook her head and turned her attention to her cell.

Crap. I was as guilty as the rest of them, but I needed a live Matlal Were to talk to. Why hadn't I thought of that a minute ago? I hadn't paused; I'd just killed.

We drifted apart, the movement echoing the feeling in my head. For a minute back there, I had felt the pack like a physical force around me, even when Ursula appeared like a horror movie monster from the shadows. The pack exulted in my kills, the elimination of our rivals. It gave me strength and speed, lifted me up and flooded me with confidence. It made me a stomping nemesis to our enemies. I'd felt as if I was shining like the sun.

That feeling was gone.

The night was cold and closed and dark.

Olivia drove up, hunched over with a shoulder pressing her cell phone to her ear. She relayed the status from the cleanup crew. They were working their way here, collecting bodies.

Two of them were ours.

One of Silas' team had been in place near the diner. Three of the Matlal werewolves had taken the route he was guarding.

One of Ursula's team had been killed at the car auction house.

Ricky and Silas arrived.

Ricky's group had split until he was chasing one, but he'd got him.

Silas had chased his quarry down a track that passed under Vasquez. An SUV had been waiting on the other side and they'd disappeared.

Six of them escaped. Seven were dead for two of ours. There were no seriously wounded on either side.

I was frustrated and edgy. The sudden loss of the pack feeling made me angry. Our casualties made me angry. There shouldn't have been any on our side. We'd gone in unprepared and under-equipped. We needed to be smarter at this.

Yearning for that pack feeling to come back made me even angrier.

Should it be *we* or *they* when I thought of the pack?

I tried to talk to Ricky and Silas, but they were distracted by more of the pack arriving.

And I got the sense of being pushed away.

The pack was coming together and it was excluding me. Whatever Alex thought, I wasn't a member, and neither was Olivia.

When the cleanup crew arrived, Ricky fought his way out of the whirl of the pack. The dead bodies had been taken from his Dodge and he handed the keys back to Olivia.

It was a dismissal. An awkward moment, with both of them wanting to do something or say something that neither of them felt they should start.

I took the opportunity to hug Alex. I could feel his distraction, and a subliminal growl from the pack, so I deliberately held him to make my point. When I looked at him, I waited for the focus to come back into his eyes. The pack wanted him, but they could damn well wait. I still stung from the rejection.

"I felt something back there," I said. "Something from the pack. Like a huge boost."

"I know," he replied. "And they know it too. That's part of what's got them so riled." He kissed my forehead. "We don't howl to communicate. What you felt was the Call. Any Were can feel it, but to get strength from it like you did means you're in the pack. It's what gives us home advantage here."

"So I'm in, or not?"

"I'd say you've proved it." He glanced back at the gathering swirl of pack members. I felt the pull on him like a physical thing. "Give them a chance to get used to it. Felix won't hold out if everyone thinks you're in."

Maybe.

"I'm in trouble with Felix again. I got involved."

Alex frowned and shook his head. "The pack approved of you joining in, otherwise you wouldn't have got the boost from it."

A thought struck me. "Does the rogue *call*?"

"No."

That felt strange. Wrong.

Silas came over. "Guys, Felix is on the move." He jerked his thumb at the pack. "We have to get these guys away now to meet him." He turned to Olivia. "Make sure Doc knows that you had bodies in the back of Ricky's Dodge when you see him."

Olivia rolled her eyes.

Finally he came to me.

He stood close enough that I was going to get a crick in my freaking neck from looking up. He was all dark but for the gleam of the distant streetlights in his eyes. I eased my weight onto the balls of my feet. If he thought he was going to intimidate me he was going to find out—

"Good hunting," he said, and turned away.

The pack split up like fat on a hot frying pan. By the time Olivia swung the Dodge around, the cemetery was empty.

Chapter 12

We got back on Vasquez, heading for my car down in SoCo.

"What was that about Doc?" I asked.

"Doc Noble. He can't manage the physical stuff as well as the others," she said. "He's just not big enough. But he knows what he's doing with forensics, so he's the natural choice to run the cleanup team. He'll treat the back of the truck, make sure there's no evidence."

It made sense. Noble was half the size of someone like Silas, but as a doctor, he would be useful on the cleanup team. With my old police hat on, removing evidence made me uneasy, but the pack couldn't afford to bring attention to themselves.

"I'm normally on the cleanup team too, seeing as I can't—" She stopped and took a sudden interest in her wing mirror.

"And what happens to the bodies?" I asked, to change the subject.

"Fertilizer. The pack owns a couple of plants for emergencies like this. Bodies go in and come out as pellets. We sell bulk and trade, all over the country. We also have a couple of farms with incinerators."

Neat. Not perfect, but efficient and good enough for the odd occasion. I wondered what the Altau did, and whether it was time for both Athanate and Were to think more about the advances in forensics.

But that was for another time. Olivia needed distracting. I changed tack and started talking topics I was sure would work. Like Ricky, and what she should be doing about it.

∞ ∞ ∞ ∞ ∞

We turned into the street where I'd left my car. Halfway down, there were sidelights flashing and a horn beeping.

"Someone's alarm's gone off," Olivia said.

"Shit. It's mine."

Olivia slowed.

"Keep going," I said quickly. "Drive past. Go around the block."

I pulled my HK out and my fingers checked it while my eyes scanned the cars and buildings around us.

We turned and I got a good look down the length of the block. Nothing.

"What's up?" Olivia asked.

"Maybe nothing." I huffed. "Maybe some of Matlal's crew."

We passed it twice more before I told her to park on the crossroad approach and wait. I pressed the alarm reset on my key fob and the car didn't explode as I half-expected.

Holding a flashlight I'd found in Ricky's toolbox, I walked down the street, listening and looking, taking deep, even breaths through my nose. There was nothing out of place.

A smell of cooking came from a takeout place around the corner, a hint of someone's cologne, long passed by. The noise of passing traffic, a distant siren. Buildings and cars dark and still.

I played the flashlight over and under the car. Nothing, except a damaged trunk lid.

Gingerly, I lifted the lid. The trunk was empty.

Oh, crap.

I waved to Olivia and she drove up alongside.

"I've been burgled," I replied to her question. "My spare clothes. And my boots."

"Not your cowboy boots? The handmade ones? Oh, no! They must cost a fortune."

"They're replaceable," I said shortly, not wanting to explain. The boots had been free, given to me by Werner Schumaker, and I knew he'd make me another pair. My distress was because the boots meant much more to both of us than simply footwear. A year ago I'd rescued his daughter from three rogue Athanate. These were the thanks of his hands when words had failed him. He'd promised that he'd never use the style for anyone else and I'd never be without a pair of the boots. Even though it wasn't my fault they'd been stolen, I felt somehow as though I'd been careless of his gratitude.

"It's kinda creepy," Olivia said.

"Yeah." It did feel creepy, but it was my problem, not Olivia's. "It's not worth worrying about. Go on home, Olivia. See you tomorrow."

"Okay." She looked a bit uncertain, but she drove off.

I walked up and down the street. A row of cars to choose from and the thief had picked on mine. For clothes? He or she couldn't have known they were in the trunk. Two of the parked cars had jackets tossed on the back seat. One had a pair of running shoes as well.

I didn't believe in coincidences.

Back at my car I tried closing my eyes and inhaling next to the open trunk. I ignored the car exhausts and the everyday smells. Dug down. My nose wrinkled and I sneezed.

Chili? WTF?

Maybe the takeout—someone had walked past with something spicy? Why so strong near my trunk? Had they walked past and brushed the car?

Deep underneath that, something else prickled my senses. But all I could think of was an R&R session Keith and I had taken in Hawaii. Not useful.

The lingering sense of intrusion into my private space was unpleasant.

I shook my head and wiped my hands on my jeans. I needed to get back home and shower again.

∞ ∞ ∞ ∞ ∞

The guards were back on the gate and in the grounds at Manassah, but the house was silent.

Not everyone was asleep. Julie had found a cot and taken up a post in the hall, just past the door to Jen's bedroom.

It was pitch black, but my wolfy eyes caught her subtle movement and my nose told me who it was.

"Evening, Julie. You can put the Sig back down."

She snorted quietly. "You can really see in the dark?"

"I can," I whispered back.

I stood awkwardly at the foot of her bed. "Sorry, I kinda threw you in the deep end here. How's it working?"

She shrugged. "Insufficient information on threats and allies, probably outnumbered, short on equipment, lacking precise objectives, unclear chain of command. Feels like home."

"I can't tell you how much I missed your sunny optimism and perceptive sitreps."

We laughed quietly, and a little of the uneasy feeling disappeared.

"How did it go today?"

"Easy. Ms. Kingslund did everything from here, so I was able to talk to Pia and David. Tomorrow, Jen needs to be in the office."

"You can handle that?"

"As long as I've got some backup and we stay at the office. She's not arguing."

"Weapons?" I asked.

"Yours are back in your suite. I've got a shorty shotgun and this Sig borrowed from Victor."

"I have some spare guns. I've been kinda collecting them from the opposition. I'll give them to you tomorrow. We'll sort out paperwork as soon as I can."

"It's not all up to you," she said. "Got to delegate, Sergeant. Anyway, I spoke to Ms. Kingslund and she has an assistant who's handling my shopping list. I'd prefer clean weapons."

I smiled in the darkness. I'd wondered how I was going to make illegal weapons with the serial numbers taken off magically legal again. One less job on my list. And she was absolutely right—there were things I needed to let others do.

I yawned and took another sniff. Her scent carried a tingling of unease beneath the humor.

"What's up? Worried about Keith?"

"Yeah."

I didn't think that was all of it. "And?"

She was silent for a few moments. "Heard a lot from Pia. It all makes me nervous. The biting thing. The mind voodoo. The secrecy."

"I make you nervous, you mean."

"And David, and Pia. And the thought of what happens afterwards."

I sighed. "We've all ended up in a place with no easy choices. The Athanate, me included, can't let you walk out with all our secrets." I felt my Athanate stir. "But you have my word, there'd be no damage. On the other hand, if you stay, you may find you start to like the idea of being bitten."

She huffed. "Awesome pep talk. Thanks for that."

"Yeah, I'm fresh out of pep." I stood. "There are worse things than being bitten by Panethus Athanate. Sleep well."

"Yeah. Night."

Jen's door on the left. Mine on the right.

I felt the stir of wolf and Athanate again, not so far beneath the surface. I didn't feel in control. I knew at some point soon I'd have to accept my Athanate's need to bite. I'd need Blood. But I'd promised Diana I would wait until she could guide me through and test the effect my bite would have. And after this evening, the wolf seemed too close to the trigger.

I'd hired Julie to protect Jen. I didn't want to be briefing her that I was a threat.

And I needed a long, hot shower.

I took the safe option and went into my room.

Chapter 13

TUESDAY

About quarter to seven the next morning, I parked on Grant Street and walked to the Schumachers' shop, wearing my stockman's coat with the collar up and the Stetson planted on my head.

Werner let me in.

"Look! Look at my American daughter, pretending to be a spy." He laughed and grabbed me in a hug. The Stetson fell off and I had to laugh too. Werner was like that.

Hat retrieved, I was bustled into the kitchen. Klara made the best coffee in town. Of course, not what I had come for. Not even for the pancakes and maple syrup that appeared in front of me.

In truth, I wasn't looking forward to this visit.

Klara and Werner immediately understood when I told them, but a few minutes later, when Emily came rushing in to hug me, my heart crashed.

She knew at once that something was wrong.

"Amber?" Her eyes were already misted.

We sat back down and I gathered her hands between mine.

"Em, I have a problem." Klara refilled my cup and stood behind Emily, resting a hand on her shoulder.

"I can't say too much, but there's something going on," I said, "and it's going to cause a lot of trouble for me. I don't want you to get caught up in it. I'm going to have to stay away for a while."

Emily looked shocked.

"Did you do something wrong? Is that why you're in trouble?"

"No. I do what I think is right. It's just—"

"It's not fair!" she shouted. Tears beaded in her eyes. "You do the right thing. You *always* do the right thing, Amber. How come you're always in trouble?"

"No, it's not fair. You're right. But no one ever said life was fair, Em. It should be, but it isn't. That's no excuse for me to behave differently."

I tried to pull her back into a hug, but she tore away from Klara and me, tears spilling down her cheeks, and ran back up the stairs.

I was half out of my chair to follow, but Werner touched my arm and shook his head.

"She is very upset," he said. "But it is better to leave her now. I will drive her to school later."

"It shows how much she cares," Klara said. "The tears will dry and that will not change. Come, sit a while."

I sighed and bent my head. They were right, but it still made me feel awful. "I have to go. I have a meeting."

"Yes, yes." Werner waved a hand. "But it will do them good to wait for you sometimes."

I snorted.

"And there's another thing," I muttered. "Your boots. They were stolen from my car."

"*Your* boots," Werner said, and shrugged. "They will not suit another, and I bet," he leaned back and chuckled, "I bet she will not dare to wear them in Denver."

"He or she had better not," I said.

"I have another pair made up ready. I must just stitch. A day or two."

"Thank you."

He patted my shoulder and shrugged again as he got to his feet and made his way into the front of the shop.

"He never forgets," Klara said quietly. "We never forget."

∞ ∞ ∞ ∞ ∞

I finished my coffee quickly and left; I had a date with the Denver PD Major Crimes division at their office on Cherokee Street. José Morales was a busy man, and it wouldn't be good to be late. Still, I walked. I preferred the fifteen-minute walk to spending ten minutes parking after a five minute drive.

But I never made it.

Chapter 14

I picked up a tail a block shy of the Denver PD building.

He—or actually, she—I amended as I crossed the street and watched behind me in the mirrored windows, wasn't a pro. Or this was a double bluff to get me looking the wrong way.

It'd warmed up and I was well away from the Schumachers', so I was carrying the coat. I still had the Stetson and sunglasses, so whoever she was, she was good enough to have spotted me even with those on.

Nagas? A takedown right in front of the PD?

No. There was no one suspicious ahead of me, no net of people casually heading toward me. She was acting solo.

Who in the hell was she then?

Without wanting to turn around and stare, I had the feeling she was somehow familiar. It was difficult to be sure with her wearing a hoodie.

Journalist?

Bian would kill me if I got slack enough to allow the media any inkling of what was going on beneath the surface in Denver. She'd probably do it in front of others to provide an example. And she'd be within her rights.

Who knew I would be here today?

I walked past the PD and called José on my cell.

"José, I've got someone following me."

"How far away are you?"

"I just walked past the front door. I want this out of sight. I'm heading around to the parking garage behind the post office on Delaware."

"Give me four minutes and I'll come in behind you. Should I have backup?"

"No. We should be okay."

"See you there."

It was a measure of how much we'd come to trust each other that he accepted my word on it.

I dawdled, slowing as I went around the block, pretending to look repeatedly at a watch I didn't have, as if I was expecting to meet someone. Then, with half a minute to go, I made my way down the road and into the garage.

My getting off the street like that should have warned her, but she came in, *and* she came up the fire escape stairs after me. There's a reason why successful tails involve lots of people, and one of those is you don't put yourself in a situation like that. She'd attended some basic training in following people, but I wasn't sure she'd passed.

Still, I was getting twitchy. This was too easy. It seemed more and more likely that this was just a journalist. But in that case, I really wanted to know how the hell she'd known where I would be. And what she was trying to find out.

I heard the door on the ground floor. Hopefully that was José. I stopped and listened.

The feet on the stairs behind her finally spooked her. I heard the door on the level below open and bang shut. Then heavy feet hurrying back down and another door opening—José going back to the ramp to cut her off. I opened and shut the door on my level and waited, listening.

Clever woman. She hadn't gone out at all. She was running back downstairs. Sneaky.

I swung over the railing and jumped. In three jumps I had her as she hauled open a door to escape into the ranks of cars. I had her wrapped up and bundled back into the stairwell before she could draw breath to scream. José must have seen the door swinging and he burst in as I pushed her roughly to the ground and snared both her hands.

Her hood slipped back.

"Melissa!" José yelled. "For God's sake!"

I froze. As soon as the hoodie came down I recognized her too.

What the hell?

Melissa Owen had been the star of the CSI department when I had been working for the police a year ago. As in when I worked for the police for pay, rather than did things pro bono. She was pretty, at a glance, but kinda ruined it with a perpetual frown of concentration that made her look manically intense. Her gray eyes were narrowed and her streaky blond hair pulled back into a tight bun, only a stray lock escaping to soften the effect.

I hauled her roughly to her feet and she dusted down her gray pants, glaring at José and me. I had no time for this shit.

"Someone going to tell me what's going on?" I asked. "Workload gotten too light in CSI?"

"No," said José. "The workload has just gotten a whole lot worse. Especially since Melissa was suspended."

He seemed as pissed as I was.

My eyebrows rose. "Take her to an interview room?" I suggested.

"We can't," said José. "I can't even be seen with her." He ground his teeth and elaborated. "Employment regulations."

Melissa hadn't said a word yet.

"What were you thinking, stalking me?" I asked her.

"I need to talk to you. I'm perfectly aware of the problems that might cause if we're seen." She and José continued their staring match. "So I was trying to make it discreet."

"The last person to stalk me around here was the hit man for a drug gang." I opened my jacket enough for the butt of the HK to show.

Melissa's eyes widened and she swallowed, suddenly looking less defiant than she had.

"Really dumb," she said. "Sorry."

"And how did you know I was going to be here at this time?"

She blinked. "I didn't. I was coming in to meet my legal rep and I saw you." She peeled the hoodie off and revealed that the pants I'd nearly ruined were part of a charcoal gray business suit. "I just got the sweatshirt from a shop and followed you. I didn't want to talk to you in full view of the HQ, just in case anyone saw. I was about to give up when you came in here, and I thought that would be ideal."

A couple came down the stairs, looking curiously at the three of us before heading out the door.

Melissa handed me a card with her cell number. "I better get to my appointment. I'm sure the captain will fill you in about me." With a final glare at José, she edged out between us and away.

"Am I missing a story here?" I looked at him.

"Yeah. Not my doing. Her department head suspended her last week because of the time she's spent on her own investigation. It's gotten worse and worse over the last year."

He jerked his head and we started walking toward the exit.

If she thought she needed a quiet word with me, I suddenly had a sinking feeling I knew what Melissa's private investigation was about. I squeezed my eyes tight shut. I'd been getting worried it was a journalist following me. Melissa was in a different league of problem.

José didn't notice my reaction. "Suspending her has stalled about a dozen investigations," he complained. "She has no friends at the PD now. She thought I would be able to overrule the suspension for some reason."

His next words confirmed my worst fears.

"I was going to talk to Colonel Laine about her, but something happened last week," he said. "Can't raise him, and suddenly I'm getting those priority DoD requests for a liaison meeting with some other colonel. On top of that, I've got FBI SWAT teams charging around the city arresting army people and telling me to mind my own business."

"Damn. One thing at a time. Melissa's personal investigation is about the Athanate?"

José shrugged. "She won't say what it's about, but I'm guessing that's it. Apparently she's been trawling every crime database and incident report since last year. First on her own time, then more and more while she's supposed to be working."

"Last year? You mean since the colonel had the bodies of those three rogues snatched out of the morgue under her nose and we came up with a bunch of bullshit about what had happened?"

He nodded. "That's about the size of it. Of course, she's absolutely right, there *is* something there, but I can't tell her, or her department head. Ideally, I was hoping I'd get the colonel's agreement to take her into the Snakebite team, bring her fully onboard, but I guess events have just run away with us. No Snakebite team, no colonel and the goddamn FBI sticking their noses into everything."

We walked out of the parking garage and crossed the road back to the HQ.

"Crap," I said. Like it or not, this had landed in my lap. I was going to have to deal with it. "It's not a problem for you if I meet with her?"

He shook his head, raised a brow in question.

"I have an idea." The seed of a plan had started to form, but I'd have to think it through and run it past others.

In the meantime, José needed to be aware of what else was going on. "The colonel who's trying to meet with you is called Petersen?"

"That's the one. You know him?"

"He's responsible for…" My guts clenched and I couldn't go on. "Forget it. This is with the FBI now. If Petersen goes ahead and makes an appointment, make sure you pass that on to Agent Ingram." I stopped and took a deep breath. "Petersen's from the same special ops group I was, but he's…"

What? I didn't know what Petersen had done, or what he expected to get out of this. Surely, someone had to be about to step in, even if his immediate superiors were part of the problem? Someone, somewhere?

We'd gotten to the PD entrance, but neither of us wanted to pass through the building having this conversation, so we stood there.

"You're saying he's gone rogue?" José prompted me.

"Yeah. In the non-paranormal sense of the word."

I shivered. Rogue. Insane? No, something about the way Petersen behaved told me he wasn't insane. I could imagine him making a compelling case to that committee about how much benefit the military would derive from harnessing paranormal capabilities. But they had to have kept it within their group, didn't they? Forget the oversight issues, keeping a project like that secret would be impossible. Maybe there wasn't anyone else involved. Maybe Ingram was right.

Or should I start to wonder about Area 51 and UFOs?

"Hey?" José's gentle inquiry brought me back. He was looking concerned.

"Sorry," I said, giving myself a shake. "The word rogue is kinda in my face at the moment."

"Tell me about it."

José had understood, early on, the need for secrecy around Ops 4-10's handling of me. He'd accepted and supported the way Colonel Laine and I were proceeding. Hell, he'd even become a friend. But he was still the boss of the Major Crimes division in Denver, and he needed to know more than Skylur and Felix would like him to.

He was halfway between inviting me to talk and telling me.

"Petersen first. He's taken control of Ops 4-10, the group Colonel Laine and I used to be in. I've got to believe that most of 4-10 wouldn't accept running operations in the US, but he's also in control of another battalion, Ops 4-16."

"Let me guess," José said tiredly. "4-10 without the moral compass?"

I nodded. "I'd advise leaving all that to Ingram."

"That's what was happening yesterday in Aurora?"

"I think so. I haven't had time to talk to Ingram. Do you know how it went?"

He shrugged. "No shots fired, some people taken into custody and a couple of vehicles impounded. I understand they were trying to track some other guys from a police helicopter, but they lost them. Good result overall."

"Yeah. Let's hope it doesn't ever get to a shooting match."

"These 4-16 guys are good?"

"Uh huh. Pretty much the same skillset as 4-10."

"Shit. And lots of them?"

"A battalion back in Carolina. But I don't know how many here." My cell was beeping. I sent it to voicemail. "There's lots more going on, and we'll have to talk sometime, but at the top of my list is the werewolves."

José looked expectant. He'd provided me with the initial police report into unexplained animal attacks that had been the start of my investigation into the rogue, back when I'd been trying to prove that werewolves weren't involved.

"There's a rogue werewolf in Denver," I said flatly. "Responsible for at least some of those animal attacks in your report and probably some that haven't been found yet. I've been volunteered by the Were and Athanate to track him down."

"Oh, shit," he said, but it wasn't the news he was talking about. His eyes had fixed on a new arrival in front of the building. His voice dropped. "Meet the FBI agent who's just been put in charge of the unexplained animal attack case."

Agent Griffith.

"What? He's in on the Anthracite project now?"

José's eyes flicked away. "I didn't hear you say that name."

Crap. Crap. Crap.

The problem with all this secrecy was keeping track of where the hell I was with each person. Project Anthracite was a secret FBI team investigating patterns of unexplained crimes. I wasn't supposed to have heard of it, even though Agent Ingram knew I knew. I could work with Ingram. If his partner, Griffith, was now involved, José was right, I had a problem. I couldn't work with Griffith.

This was what Ingram had been trying to warn me about yesterday.

"Well, well, well," Griffith said. "Two of the most *interesting* people in Denver, having a talk out on the street." The way he said it, he meant 'person of interest'. "A meeting without minutes? Getting your stories straight?"

"No," I said. "Not having a meeting at all. I know it's kinda hard for you to understand, but sometimes people are friends and take time to say hi." I reached into my jacket and handed José a folded file of paper. "While delivering my statement on events in Longmont to the police as requested."

Griffith glared. "You." He jabbed at me with his finger. "You are in this stuff up to your ugly, butch neck and I'll prove it. Your only chance is going to be WITSEC. You want to start thinking long and hard about that."

I wanted him gone, so I throttled my demon's comeback and gritted my teeth.

"Captain Morales, we have an appointment. Now." Griffith shouldered past me.

"Talk when we can," I whispered to José, and he followed Griffith into the building.

I checked the cell. Tullah.

Call me.

Chapter 15

"Tullah, are you okay?" I asked as I started to retrace my steps back to the car. I hadn't seen or talked to her since Saturday after the firefight with Hoben's men, when she'd refused to go back to Haven with the rest of us. Adepts and Athanate didn't normally mix, and Tullah didn't yet have control over her dragon spirit guide, Kaothos. As witnessed by the spectacular explosion Kaothos had caused at the warehouse in Longmont, mostly without Tullah's permission or cooperation. No wonder she didn't sound good.

"I'm fine," she said, but I could hear she meant the opposite.

"Talk to me." I tried to lighten it up. "Is Mary going to kill me for involving you in Athanate stuff?"

"Ma's calmed down some. She and Pa would like to see you at the Kwan. Can you head over there now?"

"Sure." Tullah's mother was a powerful Adept; her father was a martial arts master. Either one of them could kick my ass, and they both probably wanted to. This was going to be so much fun. "What about you? Will you be there?"

The pause seemed to stretch forever. "I can't," she said at last. "I'm sorry, I need to talk this through with you over the phone. I'm such a coward."

My heart skipped. I relied on Tullah; more, she was like a little sister to me. The idea that she couldn't face me hurt.

"You're not a coward, Tullah. What do you need to talk about?"

"Kaothos."

Tullah's spirit guide had spoken to me twice. I hadn't told her at the time.

"Look, I'm sorry I didn't tell you I'd spoken to your dragon, but honestly, I wasn't sure whether I was dreaming or not."

"I know. I was upset about that at first, but I've spoken to her and she's admitted that she approached you. This is something else."

I didn't like the sound of this. Mary had warned me that dragon spirits were unpredictable, and tended to try to influence their hosts. "So what is it?"

"It's what she wants. You remember the explosion at Longmont?"

The vision of Tullah standing there with a shadowy glimpse of Kaothos towering above, reaching into the sky and feeding on the storm, was fresh and stark in my mind.

"Kinda hard to forget."

"I don't have the depth to handle that amount of energy on my own. When you touched me, she used both of us to create the blast that destroyed the factory."

"Yeah, well, you can't argue with the result, Tullah. If she hadn't done it, both of us would probably be dead."

"I know," she said. "But a spirit guide should *never* take control like that. Ma says she's probably damaged us—you, me, your spirit guide, Hana." She sounded like she was crying. "Ma was right. Once it starts acting on its own, using people, what's to stop it? That's why dragon spirit guides are so dangerous."

"Whoa. Hold on there. Damaged us? What kind of damage are we talking about?"

"We don't know!" She was practically hissing with frustration. "People here know squat about dragons. Or hybrids." She hesitated. "Has Hana stopped talking to you?"

That was an odd question. "Hana? No. I mean, she hasn't ever really spoken to me. One word at Haven after the Assembly. And maybe something last night. Why?" I felt a stir of worry.

"Ma says the channeling of that much energy..." she stopped again. She seemed to gather her courage, and then blurted out, "It might have damaged Hana. It might destroy your ability to channel, like permanently."

That was chilling. I hadn't had much contact with my spirit guide, but I'd felt comforted knowing she was there, and that when the time was right we might learn to channel power together. I hated to think of Hana, the wolf pup, being hurt. But as I thought about it, it didn't feel right or true. Damage, yes, maybe. But permanent? No. Surely I would feel it. And even if it was true, it wasn't Tullah's fault.

"I don't think so," I told her. "And you said it yourself, no one knows."

This sounded like a kind of panic reaction to me, and completely outside of Tullah's normal attitude. However, telling her that was guaranteed to be unhelpful.

"Okay, so we shouldn't link up like that again," I said, "but are you suggesting we can't see each other at all?"

She went silent again. "I just can't at the moment. It's not just the damage. I know what she wants, Amber. Kaothos. I don't trust myself to be able to fight it yet."

This was disturbing. "What exactly are you saying she wants?" I reached my car and leaned against it, looking around.

"You remember Adepts form communities to teach and support spirit guides? Well, Kaothos thinks your Athanate House would be the right community."

Oh, shit. I suddenly understood what she was saying. I hadn't when Kaothos had spoken about it. Kaothos might not have meant Tullah should become kin; surely she'd have said. But my *House*—that meant bound to me. That meant biting. *That* got a response. My Athanate stirred inside. *Yessss.* I got a glimpse of what Bian must have felt—to have an Adept, especially one with such ability, in my House. My Athanate wanted it.

I got in the car and slumped in the seat.

Oh, shit all right.

"Ahh. Yeah, she said something about that."

"See! She planted the idea in your mind. You didn't even want a House before."

"Tullah, I've changed." I tried to think how to put it, but all I could think of was: "The House is just part of what's me now."

"And she wants you to bite me."

I swallowed.

Mary is going to kill me. Slowly.

If she got to me first. Every other Adept would be after me too.

"She says that's the way to increase my abilities to channel energy."

"I would never bite you." My Athanate lashed around inside me in disagreement. *Yesss.*

No!

"Unless you really wanted me to," I compromised.

"I know. I trust you. The trouble is, Kaothos is trying to argue me around to wanting it." She sighed. "Look, it's best just to stay away from each other for the moment."

That hurt, on all sorts of levels. I tried to damp it down, get off the emotional stuff and deal with the practical. "What about the PI company?"

"Amber, I would never let you down like that. Of course I'm still working. I'm handling all the normal cases fine at the moment. I've got myself a gun like you said and I'm practicing at the range. It's all going well. Oh, and I've emailed you one case you have to do. It's a Mrs. de Vries. She's a friend of Mrs. Harriman. In fact, Mrs. Harriman is the client and she's asking for you."

"Huh?"

"It's all in the email."

Mrs. Harriman was half of the McIntire-Harriman duo that ran the annual Foundation Charity Ball. I'd met her at the Ball and immediately liked her. Of course I'd look at the case. Eagerly. If she became a happy client, that would be the best advertising I could have.

"Well, okay." I stuck the key in the ignition. "Anything else?"

"Yeah. We're actually doing better than you think. The company. I've emailed you a summary. I'm out a lot. I've…err…hired someone to handle the phones. Casual work, part time of course. We're not obligated."

My ears pricked up. "Do I know this person?"

"Umm. Jofranka."

"As in Rom's niece? Tullah, he's going to frigging kill me."

"No he isn't. He's really pleased, I swear. I had to make him promise not to thank you before I told you."

"But it's dangerous."

"She's not working at the office. All the phones are on forward to our cells. She's sensible and she's smart. It makes sense; she's bringing in the work and I'm doing it or subcontracting. She does the billing and chasing. It works. It's cool and—"

"Just stop." I closed my eyes and silently counted backwards. It didn't help much. "I'm done pussyfooting around all these issues. The pair of you want this? Right. You both meet me, tomorrow morning. *If* you get me to agree, then I will set rules and you will follow them." Tullah tried to interrupt and I overrode her. "That or nothing. I've got too much going on to be distracted worrying about what you and Jofranka might be getting into."

I had no idea what I'd do without Tullah in the company, but I couldn't let this go.

"But Kaothos—"

"If you can't deal with her and me in the same room, I can't trust you to be handling the kind of shit you'll be coming up against out there." I softened my voice. "I'm sorry, Tullah, but that's just how it's got to be."

She realized I wasn't moving on this. We agreed to meet at Manassah and ended the call.

The whole thing left me unsatisfied. Not just having to rein Tullah in and get some semblance of control over things with my PI firm, but the little questions it started echoing in my head.

Had Kaothos done something to me while we were talking in those strange dreamy conversations? What could a dragon spirit guide do? Was a nudge in the right direction all that was needed? And was that me, pushing Tullah to come see me, or my Athanate?

I needed to talk to someone who didn't have a side in this. *Not* Tullah or Mary.

Who?

∞ ∞ ∞ ∞ ∞

I made good time getting across town and I parked right in front of the Kwan.

I'd made one stop, at Zenia's, for a takeout of Greek finger food. Mary loved the baklavas, so it was a kind of peace offering to her. I had allowed Tullah to accompany us out to Longmont, and I wasn't going to apologize to Mary for it. As I'd said to Tullah, I'd probably be dead if she hadn't been there. Mary might not see it like that.

Anyhow, picking up takeout looked like the only way I was going to get lunch today.

I felt awkward about even that small delay when I saw the handwritten sign outside the Kwan.

Classes canceled today.

I frowned. How bad was this? The Kwan was always open. Classes did not get canceled.

The door was not locked, but as I slipped inside I felt a prickle over my whole body. Was that a magical ward? The sensation was similar to the one I got from my bracelet when someone was trying to kill me, but there was no threat with this one. And that sharp smell…something important tugged at my memory, but I lost it as Mary came out and greeted me.

"I brought mezes," I said, holding up the bags. "Shredded lamb in pastry, minced lamb wrapped in vine leaves, fresh salad and a sadziki dip. Baklavas for dessert."

She didn't look angry, but there was an unsettling tension radiating from her.

"Thank you," Mary said. She was normally so calm and confident. Not today. "We have a friend here, but it looks as if it'll stretch, if you're okay with that."

"Sure."

"Come on back."

We walked through the empty Kwan to the offices at the back. Liu was making tea in the little rest area and waved; little appearances of normalcy masking an underlying strain.

"Please bring some paper plates and napkins, Shi Fu," I said to him, indicating the bags again.

He nodded distractedly and went back to his tea ritual. Rinse the tea leaves and pot with the hot water, half fill the pot, wait, then add the rest of the water. No stirring. And never allow the water to actually boil. No variations allowed.

We reached the little office.

"This is Ken Weaver, a…colleague." Mary introduced the man waiting for us inside.

An Adept. They didn't have a marque like Athanate or Were, but there was definitely a presence about him that was similar to Mary and Liu. An Adept, and a high-ranking one too.

I put out my hand, but that was as far as I got.

"What is this?" His eyes went wide with shock.

"Ken, no—"

"Spirit guide me! You think I'd talk to Basilikos?" he shouted, backing away from me. That wasn't to run away—it was to free his arms to swirl about him. Behind him and around him a smoky apparition of a buffalo formed and my bracelet started to pulse urgently, making my whole arm prickle.

My own wolf spirit guide, Hana, started to snarl, but I had no idea what to do to defend myself from an Adept's attack. I staggered, bewildered at the sudden threat and assaulted inside by Athanate and Were rapidly descending into fight mode.

Mary shoved Ken back. Her spirit guide formed, and that was one angry mama bear she had there.

"Stop!"

We all froze. I sensed Liu behind me, tea rituals abandoned.

The spirit guides wavered and flowed like wood smoke in the wind, disappearing.

"She's not Basilikos," Liu said.

"You say! Look with your own eyes. Are you blinded?"

Ken edged around the other side of the office, keeping the table between us. I moved away from the door. If he wanted out, that was fine by me.

Liu stepped back and held his hands up.

"Just wait, Ken. There will be a reason for this."

"A reason? Or an excuse? I should have listened to the others. This is madness. You're on your own." Ken backed out into the Kwan, spun on his heel and strode angrily away.

The sound of the outer door slamming echoed through the empty building.

I closed my eyes for a moment and waited for my heart rate to come back down. Mary and Liu just looked at each other. An *Oh, God, what have we done* look.

"What just happened?"

They stared at me as if I'd grown another head.

My demon took over and I looked down. "Eh? Shoes on the right feet. No double denim. It was the mezes, wasn't it? Too much lamb. He can't eat lamb."

"Amber!" Mary snapped. "This is no joke."

Liu touched her arm gently. "I think maybe I will fill the big pot for the tea," he said, and returned to the rest area.

We sat subdued until the food and tea were ready.

"Thank you. Very thoughtful of you to bring food." Liu poured me a tea and left the huge pot in the middle of the table.

"De nada. So what spooked Ken?"

"Your aura," replied Mary. She reached across the table, gripped my hands and stared into my eyes. I felt dizzy, as if the whole room had suddenly swiveled and I was looking down the side of a skyscraper. Mindless fear blossomed in my chest.

"Amber," Liu said, "tell us what happened."

I snatched my hands back and the room righted itself. "I have no idea what you're talking about."

"Your aura has changed—"

"You've fed on fear," Mary cut across him.

"No," Liu said. "Look again. That is not feeding."

He offered his hand and I put mine reluctantly into his. There was no dizzy sensation with Liu, no sense of Diana's bottomless power, or Skylur's sharpness, but a blend of every sensation I'd felt when someone was messing around in my head. I started to tremble.

"You've taken something, using your Athanate telergy. Something very unpleasant," Liu said, and let go of my hand.

"Stolen?" Mary frowned.

"Why steal something unpleasant? Something full of violence and fear." He looked at me, waiting.

I slumped in the chair, the adrenaline surge leaving my body feeling weak. I had stolen the memories, in a way. I had to make them understand why I'd done it. And maybe they would know of a way it could be fixed.

I told them everything about that day, from the time that Jen had been kidnapped right to the scene in the back of the van, where Bian forced me to heal Jen without knowing how to do it. Of course, that included Tullah coming along on the rescue mission, but I found they already knew all about the part where Tullah and I had somehow joined forces to channel Kaothos's energy into blowing up the factory.

Mary was still frowning, but Liu seemed to understand.

"I thought I could handle it," I said, wrapping up about the healing session with Jen. "They're not my memories, after all."

"They're not memories, Amber, they're emotions." He sighed. "Whether you meant to or not, it's as if you're feeding on them. You've locked them away," he laced his fingers together tightly and then slowly released them, "but they're leaking. And these are not the emotions that Panethus should feed on. That's what we're seeing in your aura."

"Eukori," I muttered.

"No. That's the Athanate word for what you sense," Mary said, and stopped. There was something there that the Adepts felt was different, but she wasn't going to tell me. "It's their fault; the Altau must fix this. They're the ones with all the experience of manipulating memories."

"They already know about it." I'd told Bian. I needed to wait for Diana to come back and fix me, but I shouldn't be telling Mary and Liu about Altau's leaders.

"Then explain to them again," Mary said impatiently. "They've missed the point. This will pull you more and more to the Basilikos side." She rested her head in her hands. "On top of everything else..."

"Talk to them soon. Today." Liu licked his lips. He and Mary exchanged a guilty glance. "And...we also have a request we'd like you to put to them."

I snorted. "You want something from the evil Athanate?"

They had the grace to look embarrassed.

"The community we talked about before," Liu said. "Obviously, we have to persuade Tullah and Kaothos to join. We need to give Kaothos a reason to participate. We need to know how a community is formed with a dragon. We talked to all the communities we could in this country and no one has any suggestions."

"Tell it like it is," Mary said. "They've abandoned us to our crazy scheme. Ken's the only one willing to help. Was."

Liu's hand came to rest gently on Mary's shoulder.

"Which leaves us with a problem," he said. "However, we know that communities have been built around dragon spirit guides in China. The trouble is, we have no contacts with them."

Mary looked up. "But the Athanate in China have."

I connected the dots. "So, you're looking for Altau to make contact with the Empire of Heaven and ask them to put us in contact with Adepts living in China."

"Yes," Liu said. "Do you think this would be a problem? Would they do this for us?"

He genuinely didn't know.

I licked my lips and prepared a rant on the problems I could see. There were no official connections between the Empire of Heaven and the Panethus Athanate, except through the Warders. Who'd just been disbanded. Panethus and Basilikos were on the edge of a war, and the Empire wouldn't want to get involved in anything that dragged them into it. And Altau was maxed out playing the hand it'd dealt in the Assembly.

I stopped. I could almost hear Bian's whisper in my ear. Athanate issues stayed inside the Athanate. It left a sour taste in my mouth.

"I don't know," I said. "I'll ask if there are lines of communication we can use."

Calmer finally, we spoke in general about a community built around just the four of us, if we could get Kaothos and Tullah to agree. We finished the mezes and drank the tea.

All of what they said was dependent on finding out how to form a community that included a dragon spirit guide.

And somehow, this had ended up on me.

∞ ∞ ∞ ∞ ∞

At the door as I was leaving, I pushed my hand through and back, feeling the prickle of energy on my skin.

"Is that a warning spell?"

Liu nodded. "A very simple working. We use it when we're not open for classes. We know as soon as someone comes through the door. It's very faint; only someone like an Athanate or Were would notice."

"Or an Adept?"

He nodded.

"But I can smell something, too," I went on. "That's not a smell that identifies this type of working, is it?"

"No," said Liu. "Again, only a few paranormals would even notice it, but it's the same for all external workings. It fades over time. Internal workings, those entirely inside the body, they do not have this signature."

The smell was tantalizingly familiar. From where? The night at Longmont, obviously. When had I smelled it again? What did it remind me of?

My mind skipped and I remembered getting off a flight in Hawaii with Keith, heading for the beach, a whole four days of R&R between the end of one mission and the start of training for the next. The wind had been blowing across the strip and the smell of aviation fuel was gently pushed aside by the smell of the ocean.

I skipped again. My car's trunk open. The clothes and boots missing.

"What?" Liu said.

"I had something stolen from my car and smelled this."

Liu's eyes widened. "What was stolen?"

"Just clothes, and my boots."

Mary emerged silently behind Liu. She was pale and frowning. "Show us," she demanded.

I took them outside to the car and Mary stood in front of the open trunk, running her hands over the lip and the floor. Her frown deepened.

"It's nearly gone," she said finally. "It's…strange. Bizarrely formed. Like an untrained novice, but strong."

Liu was running his hands over the sill. "Was it hiding something?" he said, his voice uncertain.

"A masking, yes," Mary said. "To hide who did this."

"But why? An Adept could break open a trunk without leaving any traces," Liu said. "Why then make a working and leave evidence?"

Mary stood back and folded her arms. "Exactly. But an Athanate would leave a trace. The marque would linger. That's what this hid."

I tried to absorb that. Vega Martine? One of Matlal's Athanate? "So, an Athanate who can cast broke into my car and stole my clothes? Why?"

Liu and Mary had another silent contest of wills. More Adept secrets Mary didn't want to share.

Eventually, Liu spoke. "We can't say exactly. Adepts do not use this, but someone who has been trained differently might use tokens, you understand, a technique in rituals where the part stands in for the whole."

I felt a shiver of apprehension. "Someone can do a working on my clothes and it transfers to me?"

Liu shook his head. "That's superstition. Remote spells don't work like that. That's why Adepts don't bother with tokens."

"But for someone who believes in it, it might help create a link or a focus," Mary said. "I just can't think why."

Liu looked troubled.

"Practice?" he said thoughtfully.

Chapter 16

My cell rang as soon as I put it on again. Voicemail from Ingram.

"Ms. Farrell, you're having a busy day," he said when I got through.

"You could say that. One of those."

"Me too. You been anywhere I could check this morning?"

I wanted to beat my head against the steering wheel. It was a good thing I had a solid reply for him.

"Yeah. Ask Agent Griffith. He was at the PD office on Cherokee and he suggested I start thinking about WITSEC."

"Ah. Then I guess you've been apprised of the changes here."

I snorted. I'd let him know my thoughts at our next meeting. "What happened this morning?"

"Well, let's see. I got Sergeant Alverson into an isolation ward, on account of that rash, and we were having a real interesting conversation. 'Bout that time, all the other army fellahs we'd picked up yesterday and last Friday, they were being transferred from the CBI to the secure military facilities down in Springs, pending them all being picked up by that JF-CoStPROE committee. Thing is, they didn't make it."

"How do you mean? They escaped?"

"No, ma'am. The van got hit by something as it came off I-25. Just been told it likely was a TGB-7V." He spoke slowly, as if he was reading the designation off a report.

"Shit."

The whole team, wiped out? It had to be Nagas. Killing people they'd worked with? What did they do to these guys to make them capable of that?

Ingram gave me a second, then: "You're familiar with this weapon?"

"Of course I am. Round launched from a standard RPG. Thermobaric explosive specifically designed to take out armored personnel carriers and leave no survivors."

The fuel-air explosion from the TGB-7V was intense in the open air. In the confines of a prison van it would have been like a compressed piece of hell.

"Guards as well?" I asked.

He grunted. "No survivors."

I shook off another chill. The Nagas had to be taken out as quickly as possible. If they did that to each other, fine, but this way, innocent people were dying.

Ingram was waiting for me to speak.

"And you thought of me?" I said. "Sweet."

He coughed. "Just covering bases, Ms. Farrell. And be assured, Sergeant Alverson is now in a most secure location."

"Can I see him?" I didn't really want to. I was just trying to get a feel for how secure it was.

"You could maybe bring your Sergeant Alverson to see him," Ingram said.

"Hmm. And are the CoStPROE committee aware you have him?"

"Been busier than a hog in a wallow, so might just have slipped my mind to mention it. And of course now, they're all technically persons of interest to me."

I liked his paranoia.

"Wrap them up, Agent Ingram. Reel them in and wrap them up now."

"Uh huh. Just a little issue of jurisdiction we gotta get over. Can hardly blow trumpets about bypassing the laws if we do it ourselves."

I couldn't argue with him. You start like that and you end where Petersen was—killing his own soldiers in cold blood. And for what? The possibility that they might let his secrets out?

We ended the call on a vague agreement to meet soon.

∞ ∞ ∞ ∞ ∞

Neither Bian nor Skylur picked up.

I tried Melissa. She was short to the point of being spiky. "You still run?" she said.

"Of course."

"The trail out by Bluff Lake. Tomorrow, 3pm."

"Make it the Cherry Creek, meet at the parking garage behind the shopping center."

"Done." She ended the call.

By that time I was back at Manassah without having had a chance to get through to Julie.

She met me at the front door.

"Everything okay?" I asked. It was early for Jen to be back.

"It went smoothly," she said. "No problems. And you?"

"I spoke to Ingram. The important thing is Keith is safe. The rest of his team got taken out this morning while they were being transferred."

She was good at keeping her face under control, but I could hear her heart skip a beat at how close she had come to losing Keith.

"He's safe," I repeated. "Moved to a secure location, and Ingram's no dummy."

Julie flashed a smile of thanks for that, but then she thought about it and frowned. "Why kill them? Makes no sense."

That had been bugging me the whole way back.

"Nagas and the committee working against each other? Or they realized they knew too much about everything and were too visible?"

"But there's a whole battalion where they came from," said Julie. "Or was it just specifically this op that had to be hushed up?"

"But even if it were just this op, there's the entire Ops 4 group base. All the support and infrastructure. There's got to be traces everywhere."

"You'd only need a day or two to take the IT and records down."

"Huh. Just the sort of time a jurisdiction dispute would take. Like the one Ingram says he's fighting through now."

"And the people?"

Julie and I looked at each other. I could see my own growing concern mirrored in her eyes. I didn't give a rat's ass for the Nagas, but my old unit was something else entirely. If the committee was cleaning up loose ends, there was a battalion of people Julie and I cared about.

"I can't call anyone," she said. "They'd trace me in ten."

"You don't need to worry about that." I took her to the study I'd used as an office and sat her down with my laptop.

Tullah's wizard-geek boyfriend, Matt, had provided me with the ideal tool for getting around call tracers. I gave her the headset and introduced her to the octopus, explaining how the system worked, as much as I understood it.

"...so they can backtrack as far as some server in the middle of Africa somewhere and then they're stuck. Even the FBI didn't manage to trace me, so you're safe. Find out what's happening at the base. Call only people you trust," I said, and earned an exasperated sigh from her.

"Eggs, suck, etcetera." She slipped the headset on.

"Where's Jen?" I asked, before she started dialing.

Julie pointed down the hall, her face going professionally blank. "In your suite, ma'am."

She couldn't fail to understand the relationship with Jen, but she'd yet to comment.

Maybe that only meant I had a prolonged and merciless teasing session to look forward to.

Down the hall, Jen wasn't the only person in my suite.

"Lisa? Hi," I replied awkwardly to my unexpected visitor's greeting.

Lisa Macy was a magician; she took cloth and turned it into dreams. That's what she'd done for me at the McIntire-Harriman charity ball. I still felt giddy when I remembered walking in wearing that dress.

Lisa was standing in my bedroom, surrounded by unfinished dresses. She smiled at me and pulled me forward into the middle of the chaos.

"What's this?"

"Forgotten about the reception?" Jen said.

"No, of course not."

Lisa began holding dresses up against me and swiftly making two piles—rejects and possibles, judging by her expression.

"But—"

"Bian warned us it'll be formal. It's important for you." Jen stopped abruptly. "For us," she amended.

"I thought we could wear the same as we did at the charity ball. I love that green dress."

Lisa's eyes bulged slightly, but she remained silent. She started going back through one of the piles she'd made.

"Impossible," Jen said. "We can't wear the same dress twice." She saw my expression. "Not this soon afterwards," she added smoothly.

"This one, I believe, Ms. Kingslund." Lisa was holding a strapless gold dress against me.

Could I bend over in that? I didn't have the front to carry that off. Wouldn't it just fall down?

"Silver and gold," Jen said thoughtfully, tapping her cheek with a finger. "I like it."

"But what is this going to—"

"I'll leave you to the fitting." Jen kissed my cheek and marched out, closing the door behind her.

"Ms. Kingslund is paying, Amber." The slightest crinkle at the edges of her eyes was all the sympathy she allowed herself to show me.

I knew how much these contracts meant to Lisa and I couldn't take it out on her.

"If you would undress, please, then I can see how much alteration needs to be done."

I'd have to save my temper for Jen. I stripped and she draped me in the dress and started pulling the fabric and pinning it carefully. It was mostly complete and I guessed the measurements were based on the dress she'd made me before, so they were close. But Lisa aimed for perfection.

"Back and shoulders bare. Here at the side, it will follow your line from here to here," she explained. "Then just below the mid-point of the hips, after the body starts to curve back in, the material is doubled and layered, so it flares, so..." She demonstrated. "The materials here are lighter too, so they will float. A hint of flamenco in the shape, an exuberance in contrast with the pure, classic color. Ms. Kingslund's dress will be a matching one in silver. They will be absolutely exquisite."

Jen would be exquisite. I'd probably look like a donkey at the races. With ribbons on it.

Then again, to give Lisa due credit, she'd worked the impossible for me once, at the charity ball. I forced a smile. And of course, it was the politics that were important at the reception, not the clothes. I'd endured worse than being dressed up in something that made me feel out of place.

I was so going to throttle Jen.

∞ ∞ ∞ ∞ ∞

After Lisa had left, Jen had a glass of rum waiting for me in the living room as a peace token. Wise woman.

"There, all done," she said. "Those shoes that Werner made for the ball will work with this dress as well."

"Oh, so I'm allowed to wear the same shoes, am I?"

"Yes, honey, of course. They're long dresses. You can get away with the same shoes."

"I still don't see—"

"It's not just for you. It's for me as well, Amber. I have a position in this Athanate society. I'm kin." She stumbled a little at the term before resuming. "Of course, any of them who were at the ball will have met me, but I wasn't part of their society then. Now I am. I intend to make a good impression, for both of us."

"But all this preparation. And what about Alex?"

"I can't answer for Deauville. I don't think Lisa would have the right clothes for him."

"It's Alex," I said.

Temper flared in her blue eyes, making them icy. She turned away and took a sip of her brandy. "Alex, then."

A knock interrupted us, and Carmen came in with a tray of her mouth-watering tapas. More careful planning by Jen. But there was nothing quite like sharing food to calm me down, especially since Carmen's cooking was so good. We sat side by side on the sofa with the tray on the coffee table in front of us.

"Oh, try this one," Jen said, holding up a bite-sized taco for me. Instead of the standard open purse shape, it was closed and folded in the shape of a rosebud. I opened my mouth and she popped it in.

At the same time the crunchy corn wrapping burst, releasing the tang of beef chili, cream and chives onto my tongue, our eyes met and lingered.

I blushed. Tingles ran all the way down to my toes.

"Didn't realize you'd find it that spicy," Jen murmured. "I'm so sorry."

We started laughing and it was hard to stop as we fed each other from the tray.

When we'd finished, Jen kicked off her shoes and curled up contentedly.

"So," she said. "Are we good?"

"We are excellent. I have somehow lost my intention to throttle you."

She wriggled closer. I felt the gentle pressure of her knees resting on my thighs, and then the odd flip where I sensed what that felt like to her, and the flavor in my mouth was brandy instead of rum.

"Is this part of the binding?" she said. "It's not my imagination, is it?"

"It's not your imagination." I cleared my throat. "It's called eukori. Whether it's part of binding, you need to ask Pia or someone like that. I'm as new to this as you are."

Her hands took mine, or mine took hers.

She sighed. "Well, we'll explore it together." She stroked my arm.

Of course, she immediately felt it as I tensed, just as I felt the pain that caused her.

"Sorry," I said quickly.

"It's okay."

The breathless sense of sharing blurred into disappointment and faded away.

"It's not okay," I said. "It's complete shit."

"What's the problem? Too much, too quickly?"

I managed a weak laugh. "That ran out about a week ago." I eased closer to her and concentrated on breathing evenly and slowly for a while. It helped to remember we might be interrupted at any time. I could hear Julie's voice in the study and I could sense David in the house, though not Pia.

She rested her head carefully on my shoulder and we were fine. After a moment, our hearts fell into sync and the sense of sharing came back a little.

"So tell me," she said.

"Pia filled you in on the details of the cross-infusion between Were and Athanate?"

"She said that the Were might influence the development of your Athanate side. It might make you become like the Basilikos. That Altau would be worried about you even without that, because you've developed in isolation and the Athanate that bit you sounds like he must have been Basilikos. Yadda, yadda." She stopped abruptly. "Sorry, I shouldn't dismiss it like that. I know it's complicated. I know it's a potential problem and I *am* worried for your sake. But why—"

"Pia should also have told you that newly infused Athanate are usually kept away from humans except under supervision."

"Why?"

"The lure of Blood and sex," I said and she laughed. "The problem is that new Athanate get carried away with it and, if they were with humans, they would end up unconsciously trying to change them. The process of successfully getting a human to become Athanate is long and careful. Someone unprepared like you, bitten by a new Athanate, would likely end up dead, or insane."

"So what do new Athanate do?"

"They bump bellies with other Athanate," I said, "or maybe Were, who are pretty tough and can't be infused. Supposedly."

"I see." I wasn't looking at her eyes, but her eukori took on that same steely blue sharpness. "So, you can make love with Deauville but not with me."

"Alex. At the moment."

"And Pia and David? Bian?"

"Not going to happen, Jen. I don't care what the Athanate usually do or don't do. To me, kin is different from House and affiliation. Kin is special."

Her head came up and our eyes met.

My heart was hammering in my chest. I was gambling everything on being completely truthful with her, even though so many of those truths she wouldn't want to hear. Any one of them might finally convince her I was a monster and she was better off alone.

A year ago, a woman called Dominé had fastened an *angoisse* around my neck. It was a mesh collar with the spikes pointing inward, like a choker made of barbed wire. She'd done it to show me how she felt I was living my life, a tightrope walk with pain on every side.

At that stage, one of the spikes had been the fear of becoming Athanate, another was losing my job, another letting the army down.

The spikes were all different, but I hadn't changed my situation much.

David barged in noisily, carrying a laptop. "There you are. I've built a spreadsheet to show you what I was talking about on your P&L."

Jen blinked. "Ahh. The boy wonder," she muttered. She gave my hand a quick squeeze and swiveled around. "Okay, show me."

I slipped out to check on Julie.

She'd had no luck—no one at Ops 4-10 was picking up calls from an unknown caller. We worked out how to set up the octopus so it looked as if the call was coming from a mutual friend and I left her to it, calling ahead to set up my next event.

The one that sent sudden, unexplained chills down my back.

∞ ∞ ∞ ∞ ∞

Olivia and I crouched in the shadows of a fragrant screen of mountain mahogany shrubs. Leaves shivered around us in the breeze. Our target was an ordinary house, no security, lights bright enough in the rear-facing living room to ruin night vision for anyone who happened to look outside. Piece of cake—a ten-year-old could sneak in. So why was I anxious?

I was okay. Of course I was. I'd done this sort of thing before; I could handle this. My worry was Olivia. I was feeling guilty for persuading her to take this on.

Bit late for that.

Why hadn't I had second thoughts earlier? Was werewolf impulsiveness leaking through into everything I did?

Oblivious to my thoughts, Olivia's face was set—tense determination in every muscle. So much for the surface; I could sense the near-paralyzing uncertainty underneath. This wasn't what she was used to.

"You sure?" I whispered. "We can still back off."

"I said I would do it." She bit her lip and then took a couple of deep, steadying breaths. "I need to do it for myself."

"Okay." There wasn't any point in delaying any longer. "Let's go." I clapped her shoulder and gave her a little shove.

She got up and started walking forwards.

Now *my* nerves threatened to paralyze me.

I wiped my hands on my jeans.

Crap! What the hell was wrong with me? Was I channeling Olivia's fear? Was I worried what Ricky was going to say?

Come on! This should be easy. A walk in the park. A meeting of lovers, not a struggle to the death.

I reckoned there was only one way to get rid of the nerves.

In seven strides I was at the fence and vaulting soundlessly over it into the unlit back yard beyond.

A broad picture window overlooked the neat lawn. The lights were on in the living room behind it, but the curtains were drawn.

I crept forward along the side of the tool shed, careful of a coiled hose tossed carelessly nearby. A wide barbeque grill smelling of yesterday's steaks distracted me as I slipped past, but underneath that was the smell I was hunting.

Something was wrong. I could lie to myself all night, but every step was more and more reluctant. My body was screaming at me to get out. My hands trembled. Fearful, formless images boiled out of some unmappable corner of my mind.

I froze, unable to go further.

And strong arms reached out of the blackness and snatched me into a nightmare.

Chapter 17

Fear exploding in my gut. Helplessness. Violation. Shame.

I lash out. There's nothing there, it's not me, but I have to strike out. There's nothing solid behind the swamping wave of emotion, but if I don't fight, I'll drown.

It's not me! It's just Jen's emotions boiling out of my strongbox. They can't harm me. Just emotions. No memories to tie them to.

But what follows out of the strongbox is different, and it is mine, and it does have memories.

Hands gripping me, wrist and ankle, even though I'm barely struggling. I can't fight. Something very wrong. Weak. Can't focus. Pain. Oh, no. No. Stop. Please. I'm screaming and screaming and they don't listen.

On and on.

Couldn't fight there. But I can fight here. Now. Training forgotten. Mindless swinging and kicking. Screaming. Pathetic, thin sound. So scared. Pain as I connect. Blood. Wooden bench rocking, gardening tools scattering, flesh. Hit there, there! Fight.

A grip on my wrists. So strong.

NO! NO! Desperation. Must fight.

Helpless.

Defenseless.

Drowning in despair.

"Amber! Amber! For God's sake, it's me."

The screaming stopped. It had been my voice.

Pack!

Alex is here. Alex. Pack!

I was safe if it was Alex. Safe. There was nothing behind the emotions. They weren't even mine.

I twisted away. He let me go and I fell onto my knees in the doorway of the shed, and vomited on the ground until my wracked and twisted gut told me there was nothing left.

I felt his hand on my back and shuddered. He took it away quickly.

A breeze blew across the garden and cooled the sweat on my face.

I sat back on my heels, concentrated on deep, even breathing.

Behind the maelstrom of stolen emotions came my own anger. Anger at myself for getting into this situation, and anger at everyone else who'd been involved. It was unjustified, but it was clean and clear anger, it was my anger, it had a source and a reason. I used it to push the other emotions back.

Pack it all back into the strongbox.

Only, it didn't seem to fit anymore, like a vacation suitcase on the trip home. Random chills continued to slither through me, echoes of the tumult that had struck me. My skin prickled.

On instinct, I took off my bracelet. Mary had given it to me. It had an Adept energy cast on it that had reliably warned me of danger in the past.

The skin sensations died away.

A quiet corner of my mind noted that Adept workings could go wrong. Like a computer program, the bracelet spell needed information from me and if I gave it the wrong information, it gave the wrong result.

What a frigging wreck. While Olivia was distracting Ricky in his house, I was supposed to be in Ricky's garden making out with Alex. Instead, we'd triggered a meltdown, Jen's emotions and long-buried memories of my own like a volcano exploding in my head.

I was so broken I couldn't get intimate with either of my kin.

As hesitantly as Alex's hand, the feeling of our bond link crept into my mind. Clever man to use that. The sense of him was as dark as Jen's was light, but warm and welcoming.

Alex radiated comfort. And underneath that, bewilderment.

You and me both.

The gentle pressure that was Alex in my mind seemed to flow suddenly. I looked around and came eye to eye with his wolf.

That spiked my heart, but I could handle it. He was scary, but I could see him; he wasn't some formless, overwhelming panic that had sprung out of nowhere.

Cautiously, he sidled alongside. In this form, his worry for me made his breath whine, but it didn't trigger a reaction from me. The strongbox stayed mostly closed. I slipped my arms around him and buried my face in his pale ruff.

"That's clever, wolfy," I whispered, crying into his fur. "I'm sorry. I'm sorry."

I got a cold, wet nose against my shoulder for that, and a tender little gnawing of teeth against my skin. Dumb to be less scared by that than the phantoms in my head. Teeth like those were dangerous, capable of breaking my bones with a single bite. But that I could manage. That was about as back-to-front broken as I could imagine.

∞ ∞ ∞ ∞ ∞

"It's shit, Bian, complete shit."

"Calm down."

That wasn't a mistake she would have made if we were face to face. As it was, I was calling her while driving back to Manassah and her comment made everything worse. I was alone, having left Olivia so successfully distracting Ricky that the man had no idea what had been happening in his back yard.

At least my plan for Olivia and Ricky had worked.

And it was good I was alone, because that gave me the leeway to shout at Bian.

"I'll calm down when I'm dead. I don't care about being thrown in the deep end, but it's not just me. Saving David's life nearly cost three lives because nothing had been explained to me. You and Skylur forced me into healing Jen without any idea what I was doing, and that's completely screwed things with both my kin. I have to stay away from Jen because I might infuse her, and I can't get near Alex without having flashbacks of Jen's rape. Why the hell should I be calming down?"

"Because yelling isn't helping."

"Nothing's helping. No one's helping. I need time to get help. We all need Diana back in Denver. That's what I should be doing."

"I understand this is causing problems with your kin—"

"My kin are being so frigging understanding, it's setting my teeth on edge."

"But you've agreed to help the pack find the rogue."

"I can't handle the hunt for the rogue if I'm liable to have a breakdown any second, however much Skylur wants me to do it for Altau. For that matter, you're all telling me I could go rogue myself at any time. And I can't be a liaison with the Were because I don't know what Altau wants and Skylur doesn't trust me enough to tell me. I'm neither Were nor Athanate. I'm not going to—"

"But you are our liaison."

"I was and I've reported back that the pack isn't going to do what you asked. Now I've resigned. Access to my Mentor is a right, isn't it? As far as we know, Diana's in New Mexico. I'm going there to find her."

I hated this. I *never* backed away from tasks I'd taken on. It made me even madder that I couldn't see any way around it. And going on like this with Bian was hardly likely to get me the favor I needed for Tullah—an introduction to someone in the Empire of Heaven so I could arrange contacts between the Chinese Adepts and Mary.

Whichever way I went, something failed.

If I went to New Mexico and found Diana, maybe she could help me with the mess inside my head. Then I might have a chance of learning to being useful around here instead of a liability. I needed to visit New Mexico anyway. When I'd offered to help Larry escape from Matlal just before the Assembly, I'd taken on an obligation to him. And even though he'd been killed by Matlal, the obligation remained to rescue his kin down in Albuquerque.

"Let's discuss this with Skylur at the reception tomorrow," she said. "You think you're okay for that?"

"I don't know, Bian. Tell me everything I could possibly do at the reception that might get me into trouble."

"Amber—"

I'd been so focused on the conversation, the squawk of the siren and single, lazy spin of the blue police lights in my mirror shocked me.

"Crap, got to go. Police." I ended the call, kicking myself as I slowed. What kind of a blind, dumb-ass, walking target was I making of myself if I couldn't even spot a police cruiser coming up behind me?

And why the hell was I being pulled over?

How easy would it be for the Nagas to lift a police car?

I slid the HK out and sank into my seat. Trying to make myself a smaller target was pretty futile when the Nagas were taking out vans with RPGs.

But I recognized the figure trotting up to my door and let the HK go.

I tried for normality. "José, you been demoted back to cruisers?"

"Can it. Got a call from Edmunds, gotta go, *now*."

We ran back to his cruiser and he drove us away with roadside gravel spraying from the wheels.

"What is it?"

"It's a murder. I don't know what else," he said. He looked embarrassed. "Wally and I, we worked out a code for talking over the radio with other people listening."

"I remember. You called Lieutenant Edmunds on his cell and said 'game's off' when you had to close down Project Snakebite."

"Yeah. Maybe not that dramatic tonight, but he used a couple of words, 'timely' and 'cowboy'. That's top priority, get here now, and bring you. Couldn't raise you on your cell, and Jen said she didn't know when you'd be back in. I was driving by on the chance. Just plain luck I spotted your car."

I rubbed my face with my hands. "I'm not sure I can help, José, I'm kinda losing it here. In fact, I may need to go away for a while."

"Huh?" He looked surprised.

"I don't want to talk about it now. How far have we got to go?"

"Here already," he said. We'd barely gone a mile. "Wash Park." And he turned onto South Vineyard Street.

"No." I felt the first premonition of what was about to hit me. My voice shook. I couldn't handle this. I was still a mess from my disaster with Alex.

José turned and looked at me. "What's up?"

"Number?" My voice sounded hoarse.

"971."

"No," I said again, as if repeating it would make it change. I stared at the familiar small bungalow coming up. "No."

Another cruiser was already there. The house lights were on. Curtains drawn. Yellow crime scene tape. Uniforms standing guard.

José pulled up outside the house my family and I had been living in, all those years ago, when my dad died.

Chapter 18

It got worse inside.

From the hall, we could see an elderly man who had been tied up and killed. His throat had been torn open in the living room. Blood soaked the carpet and had sprayed over the furniture and walls. Around the body, there were what looked like paw prints in blood.

But I knew, somehow, that wasn't what I'd been brought to see.

José hadn't known this was where I'd once lived, and I doubted Edmunds had any idea either. I wasn't going to believe the choice of this house for a murder was a coincidence. This was aimed at me. That told me that there was one specific room in the house that the killer would use for whatever sick message they wanted to communicate.

We took plastic booties and gloves from the crime scene kit beside the front door, and I put them on with trembling fingers and a churning stomach. I breathed shallowly. My Were sense of smell was an advantage in warning me there was more to come, and it was a massive liability in the depth of detail it was feeding me. It was fortunate I had nothing left in my stomach.

Edmunds started to say something to me, but I moved past him as if I was in a trance.

Narrow corridor to the side. Door at the end. The second bedroom. The bedroom that an older child would have. My bedroom. The one where Dad had died, surrounded by machines we couldn't afford and which had failed him anyway.

All the furniture had been moved out. A part of my mind noted the planning and preparation, the time needed. And the sheer inhumanity of it. She—I already knew it was a she—would have been alive while the killer calmly stacked things out of the way. She must have known what was coming.

I stepped carefully into the room.

At a word from Edmunds, the CSI agent slipped out.

She was lying face up in the middle of the room. Four foot-long marlinspikes had been driven into the floor and she was tied, spread-eagled, to them.

She was about my size and hair color.

She had been dressed in my clothes, though the shirt was unrecognizable; all that was left was shredded strips of cotton soaked in her blood. The jeans were pulled up, open, and splattered with blood, badly torn about the left thigh. My unmistakable boots were on her feet, soft shafts pinched tightly by the restraining rope, but looking bizarrely undamaged.

Her right cheek had three chevrons cut into it as a parody of a sergeant's badge of rank. Other than that, her face hadn't been mutilated. She looked shocked, but oddly calm beneath all the blood.

I prayed her body had shut down at the end and she wasn't conscious. She hadn't died quickly or easily. She'd been eviscerated.

"We got a fingerprint match off AFIS," Edmunds said behind me. "Lucky break. She's a vet."

Of course she was. There was nothing lucky about it. Another of the tokens that Liu talked about.

I knelt down beside her, careful not to touch anything.

"Tell me," I said.

"Barbara Green, originally from Colorado Springs, no immediate family, seven years in the Cavalry, two tours in Iraq, honorable discharge." He slowed and I glanced back. He was flicking through screens on a tablet computer. "Looks like she had problems since then. No police record, but no continuous employment either. Diagnosed with PTSD. Treated at the VA medical center...initially." He cleared his throat.

Treated. I bit off the rising anger. Not useful at the moment.

"Also registered at the St. Francis Shelter on Curtis. No known permanent address." He trailed off.

I'd never met Barbara, but I knew her and many like her.

Some soldiers come back to the love of their family and the greetings of their friends. They ease back into their civilian lives and carry the price of their service lightly, but no less honorably. Some soldiers come back in a coffin draped with a flag and everyone can gauge the price of their service. Some soldiers don't really come back and the price of their service is beyond understanding.

I heard the commotion outside before the others, but I ignored it.

I concentrated on the repulsive visible facts in front of me.

Her abdominal organs had been removed. From the amount of blood spray, she'd been alive when the killer started. She'd been hollowed out; even the front of her ribs were gone. There was no sign of the organs or missing rib bones. Her thighbone looked to have been bitten through. I'd leave confirmation to the ME, but I guessed postmortem.

There was a trace of Were scent, but thin, as if it had been masked.

I leaned forward, trying to learn everything I could in the few moments I had left with her.

I was trying not to even breathe on her, not to add to the horrors that had been done to her and the indignities that were to come. Trying to apologize that I never knew her and had done nothing for her.

Apologize; for what had been done to her was my fault.

And imprint her face into my mind, so I would never forget it.

"This case and site is now under FBI jurisdiction," Agent Griffith's voice came loudly from the corridor. "You will hand over any and all evidence or observations you have gathered and then you will leave."

I stood and turned to go with the others.

Griffith did a double take and rounded on José. "Morales, what kind of an operation are you running? What's she doing here?"

"She's here as a consultant," José said calmly, hiding his anger.

"On what?"

"Veterans." He turned and walked away.

Griffith caught my arm as I passed.

"Stay away, Farrell. If I find you've tampered with evidence, or in fact, if you ever get involved again at any site under this investigation, I will arrest you for obstruction."

I said nothing. I looked down at his hand and he let me go.

Edmunds and I followed José, stripping off the gloves and boots by the front door.

Outside, we stood by José's cruiser and watched as Griffith's team moved in and took over.

"How did Griffith get on it so quick?" I asked.

"He's probably got an alert on AFIS matches requested from Denver." José sighed. "He also has a team listening to the radio." He glanced at Edmunds, unable to turn off his detective mind, even after the FBI had taken the case. "So, anything else? Neighbors? Who reported it?"

Edmunds shrugged. "Lady next door saw a green van parked in the drive this afternoon. 'Some kind of commercial van', she said. Driver wore blue overalls. Didn't see anything else. Old man's daughter called him. When he didn't answer the phone, she called the neighbor. Neighbor said he wasn't answering the door either and the curtains were drawn. It was at about 9 p.m. she got here. Called us right after that."

Edmunds flicked through his notebook. "Looks as if the rope and tape could've come from any hardware store. Perp used the shower to wash off the blood, then sprayed the bathroom with bleach. But CSI are pretty sure there's got to be DNA somewhere. And partials, epithelials, and so on. You can't do this and not leave evidence."

He and José talked on, but I tuned them out.

Barbara had been tied up. The rogue had to have been in human form up to then. But I was sure her thigh and the old man's throat had been bitten. I had no idea what DNA did when a Were changed. Would they find two sets of DNA? One with peculiarities?

How much of a problem was this for the whole paranormal community?

Why had the rogue gone from painstaking secrecy to a blatant murder he wanted to be discovered? Maybe that was part of the message.

How had he figured out he was being hunted?

How had he masked his scent?

And, especially, how did he know about me? Not just old details like where I lived fifteen years ago, but my car, and the fact that I'd be meeting with Ricky and Alex at the restaurant yesterday.

He or she, I reminded myself, until proven otherwise.

A silence fell over us. There was a feeling of depression from Edmunds. No one likes a murder, but as a detective in Major Crimes, he lived for solving this sort of case and the FBI had just pushed him aside.

After a minute, José leaned over to me and spoke quietly. "You said you're going to be away?"

"No," I said, staring at the house. "I'm not going anywhere."

Chapter 19

WEDNESDAY

It took me a long time to get to sleep, and once I had, nightmares kept jerking me awake. Barbara Green's staring eyes. The taste of blood. Formless, screaming panic.

I gave up. The pale pre-dawn found me exercising silently in the gardens at Manassah.

Julie joined me to greet the dawn, then Pia.

Dew lay like a veil across the grass. A wintery wind tugged the tips of sleepy larch and cypress, while the shadows of guards passed silently beneath them. Deep, clean lungfuls of chill air chased the night thoughts away.

Good. I needed to be at my best, today and every day until I hunted the rogue down.

With the sun up, we went inside for breakfast.

Carmen wasn't going to be in until later, so I massacred some eggs under Pia's dubious gaze. Julie handled the coffee and toast while updating me on her calls to Ops 4-10.

She'd gotten through to a dozen people and delivered her message, as vague as it was. The difficulty was that she'd gone AWOL, which raised questions in their minds about the validity of her warnings. I could hear the hurt in her voice as she listed those she'd spoken to who simply hadn't believed her. Even those who had believed her could take no positive actions at the moment. Petersen was still their commanding officer and they were under military law. But they'd be cautious.

Jen came in, sleepy-eyed and finger-combing her tousled hair. Why didn't I look like that when I got up?

"Frambled or scried?" Julie asked her, dishing out the results of my cooking onto plates while I was looking for the coffee mugs.

"Whichever." Jen kissed my cheek. "Hmm, smells good."

Julie snorted.

We perched on stools in the warm kitchen, and I took the opportunity to brief them all about the rogue and my role in hunting him. Or her. And I got Jen's permission to use the downstairs study as an incident room.

I shied away from the details of last night, other than to explain why I thought the rogue was aware of the hunt and had changed his behavior drastically.

As I reached the end, David came bustling in, fully dressed and wafting in cold air from outside. He turned down eggs but greedily emptied the coffee pot.

Then the others went off to change, leaving me with David. I washed and he dried.

"That your best work suit?" I said.

He nodded. "More appropriate for the Kingslund office. They're very formal."

I could understand. He was there as a bodyguard and it was smart to blend in.

The dishes done, we walked into the living room to finish off our coffees.

"Everything okay with you and Pia?" I asked.

He looked puzzled. "Yeah. Why?"

"Pia wasn't here yesterday evening and then you weren't here last night."

"Oh. That." His eyes flicked up as Jen rejoined us, elegant heels clicking on the floor. Louboutin or Blahnik—she'd been tutoring me, but I wasn't up to telling the difference at a glance yet. She was sleek in a royal blue power suit with a cream silk scarf at her throat. A night in her own home had done wonders for her. She looked as if she was back to the confident woman that I knew, and I wouldn't want anything to change that.

"That what?" I prompted David as he hesitated. Anything that could be said to me could be said to my kin.

He cleared his throat. "We had to feed."

Well, I had asked. I glanced at Jen, who appeared unfazed.

"You have kin?" she asked David.

He leaned forward, carefully placing his empty mug on the table. "Not exactly. New Athanate take time to learn control, and—"

"I get that," Jen said sharply. "It's dangerous to have kin until you have control. So what's the alternative?"

David gave me a fleeting look to see if I was going to help him out, but I didn't have a clue. I wanted to hear what he had to say.

"For most, they have to return to Haven and they feed under the supervision of a Mentor," Pia said as she came in and leaned against the sofa behind David. "But it's different for David. When Athanate form bonds with other Athanate, the bond includes kin. It's not compulsory, of course, and sometimes it doesn't work." She reached down and massaged his neck. "I have more kin, but David and I share only one so far. They were together in a safe environment last night. Ideally, we would both be with our kin, but we didn't want to leave Julie without backup."

Jen blinked. So much to take in. "And your other kin?" she said.

"I haven't had much time with them," David replied. "It's all been a bit of a rush."

Pia smiled, obviously in no doubt as to the outcome, despite David's shyness.

Julie was standing in the doorway. I wondered how much she'd heard and what she'd made of it, but she looked to be concentrating on her comms earplug.

I did a double take on her outfit. On Monday, after the Nagas' visit to her motel, she'd been left with only the clothes on her back. Somewhere along the way, she'd gotten hold of an elegant black pants suit. It fit so well, the slight bulge under her arm was only noticeable because I was looking for it.

My eyes swiveled to Jen, but I could hardly make a fuss about this. Julie needed clothes to work in, and as with David, blending in was better. Jen must have organized some shopping.

Julie nodded at something that she heard on her earplug and beckoned to the others.

"So how many kin do you have?" Jen said, getting up.

"Only three." Pia straightened. "As a Mentor, I should have had more, but at Altau, we were always struggling to catch up."

"Please invite them here for dinner on Friday." Jen picked up her briefcase. "I'd like to meet them. And why not ask them to stay?"

"Oh! Thank you," Pia said. "I'm sure they'll accept. It'll be a wonderful opportunity for all of us."

It struck me that Pia's kin were part of my House, and so part of my responsibility. I should have been issuing the invitation. If I had a house.

Jen gave me a one-arm hug and another kiss on the cheek. "And wake me up next time you're exercising, honey," she said quietly with a little smile. "I'd like to join in."

"You want to get all hot and sweaty?" my demon responded before I could stop it.

Jen's laugh was low and throaty. A throb of anticipation started in my canines and worked its way down my body despite my efforts to damp it down. I couldn't let it run away with me.

"See you later then," Jen said with emphasis, and turned away. I could see her putting on her businesswoman persona like it was a coat she just needed to shrug into.

They filed out, Jen quizzing David on some obscure financial issue highlighted by his analysis. I heard the phrase 'significant opportunity to de-leverage' and my brain slammed the shutters down on my Athanate-enhanced hearing.

Minutes later, fortified with another cup of coffee, I called Ingram.

"You cannot be serious," I said.

He knew exactly what I was talking about. "It's a tough line call, Ms. Farrell, but Griffith is the agent on site with the seniority and experience. I can't override it."

"You said he was unimaginative and that he wasn't cleared for Project Anthracite."

"And I wouldn't change a word of that."

"But..." The FBI didn't *officially* know there was anything paranormal about the series of animal-related killings stretching over the last few years in Denver. Ingram suspected it, and I'd hinted I would talk to him when the time came, but he couldn't take that to his boss. "Couldn't you just divert him for a while?"

"To allow what precisely?"

Ingram would have a recording of this conversation, and whatever leeway he might be able to give me off the record, I couldn't assume that he'd take my side against his own agency. Not if I said something on the phone.

"Just to get him off my back," I said.

"Well, there's always more work here. I can shovel it around the shop. You might find he'll be slow to get back to you."

"He wasn't slow last night."

"Eh?"

Ingram hadn't heard about it. Griffith must have been keeping everyone but his own team out of the loop. I told him about it—the theft of my clothes, the choice of my old house and a veteran as a victim. I left out any paranormal reasons for those choices.

He was quiet for a minute after I finished.

"Ms. Farrell, I take it back. I can't shovel anything around that'd slow down that investigation. I'm sure Agent Griffith's fully informed of everything he needs, and I fully intend to leave him to proceed."

He was saying he'd not give Griffith any hint of his suspicions about the rogue cases, but he wouldn't hinder him in any way either. Swearing silently, I cut my losses. "Understood. Are you any further on getting into the Ops 4 group?"

"No ma'am. I surely kicked up some shitstorm of jurisdiction over in DC. I'm going to have to fly there today."

"Well, safe flight. And more power to your kicking foot."

"I thank you." He ended the call.

Crap.

Even if Ingram didn't tell him the links that made me more involved, Griffith would eventually discover them. I wouldn't put it past him to try and take me into protective custody. My deadline for finding the rogue had just gotten squeezed again.

I'd promised to, so I called Ethel Harriman as well. She wasn't happy that I couldn't meet her immediately and that I couldn't promise a schedule, but she did brief me on Mrs. de Vries' case.

It was another distraction, but either I was serious about maintaining my independence and keeping involved in normal life, or I should just pack up my PI firm now. I wasn't ready to do that and I hoped I never would be.

But I couldn't face the rest of my call list right away. Instead, I visited the local stores for maps, stationery and office products.

An hour later I had transformed the study.

Two walls were covered in bulletin boards. The centerpieces of both were maps. One was the surrounding district, with pins showing where bodies had been found. The dates of discovery and estimated dates of death were listed down the side. The other board had a large street map of Denver. A single pin was stuck in it, on South Vineyard.

The last boards were blank. They were there for me to note ideas or gut feelings. Anything. Blank was not good. No gut feeling was really not good.

Relax. I've put the boards up and they will come.

Lots more procedural investigation remained to be done. I needed the pack to feedback on where they lived and where they were sure no intruder Weres could be staying. With that knowledge I could start removing sections of the map and trying to find a pattern that would allow me to concentrate the search.

And to do all that, I needed to call on Felix. It wasn't going to be fun. He'd already know I'd ignored his order not to get involved in fighting Matlal Were. Whatever his screwed-up reasoning, it was an order and I'd disobeyed. That wouldn't be a good introduction to the next topic I had to raise with him, which was that the operation being run by the pack to hunt down the Matlal Weres was a shambles. They had to get organized, use the right equipment and work to a plan. I could put it together, if I had his permission. And at the same time, I'd be using the pack to help in the hunt for the rogue.

Felix would see that, right away.

I was still worrying about how to finesse him when the guard on the gate buzzed me.

Chapter 20

Tullah and Jofranka slunk in like a pair of errant schoolgirls.

"Don't get comfortable," I snapped. "You're going straight back out."

I slipped on my HK harness and jacket. What I had in mind should be less dangerous than it would appear to the girls, but there was no sense in being underprepared.

I ushered them back out to Tullah's car, grabbing my backpack with my jogging gear in case I didn't get home before meeting Melissa.

"Where to?" Tullah asked.

"The office, but park behind the bank across the intersection."

She headed south on Downing Street without questioning me. I'd told her to stay away from the office when Hoben and Matlal had been looking for me. She might think it was safe to go back now. I was about to clarify that.

"How dangerous do you think it is now?" I asked.

"Well, much less than last week."

"Wrong answer," I said.

Jofranka leaned forward from the back seat. "Can I ask a question?"

"No."

They both went quiet. The fact that they were taking this so seriously was a big plus in their favor.

And I guess I should have seen this coming. I'd introduced them back when I was working in the police, mainly as a way of the pair of them exhausting each other with their enthusiasm. They'd become good friends. Jofranka would have seen Tullah working as an office assistant for me and then suddenly becoming an apprentice PI.

Oooh! Cool! Exciting!

Well, if I could impress on them that it would be boring more often than not, and that, when it was exciting, that meant frigging dangerous, then I might consider taking Jofranka on, in a *minor* role. For all her sweet looks, Tullah was physically capable of taking care of herself, even before you took her Adept abilities and Kaothos into account. Jofranka had nothing in comparison. She was a good student at the Kwan, and she was street-smart, but that was it. And she wasn't aware of any of the paranormal background.

Tullah parked and they sat there patiently. Another plus. I suspected Tullah had given Jofranka strict instructions to follow her lead. That, I wanted to reinforce.

"You've got your concealed weapon permit?"

Tullah shook her head. "Still waiting."

"Bought a weapon?"

She opened the glove compartment and brought out a holstered Sig, neatly wrapped in an underarm harness like mine, ready for the permit. I checked the gun. It was safetied, cleaned and loaded.

I ran a finger along the slide, then rubbed it against my thumb. "Wipe off the excess oil after cleaning." It was almost fun being a sergeant again.

"The reason the office is not safe," I said, putting the gun back, "is that there are still people after me. Except now, it's not bikers or drug gangs, it's a rogue military unit. They're called Ops 4-16, but I'll generally call them Nagas. They're trained in exactly the way I was trained. Since they've gone rogue, I'm assuming they'll have no concerns about collateral damage or the methods they use to achieve their objectives."

"What are their objectives?" Jofranka couldn't help herself. I'd never known a girl to ask more questions. But this was a damn good one.

"I don't know, which means I have to factor in them trying to kill or capture me." I looked at the pair of them. "The important thing is that anyone who works with me is a potential liability for me and is personally at risk."

I let them stew on that for a minute.

"There was a stakeout here. Two cars keeping an eye on the office. The FBI arrested some of their buddies and these guys got the message. They disappeared in a rush. So, Tullah. What do we do? Do we just stay away?"

"No. Well, I mean someone has to go there."

"Why?"

"If they're trying to kill you, they might have left something in the office. That's dangerous. Someone else might get hurt. It's our responsibility," she said, emphasizing the 'our'.

Oh, Tullah. You star.

I kept my face blank.

"Exactly. Which is why I want the pair of you to check the office out in fifteen minutes. That's how long you've got to set up an approach that allows you to back off if you think the office is still being observed, or if you think you can see a trap. I'll be watching."

I got out and walked away. Out of their line of sight, I did a circuit of the intersection before buying a long juice drink in a café that had a view of the office.

Their appearance, right on cue, had me smiling.

They'd found a hoodie for Tullah that matched Jofranka's, and they'd bought a skateboard from a junk shop. They spent ten minutes taking turns doing sidewalk tricks and watching. They worked their way down the side of the building and back in front. Loud, obvious and distracting.

Jofranka did some eye-catching kick and spin moves in front while Tullah inspected the door, casually leaning on the wall next to it, apparently focused on her friend.

Whether it would have fooled the Nagas or not, it showed application and resourcefulness. In the time I had, that was going to have to do.

I wandered across and opened the door.

Tullah went in and I was impressed by the quick and efficient scan she did. It wasn't to say she would have found something that the Nagas had planted. Again, it was simply a good starting point.

Tullah beckoned us inside.

"Sit," I said, and pointed at the client chairs in front of my desk.

They perched, as alert as a couple of hounds who'd just heard the cookie jar open.

"You aren't interested in just answering phones, Jo, are you?"

She shook her head, glancing nervously at Tullah for support.

"And my *apprentice*," I turned to Tullah, "isn't interested in you just answering phones either."

Tullah swallowed. "I wouldn't have let her do anything you didn't clear first. I'm sorry."

I raised a brow at the tacked-on apology.

"It was kinda underhand," she clarified.

"Good. We got that out of the way. Whose idea was the skateboard?"

Jofranka raised her hand.

"Not bad, coming up with that in a hurry," I said, and she glowed. I swung my feet up on the desk. "My apprentice assures me we can afford you part-time. I'll agree on a probationary basis," I held up a hand, "pending all the admin done by Tullah, a written report from both of you, detailing what you think you can do now and proposing a training schedule that'll take you from an apprentice and a gofer to junior PI assistants."

Jofranka practically bounced on her chair.

"Meantime," I drawled, and they both went super-still. *Oh, cookies!* I had to bite my cheek to stop laughing. "I have some *real* boring surveillance for you. Tullah, you'll supervise. Jo will do the legwork. The details are in the system under Mrs. Harriman."

Tullah had relaxed slightly when I'd said surveillance, but she came back to attention at the name. Good.

Strictly speaking, Ethel Harriman was only another client, but Tullah was smart enough to know she was the sort of client where you made sure you got everything right. The potential boost to business was as big as the potential damage from getting it wrong.

"The core of the case may be a complex financial con involving a friend of Mrs. Harriman's, a Mrs. Suzannah De Vries. That's why she came to me, and I'll have to handle that part of it. But, under the circumstances, I want an immediate feel for Mrs. De Vries' partner. Not just a standard background check; I want a fingertip feeling about this guy, good and bad: he's inappropriate in the elevator; he's kind to animals; he has a hard-on for gambling. I want to know. You will not, under any circumstances, interfere, or give him the slightest hint he's under observation. Or you fail. Do you understand?"

Big round eyes. Nods.

"Partner?" Tullah asked.

Good question.

"As in business *and* personal," I replied.

I gave them a couple of seconds for other preliminary questions, but nothing was forthcoming.

"If you think there's a serious issue with proceeding, you can come and clarify things with me after you've read the case file. Other than that, don't bug me. And Tullah," I smiled evilly at her. "You'll explain my thinking on how we're handling this case and report in writing, along with the preliminary observations that you and Jo put together. And don't let your other cases get behind; it's always harder to catch up, however tough you think it is to keep going."

I could see that any idea this was a simple practice case had gone clean out of Tullah's head.

Good. This might just work for all of us.

"Jo, give us a minute, please. Don't go far, we're going to have to head off soon."

She went out without a murmur of complaint. It was the quietest, most restrained Jofranka I had ever seen.

Tullah waited nervously.

"You knew I'd checked the office out already?" I asked.

She nodded.

"How?"

"The guys you talked about, they had you rattled. You'd never have let me in here first. You'd never have had us come here if you thought they'd still be around."

"But you still didn't let Jo in till you had checked."

"My responsibility. I can't always rely on you."

"Carve that on your soul. That'll be how we work for the moment."

Tullah didn't argue.

"She's a good friend. That's a really bad reason to get her into a PI firm. Did you have any other reasons?"

"She can get places we can't. Or where we'd stand out."

She was right.

As I understood it, Jofranka's gypsy heritage had a wild mixture of everything, but with her coffee skin, the tight ripple in her long, black hair and her streetwise aura, there were places where she'd pass unnoticed and neither of us would.

"She's going to realize we're not exactly human," I said.

Tullah ducked her head. "Adept communities sometimes include people who aren't Adept. I'm clearing it with Ma."

"It's not just Adept communities we have to worry about." I didn't know where to go with this. Mary and Liu had said we should form our own community. They'd be okay if Jofranka was involved, but what about the Were and Athanate? How would they react to Jofranka knowing about me? The thought of community, House and pack being like overlapping circles didn't feel right. I wanted them to be the same thing.

The silence built a little, and Tullah fidgeted.

"You know, you don't need to be bitten to be part of my House." That just popped out, almost as if my demon had said it. Where had it come from? *Not* Athanate approved.

"But it's what Kaothos wants. She thinks she can control Athanate Blood and strengthen my ability to channel energy."

"Do you want to be able to channel more energy?"

"It'd be cool," she admitted reluctantly.

"And dangerous. It would make it much easier to come to someone's attention."

She dipped her head again in acknowledgement, a trickle of anxiety leaking from her.

My Athanate stirred and I walked over to look out the window to hide my conflict. As I understood it from Speaks-to-Wolves, my Athanate had been held in check by Hana over the last couple of years. But that wasn't the case now. Hana seemed to have her hands—*paws*—full with the Were side of me, leaving my Athanate to develop and leaving me to come to terms with it.

If I did infuse Tullah, how would Kaothos fare in the long term? Kaothos was immeasurably stronger than Hana. Maybe she knew what she was doing.

If not, would Tullah become bound to me? An Athanate-Adept hybrid?

I could tell my hard-wired Athanate instincts wanted her within my House, but I didn't want her as kin and she didn't want to be Athanate. How was that going to resolve?

What would Altau and the rest of the Athanate think of a House comprised of Athanate, Were, Adept and human?

I could almost hear the sizzling sound of dragon laughter.

I'd spent longer here than I planned.

"Well, I'm not going to press you for anything," I said, and felt a mixture of relief and almost disappointment from Tullah. She was in a real muddle over this.

I had to move on. It was getting too close to my appointment with Noble. I didn't even have time to go back and get my car.

"Drop me off in Centennial, please," I said.

"Yessir."

Chapter 21

Noble was already at the table.

He was frowning and talking curtly to someone on his cell when I came in, but as soon as he saw me, he ended the call and smiled.

"All okay?" I nodded toward the cell as I sat.

"It never is, Ms. Farrell." He turned the cell off.

"Amber."

"Doc," he replied.

"As I understand it, werewolves heal themselves, so tell me, Doc, what does a pack need with a doctor? Surely you can't still practice?" Alex had been a doctor, and had to stop when he became Were.

"My specialization is in psychiatry now."

"I can see how that might be useful," my demon said before I could catch it.

Noble's smile twisted. He knew right where that was coming from. "Don't be too harsh on Felix. Were might not have the lifespan of Athanate, but Felix comes from a time when Athanate were immensely more intrusive into our lives."

"How do you mean?"

"By limiting Were population, for instance."

I flinched. "You mean killing Were? Altau did this?"

I couldn't stop the flare of panic in me, but Noble shook his head.

"No, no. That's one reason I keep trying to make better links with Altau. They haven't done any of that. As Athanate go, even Felix has to admit, they're decent. And even with other Panethus Athanate Houses, it seldom came to that. It was more a threat, a constraint on numbers. Always with the unarguable reason of preventing humanity from discovering us, of course."

I let the sarcasm slide by. "So, Felix has been here for what, two hundred years? And he's *still* waiting for the other shoe to drop with Altau?"

Noble conceded the point with a measured nod. "Altau haven't helped. They're not approachable," he said. "Other than the interaction of new Athanate and Were, and even with that, they're erratic. They may not be as bad as some, but they're still not our friends."

"Maybe that's going to change. I'm the new liaison, apparently."

Noble raised his eyebrows. "I'll have to take over that position from the pack's side. At least, while Felix insists that Alex is kept safe from you." He gave an apologetic shrug.

Alex had been the liaison. Had he told me that? No, Diana had.

"Fine, let's not go there," I said. "Tell me instead the real reason why I'm so important in hunting for the rogue? How difficult can it be?"

"It can be very difficult. You're probably thinking of a rogue in Athanate terms. An Athanate rogue is barely sane at any time, and it's easy to see them approaching that state. A Were rogue can appear completely rational in human form. We'll need detective work."

Alex and Ricky had hinted at this, but Noble seemed more definite about it. My job just seemed to get harder all the time.

"I'm not Sherlock Holmes."

"Indeed not, but apart from your undoubted investigative talents, you have contacts in the police which we do not. I'm sorry if that's deflating, but a large part of why we need you is because of who you can talk to without attracting more attention to us. I'm afraid, to find one person in all of Denver, we need help, we need the search narrowed down."

"I'm fine with that." I chewed on it as I looked at the menu. Right off the bat—skewers of garlic-smothered grilled shrimp with a side of salad. Sold.

"So," I said, "I'd come up with a list of possible suspects or a location…"

"And Ricky and the others would check it out. Werewolves are much better at detecting marque scents than Athanate. They'd sniff out the rogue and close in."

"And kill him."

"There is no cure." He clasped his hands in front of him and pursed his lips in distaste. "I understand this is unpleasant, but we would also need you again, before he is killed. You'd have to try and find out if there was anything we need to do to prevent it happening again. If he came from another pack, does it indicate there's a problem in that pack and that more might come? Those sorts of things."

Interrogation of a condemned prisoner, no matter how evil, twisted my gut.

"And I guess I'm better at that because I'm Athanate? I'll be better at detecting if he's lying or hiding something?"

"You could say werewolves are good with the marque scent and Athanate with the marque telergy."

"But I thought werewolves can't lie to each other."

"No, that only applies within a pack. Big difference."

The waiter interrupted us to take our orders. Noble went for the fancy lobster thermidor and ordered a half bottle of an Italian white wine that sounded good to me. Jen would have known whether it was the right one if she were here. Me, not so much.

"There's so much I don't know about the Were," I said after the waiter left.

His lips twitched. "So, talk to me. It's part of my pack duties."

"Settling in newcomers?"

"Yes."

I flapped my hands in frustration. "Where to start? What is a Were? No wait." I frowned, trying for the right words. "Why is a Were?" I said and had to laugh.

Noble waited more patiently than I'd have managed.

"Look," I said finally, "speaking as a part Athanate, I can sort of understand why there are Athanate and why we have developed in the way we have. The benefits like the extended life and improved health that require Blood to maintain. The need for the special relationship with kin who provide the Blood, the pressure to form groups like Houses. That all makes a kind of crazy sense." I paused. I was babbling like an idiot, but Noble just made an encouraging hum. "So what is the equivalent for Were? Why are there werewolves, what are they like and why?"

Noble's hands flexed and he settled happily into his seat. He was expressive with his hand gestures and body. His head moved to look at his food or nod, but other than that was very still, giving me a sense of his concentrated focus on me. I wondered if that was a psychiatrist thing.

"A perceptive question, however you put it," he said. "Such a fascinating topic. Exactly the sort of topic I want to discuss with the Athanate, if they would. Instead, here I have you, half and half, my captive audience for the next hour."

I snorted.

"Were, of course, are not just werewolves. There are werebears and werepumas and maybe others I don't know about and can't really comment on. All characterized, of course, by the ability to change form. This isn't governed by the moon or any such nonsense, but they have to change a couple of times a month once they've started. It can be fun, but that's not the point. They have extended lives and health and so on and so forth, but that's not the point either."

He'd gotten animated enough to tap the table for emphasis.

"The Athanate is all about the mind. Yes, there is Blood and sex and physical improvements, but the key to understanding the Athanate is the mind. It's why they have structures like kin and House and creed. It's not that they have no emotions, but that those emotions are channeled in directions decreed by the logic of their requirements. They observe, they discuss, they assess, they document, they govern themselves with a complex hierarchy of needs and obligations and duties." He paused. "These are all mental constructions. The Athanate is all about thinking."

I could have argued, but I saw what he was getting at and kept silent.

"The Were are all about spirit. About heart and feeling and emotion. The Athanate, I believe, will talk about Weres being *enthused*. They mean it literally. The etymology of the word means to fill a person with a sense of the divine. Putting theology aside for the moment, you don't see half-hearted Were."

I thought of Alex and Ricky and Felix. There was something in what he said. All of them had the feel of someone living completely in the moment. It was one of the things that made Alex so hot.

Noble himself was the odd one out. Apart from his enthusiasm with this topic of conversation, he'd seemed much more like the Athanate he described than the Were.

"And Adepts?" I said, just to see what he would say.

"Power." His fingers drummed the table. "The attraction of being able to change things to suit yourself." As if he'd suddenly noticed it, he stopped drumming, looked aside and shrugged again. "But they are even more secretive than the Athanate. I don't really know."

He wasn't right about Adepts and he wasn't being entirely honest there, my gut said. The Adepts I knew seemed to go out of their way to not use power. But I'd rather find out about Adepts from Mary, so I went back to the Were.

"Why does a werewolf need a pack?"

"We can sit and discuss the theory, and it would be interesting, but to truly understand why a werewolf wants to be part of a pack, it needs to be felt. Of course, having a pack is better for training newcomers and so forth." He made a dismissive brushing-off motion with one hand. "All of which is nothing in comparison to how it feels. So this, I cannot easily communicate to you, but you'll understand when you feel it."

"The Call?"

"That's a facet of it."

I sighed. "Yeah, it all feels like a million facets at the moment. Maybe I just need to wait, but what I feel now is lost."

The food arrived and we began to eat. It was excellent. As Athanate and Were sharpened my senses, food had become a rediscovery. Flavors and textures took a defined quality they hadn't had before, and under the garlic, my shrimp had clever hints of mustard and coriander.

"I've got a suggestion," Noble said, interrupting my food moment.

"Well?"

"Talk to me as often as you can. I'll send you some times that I'm free. Pick some that work for you."

"You mean talk like talk to a shrink?"

"More like a mentor."

I looked at him carefully, but he seemed unaware that he'd used an Athanate term.

"You're unusual, a statistical anomaly." He gave a small smile as he went on. "You are my lab specimen. You've become Were without any support in place. Fascinating. And why me particularly? Well, it's not dissimilar to what I went through." His brow creased. "Or if that's not good enough, think in terms of the objective. We're trying to make sure you adjust well to being both Were and Athanate so that you can provide the bridge between the two."

"Which is sadly lacking."

He nodded agreement.

"You said you've been through something similar?"

"Nothing to do with the Athanate side, of course. I was infused accidentally while unknowingly treating a fatally wounded Were. I had no knowledge of what was happening to me. I assure you it was truly bewildering. I was fortunate that I was adopted into the Denver pack before I went rogue."

I felt an unexpected rush of gratitude. As much as I'd made close ties within the Athanate in a short time, this was the first person who'd gone out of their way to make time to explain things and help me. Even if it was a shrink—well, I could use someone to talk to about the changes going on in my head.

"Okay." I scribbled my cell and email on one of the restaurant's business cards and handed it over. "You *are* different from the others."

His nose flared and he let a smile slip, quickly covered.

I carefully didn't notice. So the doctor liked being complimented? Being a psychiatrist didn't mean he couldn't be vain as well. It was kinda reassuring that he had failings.

I finished the shrimp and sat back, sipping the wine.

"So, tell me a little background about your family." He made a show of turning his attention to finishing his creamy lobster lunch, but I didn't doubt he'd focus on every word.

My stomach tensed. I took another sip of wine and willed my body to relax. Why the hell was I so secretive? And could I actually lie to him? Would his wolfy-sense spot it?

"Denver family," I said. "Father died when I was fifteen. I left high school before graduation and enlisted in the army. My younger sister went on through college and law school, and she works at the Galliard Associates Law Firm. We don't get along. Mom remarried. We're not that close either."

Not entirely true. No reaction from Noble.

And a reminder to myself that Mom had to be mad at me. She'd been back from vacation since Sunday and I hadn't even called.

"No brother?" he said, looking up.

I shook my head.

"You were a bit of a young tomboy probably."

I shifted uncomfortably. A handful of sentences and I felt I'd given him the family secrets.

He sighed. "It was hasty of me to start so quickly. Well, too late now. I will play the fearsome psychiatrist and tear open those raw, formative childhood experiences." His eyes narrowed shrewdly. "You worked at being the son you thought your father always wanted. No boy was ever going to be as bold as you, no physical skill was ever going to be beyond your reach. You took part in the things your father enjoyed because you knew that's what a good son would do."

The shrimp sat like lead in my stomach.

"In the way of these things," he laid his cutlery down and gestured with his hands, "it ceased to be something that required effort. You became this person that you thought your father wanted."

"He never said he wanted a son. He never once said he was disappointed—"

"I didn't say that, Amber. I said you *thought* that was what he wanted." He tasted his wine appreciatively, his eyes watching me. "Then, having become this person, you accepted the role and responsibility, especially after his death. You left school to get a job. I would guess you supported your family financially?" He waited on my tiny nod. "Then after that, your choice of career only reinforced the characteristics you'd adopted."

"I don't like talking about this," I said. I was lying. I absolutely hated it. What he knew wasn't half of it and there was no way I was going to blurt out anything more. Paranoid, much?

"I'm sorry it's painful for you. Am I wrong?"

"No," I muttered. "What's it got to do with me becoming a Were?"

"Because you're looking at things that impinge on you now and thinking that they stem from what's happening to you now, but they probably have roots a long way back. I'll leave out the obvious psychology about not feeling close to your mother after she remarried. Let's concentrate instead on your sister. When she was a child, you treated her as if you were an older brother, a protector. She probably adored you." He suddenly jabbed a finger at me for emphasis. "Then you went away. She was what, fourteen, fifteen at the time? She was at the age where she could only relate to events in the way they affected her personally. She was being told by everybody what a wonderful person you were, and you had *abandoned* her." He paused. "Now, you think you're not getting along with her because of everything you're going through?"

He had half a point there, unpleasant as it was to realize. But only half. I could have launched into a list of my sister's shortcomings, but I'd told him enough for one day.

"All startlingly accurate." I waved my hand in dismissal. "But how would this relate to talking to you, to becoming 'adjusted'?"

"Hmm." He finished his wine. "I would focus on exploring control and direction. As a simplification, the Athanate seem to be all about rigid control." He made his hands into tight fists. "Never letting go. The pack, they are all about directing that energy, dissipating it in useful or harmless ways." He let his hands weave to and fro. "You need to be an expert in the way these instincts conflict, but you need this before you ever face it for real. You must learn to balance and master your different sides, so they do not overwhelm you."

He'd summarized it neatly. I didn't comment.

He went on. "What I will do is direct you in mental role playing, where you can experience the interaction in a relaxed and safe environment, with me providing suggestions and reinforcements. First, of course, nothing very drastic. We must build trust and progress slowly."

I wasn't sure I had time for slow. Master Liu always said there must be no fast or slow, there must only be the right speed. Did that apply everywhere?

"And we're not sharing all this with Felix?"

"Of course not," he said. "Not Felix, not Alex, not anybody. Doctor-patient confidentiality, even in the pack. All I would ever say is that we're making progress, or not."

The waiter interrupted us to offer dessert menus, but my appetite was gone. I asked for the check.

Noble smirked. Yeah, asking for the check wasn't a girly thing to do. But I didn't do it to fit in with some image of how I should behave. However I'd gotten to this stage, this was me now. *That* little piece of the puzzle slipped comfortably into place. I'd need to think more on it.

We argued casually over the check and settled for splitting the cost.

"Put aside the picture I described earlier," he said as the waiter walked off. "At best it's a caricature of you. Nothing so quick, that works on so little data, could be anything else. It gave you a flavor of what can be done. The real work will start next time."

I nodded cautiously. There was a matter of who was paying for this.

He anticipated my question.

"It's for the pack, so no charge, of course." He glanced at his watch. "Do you have to be somewhere? Can I offer you a lift home?" he said.

"I need to be at Cherry Creek," I said. "I'll take you up on that lift if that's not too far out of your way."

∞ ∞ ∞ ∞ ∞

I settled into his Volvo and buckled the belt as he pulled out cautiously on Arapahoe, heading for I-25.

His car smelled of leather seats and some strong chemical air freshener.

"Whereabouts are you living at the moment?" he asked.

My mental heels dug in. He might have all sorts of reasons for asking, but I wasn't going to tell the pack where I lived while I wasn't even a member.

"Oh, I live half my life out of the back of my car."

What did that make me sound like? I was starting to get paranoid about what I revealed to him in casual conversation.

I had the impression he followed my thinking. And he didn't like it. So much for the first steps of setting up trust.

Well, suck it up, Doc.

He drove with care, two hands on the wheel, well under the limit, eyes on the road and mirrors. My mouth twitched at the contrast with Alex. With Noble's driving style and his solid car, I was probably safer than I'd been for weeks.

I stifled a yawn.

He'd given me useful glimpses about the Were. But the whole time I knew that he wasn't telling me everything. I wasn't imagining it. Was it because I wasn't a member of the pack?

And of course I'd told him everything and been completely honest.

No. It was like looking into a damned mirror. I'd found someone as secretive as myself.

The short, top-of-the-line analysis he'd given hadn't been pleasant at all. The image that came to mind was physical exercise after a long time off. Thinking of it that way helped. What I needed was to get to a place where I could deal with the things I had in my head. If I didn't, I was destined to go off the deep end. Probably spectacularly. So who better to prevent that than the pack's psychiatrist?

He stopped in front of the mall, carefully putting the emergency brake on.

"I understand," he said softly, seeming to shed the professional persona for a moment. "Trust is that most precious of interpersonal beliefs, and it has to be earned. Look at the times I send you. Pick a few. Let us try."

"Thanks, Doc. I will."

I watched while he drove off, the big, boxy Volvo gliding away into the traffic.

There was another voicemail on my cell.

It was Mom. The exact message I'd anticipated: back from vacation since Sunday, why hadn't I gone to see her as I promised. I could feel the hurt in her voice, but there were more hard decisions to make there that I didn't feel up to now.

Chapter 22

I found Melissa at Cherry Creek Mall, doing her stretches just by the exit from the parking garage.

"Run first, talk later," she said by way of greeting.

I shrugged and let her lead, tugging my backpack's straps till it sat comfortably.

Down on the creek trail, Melissa set a good pace and I fell in alongside her. There was no way she could outsprint me or outlast me, and the pace was easy enough that I could think through some of the implications about what the Doc had told me.

Aside from the diversion around the Country Club, we stayed on the trail, down next to the creek and away from the traffic. I was enjoying it. It was only about thirty minutes later, when I saw we were getting close to Union Street, that I started to wonder what she was trying to prove.

She came off at Wynkoop, only a couple of blocks short of the Union Street station, and I followed her to a café where we got a couple of juices to go.

We walked back down to the trail.

Her face was a picture. But beneath the flush from her exertion, there was an odd weight to her narrow-eyed look.

Damn. My head had been so full of other issues I hadn't even thought about what was happening. There was no point now trying to pretend I was suddenly tired or winded. It had been only a moderately clever ruse, but I'd been incredibly stupid.

She downed the juice, her eyes smoky with calculation as she continued to look at me.

I expected her to start questioning how I was able to run without effort, but she surprised me. She grabbed my arm, stopping me.

"Did you ever really, really want something, more than anything else in the world?"

"Yeah." I wasn't going to go there, but she barely heard me.

"When I was twelve, my dog died." She let my arm go and we started walking again. "She was just a young collie. No reason to die, no history of problems. Just died one day. I thought the neighbor had poisoned her, but no one would do anything about it. No one wanted to listen to me. They told me I'd get over it, but I wasn't like that. So, I got a book on forensics from the library."

"Did you prove it?"

She snorted. "By the time I'd earned enough money from the paper route and bought what I needed to run tests, there was nothing but bones and gunk left. I know. I looked."

"So what did you do then?"

She sighed and looked up at the sky.

"I went and got another book which covered finding chemical traces in the soil. I worked waiting tables until I realized I would never be able to afford the equipment I needed. I even tried setting up a forensics business in my Dad's garage." She shook her head. "Finally my Dad took pity on me and made a connection at a forensics lab, and they let me use their stuff."

"And did you prove it then? The poison?"

"Yeah. I nailed it." Her eyes shone.

"What happened to the neighbor?"

"Huh?" She blinked. "Oh. The neighbor had died a couple of years before. It wasn't the point any more. I'd gotten over the dog, but I'd found something else. Something really important to me. You know why I joined CSI?" she said. "I need to know. Like other people need to breathe. What, why, who. The facts. Can you understand that? It's more important to me than anything else."

I nodded. I had a good idea what was coming next, and this time I was right.

"So when a mysterious, ex-special forces, rookie policewoman starts asking questions about some oddball murders and then suddenly takes out the three guys allegedly responsible, I notice. When those bodies then disappear off the slab into some military cloak and dagger facility, I'm pissed. When I'm refused any follow-up information…"

She laughed; a short, sharp sound without humor, before continuing.

"I went looking, and the more I looked, the more I found. Interestingly, almost nothing about you, or those three guys, or for that matter, the secret squirrel army facilities."

"Must have slipped a cog in your brain, speculating what it was all about," I said.

"I don't speculate," she said, as if I'd suggested she ate children.

"Melissa, you've got to realize that I can't tell you all the things you want to know, no matter how much you think you need to know them."

"Yeah?" She smiled. "We'll see."

We walked on for a minute, while I reflected on how bizarre my life had become when I had conversations like this and they seemed almost normal.

"You were at the murder scene in Wash Park last night," she said abruptly.

"How would you know, if you're suspended?"

"I listen to the police radio. Morales and Edmunds getting involved is like waving a huge red flag to me," she snickered, "especially when they start talking in code."

"Okay, so I was there. What about it?"

"FBI threw you out, and slapped one of their labels on it. Pattern A, whatever. Meaning a homicide where there is apparent evidence of a large canine being involved. They think it's some cult thing, you know."

"But you don't."

"It may or may not be a cult. It certainly isn't an animal."

"I thought you didn't speculate?"

"I'm not." She rolled her shoulders and did some side stretches as we walked. "Tell me, what evidence do you think points to animals?"

Of course I had a string of cases, some where there had been paw prints, but I wasn't going to admit knowing anything other than this case.

"The bite."

"The thigh bites." She laughed. "All those cases that Morales had copied off and given to you. They mention paw prints, too." She sniffed. "Not a single one mentions any evidence of animals, no DNA for instance."

There seemed no point in hiding my knowledge of these cases any more.

"But there's a whole report by consultants about what kind of animal," I said. "Teeth patterns, jaw strength and so on. Those guys were experts."

"Yeah. Those guys had their heads up their asses. Too smart for their own good. What kind of canine makes one or two specific bites, in exactly the same location, every time? No evidence of chewing, no bites on other bones. Just crunch, crunch." She demonstrated with a hand, imitating a bite on her neck and thigh. "No others. Not one single instance where the 'animal' that did those two bites bit anywhere else. There were other bites on the bodies, but they were all way post mortem. They were little scavengers that couldn't break a thigh."

I didn't have all the facts memorized, but I'd take her word for it.

"There was damage to ribs at the scene last night," I said.

"Well, I wasn't there, so I won't speculate," she said, enjoying herself, "but cast your mind back to the details if you can and tell me if the bone was broken cleanly or shattered."

I thought. "Clean." Strangely, abruptly severed. She had me going here. The ends of the ribs and the shortened breastbone looked odd. Certainly not chewed or fractured.

She shrugged. "Not a bite, then."

"Okay." I played along. "Not all bodies had neck bites. Those that did, the neck bites were killing bites, and those were like an animal might make."

She nodded and shrugged.

"So if those might be a genuine animal, you've got some theory about the other bites—the ones on the thighs?"

She huffed. "What, in the simplest observation, is the thighbone in comparison to the other bones in the body?"

"The biggest."

"Yup. The biggest, *toughest* bone. The thigh bites were a test or demonstration of strength. Nothing else." She peered at me. "That doesn't sound like an animal to me."

It sounded obvious once she'd said it. But why would a Were keep testing its jaw strength?

"Tell me something else about last night," she said.

The image of the body was too fresh in my mind. "The abdominal organs were all missing."

"I knew that when you mentioned the ribs. Something else."

"She was tied down. Marlin spikes were driven into the floor."

"And left there? Oh." Her nose flared and she nodded. "Well, that fits well with my theory."

"Okay, you've hooked me," I said, frustrated. "Tell me your theory."

"He's just flipped them off. That was his goodbye."

I had a vague idea where she was going. But she was wrong, though proving that to her would mean giving her more information, and just as I had with Noble earlier, I was getting really worried about how much I gave away when I didn't mean to.

"What's your reasoning?" I asked her instead.

"You've seen cold cases going back five or six years?" She looked at me inquiringly and I nodded. "All of them with some indication of canine involvement? Well, you would have been better off trawling the whole cold case murder list."

Her words chilled me.

"There are more?"

"Lots more," she said. "He's prolific, and I predict there will be even more that we haven't found and most of them, we never will. The other thing you could have trawled is the missing persons files."

"But why are you adding all these unsolved murders together? That sounds like speculation to me. What if it's more than one killer, for instance?"

"Serial killers are rare. Prolific serial killers are even rarer. Long-term prolific serial killers…The odds against having more than one operating undetected in Denver are huge." She frowned. "Although I grant you, that's an argument for this being some kind of a cult."

"If this isn't speculation, there must be a pattern you're working on?"

We walked on a ways as she thought it through.

"I started with three types," she said. "The apparent canine attacks, attacks involving ritual and attacks with evidence of almost uncontrollable rage. Then I added the canine to the ritual, because those bites are evidence of a ritual in themselves. Finally, I added the ones involving rage, because I believe the rage was caused when something went wrong. That's the weak point. I'm not a profiler, I'm a forensic scientist, and it frustrates the hell out of me that I can't find a link to prove that gut feeling."

She saw my frown.

"The ones I labeled rage died without any indication of a ritual or bite marks. My theory is they died too early, and the killer went berserk. There was evidence of 140 stab wounds, all post mortem, on one body."

That was a chilling image of rage. Not uncontrollable, not out on the street, but pent up and discharged in hiding. But I needed to focus on the big picture, not this one bizarre element.

"Melissa, you *are* speculating. Is there a provable common thread, apart from the fact that none of them have been solved?"

"That fact is part of it. The killer is fanatically methodical and highly knowledgeable about modern forensic science."

"But there's nothing in the news. This wasn't even a topic of speculation in the police last year." I'd listened out when I worked patrols for the PD. Admittedly, I hadn't been listening for this kind of case, I'd been listening for any hint of vampires, but still, I would have registered this.

"The ones we've found are the marginals. No one's interested. No one is pushing for them."

"But—"

"But nothing, Amber. You know how it works. The PD doesn't want to link up murders because it would highlight that it should be solvable. If they say the murders are all unrelated then everyone can just throw their hands in the air and spout about how awful society is becoming when there's all this random violence. And the politicians encourage them. No politician wants to go to the polls with a serial murderer rampaging through the city. But random violence, hey, part of modern America. They set up some useless outreach initiative to show they care, and get on with winning their election."

It was on the extreme side of cynical, but it wasn't without basis.

"And the thing that will blow it all up," she said, "is if we find one, just one, of the high-profile missing cases and link it in."

"We?" I raised an eyebrow.

"The question you need to ask yourself isn't whether you use me or not, it's how to make best use of me."

"There are some huge assumptions in there. I'm a PI. Why do you think I'm responsible for hunting down this murderer? You say you don't speculate and yet you've linked up cases by picking facts that fit your theory. You're just guessing."

"I'm right though, aren't I? You are working on it."

"You're crazier than I am."

"Maybe. But I have files and files that I know you want to see. Stuff that isn't even in the police records. Ideas on where and how. Contacts with people who've looked into this." She saw my sudden sharp look. "Not the FBI."

We reached the Country Club and stopped. Melissa would be heading back to the parking garage behind the mall. I would be going around the club to get back to Manassah.

"Don't forget, I am a trained forensic scientist as well, if you should come across some evidence. And I have all the equipment we would need."

I looked skeptical.

She shrugged. "They update their equipment in CSI every couple of years. They sell the old stuff for a song."

"What do you want from this, Melissa?"

She gave an awkward half-laugh. "You weren't listening. I need to know." She turned her face away, looked down at the creek. Her voice was strained. "I need to know like some people need their fix. I need it to be me that finds out."

I needed all the help I could get. I'd contemplated hiring her when I heard she'd been suspended, but I wasn't sure if this was the help I wanted, given the problems that came with it.

It was dangerous territory; Barbara Green's murder and the message that sent to me made that plain. Having Melissa work with me meant I would have to look out for another person.

But if I wasn't working with her, and she did stumble across proof of the paranormal secrets on her own, there wouldn't be anything to stop her from broadcasting it. I'd have failed the paranormal community and, according to David and Pia's predictions at the Assembly about uncontrolled Emergence, the whole world.

And there was one other thing that I'd need to be sure on with Melissa: I wasn't hunting the killer to prove his guilt and hand him to the justice system. I was hunting to kill. What would she think of that?

There was a lot to consider.

"I'll call you," I said, and trotted off home.

Chapter 23

Back at Manassah, in the study, my mind was in a whirl as I looked at the maps. It felt as if they'd grown since this morning, like some strange mold spreading across the walls. Their blankness was accusing.

They needed to be covered in pins, according to Melissa. Could I trust her? Would her 'evidence' just confuse everything?

How could he get away with this for so long?

By being very clever, and incredibly careful.

I had to be cleverer, painstaking and quick. And I had no idea where to start. No feeling for it.

Overwhelmed by how much needed to be done, I distracted myself checking my emails. Full of trash as usual. There was even one that was gibberish—letters and numbers. My finger hovered over the delete key.

The colonel hadn't been in touch, and this was one way he used.

I ran my eyes down it. Embedded as randomly scattered digits was a phone number. Possibly. Or I was seeing things.

I swapped my sim card for an unused one and called, wondering if I'd started to get delusional. I hadn't. Yet.

"Hi," he said. He sounded very tired.

"We have to stop speaking like this. Why don't you come on over?"

"I would love to. We better keep this short rather than cryptic. I don't know what they have in the way of scanners, but I'm running out of time."

"Okay. Where are you?"

"A couple of hours east of you, hiding in an old barn a few miles off US 36."

He was out on the high plains, where you can see in every direction for miles, but to be hiding, there had to be a reason beyond visibility.

"They know where you are?"

"Roughly. They got a hit on me somewhere near the Nebraska border. They know the car and they're patrolling the roads. They know I'm somewhere between I-70 and I-76. Of course, they know where I'm heading now as well."

"That's a lot of area to cover. And you know all this how?"

I could hear him snort gently. "I picked up a TacNet node when I left, and I've got all their codes. I'm listening to them."

I grunted. The TacNet would link in with their Ops 4 group radio command circuit, as long as it was provided the right codes. They couldn't have known that the colonel had the hardware itself, but they were being sloppy if they hadn't realized their codes were compromised .

Or maybe they were being rushed. The pressure from the FBI had to have rattled them. Their behavior in Denver—killing their own team members—indicated they were panicking.

"They can't cover every little road coming in from the east."

The farmland had a grid of blacktops and dirt roads that ran like dusty veins between endless fields under a cobalt sky. There were too many to patrol. Sure, dirt tracks would kick up dust and attract attention, but he could always move at night.

"Got a couple of problems," he said quietly.

I kicked myself. I was thinking like a civilian again. This wasn't some gang of badasses out to get the colonel. This was Ops 4-16, the Nagas. A military unit, who'd be thinking like the military.

"They got eyes aloft?" I guessed.

"Yeah. Couple of light aircraft during the day. That's all they need. They can see every car that moves out here for fifty miles around. But they've brought in a helicopter for night."

"What have they got?"

"I don't know, they aren't giving specs out." Snapping at me was a sign of how wearing this had to be for him. On his own, he would have been a ghost to them, but taking his wife along for the ride must have limited his choices. Now it was close to getting him caught.

He gathered himself and sighed. "The Ops 4 group has access to two high spec birds. The Chinese Z10 and the Apache."

Oh, shit.

"They have a Naga flying those?"

Neither machine was the sort of thing you retrained a grunt to fly. At least, not if you wanted them to fly it twice. Flying any helicopter was a handful. Flying at night made it worse and the control systems in these super-helicopters pushed it even further.

"No," Colonel Laine said. "They'll have someone seconded from a flying unit."

"That's a weak point."

Possibly.

"I wouldn't want to depend on it."

No, I wouldn't either. With the colonel pinned down in the high plains, it was up to me to come up with a way to get him to Denver, whatever the Nagas threw up to stop us.

"I'll arrange something tomorrow," I said. "Maybe I can get the FBI to close the airspace down. If they haven't got spotter planes to coordinate their cars, they won't be able to concentrate their patrols. We should be able to get you out."

"I don't know, the TacNet reports make me think they've got enough people here that they're doing ground sweeps during the day, checking any hiding places like this one." I'd never heard the colonel like this before. He sounded so beaten down. "I haven't got a detailed map, but I reckon they'll find me tomorrow if I don't move."

Damn. Nothing like pressure. It had to be tonight.

My mind raced. There *are* ways to take on an attack helicopter from the ground and win, most of them involving lots of Stinger missiles. Lots. I had a problem with that on a whole load of levels.

This was the US. Stingers that missed the helicopter might select some other heat source to lock on and end up targeting a family car on the road. And if I did manage to take the helicopter down, I wasn't killing Nagas, just some pilot and gunner who'd been seconded from the Cavalry and thought they were following legal orders. Oh, and on a practical level, I couldn't go out tonight and buy a dozen Stingers in downtown Denver anyway.

All of those were good arguments for not attacking any military helicopter. There was one other point. If it was the Apache, it had a counter-measures weapon system that could backtrack and target multiple Stinger launch sites.

It wasn't a real healthy option taking on an Apache, but I had to plan for the worst case. I had to assume it would be the Apache. And I had to assume that, as a last resort, they'd forget coordinating cars to come pick us up and would try and blow us away.

I needed to counter the Apache's advantages.

The pilot would be looking at synthetic vision—a composite picture that combined images from a low light camera and an infrared scope and overlaid it on whatever he could see out the window. Like a werewolf, he would be able to see humans in the night from their body heat. Even on a moonless night like tonight. In Ops 4-10, we thought of Apache pilots as no longer completely human, which felt horribly ironic to me now.

The gunner's weapons system had the same vision capability. He could fire missiles that would lock onto a car's heat signature, and he had an armor-chewing machine gun that was slaved to the movements of his head.

The Chinese Z10 wasn't anything like as capable, but shared a lot of the same abilities. Either of these damned helicopters were capable of hunting coyote in the night desert. Humans and cars would be too easy.

All of which left me with options I'd devised as a purely theoretical exercise in Ops 4-10. The assignment had been to find the minimalist solution that could be used to escape from a hunting helicopter at night, but minimalist still required a truckload of equipment.

"You're going to have to leave it with me, Colonel. Thank God, there's no moon tonight."

"What are you going to do?"

"Set the ball rolling. Then I have to go party. But don't worry, after the party I'll gear up and come get you."

"Your sense of humor is going backwards."

"Yeah. Keep this cell handy—I'll call you."

Damn. I had two plans. One was to sneak out like a mouse, relying on the hunters to be too confident in their electronic systems. The other was the fallback. I really didn't want to go there, but there was supposedly a way to even up the odds.

I needed a combat team. I needed equipment. I needed more time.

Joking with the colonel aside, I was going to have to miss the reception at Haven. Bian was going to kill me, but it was that or save the colonel.

Jen chose that moment to arrive home, preceded by Julie and followed by David and Pia, who were laughing at something.

"What's up?" she demanded as soon as she saw my face.

"A list of things to do and no time to do them." I'd promised to tell her everything, so I explained the colonel's position, as briefly as I could. Jen would understand that our visit to Altau would need to be canceled. That would have to be my first call, to Bian, as soon as I finished talking to Jen. Then I'd need to find that truckload of equipment. In a couple of hours. At night.

"And this list of equipment?" Jen picked up a pad and a pen.

I huffed. This was just delaying me. Pia was starting to look agitated, and I made myself calm down.

"Nightscopes and a tactical comms system from Victor. The man himself. A couple of his men and an SUV. Your helicopter." I swallowed nervously, but she didn't even blink. "A motorbike. Er...survival blankets and dark-colored, lightweight blankets, paramedic first aid kit, half a dozen powerful LED torches, a couple of laser pointers, photographer's tripod..." I ran through my list, all the way down to: "...and duct tape, lots of duct tape."

"That's it?"

"No," I said. "There's one thing I can't imagine anyone will be able to provide in a hurry. Maybe I'll need to rig up an alternative—"

"Enough already and tell me."

I sighed. "An infrared communications laser. Preferably something with juice like a satellite system." I scowled. It had been a long time since I'd done the evaluation on this kind of equipment. "And Matt, for an hour, to help put it together," I added.

"There are firms here in Denver that make satellite comms equipment," said David.

"Maybe I'll have to break in somewhere..." I slowed to a halt. Jen was looking smug and reaching for the phone.

"Jen? Who're you calling?"

She smiled. "I'm starting with your friend and mine, Mr. Campbell Carter. Who, by the way, is just desperate for me to help organize his fundraising campaign."

"But—"

"He owns Merrow Technologies," Jen said, "and they are the majority shareholder in AdAstra Communications."

"Who supply satellite comms systems to NASA," David finished off and punched the air. "Touchdown!"

"And I'm sure he could arrange a loan at very short notice. What shall I say it's for?" Jen asked coyly.

"Ahh...an experiment with short, urgent messages to a vehicle."

"Well, he won't have any idea anyway." She pointed me to the hallway. "This is going to take a few hours to put together, during which time we *will* be at the party. Go change. All of you."

"But I have to—"

Pia grabbed me and started to pull me out.

"You don't have to sit here and organize everything," Jen said. "That's what I've got secretaries for."

"But—"

"Go. Your dress is on your bed. We are *not* going to be late."

∞ ∞ ∞ ∞ ∞

"Wow." Jen said, when I reentered the study.

I was scrubbed and changed, with my hair braided and my face made up by Pia as I fretted. I was still tugging the dress to see when—not if—it was going to fall off. It defied gravity and the tugging.

Lisa had done her magic again. Even distracted as I was, I loved the gold dress. It fit like a glove up my front, just covering my breasts and dramatically swooping down to my lower back. From the level of my thighs, the material was light and layered, gathered towards my left leg. As Lisa had said, dramatic as a flamenco dress.

Jen's reaction swept away any lingering worries about the outfit. It was worth it just to see the way she looked at me. She came over and inspected me, her blue eyes checking me up and down, and her fingers smoothing a ruffle here and there.

"I approve," she murmured. "I'd better go catch up." She planted a kiss on my cheek.

My Athanate stirred comfortably as she sauntered away, glancing back over her shoulder for a last look at me.

An intercom call from the guards at the gate brought me back down to earth; Alex had arrived. With Ricky—I'd forgotten that little complication.

This is going to be fun. Not.

∞ ∞ ∞ ∞ ∞

I got Alex first, leaving Ricky talking to Pia and David in the living room.

His dinner jacket was superb, the black cloth complementing his light brown hair and the cut emphasizing the broad shoulders and snake-slim hips.

I searched his eyes, green and sharp tonight. Was there any doubt, a little hesitation that told me I'd broken what had grown between us? Nothing.

Or was I seeing what I wanted to see?

His brow was creased and I reached up hesitantly to smooth the wrinkles out, just as Jen had done with my dress.

My stomach clenched in anticipation, but there was no sudden maelstrom of emotions overpowering me.

"Okay?" he said softly as I dared to lean against him.

"Yeah. I think so."

His face turned to brush the inside of my wrist with his lips, sending a shiver down me. Still no reaction from my strongbox.

I couldn't risk driving my kin away. I had to make him understand it wasn't me that had rejected him so violently in Ricky's back yard. Even more hesitantly, I *reached*. Our eukori slipped over each other like twining silken scarves. There was no hesitation in the sensuous darkness that was his true inner self.

The green of his eyes slipped subtly toward gold.

He sighed and smiled. "Has this cured you of any doubts that you used Athanate compulsion on me?"

"No," I said. As he frowned again, I went on, "But at the moment, I'll try to just deal with everything as it is, rather than how I got here."

He laughed and his hands went to circle my waist.

I skittered back. No, I wasn't ready for that yet. I wanted it but I didn't dare.

"Okay," he said, holding himself in check.

We relaxed, two paces between us.

"Anyway, I wouldn't have minded being compelled by you," he joked.

"No, you *couldn't*. That's the difference, Alex. That's where I can't go. I mustn't compel you and I have to be sure I'm not compelling you. Anything else and I'm on the slope to ending up Basilikos."

"What's the point if you never use it?" There was still humor in his tone.

I shrugged. "I'm not being unrealistic. Defensive use, where my life is threatened, would be justified. Use it on friends and family? Hell, no. I'd be no better than Basilikos."

"What about on the pack?" His eyes went past me to the living room door.

"I wouldn't," I said, turning, "but I can't guarantee what Altau would do."

We went into the living room to tackle the next problem. Ricky.

∞ ∞ ∞ ∞ ∞

"You are kidding, aren't you?"

"No, Ricky. The options are, you stay here, or you wear a blindfold. It's Altau's standing orders. No outsiders get to know where the headquarters are."

I wasn't sure how secret Haven was any more, after Matlal's attack on the Assembly, but I wasn't going to go against these orders.

"What about Alex?"

"Alex is a member of my House, and kin besides. I'm responsible for him and Alex understands that."

Ricky didn't like that, but he couldn't argue it.

"It's not just a formality either, Ricky," David said. "If Altau find out you know where Haven is, the standing orders say you'd have those memories erased."

"Memories like that aren't neat little modules, either," Pia said. "It's easy enough to blur a face, but something that relies on landmarks, for instance, links into all sorts of other memories. Having those erased would be unpleasant."

Ricky swore under his breath.

"Let Felix take it up with Skylur, and I promise you, I'll back Felix," I said. "I think this division is stupid."

At that, Ricky took a long, cool look at me, but in the end, he just nodded.

Chapter 24

House Altau didn't do things in a small way. Their style was normally restrained, but I'd had a feeling that went out the window when they decided to make an impression. I was right.

There was still a sense of disturbance about Haven, but instead of the anthill we had the swan: grace on top and frantic paddling below. All the cars that had been parked on the lawns were gone. The lawns were gone too—vanished under a pageant of marquees and tented pavilions. Somewhere in that flapping city, I figured Panethus strategists would be ignoring the party and concentrating on assessing the risks of Basilikos' actions and planning responses.

We drove through all that right to the front door of the house, and handed the keys to the valet.

A flock of greeters and ushers delivered us to the antechamber of the reception, which was in the suite that had been used for the Assembly. Julie and Ricky were directed to a separate room where others waited. I was assured that all security in Haven was Altau's responsibility, and nodded to Julie to go.

Ricky and Alex shrugged at each other. "Hope they have something good to eat while we wait," Ricky muttered and let himself be taken away. He wasn't exactly security, but I didn't want to get into a long explanation of why he was here. I guessed Felix wouldn't get to hear about this part.

∞ ∞ ∞ ∞ ∞

On the night of the Assembly, the antechamber had been all business. Now it was transformed.

Along the walls stood six-foot-tall sprays of lilies, bright and styled like explosions of fireworks, their perfume subtle but sensuous. Chandeliers glittered above. Guards in crimson jackets and black pants stood on either side of the closed doors to the reception. A wide carpet in matching crimson with gold patterns ran the length of the room.

Jen's eyes roved over it all. I could almost hear her calculating what it cost and which of her events it might suit. Alex wrinkled his nose and pretended he wasn't impressed.

I turned to look at my House, suddenly afraid we wouldn't be fancy enough. Thank God Jen had insisted on the formal dresses for us. She looked amazing, of course, her silver dress the exact match to my gold.

Alex and David looked good in their dinner jackets. David needed to remember not to slouch. Maybe Pia looked a little out of place with the rest of us, but the hint of Scheherazade in her swirling skirts made her look fabulous and exotic. She had assured me that there wasn't a unified style at these occasions, and other Athanate would be in alternative dress.

Damn, we looked good, even if I said so myself.

David stood at attention like a fresh recruit, stiff and awkward, staring over my head. "Do we pass inspection, ma'am?"

Jen rolled her eyes. The rest of them laughed.

"House Farrell."

I turned.

A blonde woman in a blue ball gown stood waiting. Despite her studied calm there was an air of wariness about her, as if she was expecting everything to go wrong the very next moment.

"I'm Elizabetta Cleve kin-Sherman of House Altau. I'm Head of Protocol for the reception."

"Pleased to meet you, Elizabetta." I looked closely at her. From the kin-Sherman name, she was kin to Tom—one of my friends among the Haven security staff. I wasn't surprised he'd found such an attractive woman to be his kin.

"Liz," she said. "But please always introduce yourself formally first. I'll be taking you in shortly and announcing you, but it's always expected that you greet people individually with your full name."

While I was wondering if I was supposed to introduce her, Jen spoke. "So I should say that I'm Jennifer Anna-Marie Kingslund of House Farrell?"

Elizabetta shook her head. "The form is Jennifer Anna-Marie Kingslund kin-Farrell. You can also add the House Farrell at the end if you wish. Here, as guests of House Altau, no one would challenge you, but it's always best for kin to state your kinship among Athanate."

A discreet gong sounded behind her.

"The last group has cleared," Elizabetta said. "Please come with me." She turned and led us to the doors.

How bad can it be? They aren't going to eat me.

Despite my brave words, my heart was in my mouth.

At the door, Elizabetta turned for a last check.

"Ah, no," she said. "Excuse me." She rearranged Alex and me, so that it was his hand coming up under my arm and resting on me rather than the other way around, mirroring the way Jen had already chosen.

Alex glowered and Jen smirked.

Enough, children.

The doors were opened and Elizabetta led us through, with David and Pia close behind.

We stopped five paces inside.

As with the antechamber, the Assembly room had been transformed. The heavy crimson carpet reached every corner, chandeliers marched down the middle of the room and the walls were hung with drapes of black, gold-embroidered silk.

A classical string quartet was playing on a balcony. They paused as another gong sounded clearly.

I'd been an unwelcome visitor in redneck bars that didn't go as quiet as the Assembly room. Every eye was on us.

Elizabetta's voice rang out. "Amber Farrell of Denver, House Farrell. Friend and ally, close affiliate and subordinate to House Altau. Her kin and House."

She repeated it in Athanate. I caught words I knew: *ykos, philos* and *perikos.*

Hell, another few years and I'll be fluent.

Bian had used those words to introduce me to the Lyssae Anubis and stop him from biting my head off. I thought they seemed useful words to know, looking around at some of the faces in the crowd.

Elizabetta ended with, "Be welcome to Haven, House Farrell."

A murmur came from the Athanate, and the quartet restarted. Some heads turned away. Some conversations restarted.

The more I looked at it, the more the gathering seemed unbalanced somehow.

I didn't have time to analyze it. Beside me, I could hear Alex and Jen both let out a breath, and both stop when they realized the other was doing it too.

"Well, Pia said there would be a reaction to us," Alex said, clearing his throat.

"It's not all about us." I frowned. I didn't have enough knowledge about the factions within the whole Panethus group, but at a glance it seemed there were two sides and a middle ground of undecided. A few of the clusters looked almost confrontational.

There didn't seem to be any consistency between them as to their reaction to us. What was going on?

Pia slid up alongside us, but at that moment Bian emerged from the throng, followed by a man and a woman. I recognized the woman from the charity ball and both of them from the Assembly.

"Amber, I'm delighted you could come," Bian said.

Yeah, I'd had a bit of a meltdown on the phone to her. I'd apologize later.

"I think you've met Eugenie," she went on, "and this is Louis."

Bian was easing us into the party.

Oh, well, here goes my first formal intro.

"Amber Farrell, House Farrell."

"Louis, Comte de Fontaines d'Argonne, House Argonne."

Oh, Gods, what had Pia told me? Titles overrode surnames. Not only was he House Argonne, he was a French count. Hadn't they chopped off all their heads in the revolution? Apparently not.

And the woman...

"Eugenie Augusta, Herzogin von Urach-Passau, House Passau." She smiled apologetically. "What a mouthful! Just Eugenie."

Didn't Herzogin mean princess? Now I felt completely disadvantaged in the name department.

She leaned forward and we kissed necks on both sides.

Diana had explained the custom which allowed Athanate, when meeting, to assess each other's marque and emotional state. It was a skill I had yet to acquire, or maybe Eugenie had her emotions under better control than me. I wondered what she made of my marque, blended as it was with Were. But I guessed that was Skylur's purpose in this whole reception, to let Panethus sniff me for themselves.

"Louis, of course," said her companion, capturing my hand in both of his. We kissed necks and he ended by bending his head over my hand. "I could not dream of being such a burden on your mouth."

"And there was me, thinking I was the one with a bit of wolf," snapped my demon.

Bian and Eugenie burst out in laughter. Louis smiled, not looking at all put out.

Jen and Alex made their greetings in turn. Neck kissing was an Athanate thing, not required for kin, to Alex's enormous relief when greeting Louis. Jen just smiled and looked relaxed, as if she did this all the time.

I could feel Alex's discomfort about all of it, but my kin found that the pompous formality of making introductions all around made it impossible to be angry for long. Maybe that's why Athanate did it.

"Not everyone will be as pleasant," murmured Bian as we kissed necks. "Try and throttle that demon in your throat, Round-eye. I have duties, but

I'll be back." She slipped out, brushing deliberately between Jen and Alex. "Keep a dance free for me later, all of you."

Louis talked to Jen and Eugenie to Alex while I was distracted by Norgaard from Denmark, who'd been supportive in the Assembly, and had come up to introduce her kin to me. They were a pair of handsome, straw-haired young men, who were twins. They looked like a couple of teenagers she'd just kidnapped off a farm in Jutland, but they claimed they were fifty years old.

While we talked, staff drew back the drapes on one side, revealing a second room with a dance floor and tables of finger snacks. The walls of the second room were mirrored panels, offset in a zigzag pattern, creating a kaleidoscopic image. I found it disorienting, but the gathering mingled more as they drifted into the new room. I lost the feeling of cliques forming in the glittering swirl of Athanate and kin.

The quartet merged into a larger group and began playing ballroom dance music.

Wait staff began to pass through, carrying trays of champagne.

"This is excellent champagne," said Jen, sipping from a glass and frowning. "But I don't think I know it."

"Ahh. These are the very fountains of Argonne," Louis said. "My life's work has been to produce a champagne truly worthy of beauty."

"Not champagne then, if it's from Argonne. It's just *méthode champenoise.*"

Ouch.

"There were vineyards producing champagne in Argonne when Champagne was muddy woodland, Ms. Kingslund, but I grant you, they've marketed their name better."

"Hmm. It's certainly better than most of those that market themselves so well. I must buy some." Jen smiled brightly at him. "And provided you don't read anything into it, it's Jen."

Louis inclined his head formally. He seemed to be enjoying the cut and thrust of talking to Jen, however sharp her strikes were.

"We need to follow Skylur's example," Eugenie was saying to Alex. "There should be much better links between Athanate and Were. Perhaps you could visit us in Germany and show us how."

My lips twitched. I had no problem with this flirting, and no worries about my kin. I wondered if Bian had selected Eugenie and Louis for exactly that reason.

For myself, after Norgaard, I had a succession of Houses introducing themselves to me. Many did it as a formality, a convention that they had to observe. The new House needed to be greeted. It wasn't that they were hostile, but few had the easy approachability of Norgaard, or the embarrassed friendliness of Lindberg, the representative for Sweden. A few were downright unhappy and not concerned that it showed in their marque scent. I might not be able to read Eugenie, but I could read some of them.

In my head, my countdown clock was ticking. In another hour or so, I had to be out of here, out of this dress and racing off onto the high plains to fetch the colonel. A shiver of the Athanate elethesine hormone burned off the little champagne I'd had and got me a startled look from the Athanate House I was greeting.

Couples drifted onto the dance floor. Long-lived Athanate and kin had had time to perfect their technique. I had noticed at the charity ball that none of them ever seemed to put a foot wrong in a dance.

Slowly, my House was lured out onto the dance floor. First Jen and Pia, then David. Finally someone decided Alex wasn't about to turn into a slavering wolf and he joined in. I was still too busy kissing necks.

Finally, I had Arvinder to contend with, leader of Theokos—the powerful Athanate subgroup that had switched allegiance from Basilikos to Panethus in the recent Assembly. He was dressed as formally as Alex, but managed only to look like a handsome, laughing pirate in a dinner suit.

Despite meeting previously, we greeted each other formally.

"No devotees here with you, Arvinder?" I teased. Many Athanate had brought kin with them, but Arvinder's creed dictated a different position for his human partners, almost worshipers. I wasn't comfortable with the idea yet, but I'd wait until I met them before I formed an opinion.

"I am tactful, and most aware that it could cause discomfort here," he replied, looking around at the swirl of dancers.

"What's the buzz here? Isn't Panethus one big, happy group?"

"Panethus isn't really Panethus anymore," he said obscurely.

I was about to dig deeper when, in the middle of the dance floor, Jen's silver dress caught my eye. I half-expected her to be with Louis, but she wasn't. She was dancing with Bian.

"Excuse me."

I sliced through the dancers to touch Bian's shoulder.

"My turn, I think."

"Oh, Amber, it must be the lighting. I never noticed before how green your eyes are," she said. "You can't dance with your kin this early in the evening." She reached out, one-handed, and snagged Alex as he passed.

He turned, and his eyes grew round at the opportunities for this to all go wrong.

Bian skillfully handed Jen over. Alex and Jen looked as if they'd each picked up a rattler. I tried to say something, but nothing emerged and Bian swept me off, leading expertly.

I was working hard not to stumble, so I could barely spare them a glance. I saw Jen pull Alex forward and he automatically moved into the steps of the waltz. They left enough space between them that I could have fit in, and maybe that was where I should have been.

Bian giggled. "Ken and Barbie wouldn't look that stiff. Leave them. They have to adapt to it eventually."

"All fun for you. It's a delicate time, Bian."

"They aren't made of glass, either of them." She turned us around and danced us away from the crowded middle of the floor. "Stop twisting your head. They aren't going anywhere. Besides, you can see them in the mirrors. Cool, huh?"

"Your design?"

"Yeah." We'd reached the edge of the room and she maneuvered us around until she had her back to the mirrored wall.

"Is it an Altau specialty?" I asked. "The mirrored room?"

"No," she said. "I got the idea from a Kung Fu film. What you think you see is not what you see. All those thousand images, which is me?"

"Hmm." She'd missed a step and I'd nearly stepped on her toe. "This kind of dancing's not your preferred style, is it?"

"You should see the parties I give," she said, distracted.

She stopped dancing, craning her neck to look around me at the other dancers.

"What the hell are you up to, Bian?"

"Trust me. Again."

And she stepped backward, pulling me with her. The whole room seemed to spin and I stumbled.

Chapter 25

The room we arrived in, *so* elegantly, was nothing like the mirrored ballroom.

It was cool and dark enough that the people inside were just outlines. The scent came through quicker than my eyes could adjust and I knew there were Basilikos in the room.

I'd underestimated my Athanate senses in the ballroom. The whole time I'd been getting a trickle of scents from marques that I knew were Panethus, reassuring me that, however unfriendly they were to me personally, they were not enemies. There was a marque in this room that was like a slap across my face.

Bian had a grip on my wrist, and she wasn't agitated. I tried to calm myself. Yeah, trust her, she said.

"We're all here now; I think we can turn the lights up."

I recognized the voice. That was Skylur.

"You are being ridiculously melodramatic."

Correia! The new leader of Basilikos, the woman who'd ousted Matlal, right here in Haven.

"Is your new affiliate about to go rogue?" Correia asked.

"Now who's being melodramatic?" Skylur said as the lights brightened, showing a small, plain room with a decorative fireplace, chairs arranged around a coffee table, and bare walls. "You're perfectly well aware that the tests presented at the Assembly were grossly distorted. Thanks to factions within Basilikos."

"I'm also aware of what my senses tell me. You have an affiliate there walking a knife edge. She's one jolt away from collapse." Correia was sitting opposite Skylur, for all the world like two old friends chatting by the fireside, instead of the leaders of two creeds of Athanate, each bent on the destruction of the other.

Skylur just smiled.

I swallowed all the questions that I wanted to ask and concentrated on standing quietly.

Behind Correia was a wedge of silent, dark-uniformed security, all House Correia by their marque. All six of them had the unblinking, coiled stillness of Athanate flooded with the elethesine hormone. If anyone here was on a knife edge, it was them.

Basilikos had been turned upside down at the Assembly. They'd found their former leader had been plotting attacks on the meeting without regard for the safety of his own allies, and from a point of almost winning the balance of power, they'd been confronted with a defection and the sudden arrival of new Houses affiliated to Altau. But these Athanate did not look beaten. They looked as if they were straining to snatch back the ground they'd lost.

This was much more interesting than kissing necks in the ballroom.

Behind Skylur, and somehow balancing the presence of all Correia's security, stood a single man, short and black-haired, his skin the olive of the Mediterranean, his eyes hooded beneath upswept brows. As if to emphasize the contrast with Correia, he wore pale chinos and a white open-necked shirt with a rounded collar. He was casually cracking and eating walnuts with his blunt hands. A bowl of them sat on the table beside a pile of discarded shells.

Bian pulled me in behind him.

Adept Emerson, the truth sensor from the Assembly, stood by the empty fireplace, one hand idly stroking the imposing eagle statue that stood there.

"Must we continue in English?" Correia asked.

"It is the language we all have in common," said Skylur mildly.

"So." Correia snorted and sat forward. "Your choice of attendees is informative. I believe we are discussing your headlong pursuit of Emergence."

"I recall your message; you requested the meeting to discuss an exchange."

I had no idea how old and experienced Correia was, but if she were trying to land a verbal blow on Skylur, I bet he would slide past her every time like that.

"Why do you have her here?" She indicated me.

"House Farrell?" suggested Skylur. "She has a fresh eye for everything we've hashed over countless times. I like old assumptions being challenged. And you must admit, her House does that."

Correia muttered something in Athanate.

"It's not a House, it's a zoo," Bian immediately translated.

I smiled. I had a sudden wolfy vision of tearing Correia's neck open, but I guessed I wasn't supposed to do that at this meeting. The smile was a far better way of getting to her.

"To move us forward, I could suggest that we concentrate on the request for exchange of prisoners and speak about specific Houses." Skylur crossed his legs and gestured to the man behind him. "Naryn?"

"We hold Houses Teugis and Madrone here—" Naryn began.

"On what grounds?" Correia interrupted.

"They were investigated for failing to attend the Assembly after a direct command, and that investigation uncovered practices which are not in accordance with our creed."

"Creed would appear to be no longer what defines us," Correia said. "You must have greater reason."

Naryn bowed slightly. "Philosophy, if you prefer. In any event, they have declared themselves unable to commit to Emergence. This is not an attitude we can now support. Panethus is now the party of Emergence. Their domains remain Panethus and so we hold them as outsiders caught within our territory, all under the rules of the Assembly."

"And you will come apart at the seams if you persist in enforcing your 'philosophy'. Teugis and Madrone are just the first." She stopped herself, and visibly relaxed back into her seat. "So, they want to join Basilikos. We allowed House Singh to lead his whole faction over to Panethus in the Assembly. Why can't you do the same?"

"You had no choice in the Assembly. That is our neutral venue," Skylur said, steel beneath the silk in his voice. "We are not in the Assembly now."

The tension behind Correia ratcheted up a notch. Naryn went back to his walnuts as if oblivious, his eye movements slow and unconcerned. Who was this man?

"Well, I will match your two Houses, with Ubbriaco and Kalinides," Correia said. "As you have realigned your geographic boundaries here in America, so have we elsewhere. These two did not see the sense in joining us, and so we're holding them as outsiders in our domains. Like you, honoring the rules of the Assembly. So: a simple exchange, two for two."

Skylur and Naryn did not respond.

"What about Romero?" I asked in the silence. According to Larry before he was killed, Romero had gone to Basilikos.

She didn't care to talk to me, but Skylur waited until she responded.

"Nothing to do with me. That was Matlal's private project. Or Vega Martine." She shuddered. "Basilikos want nothing to do with that. What was it you said about traps at the Assembly? They can bite back. Well, we will see at the end who has been bitten worse."

My eyes flicked to Adept Emerson. I assumed she was here to ensure that only the truth was told. Her expression hadn't changed. Either I was wrong about the truth sensing, or Correia was being truthful and had nothing to do with whatever had gone on in New Mexico.

"And the Matlal remaining here in Denver?" Bian asked.

"I have broadcast a call for them to leave. If they don't, they're yours to deal with as you will."

"They always were, here in my mantle," Skylur said.

"Why are they not leaving then?" Naryn chewed meditatively on a nut. "Because they have nowhere to go? Possibly because you've declared them outcast?"

Correia didn't answer.

"Then again, if they did manage to achieve something here, that might rehabilitate them in your eyes." Naryn tossed empty shells in the fireplace.

Correia put out a hand and one of her security team placed a roll of paper in it. "Here's a list of names which may help you in tracking them. That's as much as I can do. You're right; they are outcast, but that's because they've made themselves outcast. I have no responsibility for them."

"What about their...toru?" I stumbled over the Athanate word—the name Basilikos gave to the captive humans that they fed from. It meant cattle that are owned. Basilikos had been holding some here in Denver so that they could feed. As I understood Athanate laws, Altau needed to find them and free them, if any were still alive.

"How on earth would I know anything about that?" Correia snapped.

I refused to back down. "Wouldn't Matlal know?"

"He's not able to tell us anything." Correia's eyes lingered over me. I had a good idea she was suddenly remembering I was the one who was responsible for Matlal's current mental state. Personally, I didn't think it was that impressive. I suspected that in any tests of telergic strength, Matlal had been secretly supported by Vega Martine and when he lost that support, he'd proved weak.

Without any help from the rest of Basilikos on finding the toru, that left us with only what I knew: When I'd met Larry in Cheesman Park, he'd walked from wherever they were being held and he'd approached the park from the northwest. It couldn't be that difficult to find them and free them, but Altau hadn't yet.

"Why isn't Matlal dead?" Bian asked quietly.

"We need to recover things in Mexico. We'll see then."

I noticed Correia's eyes stilled, as if she wanted to look over at the Adept and was willing herself not to. But Emerson didn't say anything. Maybe what Correia said was not the whole truth, then. Interesting.

Almost as interesting as watching Naryn work with Skylur.

"What are you doing in Istanbul?" Naryn asked. It might be something of interest, but I sensed it was a topic intended to keep Correia off balance for the next question.

"Nothing." Correia looked puzzled. "We keep out—it's the Carpathian's territory, isn't it?"

"You've not given us the names of all the Houses imprisoned by you," Skylur said.

"You named two, I named two." Correia's eyes narrowed. She'd been successfully distracted enough that she allowed her marque to blossom with satisfaction. She had something she believed Skylur really wanted.

"That's not what I said."

"Very well," she replied, insincere reluctance in her voice. "We hold House Tarez. Such an old House, so very old. Their affiliations must go back centuries, deep and hidden as a great tree's roots. If Panethus were to lose that, maybe all sorts of linked affiliations will weaken. I can understand your concern."

Skylur said nothing, but I felt his anger through his marque. He was deliberately revealing his emotion. Naryn and Bian tensed. My weight unconsciously came forward onto the balls of my feet and elethesine started to flood my system as my hard-wired Athanate instincts took over. The strongbox in my mind seemed to creak and sweat sprang out on my forehead. I was *not* going to lose it now.

Correia backed down in a hurry, holding hands up as her own security flattened their formation to face the threat. "Enough! A deal, Altau, a deal."

I blinked, trying to still everything in my head. Calm. Calm.

"What have I got that you might want?" Skylur asked.

Correia turned and looked directly at me. "Isn't that what you're offering?"

Chapter 26

Skylur laughed.

Correia laughed with him.

I didn't share the joke. I'd had just enough warning to clamp down on my reaction so I wouldn't sink to my knees or lose whatever was in my stomach, but I was useless, rooted to the spot and shaking like an aspen leaf. The strongbox was open and every screaming horror wanted to rampage through me. My entire effort went to prevent my being overwhelmed by things inside my own head.

I could feel Bian's shock. She slipped across in front of me, so I was partly shielded by her and Naryn.

"Oh, your pet doesn't like the idea of sharing her Blood." That bitch Correia was enjoying this. "I'm not even sure she would obey. Would you force her to submit?"

"She would obey," Skylur said.

He might as well have spat on me. His simple words stung like a whip. Anger flooded up, threatening to complete the destruction that the leakage of formless fears had started. But it didn't. Anger I was used to dealing with. Anger was a flame I could control, and I scoured my mind with it.

"Such a temptation!" Correia was saying. "A way to even the odds and prevent Panethus from racing away and swamping poor Basilikos by gaining thousands of new recruits."

She stood and glared at Skylur.

"You think that I'm such a fool, that I'm so uncertain in my leadership that I'd fall for a sleight of hand like that? Look at her! Taste her marque! The stench of Were is making me gag. She's so close to rogue, she can barely stand there. So much for reducing crusis. You'd turn me into a freak show."

Skylur stood, pushing his hands into his pockets. "The reduction in crusis is real. You'd really turn it down?"

"If it's real, why haven't you used it?" Correia came back at him, absolute certainty in her attitude.

Skylur shrugged. "Well then, what instead?"

Correia was enjoying her moment too much. Certainly too much to see relief and belated awareness dawning in me. Skylur had never intended to offer my Blood. He'd let Correia believe he was, and in seeking the catch she'd out-thought herself. He'd tricked her and gained me some measure of security from Basilikos.

For the moment. I repeated that to myself. The longer I kept myself sane and functioning, the more attention I'd draw back from Basilikos.

Just wonderful.

"With Emergence," Correia was preaching at him, "Panethus have hitched their chariot to a pack of street cats. But just as you did with your creed of kin, your definition of yourself forces a definition on us. Basilikos are the opponents of Emergence. So be it. What you have abandoned, we will clasp to us and hold high. Basilikos are now the party of the Hidden Path."

I was glad of the distraction as I got myself back under control. I had done enough homework to know about the Hidden Path. It had been the underlying creed of all Athanate—to be so secret in their ways that they were never discovered. A path so secret, as they had it, that even the eagle could not see it. The symbol was the blindfold eagle, and a statue of that by the legendary Athanate artist Ptolomeus dominated the main entrance hall here at Haven.

The image ran through a lot of Athanate art. The shape of the eagle was used as a motif running across the edges of the fireplace. Even the artwork that Adept Emerson stood beside was an echo of that piece in the hall. In the same way Correia had described the linkage of associations as a tree's root systems, the thinking behind the Hidden Path crept deeply into everything about the Athanate, hidden until you thought about it.

I suddenly realized the sheer scope of Skylur's task—not just to remove that fundamental belief from the Athanate, but to *reverse* it. No wonder his position in the Assembly had caused such a disturbance on both sides. No wonder the reception seemed so fragmented.

And I felt Skylur wasn't happy with Correia's direction now. In taking the Hidden Path as her emblem, she was going to tap into the unconscious roots of the Athanate psyche.

He picked up the bowl of walnuts and offered one to her.

She refused to even see the bowl. She was staring directly into his eyes.

"You know that I've always been a follower of art," she said.

Naryn and Bian tensed again, responding to Skylur. I caught up shakily. I didn't think it was coming to fighting, but I couldn't tamp it down.

"Hmm?" Skylur selected a walnut and replaced the bowl on the side table.

"In exchange for House Tarez, I will take Ptolomeus' statue from your entrance hall."

I could feel the shock reverberate through Naryn and Bian.

The walnut cracked in Skylur's hand. A neat, precise sound.

"Done," he said.

Chapter 27

The deal was concluded with startling speed.

A neutral venue for the exchange was agreed and House Correia ushered out by some secret passageway to prevent anyone else knowing they'd even been here.

If Altau genuinely wanted me to review their security, I was going to have to know about passages like that. It was a measure of how much control I'd managed to establish that I was able to think that mundane thought.

Skylur took one long look at me before turning on his heel, apparently satisfied I wasn't going to go rogue in the next couple of minutes. "Naryn, Bian, a moment in the planning room." He marched out the door with them behind him.

"Well, that was amusing." Adept Emerson took Skylur's seat, and motioned me to Correia's.

"How does it work?" I said, proud that my voice was steady. "You say something like that that clearly isn't true, but isn't supposed to be believed. What would another Truth Sensor feel?"

She laughed. "The truth. Always the truth, as perceived by the teller."

I sat in Correia's seat. It wasn't infected, even if it did have a lingering scent of her marque, overlaid with a hint of triumph. She thought she'd gotten the better end of this deal. Maybe she had.

"Why are you here, Adept Emerson?"

"Three questions in one! Why am I here in Haven? Why was I in this meeting? Why am I still in this room?" She leaned back, aping Skylur's mannerisms and making a steeple of her fingers. "I'm here in Haven because there are no Warders anymore, and Altau offered. I was here in this room to make sure Correia didn't lie outright. And Skylur left me here to talk to you, to calm you down if you needed it."

"He pulled off a trick with Basilikos?"

She nodded confirmation.

"What if Correia had gone for it? Agreed to take my Blood in exchange?"

"Gone for what, Amber? Skylur didn't offer anything. She thought he did, but she was wrong. He was running that conversation from the start."

"Well, what about the statue? Skylur was shaken when she chose that."

"He *looked* shaken, I'll agree. He knew it would cost something like that, but by choosing it, she's revealed her own weakness. Basilikos is as fragmented as Skylur designed it to be, and she hopes that this symbol will unite it. It's a powerful symbol, the original statue of the Hidden Path. It will speak powerfully to the subconscious of older Athanate. It's true, there has been a heavy cost to this, but I think Skylur believes it's bearable and justifiable."

I let myself relax a little more. Skylur was one step ahead of everyone. If he never intended to offer my Blood—I felt uneasy again just at the thought of Correia biting me—then what had his intention been when he'd said I would obey? He'd made me angry. I'd used that anger to recover. It wasn't pleasant, but it was the quickest way to help me without compromising anything else. Yeah, make that several steps ahead of me.

And in the meantime, I had an Adept to question and about a thousand questions to ask that were closer to home than why Skylur offered a sanctuary to Adepts and what an Adept might get from it.

"If he's not right in this call," Emerson was saying thoughtfully, eyes unfocused on the empty fireplace, "then heaven help us. At best, we will become like footless, grey ghosts, forever fleeing the anger of the blind eagle."

She shivered.

"I have so many questions, Adept Emerson."

"I imagine you have." Her mouth twisted, highlighting the fine wrinkles that ran across her face and gathered at the corners of her eyes; a woman fond of laughing, much like Mary. "Very few of which we'll have time for. Call me Alice." She ran a hand through her hair. "I bet I can predict what you'll ask first."

I shuffled questions in my head, just because.

"Do you have contacts with Adepts in the Empire of Heaven?"

She laughed again. "You did that quite deliberately. What on earth would you—no, no time for that. No, I don't. Sorry."

I leaned back in the chair. I never seemed to get the answers I needed. I tried another. "What's a spirit guide?"

"Goodness! No time for that either. You'll have to come back and talk to me about that."

"What did you mean in the Assembly when you said I was thrice bound?"

"Ah. That was all three of you. Yes, you would want to know that. And we don't have—"

"Please."

"Very well. I wish you joy of the knowledge." She bowed her head. "What's binding? That which holds you to your House—the impress in your head? Or love—the impress on your heart? Or duty—the impress on your soul? None and all of these. And what must Basilikos say, who know not love? Or those that know not true duty?"

She stopped abruptly, rocking her body to and fro on her chair. "It's difficult to speak in modern English sometimes. I don't know how the elder Athanate manage it. Perhaps because it's all new language to them." She sighed. "It's difficult to speak of binding at all. It's too easy for Panethus to fall into seeing binding as love. Accept that as error, and ponder on what Basilikos preach to Aspirants. They talk of the opposite of love: hate. And thus they are blind too."

"Binding is the dark sister of love and hate, the daughter of need and the mother of spirit. It is anchored in desire and obsession, fascination and passion, but it is none of these. An Athanate may be bound by their head, or their heart, or their soul. Few are bound by all three, and fewer still share bindings three ways."

"I'm triple bound? And to both kin?"

"And they to each other, Amber. I made a joke—three bindings, three ways."

To each other? I wish. Were we talking about the same Jen and Alex?

She tilted her head. "Do you understand?"

"The binding bit? It's like one of those things you understand until you try to explain it," I said. "Or you see it until you try and look at it. I'll stop hunting it and let it sneak up on me."

"Yes! Exactly!" She sat straight, clasping her hands in her lap. "I forget that even though you're a child as an Athanate, you're not as a human."

I tried to settle my thoughts into some kind of order. "So I did this to them? I bound them to me?"

"Not precisely." She hesitated. "I can tell you feel guilty, as if you forced something on them. Absolutely not. They bound themselves to you as much as you did. And in turn, remember, they've bound you." My face must have reflected my hesitation. At loss to get through, Alice looked up at the ceiling for inspiration. "You were the architect and builder, but theirs was the material."

I could be happy with that, once I really believed it. Maybe I needed to let that belief sneak up on me too.

"Stop overanalyzing it, Amber. Goodness, if the first cavewoman who picked up a rock to defend her children had had to sit back down and puzzle out why the rock was hard, maybe we'd still be food for lions."

I managed a laugh at that. Yes, I'd let it sneak up on me.

"So, what was my first question supposed to be?"

She smiled tightly, the lines at the corners of her eyes gathering like a gossamer fishing net.

Bian stormed back in alone, her face set in anger.

"I was afraid I wouldn't have much time," Alice said, and we stood. She reached out and took my hands. "Come back and talk to me. Do not let any of the old ones get beneath your mental defenses, whatever anguish your mistakes are causing you. They might mean to help, but what you are, here," she let go and touched the side of my forehead gently, "is like soft wax. They will leave their impression on you and destroy what is forming there."

"But Diana—" I couldn't walk around forever with this bedlam threatening to break out in my head at every turn. And threatening to poison my relationship with Alex.

"Diana alone might be skillful enough to not harm you. But she is not here. Be brave. Be strong. Be patient. Come and talk to me—about workings and spirit guides and why you want to talk to the Chinese. And no aural sex."

"No *what*?"

"Aural." She spelled it out. "Opening your aura makes you vulnerable."

She saw my blank look and sighed in exasperation.

"Sex, all right? It's best at the moment to keep away from physical intimacy, basically," she said primly. "It lowers your mental barriers. That could be dangerous."

"Adept Emerson, Skylur wants you in the planning room," Bian said.

Alice nodded and walked off with a last glance.

"She fill your head with her indecipherable mutterings?" Bian asked as the door closed. If she'd truly been the leopard whose spots she wore, her tail would have been lashing from side to side.

"Not indecipherable, so much as difficult to grasp." I'd never seen Bian upset like this.

"There was probably a very good reason they threw her off the *Mayflower*." Bian glowered at the door.

"Bian, what's wrong?"

"Tell me you're all right first." Bian turned her glower on me. "You nearly came apart back there."

"I...yeah, you all caught me off balance. Sorry. And Alice is right, something up here," I tapped the side of my head, "tells me it isn't ready to give Blood. Skylur's trick freaked me."

"Emerson was talking about someone getting in your head, not your jugular."

"But something she said earlier makes me think it's all part of one thing. When you feed, you feed on emotion as well, don't you? Isn't that just using telergy? When you feed, aren't you in your kin's head too?"

"Maybe. Anyway, the damage has been done; Naryn, *not* a fan of yours. He thinks you're one step away from rogue. We need to get you away from here before he persuades Skylur to lock you up."

"Who the hell is he?"

"The Diakon."

"But—"

"Yes, I was the Altau Diakon."

"Oh, God, Bian, is this my fault?"

"No."

She made to move away, but I grabbed her. "Tell me what the hell happened," I said. I switched to my bad Vietnamese. "Talk to me, little sister."

Her eyes darkened like a night storm, but she didn't pull away. I waited and let the anger slowly subside. Then I hugged her.

"Careful," she breathed onto my neck. "I might get to like this."

If I was being teased, she was better. And it was worth it, despite the instinctive cringing away from her fangs that I had to control.

"It's not you, or me, it's just frigging politics." She sighed. "Naryn used to be the Altau Diakon. He'd been with Skylur forever. When Skylur started setting up sub-Houses secretly, Naryn was the obvious choice to run them and I was chosen to be the new Altau Diakon. But now we're trying to re-integrate everyone and all those sub-Houses want the person they know. It's not trust really, it's…familiarity. Anyway, Naryn's back as Diakon for the moment, and I'm tasked with local issues—the Matlal remnants, you, and so on."

"I'm a task?" I grinned.

"A damned awkward one." I could hear the smile in her voice. "But so tasty."

I figured the hug had achieved its aim and let her go before she raised the stakes again.

"Naryn is a serious problem for you, Round-eye. Don't give him the slightest excuse."

"I can't avoid coming here. I can't avoid Skylur. I've got Larimer's response to give him. He refused to help find the Matlal Athanate—"

"Already done. Alex told me. And about the colonel."

I chopped down on the reflex jealousy and tried to concentrate on the important things.

"There's an outcome from that refusal which is going to fall on you," she went on. "Best I can offer to soften the blow is to help you with your other tasks, like getting the colonel here safely."

"Huh?"

"Me. Tom." Bian made an exaggerated mime. "We. Help. You. Better than standing around here like a spare part."

The whine of Bian's secret entrance startled us. It spun around and David stepped unsteadily off the platform.

"How the hell did you work that out?" Bian asked.

"I was watching you. Monkey see, monkey do. Amber, call from Matt. Everything's ready back at Manassah. I think it's time to go."

"It is."

Bian retrieved a slim intercom from her bra. "Tom. Meet me topside in ten, please. Full combat kit and bring mine."

"I'm in too?" David asked me.

I nodded. Julie, Pia and Victor's guards should be enough for Jen. I'd need Alex as well, and I was hoping that meant Ricky too.

Bian ushered us into the corridor. "There's an elevator at the end," she said. "I'm looking forward to this. I get to see what your little accountant is made of." She grabbed David's butt.

"I'm actually not an accountant at all, I'm an actuary," David said, unfazed. "Despite the fact I work in financials, there are fundamental differences between what I do and what an accountant does. It's all to do with risks and uncertainties. It's really fascinating. See…"

Bian gave me a beseeching glance over her shoulder.

I shrugged. "You made the bed, you lie in it," I mouthed at her. Not that there was any real chance of that, given how smitten David was with Pia.

Chapter 28

My ear hissed with the noise of too many connections lashed together in a hurry.

The colonel's mil-spec TacNet was like a huge spiderweb, stretched over the high plains, fastening to the Nagas' comms system on one side and Victor's on the other. It even seamlessly relayed cell calls, all slipping down the ether to me, kneeling motionless on a blacktop in the middle of nowhere.

It was dark in a way that cities don't get: unrelieved blackness in every direction except for the diamond scatter of cold stars across the sky.

I was hot. That was good. It meant the blankets swathing me were keeping my heat signature locked in. Bian had checked on her infrared scope. Outside the duct-taped blankets, I was close to the temperature of the blacktop and invisible to infrared eyes.

I was looking east into the darkness where Colorado 52 ran, arrow-straight, and waiting for the call to slither its way through the static in my ear.

Alex's voice startled me. "Contact! Fifteen. First mark in ten." He was calling on his cell, fifteen miles east of me. Time to rock and roll.

"Affirm in ten." That was the colonel.

It went quiet, then Alex came back. "Five, four, three, two, one. Mark."

"Rolling. Five seconds to the blacktop." I heard the colonel's car engine racing. He'd be shooting out of the old barn, down the dirt track. He'd make the blacktop just around...

"Bravo, this is Eagle," said a voice I now recognized as the helicopter pilot. "I have a contact westbound on Colorado 52. Twenty miles west of us."

"Not one of ours, Eagle. Check it out." *That* was a Naga, in their command center, somewhere out on the interstates.

"Right overhead!" That was Alex again. I heard a brief rumble like thunder, then he spoke again, his voice subdued. "Apache."

Oh, joy.

It had to be the frigging Apache, not the Chinese Z10.

Fifteen miles west of me. A little over five minutes. Five miles east of me, the colonel trailed his coat and the Apache came flying down the road to see who it was. They'd pass right over me.

"Eagle. Second vehicle joined westbound on 52, eight miles. Motorcycle. Designated Oscar 3."

Bian. My pickup. Dismissed. Not their target.

But still logged in their fire control system.

It was an eerie, creepy feeling. They could probably read her license plate.

I had a moment to wonder about the wisdom of this. I was putting myself directly under the flight line of the most capable attack helicopter in the world. The beast thundering towards me had the weaponry to turn this road into a river of fire, to gouge out a grave the length of a freight train and leave nothing of me to fill it.

I had the equivalent of a strong flashlight.

Well, you always did like to see your ideas put into action.

Thanks, Tara. This was one I wanted to leave in the workshop.

"Passing overhead!" Bian's voice.

Any second now.

I had one eye on the nightscope, the other wide open and searching for the first hint in the darkness of the onrushing helicopter. The split view made my eyes ache, but I wasn't going to do what they were doing—rely on what one piece of tech was telling them.

"This is Eagle, Tango! Repeat Tango, westbound at twelve." They'd identified the colonel's car, and they were less than seven miles from me.

"All units respond, grid 5-18, Tango westbound on Colorado 52."

I tuned it out as pursuit vehicles called out positions on the Nagas' TacNet. As long as there was nothing in the immediate vicinity, we'd be fine; but we couldn't be sure of that. I didn't know how big they'd set their grid pattern, how much space there was in grid 5-18. Maybe the colonel would.

I could see Bian's headlight in the distance.

I pressed the 'charge' button. I imagined I could hear the whine of capacitors as the satellite comms system juiced up alongside my head. Then it was blotted out by the distant thudding of the Apache.

A low star above Colorado 52 blinked, reappeared. Another.

Half seen, half imagined, the sinister shape started to emerge, the infrared making it look like the air was boiling around it, and it was suddenly hurtling towards me at forty feet and over a hundred and fifty miles an hour.

It was terrifying.

Don't see me! Don't see me!

The grotesque growths on the front of the Apache took shape in my scope-enhanced eye. Front and center, the topmost cluster was the PNVS, the Lockheed Martin Pilot's Night Vision System. Left and below, the gunner's IR cluster. Right of that, the range finder and low light cluster.

Two shots, maybe. The chance for three would be like winning the lottery.

Half a mile.

All the breath went out of me. My eyes stopped fighting each other and a ghostly composite image formed of the menacing insect-headed aircraft. The blades were invisible. It was slightly nose down, as if it was looking directly at me. My mouth was dry.

Now.

I thumbed the nightscope's laser pointer. I had half a second before their countermeasures suite lit up with a threat warning. Time seemed to stretch. I leaned on the rig, pivoted it on the photographer's tripod.

Hurry, hurry.

Gently stroked the pointer onto the PNVS cluster, looking right into its malevolent, mechanical eye. Squeezed Matt's lashed-up trigger.

Silence. No bangs, no flashes.

Had it even —

"Shit! Shit! Shit! Vision system failure!" screamed the TacNet. Score one for me. Pilot *completely* freaked.

The Apache leaped upward as the pilot became almost completely blind and instantaneously allergic to flying close to the ground.

I followed it up. Gunner's cluster, dead center.

Slowly. Slowly. Last chance.

Squeezed the trigger again.

"NVS down! IR gone. What the fuck?" Gunner freaked too. Ha!

"Bravo, this is Eagle. Systems down! Complete IR system malfunction."

Dammit! Two bulls eyes! Third shot…and then it passed overhead, an angry roaring beast, visible only in that it blocked out the stars as it clawed itself up into the night sky with its head swinging and dipping, searching for the enemies that had blinded it. My wolfy eyes could see the heat coming off it like smoke in the cold air.

I threw the blanket aside and hefted the laser comms system. Maybe if they turned this way…

Bian's motorbike came racing out of the night. The tires shrieked protest as she skidded to a stop beside me.

I jumped on behind her, slotted the laser into the saddlebags and grabbed hold. "Go, go, go."

Bian redlined the big Kawasaki. We roared off along the midnight road, footless gray ghosts fleeing the anger of the blind eagle.

"And...mark," the colonel said in my ear. "Going dark."

About eight miles ahead of us, the colonel had turned off his lights and swung right onto a dirt track. His speed would drop to about thirty and he'd start counting and hope the coyotes weren't out on the road. As long as he kept the car straight there wasn't much else to hit. In five minutes he'd stop and wait for...

"Inbound, ETA ten." Victor's gravelly voice, with the thudding of Jen's helicopter as background.

Victor had a nightscope as well. The colonel would pop the hood on his car and he should light up like a burning oil rig on the IR scope.

Time for the second pinch point. The Apache had a radar system. In standard battlefield mode they kept it shut down to stop missiles from locking on to it. If the pilot got over his unexpected IR system problems and decided to fly on radar, he'd see Jen's Bell 407 helicopter, the colonel's car and our motorbike. And one flicked switch later his weapons system would acquire targets. I had hopes that a $60,000 Hellfire missile wouldn't regard the ass end of a motorbike as a suitable target, but I didn't want to find out and that wasn't going to help the colonel and Victor anyway.

So he could find targets. And then what would he do?

He wasn't a Naga. He hadn't signed on to blow away cars and civilian helicopters in the cold, high plains of Colorado.

I hope.

"Colonel's here at the meet point." David's voice on the comm. "I can see your headlight, but there's no sign of pursuit from south."

"Also clear to the north," Tom's voice followed.

"Going dark," Bian said.

The headlight died, and we had a minute slowing down along the blacktop as Bian's Athanate vision adjusted, then we turned and chased after the colonel's car along the dirt track. I could taste the dust in the air, thickening quickly as we overhauled him. Bian's eyesight allowed us to travel much faster than the colonel.

The TacNet had cleared from the confusion of pursuit cars calling out their positions.

It was down to the Apache. Bravo wasn't talking at the moment—the Naga was probably reporting up the chain of command.

"Eagle on the ground. Checking systems. Back to you in fifteen." The Apache had landed.

Silence on the TacNet. The Apache crew would be running their onboard diagnostics. I wasn't an expert, but I was betting it would take them a while to figure out I'd burned out their IR sensors with a laser.

"I see the colonel's car. ETA five." Victor.

He was coming in to land. We'd be loaded and gone before the Apache got off the ground, but how far?

"ETA two," Bian confirmed our position.

I pictured the immense country around us. Miles of flat fields and darkness crossed by scores of roads running at right angles to each other. For all the noise on the comms, they couldn't have more than a dozen cars patrolling this area. We were like a needle in a haystack while that Apache was down.

Bian slowed and we coasted alongside the colonel's car. I swung off as soon as Bian stopped, and slung the saddlebags with AdAstra Communications' expensive satellite comms system over my shoulder.

"I have headlights north of us." Tom's voice was calm, but it still shattered my premature wind-down. "I'm holding position."

At this time of night, it was vanishingly unlikely that was a farmer heading home. Of all the miserable luck, one of the Nagas had decided to take this dirt road to get down to 52. Tom could see a long way and we had a little time yet.

It depended on how fast the Naga was going.

"Shit." Bian fired up the Kawasaki again and had its tail snaking in the dirt as she took off toward Tom.

I caught a glimpse of the headlights Tom had reported just as Victor brought the Bell in to land, flying without lights and relying on his helmet IR system. Dust billowed and whipped around us as he drifted closer. I guessed Victor had to be flying blind now, feeling for the ground through the cloud he was kicking up.

"Bravo, Pursuit 6," said the comms system. "We just crossed with Pursuit 9 on 52. He must have turned off."

Crap, they had been too close. And now they knew we were on a side road. The next call would pinpoint us.

"Your flight is boarding now, people," Victor growled, as the Bell settled. "Watch your heads."

"Bravo, Pursuit 7 on uh…County 13. I have visual with some disturbance. Lights and dust. Just checking…oh, shit. I can hear a helicopter."

The colonel scurried forward, his arm around Vera and their heads bent low.

"He's shooting, people. Hurry it up," Tom called from outside the dust cloud.

The guy had to be shooting blind. He couldn't see anything, but luck wasn't running our way tonight. One bullet in the wrong place…

Then Tom's voice again. "Bian's on it."

"Tom, Bian," I called. "Leave it. Come in now. Time to go."

Vera stumbled on the uneven ground and fell. Immediately, David was there. He and the colonel lifted her into the Bell.

They climbed in quickly. David took the bulky laser from me and strapped it down. I stood in the door. Victor had the blades spun up to takeoff speed again. I could feel the Bell straining to lift.

"Done." Tom spoke from somewhere in the night.

"Forget them. Come on, come on," I called again.

The Kawasaki seemed to leap out of the night suddenly, screaming like an enraged puma. Bian slammed the back brakes and it slewed around, throwing up even more dirt into the cauldron of dust around us. She and Tom jumped off and let the bike slide away.

"Go, go, go," I yelled, shoving them inside.

I followed them through, falling into the cramped compartment as the Bell immediately snatched up its tail and swiveled to face west.

And in the confused, jumbled darkness, I could smell blood.

I twisted to my right. I was shoved up against Bian's back, the hard casing of her katana's sheath pressing against my shoulder. There was some blood there. Not Bian's or Tom's. That was fine. If there were a couple of headless Nagas back there, so much the better.

I twisted the other way.

Vera had fallen from the seat where David had lifted her. The colonel was on the other side of her. His face was blank with shock and he was cradling her in his arms, his hands touching her, searching blindly.

I tore the comms set off and knelt over her. I could see what he couldn't.

"I'm so sorry," she said hoarsely. "I seem to have got myself hit."

Chapter 29

I'd healed people before. I'd healed Jen when she was badly hurt. But I'd messed up her head and mine when I did it.

My brain was wavering but my hands were working automatically. First things first. Stop the bleeding. Tear the clothes. Open the first aid box. Compression. Bandages. The colonel was working with me, by touch. All the time I felt sick inside that I was just about to make things worse.

Bian was beside me.

"Please, Bian," I said.

She sensed what I meant. "You've done it before, Amber."

"I made a mistake—"

"You healed Jen."

The colonel was trying to see us in the blackness. He couldn't even hear what we were saying over the noise, but he could feel my uncertainty as my hands fumbled the last bandage. He'd be frantic now—he'd seen wounds bleed like this before. Vera didn't have long. We were miles from any hospital and even if we got her to one, we'd set ourselves up as stationary targets for the Nagas. They'd be looking.

The colonel knew Athanate healed themselves, but he didn't know about Athanate healing others.

Bian's hands ran over the bandage, noting the entry and exit position of the wound. She knew how much blood had been lost.

"No," Bian said. "You're right, you can't do that. It's arterial. I've got to work directly with the circulatory system." She grabbed me and started to push me out of the way, but she paused. "I'm going against Skylur's orders. Your account—you deal with him. And you owe me big time, Round-eye."

A hundred arguments flared in my brain. Skylur's last orders on this were that I had to be responsible for healing my House. Vera wasn't my House. But Skylur expected us to understand the purpose of his orders and not the letter. Bian was telling me the responsibility for this was on me. Fine, I'd take that.

And she expected something as big in return.

What was I getting myself into?

David flicked on a flashlight and shone it down on Vera. It looked even worse than it had felt.

Bian's eyes were inches away. The look in them—I'd seen that before. It wasn't about whether she'd heal Vera. I was sure she'd do that anyway. It was about me and how I'd respond.

I'd trusted her with my life.

"Blank check," I whispered, knowing she'd read my lips.

I barely had time to register the changes in her face. The eyes widening, the fangs appearing. Then she was bent over Vera.

"What's she doing?" the colonel yelled. His hands were on the verge of grabbing Bian and wrestling her back. I stopped him.

"It's her only chance," I said.

"She's not…"

"She's just healing her. Nothing else. You have to trust me." I gripped his shoulder, leaving more bloody hand smudges on his shirt.

He looked up at me. I don't know what he saw then, in the thin glow from David's flashlight. I was different from the last time I'd seen him, obviously. In that time, I'd taken huge steps to becoming Athanate and Were. I was very different inside. From my point of view, the face in the mirror was looking crazier every day. But Colonel Laine saw something different.

I felt the panic drain out of him, as if my touch had somehow provided a conductor for it to flow away. His face sagged and I realized that, for the first time, he was feeling his age.

Then he did something that only he would have thought of. He slipped his hands around one of Bian's and squeezed gently.

For an instant I could sense all four of us, like something electric passed between us.

David jerked me back. "Apache in the air," he shouted. He'd retrieved my comms headset from the floor and he'd been listening in.

I ignored the slippery, sticky feel of the blood all over the headset and put it on. I waved David back to his seat.

The colonel pulled his headset back up from around his neck. Much more sensible place to leave it.

The pilot was reporting his IR systems were wasted. He'd put lights on and was doing a sweep near where we'd been, using the low light system. I wasn't sure if the IR laser would have taken that out as well, but I'd missed my chance. Without the IR, the synthetic view the pilot would be getting wasn't good. He'd probably see the dust Victor had kicked up at the evac zone, but what then?

If he took a chance and fired up his radar, we'd light up like a beacon on his screen.

We couldn't outrun the Apache and we sure as hell couldn't outrun his missiles. I'd hoped they would have been on the ground longer, but the dice seemed to be falling against us this time.

I racked my brain, but there was no way we would stay hidden if he used all his weapons systems to look for us.

And if he found us, it came down to the biggest gamble of all.

What would that pilot do if the Nagas told him to take us out?

"Victor, head for the I-76, low as you can go," I said.

"We already there on height, girl," he grumbled. "Don't want to trip over no telephone lines."

But he swung the nose northwest and eased the power up.

"Lower, damn you. Find a road going north and follow it."

"Crazy bitch." But he banked and swooped lower and suddenly we were hurtling along a dirt track heading toward the interstate. We'd be kicking up a dust storm behind us, but the Apache would take time to find that in the darkness.

I eased around Bian and Vera, coming up on Victor's shoulder.

"ETA interstate?"

Victor jerked his head up.

Yeah, look out the window, crazy bitch.

I could see the all-night interstate traffic. The bright lights of Mack trucks swept along west to Denver, east out to Nebraska. The occasional late-night car. Way over in the distance, a haze of dim lights that marked a prairie town.

"Tuck us in behind a big, fat truck, Mr. G."

He snorted. "You are crazy, like a friggin' headless chicken."

"Or a train, if you see one going in the right direction."

"You have any idea what the slipstream from a truck does to a helicopter?" Victor's eyes remained firmly fixed on the road ahead, but I knew he wanted to glare daggers at me.

"Prefer a rough ride or Hellfire in your ass?"

He didn't reply.

On comms, the Apache pilot was arguing with the Nagas.

"Negative, Bravo. I say again, negative. Whatever took out my IR is just waiting for me to fire up my radar."

"Not a suggestion, Eagle. There are no other military aircraft involved. There's one civilian helicopter. You have countermeasures. This is Bravo, repeating direct order, commence search on radar."

The interstate was rushing up out of the night.

So were telephone and power lines.

Victor hauled back and the Bell went up with a stomach-kicking leap. I lost the interstate and hung onto the seatback, looking out at stars. The colonel fell down over Vera and Bian, wedging them into place with his body. Pia, David and Tom were the sensible ones, strapped in.

The Bell tilted and plunged down on the north side of the interstate, then the head swung back up again like a drunken dolphin. The helicopter slowed, swerved in and righted itself. Then we were abruptly holding formation with an eighteen-wheeler heading for Denver, shaking like a speedboat in choppy water as the slipstream buffeted us.

I pulled my mike out of the way. "Everyone okay?" I yelled.

Thumbs from the back. Bian paused to say something I was probably better off not hearing, then took the opportunity to lock herself more firmly against the seats and went back to her task.

"Radar system up," the gunner's voice from the Apache said, and I froze.

There was silence on the TacNet.

The colonel turned his head and looked up at me.

I shrugged. There was nothing more we could do.

"Eagle at fifteen hundred feet. Search radius fifty miles. There's nothing flying, Bravo. Nothing new on the ground between I-70 and I-76." The pilot was doing his job, but he wanted out.

"Go higher, Eagle. Initiate search pattern west of grid 5-18. Air and ground. They have to be there somewhere. Break. Pursuit cars, return to closest interstate. Monitor channel 1. Report position on channel 2."

Victor eased in closer. If the Apache kept going up, there was a point at which the radar returns would reveal a double for our shielding truck and us. How hard were they looking?

What if they came this way? We'd slowed to hide behind the truck. The Apache would overhaul us in minutes.

Closer. The juddering increased, and the sweat stood out on Victor's face as he fought the controls to keep us in place.

He'd made us safe for another few moments, but all it needed was the smallest thing to go wrong. Even the truck driver glancing back and seeing a helicopter sneaking along beside him. He was bound to hit the brakes and we'd overshoot. The Apache weapons control system would have us the second that happened.

"Eagle at three thousand. Commencing sweep to north."

Victor eased us in even more, then slid us into a position above the truck. The buffeting was less there, and if the Apache was looking straight down, our radar return would merge with the truck. What would we look like at an angle? If he saw a strange return for a truck would he come looking? There was enough light on the interstate for his low light system to show him what we were doing.

And how long could we keep this up? We were about thirty minutes away from the outskirts of Denver at the truck's speed, if Victor could hold it. I tried to do the math. If the Apache missed us this sweep, their search pattern would take them down as far as I-70 and back. That'd have to take fifteen minutes this sweep, then maybe ten on the next—the interstates got closer. Five minutes for the next sweep. We had two search sweeps, maybe three, to evade before we got too close to Denver and Petersen called it off.

He would call it off, wouldn't he? How desperate was he getting?

"Eagle! Pursuit 7 reports helicopter flying along I-76 westbound, three miles west of the town of Wiggins."

Shit! Our luck just wasn't holding tonight.

The colonel pulled himself up alongside me, both of us looking out at the expanse of night around us.

"Nothing on our screens," the gunner said.

"They're in tight behind a truck. I'm closing." Different voice. Pursuit 7 must have got on the interstate at just the wrong point.

Damn our luck. We'd have to move. A car on the highway wasn't an ideal platform for firing, but I didn't want him firing up into our belly. We were caught between the rock and the real hard place, and we were down to our last gamble.

I tapped Victor and pointed to where I thought Denver was, over the horizon.

Victor lifted us out of the slipstream and poured on the gas. We angled away from the interstate, racing away into the unrelieved blackness of the prairie.

"Got them." The gunner.

"This is Bravo. Eagle, you are cleared to engage."

"What? No! Are you crazy?" the pilot yelled. "Negative, negative."

The colonel's eyes met mine in the weak glow from Victor's instruments. I could see the same thoughts in his head as in mine. The last roll of the dice came down to the conscience of a couple of soldiers in the night sky over Colorado.

"Eagle, engage that helicopter. This is a matter of national emergency."

"Bullshit, Bravo. We came here to spot for you. We've got him, and he isn't getting away. He's got to land sometime." The pilot.

"There is no way we're going to fire on an unarmed civilian aircraft without legal authority." The gunner.

"Eagle, this is Bravo. We constitute that legal authority. This is a direct order. Fire on the target."

"Is this some kind of crazy test?" The gunner couldn't believe his orders, but how long would he hold off? As far as he knew, Petersen was legal authority.

The colonel's hand played over the switches of his TacNet controller.

"All life is a test, son."

My head snapped around. He'd patched himself into their comms system. He spoke with his eyes closed, and his face so sad, so tired.

"It's a decision that comes down to you," he said quietly, "to your honor and integrity. There are no other guides here. And no good outcome. Do your duty and God bless you."

There was a second of silence. Bravo started to yell something, but the Apache gunner overrode it all.

"This is Eagle. Weapons locked down."

He hadn't said he wouldn't track us, but it sure as hell beat being blown out of the sky. There'd be something we could do to sneak us away on the ground. I wanted to punch the air and shout, but the colonel just dropped his head into his hands.

What the hell?

There was a double flash in the darkness behind us. Victor swore and hauled the Bell into a tight curve. At the far point of the swing, I looked back to the east and saw the remains of the Apache aflame. It seemed to fall so slowly; a huge, red flower floating gently down to the waiting blackness.

Chapter 30

THURSDAY

"Ingram, can you not bypass this DC bullshit?"

"Well, an' I jus' might, Ms. Farrell, but for what justifiable cause? Those army folks aren't going anywhere. You can't spirit a whole damn battalion from under my nose." His voice was tinny coming from the speaker.

"They can. They have been, for a dozen years."

The colonel and I were sitting in the study at Manassah, surrounded by the boards displaying my stalled investigation into the rogue. With Jen's furniture in mind, we'd changed out of our blood-soaked clothes into the spare sweats we'd gotten from Haven. Both of us looked like extras from a horror movie, with Vera's blood smudged over our hands and faces. She was stable and unconscious, lying quietly in a guest bedroom. Bian was with her at the moment.

Jen and Pia were in the living room, getting the story from David. Julie was in the dining room, calling every number she could in Ops 4-10. And we were on the telephone to Ingram in Washington trying to whip him into a gallop without getting slowed down by detail. It wasn't working.

"I can hear something's riled you up good, Ms. Farrell, but I can't—"

"They blew up an Apache Longbow last night." The colonel had been silent until then.

"Jesus! And who might you be?"

"Colonel Laine. Former OC Ops 4-10 and the Ops 4 Observation Facility."

"Umm. Well, good morning to you, sir. Now, when Ms. Farrell promised me a talk with you, I had envisaged us sitting down over a cup of coffee." He sighed. "I guess that'll have to wait on opportunity. So tell me your story."

"I understand you're aware of my situation, as far as it will have been described by Colonel Petersen to law enforcement?"

"I am."

"Well, I'll skip ahead." The colonel ran a hand through his hair. He didn't bother dismissing the charges that had been made against him, nor did he justify his decision to run and hide rather than surrender. "I knew I'd been seen when I crossed into Kansas. I had jinked around, kept off the interstates and major roads thinking they'd be stretched too thin to catch me, but either I was wrong or they got lucky. I'd brought an Ops 4 TacNet system with me, and I patched into their circuit so I knew approximately where they were and what they were doing. That got me a couple more hours driving, but I was still more than an hour short of Denver when they put enough resources in the area that I had to hide out in a barn. I was stuck. They had light aircraft overhead during the day and a helicopter at night. I called Sergeant Farrell."

"If I can stop you there for a moment, Colonel. As you say, I do understand your situation and Apache helicopters are a big headline, but I'm puzzled. I can understand you not wanting to put yourself in the hands of local law enforcement officers, especially after what happened to the Ops 4-16 team that we had in custody, but what is it about Denver that makes you so sure it's safer there? Ms. Farrell is admirable, but hardly sufficient against the forces you say are chasing you."

A typical Ingram question. The colonel hoped that the Athanate, with all their centuries of living hidden, were capable of making him and Vera disappear for as long as it took. But we couldn't talk to Ingram about that, and I really didn't want to start lying.

"I'm going to have to leave those details out for the moment," the colonel said. "They're not mine to reveal."

Great. Back in my court. I couldn't blame him.

The speaker was silent for long seconds. I didn't dare breathe.

"Very well. We must speak when we can, Ms. Farrell. And that 'when', it's gonna have to be sooner. Proceed, Colonel."

The colonel took him through a condensed version of the night's events, ending with the explosion of the Apache.

There was another ominous silence from Ingram in Washington, then, "Help me out here. They have an Apache on your tail tracking you but refusing to fire, so they blow it up?"

"The important question in there, is why they placed a bomb in the Apache in the first place." The colonel had just out-Ingramed Ingram.

"I hear they call it 'tying up loose ends' on bad TV," Ingram said, after another pause. "They couldn't chase your helicopter into Denver; too many witnesses, too likely to come across people who would ask what the hell they were doing. So the Apache crew became a liability. I have said to Ms. Farrell before, you guys play hardball."

"Even against their own team, once you'd gotten them into custody," the colonel said. "Let me guess, they originally asked for them to be handed over directly to Ops 4. You insisted on going through some official channel handover."

"I did. I guess that was the point those boys got taken off the playlist."

"I believe so. The next question is, if they're willing to kill some of their own men and blow up helicopters, what's their next move?"

"Suppose you lead me there, Colonel."

"This is their endgame for their project with Ops 4-16. Whatever they planned is either in motion or is being abandoned. The FBI is on their case and they're going to run. The bulk of them might already have run."

"So, if they're running, why stop to try and get you, or Ms. Farrell? Why kill their own team?"

"Because not everyone is running. They're covering for someone," the colonel said.

"But, if you'll excuse me, Ms. Farrell don't know sh—"

"She may not know what she knows."

"There, you've done lost me like a dog in the desert, colonel. All that stuff about not knowing what you don't know is all over my head."

I huffed. Agent Ingram's mouth was just running on to give him time to get ahead of the conversation. But for me, I was truly that dog in the desert, as he put it. What the hell was Colonel Laine talking about?

The colonel stared at the phone. "I'll explain that later. It's not on the critical path." He shifted forward in his seat. "The critical path is stopping any more loose ends from being cleaned up, and the danger of doing things by the book is that somewhere in the chain of command is the person or persons that Petersen is trying to cover for. They'll delay things. It'll risk bringing attention to themselves, but their hope will be to prevent any proof from being captured."

"Someone in my meetings today might be working with Petersen?"

"More like Petersen is working for that person."

"So you're suggesting I just press the button on the operation down in Carolina and hope."

"Speak to the most senior person in your chain of command that you can absolutely trust, if you have to," the colonel said, "but every hour is critical now."

The door opened and Julie came in, her face pale.

"Sorry to interrupt, sir. I have something."

The colonel gestured to the phone and Julie nodded. This was for sharing. He waved her on and sat back.

"Sergeant Alverson here, Agent Ingram. I've been calling friends in Ops 4-10. You have no time. The base has gone to lockdown. All the Command, Admin and Medical blocks are closed. Most of Ops 4-16 have gone already. They're trying to load 4-10 on some Hercules transports—"

"Ingram," I interrupted Julie. The nightmare image of a huge red flower floating down in the night blotted everything else out of my mind. "Get on to air traffic. Ground everything out of the base. Every transporter off the ground means a hundred or more dead. And shut the power down to the whole complex. Every minute you leave power on means more records trashed."

"Whoa, I can't do that," he complained. "You're leaping to some huge conclusions there."

"You have to go in now. If they're willing to take out their own men with RPGs and blow up Apaches, they're not going to hesitate over blowing a Hercules. And I'd lay my last dollar that there are 4-16 teams in those closed blocks, right now, destroying every record they can find."

"That's crazy," Ingram said. "Everyone does off-site backup."

"They know that as well, and they know where," the colonel said. "You'll have a few unexplained fires that happened last night. Agent Ingram, we're wasting time."

There was a long pause before he growled, "Damn. I'm on it." The call cut off.

We looked at each other, stunned by the magnitude and swiftness of it all.

"Those Hercs—"

"I think I've persuaded enough people to delay that a few hours," Julie said. "The whole operation was strange enough that people were already asking questions. I think it'd help if you called some people as well, sir."

"I will," Colonel Laine said, getting up. "Trouble is, this is a planned operation for Petersen and whoever's backing him. The FBI, on the other hand, will be going in with no plan, no clear view of the scale or direction." He shook his head and went to join her in the dining room where Matt's untraceable telephone system was set up.

I checked on Vera. There was only so much Bian had been able to do for her, given the amount of blood she'd lost.

As Victor had brought the Bell over Denver, heading for the landing pad at Manassah, Bian had managed to get a cell phone call out to Paul and Mykayla at Haven. They'd arrived with an emergency transfusion kit a while after we'd landed, and between them they'd done everything they could for Vera.

Bian had said all Vera needed was rest now. I'd have liked Alex's medical opinion as well, but he hadn't gotten back yet. He should have called. I put it out of my mind. He was with Ricky, and whoever took on the pair of them had better know what they were doing.

Vera was sleeping peacefully in one of the guest rooms. Paul was sprawled in a chair alongside her, half-dozing when I looked in. He made it halfway to his feet before I pressed him back down and left them.

A glance in through the open door of the living room showed me Jen and Mykayla talking on the sofa. Bian sat in the window seat, totally absorbed in cleaning her katana with my gun oil.

I was too nervy to sit with them. Outside, Victor was shooting the breeze with some of the guards and I slipped out to join them. Dawn had started painting the eastern sky with moody pinks and I shivered at the chill in the air.

Faces turned to me—eyes a little wide, faces a little shocked. Victor must have been entertaining them with stories of the crazy bitch.

"You okay, big man?"

He grumbled. "Another liter of coffee with a bourbon chaser and I'll be right," he said. "You?"

"I'm good. That was some flying you did last night."

He grunted. His eyes swiveled to the house and he frowned. His men picked up the tension and left us alone.

It wouldn't be the first time Victor had flown with wounded people. It probably wasn't the first time he'd brought in someone bleeding from a damaged artery. But it might very well have been the first time someone with that kind of injury had survived the flight.

We hadn't called an ambulance. We'd spirited her away from the blood-splattered helicopter and Victor could see that everything had calmed down. He was professionally not curious about clients' private business, but this had all gone way beyond the normal parameters.

"I owe you some kind of explanations," I said.

My Athanate uncoiled. It'd been completely unconcerned with my talking about the Athanate to Jen, for instance, but this was different. Victor wasn't House.

What if he was? Would he be an asset? My Athanate thought so.

I turned away in frustration, hugging myself against the cold. I couldn't go around adopting everyone. I had enough problems as it was, without trying to find out how to run a large Athanate House.

Victor patted my shoulder clumsily. "Well, what you can, when you can, woman. Mainly. But what I need right now is enough to make sure my team are briefed on what they're facin'."

It was more than fair.

"Those guys last night were soldiers from another covert special ops battalion." I frowned, thinking over the colonel's comments to Ingram. "We call them Nagas and they're not good guys. They're well-trained and well-equipped. They're after the colonel and me. Unfortunately, they'll have enough info to know I'm likely to be found here. The colonel is going to disappear for a while, but I can't. It's going to come down to a race between the FBI closing them down and the Nagas finding me."

"Can't you get some FBI help here?"

I shrugged. "I doubt it. They're stretched like everyone else. Their solution would be to put me in protective custody. No use for me, and anyway, that'd leave Jen out in the open."

Victor's eyes swept the front of the house, the drive, the gate, the guards. I could see him looking at the hundred ways the place could be attacked by people who were committed enough to try.

"Too many ways in. The gate's good, but that house," he waved to the adjoining building, then down to the boundary of Manassah, the larch and cypress adorned with tendrils of mist, "the gardens, the club grounds. It's a mess. I need more people," he said. "An' that's a problem. I'm using everyone on this one contract at the moment. Not good business."

He frowned and stomped his feet in the cold. He'd moved Jen out once before on the basis that the house was too open, and she'd hated it. But if it was a choice of that or Victor pulling out of his security contract, Jen would have to take it.

"I'll talk to Ms. Kingslund," he said finally, and moved off to get feedback from his team.

I retreated to the warm study and ignored the accusing stares of the blank project boards. It was quiet. I could faintly sense David and Pia. Jen was still in conversation in the living room; something Mykayla had to say was fascinating her.

Still nothing from Alex.

I knew what I needed to do to settle myself. Everyone has their post-mission ritual, even if some hid them in rowdy drinking or horseplay. Mine was silent and contemplative. I took an old piece of knotted string out of my desk drawer and sat on the floor, legs hitched up into a half lotus, and closed my eyes.

My fingers began to play the string. The knots weren't any code or anything, just a tactile prompt for my ghosts.

Joe was first. Handsome Joe from Nevada with the pretty eyes and the quiet smile. My nineteenth birthday. Green. Sweating in the cold. Jungle all around us. He'd taken a bullet that had had my name all over it. I'd carried his body out.

On I went, fingers and thoughts threading their way through ten years of special ops. Not everyone who died, just the people who put themselves in the way for me. On, through the five dark ones. My team at Hacha del Diablo. On, to Larry. Reeking of cheap bourbon and leading Matlal's elite hunters away from me in Cheesman Park.

To the end. My fingers twisted two knots close together. A huge, red flower in the dark. Pilot, Gunner, names presently unknown, crew of an Apache codenamed Eagle. Duty, honor and integrity.

"Roll call?" Julie's voice was quiet, her hand on my shoulder gentle. She knew my ritual as I knew hers.

I nodded.

"We have to go," she said.

Life went on. Jen needed to be at her office and I needed to track Alex down.

I stood. Jen was at the door watching.

Julie slipped out and Jen flowed into an embrace.

"However bad it gets, and it got real bad last night waiting here," she whispered, "there's not a thing I would change about you."

She broke away, her hand trailing down my arm, to my hand, till her fingers played over the memory knots in my string. Calm, blue eyes held me. "I hope, one day, you'll share all of this with me."

Chapter 31

"Sit," I said to Tullah and Jofranka. It was getting like I had a pair of hounds.

The two of them had arrived with their report as Jen was leaving.

They were both nervous, but Jofranka's anxiety had an edge to it. Her eyes slid past me, before she steeled herself and brought them back. I glanced at Tullah and a tiny nod confirmed it.

I wondered how that conversation had gone: *So, Jo, thing is, I'm a witch and our boss is a vampire.*

I was running on trust here; I trusted Tullah who trusted Jofranka. My Athanate side was twitchy with worry. Not for the first time, I wondered about the wisdom of this. What would happen if Jofranka started babbling to people about the paranormal? It wasn't that Altau weren't capable of coming in and fixing things, it was the fallout from that; the damage to Jofranka from having her memories suppressed. And it'd kill any chance of my living anything like a normal life in Denver stone dead. I'd be carted off to Haven and prevented from leaving the grounds. I knew Tullah would have made that clear to Jofranka, but I needed to as well. Soon.

My thoughtful delay hadn't calmed their nerves. I flipped open the executive summary and started to read, with a suppressed smile at the situation. A year ago, the thought that I would be getting reports from a couple of apprentice PIs would have made me laugh. Now, I shared their nerves.

It wasn't just the paranormal aspects of our relationship. Was I doing the right thing for my PI company? There wasn't enough of me to go around. I was gambling on being able to crack this case, using them, while I hunted the rogue and fought off whatever stumbling blocks the paranormal community and Nagas dumped on me.

The trouble was, I was probably gambling with the future of my little company.

The file gave me the summary background on the de Vries case, filling out what Mrs. Harriman had told me when she hired me.

The de Vries, Schalk and Suzannah, had come to Denver in 2000. He'd made his fortune in South Africa, but had decided to emigrate. With his resources, it was relatively easy for him to engineer a move to America under the banner of inward investment. But his company here, Auradamas, didn't much resemble what he'd created in Africa. It was what was sometimes called a ticket company, not just because he'd used it to make the move to America but because it was designed simply to support his lifestyle here, with the minimum impact on that lifestyle. He might have worked two days a week. When he felt like it.

Auradamas was a trader in gold and gems, mainly diamonds. De Vries had good contacts back in South Africa with firms like the de Beers and AngloGold Ashanti corporations. He'd set up buddy contracts, he imported valuable raw goods, and sold them in the States at a markup. His company had a dozen people in a small office tucked away behind the Alameda shopping center, a few minutes' drive from his house. The company's profits had been a few hundred thousand a year, most of which had gone in dividends to the shareholders. That was mainly Mr. and Mrs. De Vries, but Ethel Harriman and Lloyd McIntire held shares.

The setup was about as simple as you could get.

They'd settled in, made friends with the right people, joined clubs, supported the ballet company, done good works.

Then he'd died twenty months ago, at the age of 49, of a heart attack.

Mrs. de Vries had promoted Forster Sloan, the relatively new vice president, to run the company, and from the numbers, it had been a smart move. Turnover had risen steeply and profits had gone up 45% in tough times.

Their relationship had moved from professional to personal.

And Mrs. Harriman had called me on a gut instinct about a friend who was going through a difficult emotional time and *might* have made some poor choices.

She wanted to be right, but there was nothing in the summary to support her concerns. The worldwide diamond business was run by de Beers, and they had a vested interest in dealing with people they trusted. Practically every diamond of any significant size was logged on the de Beers database and traders were locked into contracts with de Beers. A trader stepping outside of that contract would suddenly lose their supply and simultaneously find every other business that wanted to stay on good terms with de Beers would refuse to deal with them. It was more efficient than government regulation and Auradamas was in de Beers' good books.

On the legal side, Auradamas played by the rules as far as I could see: businesses importing goods like these attracted federal attention and the company had been looked over very thoroughly. Squeaky clean.

I checked the last date of government review. Only eight months ago. What could you do in that time?

I skimmed to the end of the file.

Knowing my preferred format for internal reports, Tullah had put in photos.

Schalk de Vries had been a big, red-faced man with floppy dark hair and a loose smile. He looked like the sort of guy that had been large and loud in life. Suzannah de Vries, in contrast, was blonde, petite and looked quiet. I didn't want to jump to conclusions, but I'd lay good money on her being overshadowed by him when he was alive. Had she just flourished out of his shade? Was Mrs. Harriman's worry based on a change in her friend that would have happened anyway?

I looked at the last photo. Forster Sloan I loathed on sight. He had the sort of bright, shiny look that made me wary of insurance salespeople and television evangelists. I stomped on that. Maybe it had influenced Mrs. Harriman as well.

I tossed the file back on the desk and looked at my apprentices.

"So much for the overview. I'll get into the detail section later." I sat back and crossed my legs. "Give me your gut feelings."

"Like it says, straight up and down from everything I've been able to find," Tullah said.

"Sloan's personal background?"

"Vague. Nothing big one way or the other. Not a saint, not a sinner. Moved around in different jobs. Worked in the gems and import businesses. All recent stuff, within the last ten years."

Oh yeah?

But Tullah didn't go any deeper. Jofranka hadn't said a thing yet, but I wasn't going to push hard. I was interested to see how Tullah would handle this.

"I don't like vague," I said, as neutrally as possible.

"Yup. So, I thought, first off, we should get a close view." Tullah wriggled a little.

I sighed. I should have known. The fact that they were in front of me and I wasn't picking them up at the police station suggested the closer view had gone all right.

"And?"

"We set up a fake company. Head and neck massages at work. It's cool. All the big companies are offering it to their staff."

"And you went and offered them a free trial?"

Tullah nodded apprehensively.

I snorted. Not bad.

"How'd it go?"

She relaxed. "We got a meeting room set aside and we got most of them in there on their own. We massaged them and they talked." She shrugged. "But same old. Not everyone likes him, he works them hard, he brought the business in big time last year. No one had anything really bad to say."

"He works hard too?"

"Long hours. A couple of them actually mentioned it as a good contrast to Mr. de Vries."

I turned the file on the desk back to Sloan's picture. If he'd been a runner, I would have had him down for sprints, not marathons. He didn't look like a long hours man. Not without his own good reasons.

I didn't let my thoughts show. "So we have nothing other than what might turn up in the accounts?"

Tullah shook her head. Her face was as innocent as ever. And she was waiting for something.

Jofranka sat silently. Her whole body radiated disagreement.

"Did you get to massage Sloan himself?" I asked.

"I did," Jofranka said.

"Who chose?"

"He did."

Now that might be interesting. Why Jofranka? Both of them were attractive. What basis did he use and could I draw any conclusion from it?

Or alternatively, why was I expecting that there was a reason for it? That photograph had biased me.

Tullah exuded a sense of confidence. Jofranka was a lot stronger and more self-sufficient than you'd realize from looking at her. But home life had given her mannerisms she hadn't cast off yet—the eyes slid down when she met someone, the head wasn't held as high as Tullah's. She looked the more vulnerable of the two.

Could I base any reading of Sloan's motivation on it?

I waited until Jofranka's eyes came back up to mine.

"And?" I prompted her.

"I don't know what you expect of me," she said, glancing over at Tullah. "You've done this sort of thing before. You have...skills. What does it matter what I—"

I held up a hand. "Jo. Just tell us what you think."

Her lips thinned and she frowned. "He's a slimeball," she said.

We waited.

"Nothing obvious." She looked frustrated. "This is just a gut feeling. I can't expect you to rely on that." She stared up at the ceiling. "Oh, one thing. He's supposed to have some problem with his leg. He says he's supposed to use a cane to walk. It's fake."

"How'd you know?"

"I watched him in the reflection off his window when he thought I couldn't see him. There's nothing wrong with his leg."

"Okay. But 'slimeball', Jo. What made you so sure about that? Did he say something?"

"No. He asked about my family and my job. Hobbies. Just ordinary questions, but..." she trailed off.

"But you sensed something?"

She nodded.

And 'ordinary' questions about family and job; I shuddered at what conclusions someone trained, someone like Ben-Haim or Doc Noble for instance, could make from a few seemingly innocent questions and answers.

"Then we need to go to the next level," I said. "I don't want vague background and gut feelings. I want you to go back and dig until you're satisfied, because until you're satisfied you can't expect me to be satisfied."

"Is it okay to use Matt?" Tullah asked.

"As long as he does the digital ninja stuff and leaves no trace."

From the gleam in her eyes, this had gone exactly the way Tullah had wanted. And she'd be expecting me to cap off the meeting with a message to underline the lesson.

"Good call," I said to her, knowing she'd understand I was talking about her whole presentation here today. "And Jo, we don't draw conclusions on gut feelings, but sometimes it's all we have to point us in the right direction. It's not something that can be taught, so your gut feelings are as valid as ours." She sat straighter and smiled for the first time that day. "That's not to say it can't be developed. Taking in lots of difficult, boring background detail gives your gut much more to work with." I closed the file. "This was a good start. Along with clearing up that vagueness, I want you to visit Mrs. Harriman. She was the first one who got a gut feeling about this, and there'll be stuff she noticed that will give you leads. I want to know anything she says, whether you think it's relevant or not—what he said to her about the arts that Mrs. de Vries supports, how he talks to different types of people, what *his* hobbies are, who *his* family are. Everything."

I paused and held their eyes. "We good on everything?"

There was no hesitation from either of them. Jofranka's anxiety from the start had gone. Maybe that's all that was needed—to show that this was business and she had a valid part to play in it. I was still going to need to talk to them and make sure Jofranka completely understood the position we were in. But not today.

"Now get going, the pair of you," I said. "And stay safe. Call me tomorrow."

When they'd gone, I flicked through the shareholder company accounts that Mrs. Harriman had been able to get me.

Forster Sloan had reinvigorated the company, pushing it out of the quiet tickover that Mr. de Vries had set up. There wasn't any huge trick to what he'd done. He'd gambled the company's money on buying more stock at better margins. He'd delivered the new sales that justified it. That all fed the additional margin straight into the profit line.

Take a gamble, albeit with someone else's money, then work hard for long hours to make it pay. Well done, Mr. Sloan. The relationship with the founder's widow? Just one of those things that might happen when people work together.

Why was my gut feeling so dead against him?

I went back to the photo.

A sprinter, not a marathon runner.

How long was he going to keep it up?

And then back to the last audit. Eight months ago. How much could you achieve between audits? How long could you bypass de Beers' rules before they noticed? What if you didn't care about the long-term future of the company? What if, like Petersen, you were in the endgame?

The accounts showed the heavier buying pattern was continuing. The profit figures weren't available yet, but some of the marginal data suggested profits weren't as high. What difference was I talking? Half a million? A million? Diverted into an offshore account?

I slumped back in my chair. It wasn't chickenfeed, but it didn't seem enough of a prize. Not for the smiling man in the photo who'd burrowed himself into such a good position.

I wanted to go digging myself, but needed to get back on track with my own investigation. Those blank boards in the study were still reminding me that I had no gut feeling in the hunt for the rogue, and no progress.

I slipped the de Vries folders back into the cabinet and locked it. That didn't quite get the case out of my mind.

If, *if* he was bypassing his existing contracts on buying with de Beers and AngloGold Ashanti, what better margins could he be getting elsewhere to boost the value of that prize?

Stolen goods could be bought at a tenth of their face value, but that would leave a big trail and bring a huge additional risk into it.

Gold was difficult; forget AngloGold Ashanti. Gems were uncertain.

But diamonds...diamonds were small and light in relation to their value. There were all sorts of legal barriers here in the States to importing diamonds from anywhere other than approved sources. But if you didn't intend to stay, they were relatively easy to smuggle to places that didn't care so much where they'd come from.

I texted Tullah to get Matt to do some extra digging.

Definitely find out what Sloan did further back than the ten year history we had, and then build on that. And did he have a boat or a plane? Property or business interests overseas? A pattern of visits to other countries? Especially visits to countries with lax fiscal attitudes.

And, just as a matter of interest, could Matt please find out what Blood Diamonds cost?

Chapter 32

I was about to get an update from Bian on Vera, when the gate intercom sounded at exactly the same time my cell beeped. Someone in a green van wanting to see me, and Alex finally on the phone.

"Don't let them through the gate yet," I said. "I'll be out in a minute. Hello?"

"...Ursula at the gate," Alex said, his voice blurred by background noises. He seemed to be able to hear me okay, but I could barely make him out.

"Are you okay?" Ursula could wait, whatever she wanted. Alex had been supposed to come straight back to Manassah. What had happened?

"Fine. Look...problem." The signal was breaking up. "...need...right away. Ursula..."

"We got a bad signal here. There's a problem where? What kind of problem?"

Silence. I tried calling back and got voicemail.

Bian raised a brow.

I shrugged and put my HK shoulder holster on underneath a jacket before going out. Bian slung her katana sheath over her back and joined me.

Ursula was standing impatiently at the gate, ignoring the guards. She looked even bigger in daylight than she had at the cemetery on Monday night. Her wavy, blue-black hair was drawn tightly back, and she had frown lines that seemed permanent over dark, deep-set eyes. Sort of a mix of Xena and Wonder Woman, with a sore head.

"We need to go," she said, as if that was all that was needed.

"Pleased to see you too. Why and where?"

"Alex should have called and explained."

"The signal cut out."

"Felix says it's urgent. Now you know as much as me."

I leaned against the gate, not going anywhere, until Bian spoke. "Okay, let's go. We can try calling again on the way."

I looked at her in surprise, but there was no clue to her thinking on her face.

"Wasn't an invite for you," Ursula said.

Bian smiled. "But he didn't say I couldn't come, did he?"

Ursula's hands flexed like claws for a second. She looked as if she wanted to pull Bian through the bars of the gate, in little bits. I didn't understand why Bian was goading her, but I was irritated enough by the unexplained summons to play along.

"You were in a hurry?" Bian prompted.

"Come on then," Ursula growled, and got back into her van.

Bian and I joined her, climbing into the second row of seats before my mind caught up.

What was I missing here? Lack of sleep over the last couple of nights had made my thinking fuzzy. I'd gotten into a van with a Were I barely knew based on a fragment of a telephone call that sounded like Alex. A van, what's more, that shared the basic characteristics of a van seen outside the horrific murder scene in Wash Park. And a with a Were that was plenty big enough to chew thigh bones.

I didn't really think Ursula was the rogue, and I had Bian with me, but I really needed to raise my game. Between the rogue and the Nagas, I couldn't expect second chances.

The interior of the van was a mess of emergency gear. Towing and climbing ropes, axes and shovels along one side, flame jackets and lifejackets on the other. A large red box of medical supplies was bolted to the floor behind our seat. Across the top of the box, National Park Service had been stenciled in white.

Bian reached over and picked up a ranger hat. "Oh, cool. Smokey the Bear. I love these." She put it on. It was about five sizes too big, and I tried to think of a joke about that.

"Put it down," Ursula snapped, glaring at us in the rearview mirror.

"This your van?" I asked over her shoulder.

"No. Why?"

"Curious. Why are you driving someone else's van?"

"Silas borrowed mine."

"You both work for the Parks?"

"No," Ursula said. Then so quietly I almost missed it, "Silas is the Park Ranger. I'm a veterinarian."

"No sick poodles today?"

"I was working when I got the call from Felix. I have a backup. I work with farm animals, not poodles, as if that's any concern of yours."

So she could speak in whole sentences, sort of strung together. A veterinarian werewolf. Awesome. I wondered what the animals thought of that.

"Where are we going?" asked Bian.

"The fertilizer factory in Aurora."

That was as much as we could get from her.

I called Julie and explained where we were, but Alex's cell remained offline.

From something Alex had said previously, I knew the factory was alongside I-70, so Alex and Ricky would have been coming back that way. Maybe they'd stopped and found something, but what would cause this emergency summons?

∞ ∞ ∞ ∞ ∞ ∞

We came off Colfax, picking up a smaller road that ended at the factory. It was a wholesale and professional supply facility, with a neat, white front and loading docks running down one side. If I hadn't been looking hard, I would have missed the small sign that told me it was the depot for Larimer Agricultural Fertilizers.

Ursula drove us around to the back, where what appeared to be the original warehouse still stood. It was an old iron framework construction covered with corroding corrugated sheet metal. A man in blue coveralls saw us and heaved on a sliding door, big enough for an eighteen-wheeler to pass.

We stopped just inside. It was gloomy as a cave and, with the echoes of the truck's engine falling silent, the ungreased squeal of the door runners sliding shut was ominous. Spears of sunlight shone through rust gaps in the walls and ceiling, highlighting the dust in the air and picking out the decomposing hulks of old machinery lined along the side.

We were parked beside Alex's SUV. He and Ricky were standing at the far end with Felix, Silas and a couple more men in coveralls who I thought I recognized from the Matlal ambush on Monday evening. Underneath a nose-prickling odor of chemicals from the fertilizer factory, there was a smell of blood and violence in the air that made me hurry across to Alex.

We met halfway. I steeled myself and hugged him. There was no reaction from my strongbox, so I held it for a few moments more, letting his warmth seep into me. It wasn't his blood I could smell.

"The colonel?" he asked.

"Back at Manassah. His wife was wounded, but Bian healed her. Everyone else is fine."

"Sorry we couldn't talk earlier," he said. "Ricky got a call and we had to come in here. It's been pretty tense. We stopped —"

He went silent as Felix and the others joined us.

A very unhappy Felix. I wondered if there was any other kind. Then again, I had disobeyed his orders.

"What the hell are you playing at, Farrell?" Felix said.

Bian chose that moment to amble up alongside me. "And what are you doing here?" Felix said to her.

"Chillin'," Bian said casually. "What's the big deal?"

I'd seen Bian in action with the katana that she was wearing. Maybe the pack had too, because I could feel the atmosphere changing. The balance felt different with her next to me. I offered up a little prayer of thanks that she'd decided to come along.

"The big deal is spying," Silas said.

I'd had it with this Were attitude, always expecting me to know what they were talking about; this bullshit superiority; the feeling I was always under some kind of threat from them. They seemed to be forever looking for the ways I didn't fit with them and never thinking that they might be the cause of it.

"I'm glad you raised it," I said, "because I've got a real problem with betrayals."

That rocked Silas back.

But what happened next did the same for me. As Silas swelled menacingly, Felix grabbed and held his arm.

"Let's hear this complaint," he said, his voice low and quiet.

Felix's anger wasn't gone, but he was holding it in check.

"Monday night," I said. "I was at the restaurant with Ricky, Alex and Olivia. Who else knew?"

Felix shrugged. "The doctor and I, of course. Possibly the guards at Coykuti. Silas and Ursula." He glanced at his enforcers to see if anyone had any other suggestions. No one spoke. "So why?"

"Which one of you told the rogue?"

Ursula's face rippled. She didn't change, but with the movement across it, I caught a glimpse of the wolf-snarl behind. Silas took another step. I felt Bian's weight come up on the balls of her feet, but nothing more. If it all went south, she had to judge the time—drawing her katana would be provocation, but she needed space to get that blade free. I felt the weight of the HK under my arm, visualized the moves that would draw it and flick the safety off.

And Alex turned subtly from his neutral position to face his own pack.

Oh, shit. All in all, maybe I had pushed too hard.

Of all of us, Felix stayed completely still.

"Olivia told me you'd had trouble," he murmured. "But she said nothing about the rogue."

The dynamics shifted again. Ursula and Silas took their lead from Felix and calmed down. Ricky eased back a step.

All of them noted Alex's new position. Damn, I'd caused him problems again.

"All Olivia knew was my clothes and boots were stolen out of the back of my car." I met Felix's eyes and held them. The hell with werewolf dominance posturing; I would not lower my eyes. "Then the next night, those clothes turned up on the rogue's latest victim. It's the first time he's wanted a body discovered immediately," I paused, "and he dressed her in my clothes. Message, you think?"

I let the silence build a moment.

"So, the whole pack and Altau know I'm working on the hunt; that's not a secret. My car's not a secret. But only a handful of people knew where I'd be on Monday night. The rogue didn't find it accidentally."

"Your House knew as well," Felix pointed out.

"You can't believe one of my House would betray me," I snapped, without thinking.

"You can't believe one of the pack would betray you."

I'd fallen right into that one.

"But I'm not pack. You haven't accepted me. They all made that plain on Monday after the fight with Matlal's pack."

"The fight I explicitly told you not to get involved in."

The argument seemed to be slipping away from me. I was digging myself in a hole and letting him get out of his.

"You're going to have to decide whether she's in or out, Felix," Bian said. "If she's not in the pack, why are you trying to tell her what to do? Hmm? And from what I hear, she was an asset on Monday night. But, anyhow, we should get back to who told the rogue. If you're so sure no one would deliberately tell the rogue, who might have spoken to someone outside the pack? Or had a conversation in the hearing of someone else?"

Thank you, Bian.

Felix exchanged looks with his enforcers. "I'll question everyone individually and see if they discussed the meeting at the restaurant with anyone."

"And they can't lie to you," Bian said quietly.

"They can't," Felix barked. "But it'll take some time to organize. On the other hand, you can explain *this* right now."

He gestured. The two in coveralls went and dragged a long, patchwork bag from the shadows where they'd been standing when we arrived.

As they approached, I saw they weren't dragging a bag by its handles, they were dragging a body by its bound arms. A light body. Female. And that's where the smell of blood came from.

They thought whoever it was worked for me.

Tullah? Jofranka? Anger surged in me as I shoved them aside and turned the woman over carefully, kneeling down to hold her.

Too slight for Tullah. The skin of her hands too pale for Jofranka. Who the hell?

Her head had been covered in a dirty burlap sack. I untied it and pulled it off.

Melissa blinked up at me. Her face was swollen, bruised and bloody. Her eyes could barely open. She was shivering, I guessed partly from cold and partly from fear. But incredibly, through all that, there was a gleam of satisfaction at seeing me.

I undid the gag.

"Knew it," she whispered through bleeding lips.

What the hell was she doing here? But that would wait; anger swamped the bewilderment.

"Which of you bastards did this to her?"

"So, you do know her," Felix said from behind me. "Lucky for her."

"You call this lucky?"

"The alternative was helping crops grow, so, yes. If she'd just said she was working for you from the beginning, this wouldn't have happened," he growled. "But you'd still be here explaining what you think you're doing spying on us."

She said she was working for me? Shit.

"My fault," croaked Melissa. "Di'n't clear it with Amber. She di'n't know."

Alex handed me a bottle of water and I carefully drizzled some into her mouth while I thought furiously.

The pack expected me to have good links with the police and to somehow use that to help in my hunting for the rogue. Even if she was suspended, Melissa had those links, and Agent Griffith wouldn't be watching her like he was watching José. She was a forensic scientist, if we happened to stumble across clues that needed that. She'd already proved she had some insights, and claimed more. She'd managed to find this place, so she had to have a nose for investigation. Maybe she *should* be working for me.

Against all that, I'd have to keep her from talking to others about anything paranormal that she'd come across. Like a werewolf body disposal facility, for instance.

And she'd not just showed up here, she'd been caught; not what I wanted in a field agent.

Or did it just come down to saving her life?

Indecision, as much as anything else, kept me from saying anything.

"Didn't clear what?" Felix said.

Melissa cleared her throat. "I've been investigating the cases Amber's working on," she said. "Independently. I can help, but we didn't have time to discuss what I was doing."

She was skirting the truth by a fair margin, but luckily none of them caught it.

"What part of your *independent investigation* would have brought you here?" Silas asked suspiciously. "How did you find out this belongs to us?"

"No one told me, if that's what you're asking." Melissa coughed quietly. "This was just the next on my list of factories to check."

"Explain." Silas knelt down beside us and frowned at her.

I pulled Melissa closer. There wasn't a lot I could do alone against Silas, but I didn't want him threatening her. She'd had enough.

"Fertilizer dust." She tried to lift her hands, but they were still tied. She gestured upwards with her chin and our eyes followed. One of the beams of sunlight passed a couple of yards above us, turning all the dust floating in the air into tiny, incandescent stars. "Some of the bodies dumped up in the mountains had traces of fertilizer, like you'd get from transporting it in a van used at a factory. Or if the killer worked at a factory."

"But that wasn't in the records," I said, despite myself.

"The department didn't want to include it," she said. "Too remote a chance. Might be a false connection. Bunch of bullshit reasons. Not too remote for me. Been checking them all."

"That's crazy. There are dozens of these kinds of factories," Silas said.

"What's it to you anyway?" Ursula asked.

Silas edged closer.

I pushed them back. "Give us some space."

"What it comes down to," Bian's voice cut through the tension that was growing again, "is this woman's status. Is she part of your House, Amber?"

And part of Altau by association. Bian was verbally pushing them all back. The one thing that definitely would make them back off was the thought that they were stepping on Skylur's toes.

Damn. Damn. Damn. I was being hustled into a decision.

My House or not?

I looked down at Melissa and my Athanate suddenly made my mind up for me.

"Mine," I said, exasperated by the feeling of Athanate pleasure that gave me.

"Good," Bian said. "You all can give us some time here for a few running repairs, then we'll answer your questions." She motioned them away.

Bain and I lifted Melissa gently to her feet. One of the workers motioned to the back of the building. "Restroom there," he growled.

We just got her there when a door opened at the back and Dr. Noble arrived, pissed at not being called earlier and even more pissed that he'd had to postpone a consultation to find out what was going on.

"Jumped-up quack," muttered Bian as we closed the restroom door behind us.

"What the hell did you think you were doing?" I hissed in Melissa's ear as I started to untie her.

"Just the job I was supposed to be—" she complained before I stuck my hand over her mouth, muffling the cry of pain from her bruised lips.

"Time for a few hard truths," I whispered, "seeing as I've had to take you on board."

She nodded carefully. There was still that look of satisfaction in her eyes. She was on a lead that was yielding big results. Forget that she'd nearly been killed. And they called *me* a crazy bitch.

I dropped my hand. "Everyone in this building, except you, isn't human." Her eyes widened, but the threat of my hand kept her silent. "Among other things, we have very good hearing. They can hear us outside if we raise our voices. And when we go back out, remember this: everyone will be able to hear how quickly your heart is beating. Everyone will be able to smell how nervous or scared you are. We'll even be able to tell your reaction to a question. So avoid lying, starting now."

I was watching her as she nodded again. Her breathing was rapid and her heartbeat was all over the place, which wasn't surprising. She was scared. Well, she damn well ought to be.

"You lied about checking all the factories, for instance." That worked like a slap in her face. "What made you come here?"

"Anomalies," she said quietly.

I freed her hands.

Bian wet some paper towels and handed them over to start cleaning her face.

"Family-owned for over fifty years," she explained. "Only just covering costs. All the other little independents like that have been bought out." She tried shrugging and ended up wincing as she added ruefully, "Unfortunately, also the only one with someone on the premises, 24/7, as it turns out."

"You're telling me this is the only uneconomical, family-owned fertilizer business left in Denver?"

"No, there are ten. I've been checking one a week for the last couple of months. Testing the dust. No matches." She cleared her throat, eyes flicking desperately between Bian and me. "Is this the...are you...are they all in it?"

"No. This isn't a cult responsible for those murders. Or not that I know of. But if they really were killing them, they'd have just processed the bodies here, not dumped them out in the mountains."

"You've blundered into something just as dangerous, though," Bian said.

Her eyes went back to the door. "What—"

"They're werewolves, okay? I can't explain it now. Sometimes there are casualties and they can't leave them lying around for forensics to have a look at. This is one way to dispose of the evidence. In the fertilizer, like you would have been."

"Werewolves." It wasn't a question. It hadn't thrown her. Even in her shocked state, her mind started working on what she knew about the cases and how this new fact might fit in. It was probably her coping strategy. The trouble was, her idea of werewolves was a product of modern entertainment. "But—"

Bian came and rested her chin on my shoulder. "Do we bite her now, or keep her to play with later?" she purred.

I could smell the elethesine hormone that triggers the Athanate changes, and manifests the fangs. From Melissa's startled reaction, I knew that Bian's fangs were out.

The question was why.

Bian loved being shocking, but the real message was for me. I'd been maneuvered into accepting Melissa as part of my House, and Bian was reminding me it was now my responsibility to ensure that the Athanate remained secret. Or she would.

"Oh God! Vamp—" Too loud. I shoved my hand over Melissa's mouth again until she calmed down.

"Not vampires. Do not say that word out there."

"But, the fangs… Oh! You mean they don't know?" So much for never speculating. Her mind was leaping from the facts into the big blue sky.

"We're Athanate, not vampires. Vampires don't exist and the werewolves know that." I sighed. "There's a whole bunch of stuff you're going to need to know, but for the moment, just say as little as possible."

I felt Bian's presence prompting me.

"And everything paranormal you find out is secret. So either you're stuck in my House keeping it a secret, or we erase your memories. That's not pleasant. It spills over. You might lose years of memories."

That hit her. Maybe she shared my phobia—lose a little and how do you know how much you've lost?

"Stuck in your *House*?" she asked tentatively. She'd picked up it didn't mean where I lived.

I nodded. Detailed explanation would have to wait: Bian tapped my shoulder and jerked her thumb at the door. Noble had finished his rant. Someone was coming over to check on us.

"We're back on," I whispered in her ear. "Say as little as possible; don't lie. Yes, I've taken you on in my House. Think of it as my Athanate clan if you like. Your job is to do back-office investigations—forensics, databases, that sort of thing. Out there, you're going to need to do exactly what I tell you, without question, to convince them that's true. If they think it's not true, their instinct will tell them to kill you. Understood?"

She lowered her head. Maybe the extent of what she'd gotten into was becoming a little clearer.

We walked her back to the waiting group.

Melissa had been wearing her glasses rather than her contact lenses. They'd barely survived the beating they'd given her. One lens was cracked down the middle. Silas handed them over and towered over us.

"Pretty eyes," he said to Melissa. "Keep them that way. Don't spy on us, don't get clever, or I'll rip those eyes out myself."

I shoved him back. He moved, not as angry as I thought he might be. Dr. Noble, his own ranting aside, seemed to have had a calming influence on the group.

"Since you're investigating, do you have anything new to tell us?" Felix said. He sounded almost reasonable now.

Melissa leaned shakily on me. "I don't know how much of what Amber and I have discussed has been passed on yet," she said, cleverly implying there was a lot in progress between her and me. "I don't have conclusions. Background stuff? How about this: Unless the perp is just using something mechanical, he's getting bigger and stronger over time."

"What do you mean bigger?" Felix's eyes narrowed. I picked up that was something he'd suspected.

"The test bites—"

I stopped her. "From the top, please."

Melissa took a breath and steadied herself before rerunning the argument that the thigh bites were a test or demonstration of strength.

"And the damage to the bones shows both a bigger jaw and more force over time," she concluded.

"Not a characteristic," Felix said triumphantly, looking across at Noble. He'd gone quiet and just dipped his head to acknowledge, his mouth curving down thoughtfully. Silas and Ricky shook their heads. Ursula folded her arms.

There was obviously disagreement in the pack, but about what? And why hadn't they told me?

Alex explained. "Weres come from mature humans. Weres don't grow usually, and even when they do, it's by very little. How much are we talking? Ten percent?"

"No." Melissa had stopped shivering, focused on discussing her findings rather than her situation. "The progression shows an increase of at least twenty percent in size and at least thirty percent in force."

"How do you mean, 'at least'?" Alex queried.

"That's the observable range in the bodies I have had access to, the newest of which is at least six months old. There's no certainty that whatever made the bites was exerting maximum effort and, in fact, cleaner breaks in the more recent would be consistent with greater control of greater strength. Also, the force wouldn't vary arithmetically by size, more..." She stopped, aware she'd lost her audience.

"Okay, bigger. Backtrack a moment," Ricky said. "You said something mechanical?"

"I made a clamp to replicate the bite mark and measure the force." Melissa shuffled her feet. "Until I get fresher evidence, I can't rule out that it isn't some psycho using a similar device."

"So, it could be faked. And it's grown," Ricky said. "Weres don't do that. It's not a Were. There's no Call. No marque. We know, we've looked."

"Well, if you've looked like you're searching for the Matlal Were, how do you know you haven't just missed it?"

"What do you mean?" Ricky said.

"Your organization for your search is a freaking disaster. The Matlal Were have a comms system, and you use a bunch of cell phones. You're all over Denver, with no ability to concentrate your force when you come across the Matlal Were. No one even knows who's searching and who's not. You got lucky on Monday and still lost people. You can't even tell me if the Confederation are already in touch with the Matlal."

Felix's eyes darted to Bian.

I'd gotten carried away. The threat from the Confederation wasn't meant to be shared with Altau.

"Oh, don't worry, Felix," Bian said. "They've already been to see us and we kicked them out."

She spun on her heel in front of me, so her back was to the others. "We've got to tell them sometime," she said, loudly.

"Huh?" Not my cleverest response.

Bian's mouth moved silently. I read her lips.

You owe me, Round-eye. I'm calling. Just go along.

Oh, crap. I shrugged. I had promised. After all, how much worse could it get?

Bian turned back to the rest of the group.

"House Altau has been forced into a corner by House Farrell. Since we're fully committed throughout the rest of the country, we can't spare teams to hunt for the remains of House Matlal in Denver. Organization of that task has been delegated to House Farrell."

Huh, again. But she hadn't nearly finished.

"We asked, through House Farrell, if the Denver pack could assist her, and for your own reasons, you refused. House Altau is obligated to provide assistance to Farrell in Denver, and she's used that to pressure us into hiring mercenary trackers who are skilled at the job."

The pack liked that—the concept that I'd forced Skylur to do something. Hell, *I* liked that and I knew it wasn't true.

"Bounty hunters?" Silas said.

"Yeah. No half measures. We've got two of the best," Bian said. "I've arranged a meeting with them for you."

"Why? What's it got to do with us?" asked Felix.

"Because this is an opportunity to work together. Amber's already hunting the rogue for you and she'll organize these hunters to go after the Matlal Athanate for us. I want the pack to add in the hunt for the Matlal Were. Even add in checking for the Confederation trying to slip someone into Denver. Get the full benefit of the hunters and the use of Amber's military experience." She hesitated. "Oh, and because these hunters...they're Were."

Chapter 33

"Airfields are always much colder than their surroundings," I said. "I'm sure it's been scientifically proven."

"Even if it's a disused airfield?" Bian said.

"Especially if it's disused."

"Well, blame the pack."

Felix was still furious, but at least he was here. He and his enforcers formed a snarling knot around Silas' truck, far enough away that we couldn't hear the words, but close enough for the tone to carry. Noble had left to return to work. Alex paced halfway between the two groups, cell glued to his ear, trying to run his business remotely. Melissa was dozing in the back of his SUV. I'd thought about Bian doing healing on her, but in the end decided the bruises would serve as a good reminder.

It'd taken an hour of Bian's patient argument to wear Felix down to this point. At one point, I thought he'd been about to crack and say he'd take over the hunt for the Matlal Athanate as well, just to keep other Weres out of Denver, but Silas and Ursula didn't want that. They didn't want bounty hunting Weres on their territory either, but Bian had kept hammering on the selling point—the faster they got this under control, the less opportunity there was for the Confederation to sneak in. Bounty hunters would pack up and go when they finished. Getting rid of a Confederation-sponsored rival pack might weaken the Denver pack to the point where the Confederation could just walk in anyway.

I didn't know how much of Bian's staging of it helped, but what I thought was a minor point, that I'd somehow forced Altau into this position, seemed to count more as far as the pack were concerned. They'd all yelled at me and Bian, but it was as if having two targets reduced the force of their arguments against either one.

The one thing they'd all been inflexible on was that we meet on neutral territory. And so we were shivering on the crumbling strip of the old Colfax airfield, further along I-70, waiting for the bounty hunters.

Bian explained that one, Verano, was a small pack; the other, Gray, was a solo operator. Verano had been highly recommended by the Houses of the Eastern Seaboard for tracking down Basilikos trying to infiltrate their mantles. Gray had come with the recommendations of the central Canadian Houses in the wilds of Manitoba and eastern Ontario. He'd also just finished working for one of Altau's formerly secret affiliates in the

Dakotas and Bian seemed to think we'd been lucky to get him. I was just intrigued by the thought of a solo werewolf.

A black limo with dark windows cruised down off the interstate and stopped short of the strip, unwilling to risk the uneven boundary with its low-slung chassis.

I slipped my hand inside my jacket to rest on the HK. There could be anything behind those windows.

"If that's Verano, then bounty hunting is good business," I said.

"Better believe it," muttered Bian.

I edged closer to Alex's SUV. Melissa sat up inside, bleary-eyed and wincing at the movement.

Alex ended his call and joined us, making us two obviously distinct groups welcoming the hunters. We should have thought of that earlier.

The car came to a halt and the door opened.

A werewolf flowed out, long and sharp and the colors of steel in snow.

Ursula and Ricky immediately shucked their clothes and changed with that eye-twisting shimmer. Ricky's wolf I recognized from the first meeting out at Coykuti. He was pale with russet tints. Ursula was unrelieved midnight black and the pair of them were huge, much bigger than the Verano wolf.

"Freaking hell," Melissa whispered.

"Just werewolf formalities. And that's Verano," Bian said quietly, as a man followed the wolf out of the limo.

Verano wore a black suit with white shirt and thin tie, the color of the suit and tie exactly matching his big, frameless sunglasses. A white woolen coat with a matching fur collar was draped over his shoulders. His hair was so white it had to have been dyed.

And his big, square face was expressionless as he looked between the two groups waiting.

A second wolf, the twin of the first, slunk out of the car and took station on his right.

"Shit, is he here to hunt Matlal or to design dresses?" I was talking to myself, but Bian heard me and grinned crookedly.

We walked forward, Melissa scrambling out of the SUV to join us. Felix and his enforcers set a path to meet us all halfway.

With excellent timing, a Harley hardtail came grumbling down the same road. My recent history with bikers being what it was, I closed my hand around the reassuring butt of the HK and pulled it just clear of the holster, but left it hidden.

"Gray," Bian said.

He was encased in leather, as he needed to be with the cold. Not a slick racing suit, but a jumble of pieces, topped off with an old brown World War II flying jacket and a Russian hat with earpieces.

He bounced over the edge of the runway, and brought the Harley to a halt near us.

The throb of the Harley died. He tossed his gloves and lifted his fur hat to scratch his scalp under his long, black hair.

"How very…picturesque." Verano's voice was cold as the wind.

It was amusing, given how staged his arrival had been.

Gray leaned the hog on its kickstand and walked over to us.

"You must be Bian." He held his hand out and they shook.

"What gave that away?"

"You're the exact height I imagined from your voice," he said, making Bian laugh. He offered his hand to me. "Nick Gray."

"Amber Farrell, House Farrell," I replied automatically and shook.

For all his English name, Nick Gray looked full Native American. He had the wind-burned, chiseled-down cheeks and steady stare of a backwoods hunter. His eyes were the brown of walnut heartwood, polished to a fine sheen.

And his marque was strange, as polished and glossy and full of secrets as his eyes.

We froze, looking at each other long enough that I felt the rumble of jealous anger building in Alex.

He blinked and smiled. "Chippewa," he said, as if that's what I'd been puzzling over.

"Arapaho," I responded. "Only a little, though. And this is—"

"Alexander Deauville *kin-Farrell*," Alex interrupted me, leaning across to shake Gray's hand, maybe too firmly.

Down, boy.

And not the best way of introducing himself, with Felix listening.

The moment passed. Gray moved to greet Felix and Silas while Verano introduced himself.

His was a clear werewolf marque—the scent and whatever else it was I was sensing. The eukori. What made Gray so different?

Greetings over, the groups separated out into the corners of a square, emphasizing the tensions between us. Bian started to explain what we had agreed. All the searches were combined together and I would co-ordinate between the Denver pack, Verano and Gray. That meant setting up areas, times, schedules, routines, procedures and other fun stuff.

I laid down some objectives to be met if at all possible. When we caught up with the Matlal Athanate, Bian would have to be involved. Matlal or Confederation Were had to be delivered alive to the Denver pack. I needed to be there when we tracked down the rogue.

Between the colonel's TacNet system and headsets borrowed from Victor, we'd have a workable comms and I promised to list some protocols for the next meeting.

Everyone had personal weapons. I had a list of equipment that I wanted and Bian agreed Altau would fund.

Wonderful. Except Verano and Gray had disliked each other on sight, and Verano made it known through every step of the discussion.

That was a personal problem for me. I didn't like Verano either, but there were twenty in his pack of hunters and feet on the ground was a big consideration. I'd have to choose Verano over Gray, if it came to it.

Verano was already pushing for it, querying the contract with Gray, saying he could bring another two or three to replace him and take over his contract. Gray smiled and Bian refused to discuss it.

"I don't understand what a solo operator brings to this mission," Verano said finally. "It's complicated enough." His eyes roved over the groups. He had a point there.

"Don't worry, I'm sure I'll get assigned all those places where you'd stand out," Gray dismissed it. "Are we done?"

Bian nodded to me.

"We are, until the 09:00 meeting tomorrow at the Oxford Hotel, just across from the station. The meeting room is booked in the name of Rose Cooper." I stepped forward into the empty space between the groups.

Verano was still flanked by his escort of wolves.

I stared at where his eyes were hidden behind his glasses. "Invitation-only meeting. You, you and you." I flicked eyes between Verano, Silas and Gray. "Leave the doggies behind. Along with the attitudes."

"I'll be there." Verano sneered and turned on the heel of his well-polished shoe.

Gray straddled his hog, but waited for the limo to complete its painful 180 turn on the narrow track.

That gave Alex time to stalk over, all stiff-legged and prickly.

Crap. I followed.

"I'd like a chance to talk," Alex said to Gray, looming over him.

Gray squinted up, unfazed. "Okay. What about?"

"Chippewa oral tradition, specially to do with Were."

I relaxed. Alex's pet obsession with the Were among Native Americans.

"Hmm. I'd be glad to have the opportunity to meet the pair of you off-duty," Gray said, putting his fur hat back on.

Not the best response, but thankfully Alex didn't get any more territorial.

And it served my purposes. Diana had told me taking a werewolf out of a pack would end with them going rogue. I hadn't thought that through until Gray triggered it—what if I never had a pack? Or was Gray his own pack and his own alpha? Was one of those a way out for me? Could I be part-Were and not wrapped up in the Denver pack? Please.

Oh, yes, I wanted to talk to Gray, to hear about how he came to be solo. *And* to find out what was behind that strange marque.

Chapter 34

I'd gotten in the front with Alex in his SUV when we headed back. Melissa was in the back with Bian, and nervous. Good. It might serve to underline the seriousness of the situation she was in. I couldn't spare the time to worry about her. I was tired and confused. I needed answers from Alex. He had to have known what Felix was thinking, but he hadn't told me.

"So Felix thinks the rogue isn't a werewolf," I said calmly.

"Sorry," he said.

"Time to tell all, Alex," Bian said from the back.

She didn't mention the tension between Alex and the rest of the Denver pack. She didn't need to. The fact he'd been prepared to stand with me was another reason I wasn't going to give him a hard time about keeping secrets from me. He was already in a difficult position with the pack, and siding with me might mean he never got back in.

Alex grunted. "Felix went ballistic after your news about the rogue. He pulled the pack off everything else and sent us looking. People had to call in sick to work, or take vacation. They worked around the clock."

"But you were already maxed out chasing down the Matlal Were," I interrupted him. "And he provided some of the pack to guard your house over the weekend."

"Yes, and the pack went and killed the Matlal Were down in Cherry Creek. All of that," he said. "You're not seeing the problems Felix's facing. If it gets out that there's a rogue loose in Denver, the Confederation would use that as an excuse to come and 'help'. Then we'd never get rid of them. We're between a rock and a hard place. That's why it was so easy for you to get the hunters in."

"That was easy?" Bian snorted. "I wouldn't like to see—"

"Hold on." I shushed Bian. "There are rules for Were? The Confederation can come in here if there's a rogue?"

"Not like that," Alex said. "But they are concerned for the opinion of other packs. They'd rather grow by accumulation. If they're seen as aggressors, they might even be attacked. But a rogue, and the local pack not able to catch it? Open door."

"Back to your hunt for the rogue," Bian said. "What did you find?"

"Nothing. That's the point. Even in a place as big as Denver, even in the limited time, it's near impossible that the whole pack could look and not find even the slightest trace of another marque."

I didn't know how realistic that was, but I realized I hadn't told him everything I knew. I guessed that made us equal.

"He's using some kind of a spell to hide it."

The SUV swerved as Alex turned to stare at me.

"What?"

"The road's out there—the thing in front of us." I waited until he focused on it again. "When my clothes were stolen from my car, the marque was hidden. I didn't know it at the time. It wasn't until I had Mary and Liu look at it that I knew."

I glanced in the back. Melissa was so bemused by all the talk she'd forgotten to be anxious about Bian. And Bian herself was looking very interested.

"So," I said. "Maybe a Were who uses magic."

Bian grimaced. "Hate that word. Anyway, we all use 'magic'. Athanate use it to manifest fangs, Were use it to change shape."

"Athanate work at using it more."

Bian eyes flickered. She wasn't eager to talk more about how Athanate might channel the energy, probably because she didn't want any chance of it getting back to the Adepts and the Were. "There's nothing to stop a werewolf from developing his or her capabilities the same way."

"It takes time?" I asked and Bian nodded. "So who's the oldest werewolf?" I asked Alex.

"Larimer, by quite a bit. But that doesn't mean—"

"No, it doesn't mean he's the rogue, throwing everybody else off track and telling us it can't be anyone in the pack because he's asked them all. Or that it can't possibly be a Were. But it's a possibility. What is he saying to you?"

"He thinks it's an Adept who's used the energy to shape shift. That's why there's no Call and no trace of marque."

Was that even possible? I had something more to ask Mary, or Alice. In the meantime, another thought struck me.

"Assuming it isn't Larimer, is that the reason he wanted me to do this investigation? That I have links with the Adepts?"

"Wasn't just that," Alex said.

Bian leaned between the seats, Melissa forgotten for the moment. "Explain," she said.

"Larimer's playing it safe. If Amber's just a ploy by Altau, he'll find out, and in the meantime, either Amber will find the rogue and he claims credit, or she won't and he'll blame Skylur."

"Why the unending suspicion of Altau? Of me?" I asked.

Bian laughed. "It's the mind voodoo he doesn't like. Larimer's afraid Skylur will seduce him."

"Bian, stop it, that's just a distraction."

"Skylur has tried to manipulate Felix," Alex said. "Back when you were the liaison with the pack, Bian."

She didn't deny it.

"Why?" I asked her.

She sat back and looked away. I thought she wasn't going to reply, but she did. "The Confederation is anti-Emergence. Skylur doesn't want that on his doorstep. Larimer's at least more flexible."

"Altau will push Emergence too quickly," Alex said.

"It'll always be too soon, too quick for some," Bian snapped back.

"It's not Altau pushing," I stopped them. "It's human agencies getting a sniff of what's been there all along. Like Melissa did. You both saw David and Pia go through the likely outcomes if it comes out accidentally. Nothing is too quick if it's only quicker than discovery."

"It is if Altau reveal the paranormal in the middle of a war which is all about Athanate politics." Alex was not going to let this go.

"It's not about politics," Bian said. "It's about behaving in a way that will be acceptable to the rest of the world. At least we have societies and rules that we follow. Your rules are just whatever the alpha makes up."

We'd reached Melissa's apartment in Glendale. Alex slammed the brakes on and killed the engine. He was furious.

Before he could get out, I swiveled in my seat and reached across to hug him. Both of us were stiff as dummies. I was scared of what might set my strongbox off again, scared if I didn't do this he'd think I was moving away from him. And he was angry.

"Hey," I whispered. The tension eased.

"Sorry," he mouthed back against my ear, his anger fading like mist.

I knew it wouldn't always be this easy, and that scared me. If I wasn't able to control myself, how could I be sure of keeping it steady between me and my kin?

In the back, Bian mimed putting fingers down her throat.

"Come on," she said. "Let's go see Mel's pad."

Alex waited in the car while we went up the stairs. Melissa had a corner apartment on the third floor: small rooms, but light and plenty of space for one person.

She let us in and stood there looking around. I had a feeling that not many people came here. But we weren't here to comment on the décor.

I elbowed her into action. "Box up all your files on this case, anything you think might be useful. And pack for a couple of weeks. Change the phone message. You've got ten minutes."

She found her second pair of glasses and discarded the broken ones with an audible sigh of relief.

"I'm not coming back here?" she asked.

"Not until the rogue is found."

"But—"

"Melissa, some of the best suspects for being our leak or our rogue all heard you describing how you've been investigating this. Even if they're not the leak, he finds things out quickly. It took him no more than a day to learn I was working the case. You've seen his work. You've heard about the murder in Wash Park. You want to wait around for him here? Or come help us find him?"

Melissa nodded, looking even paler, and disappeared into her bedroom.

"She needs healing," murmured Bian. "And she's kinda cute."

"Stop it, Bian. Pia will take care of that, when we're all back at Manassah. Until then, her injuries may actually bring it home to her how bad it could have been."

"And then, Amber? After she's healed? Kin?"

"I have my kin. Jen and Alex."

"They won't sustain you. Athanate need three or four kin." She leaned on my shoulder, Leopard Bian body language mixed with Diakon Bian talk. "It's not so bad for you as House. You have access to all your House kin."

"Bian!"

"Just telling it how it is, Round-eye. Skylur's only got a couple of kin. He feeds on everyone. The House is like a hive. It's healthy for Skylur to feed widely. All those Altau pheromones need spreading around."

"It works for him, fine. It's not going to work like that for me."

"Hmm. Not always going to be an option. And you'll find the need changes you."

"You're guessing. Neither of us know how many I'll need. I'm as much Were as Athanate."

"Fair point. Anyway, at the moment, you should be more concerned for the rest of your House. David and Pia. Unless David's gone out and hauled in some kin in a hurry, they'll be sharing Pia's kin. Again, not enough."

"We'll manage."

"As long as you know what needs managing. I'm not teasing you, Amber. Well, not just teasing you. Keep talking to me and Pia."

"That's one thing Naryn has done which is good. He's made you easier to get through to."

We laughed.

"He'd so like that," Bian said. "Seriously, it's not always to do with Blood. Or sex. Vega Martine was partly right when she spoke to you before the Assembly. The marque does not always concern itself with love or desire. Sometimes, it does things for need. And House Farrell needs. Keep listening to your instincts."

I shivered. "That sounds no better than Basilikos."

"There's a long way between that and Basilikos."

Melissa brought out a suitcase. She saw Bian draped over me, blushed and hurried back into the bedroom.

I laughed again. I had changed, I was different. Time was when I'd have gone scarlet too, if someone saw me standing like this.

"You have too many unbound, Amber. Victor, Julie, the colonel and his wife. Now Melissa. Even I couldn't turn a blind eye to that. Think what Naryn's going to say."

"The hell with him. What's he going to do about the whole Ops 4 group? Bite them all?"

"There's a difference between them and your House."

I had to concede the point. "What about Vera? Did you do anything?"

"I just healed her. But sometimes that starts the binding anyway."

Melissa laid another small suitcase down and darted into a small study room.

I caught a glimpse of the equipment through the door. Presumably that was the forensics stuff she was talking about.

"Only the really important bits, Melissa," I called out. "If you need it all, we're going to have to bring a truck."

She came out with a large box.

"Uhh. I'll need all the rest of it. Just in case."

Where the hell was I going to put all this? I needed Melissa right under my wing to keep her safe. That meant Manassah. But at some point soon Jen was going to put her foot down.

Tomorrow's problem. "Right. Someone will come and get it." I grabbed a pad of luminous yellow sticky notes. "Mark the ones that are delicate."

Everything got a sticker. Bian snorted.

She changed her answering machine message and we carried her suitcases downstairs.

"No neighbors to inform? Boyfriend to call?"

Melissa shook her head silently.

"Back to Manassah?" Alex asked.

"We could go get a bite to eat," Bian said. "I'm getting hungry."

Melissa edged closer to me.

Oh, that's a great decision, girl. Yes, Bian will bite you, but you're safe with her. Apart from the all-night leopard sex you'd end up having. But you'd rather come to me. I lose control and bite you and you'd end up rogue. If you survived.

There was a lot we needed to tell her.

∞ ∞ ∞ ∞ ∞

Alex headed for a restaurant he knew. Bian and I started briefing Melissa, but I let Bian take over. I was tired and unsure when I'd get another chance to think about the whole case. I'd be working tonight getting a schedule of operations ready for the bounty hunters tomorrow morning. Bian didn't seem to mind.

Felix wanted it to be someone else's problem. Despite what I'd said, I didn't think he was the rogue and I didn't think he was covering for the rogue. He couldn't be the rogue and keep his pack sane. If he wasn't the rogue, he had no reason to cover for him. I had issues with Felix, but from Alex's comments, he deserved a slice more leeway from me. He was juggling the same kind of rocks and hard places as Skylur. And he was the alpha of the Denver pack, they couldn't lie to him, so it wasn't any of the pack, despite the clues of fertilizer dust or big green vans or blue coveralls.

That left some*thing* that could become a wolf, which had some Adept abilities. It either had a marque and covered it, or it had no marque to cover.

My gut was as empty of feeling as the boards back in the study at Manassah. That might change after I squeezed every drop of information out of Melissa, but before I had a chance to do that, I needed to organize the bounty hunters and the Denver pack to handle all the groundwork of finding the rogue and the remnants of House Matlal.

My cell startled me. Unknown number.

"Yes?"

"Ms. Farrell, it's Bud from Victor's team on the gate at Manassah this afternoon."

I jerked upright. "What's the problem?"

"Just a decision I want to run by you," he said, hearing the tautness in my voice. "Ms. Autplumes has requisitioned me to leave the gate and do a stake-out for your firm on another case. Standing orders are to clear that with Sergeant Alverson, but she said she wanted you to decide."

The only other case was Mrs. de Vries. How the hell had that progressed to a stakeout?

With the sinking feeling in my stomach, I knew I'd come to a point I'd anticipated, but expected to happen way down the line. Tullah was making a call here. She knew perfectly well what the guards on the gate were for and how vital they were. She thought she had something more important, even if it was only for one evening.

My cell beeped in my ear. Someone trying to get through. Probably Tullah.

I trusted her, but did I trust her judgment call on this? Whatever I chose would send a signal.

"Do what she says," I said to Bud.

I ended that call and connected to the other.

"Amber, we need you now," Tullah said. "I can brief you as we go."

I could hear the excitement in her voice. Slam dunk, finish the job and put in the bill excitement. Do it right now.

If Mrs. Harriman was happy by the end of it, my little company was going to float for a good while more. If Tullah had misread it, she'd be back at college, and Jofranka and I would be looking for day jobs.

If I hadn't wanted to make this decision, I shouldn't have handed the case to her.

Trust and Jump.

I motioned to Alex to turn around.

"We're coming back, Tullah. Hold on a second." I turned to Bian. "If it's okay with Jen, would you stay at Manassah until I get back?"

"Leaving me with all the cookies," she said. "Of course."

I had to grin and bear it.

"Meet where?" I said to Tullah.

Chapter 35

"Thank you for agreeing to meet us, Suzannah, especially at such short notice." Ethel Harriman's face gave no clue to what we were here for.

"Goodness, Ethel, such a mysterious message. Urgent, you said." Suzannah de Vries laughed nervously. "I could hardly turn it down."

We were at her house on Sunset Drive in the upscale Glenmore Hills Village suburb. The house was set back behind a veil of well-spaced spruce and pine. The sort of house that had a fountain in front with a drive that curved around it like a big lasso.

Mrs. Harriman—Ethel, as she reminded me I had to call her—had gotten us in with a phone call.

In the flesh, Suzannah de Vries was mostly what I'd imagined from her photo: small and well-dressed but not imposing. Her clipped South African accent had faded, but was still there under the surface. She showed us into the living room and we sat. Whether it was the unexplained meeting or her normal behavior, Mrs. de Vries was nervous. Her eyes darted back and forth and her hands twisted together briefly in her lap before she got them under control.

"I'm afraid it's not pleasant." Ethel looked as if she wanted to pace the room, but managed to remain seated and radiated a calmness I didn't share. "We have one more guest to impose on you. He'll be here at any moment."

Mrs. de Vries suddenly looked alarmed and clutched the arms of her chair. "It's not an accident is it? Forster?"

"Nothing like that."

The doorbell chimed and Tullah slipped out before Mrs. de Vries could rise.

"Ethel, you're scaring me."

"I know, my dear, and I am so sorry. I couldn't think of how else to do this."

Tullah returned with Scott Borders in tow.

Borders was one of the big men of the Denver banking sector, and though he was in no way connected with the day-to-day running of any branches, he'd been a friend of Schalk de Vries and still managed the company's financials at the bank. He'd fought to avoid this encounter, but Ethel was not easily refused.

"Scott! Hello. What a surprise." Mrs. de Vries looked confused. "If this is about the company, I really must have Forster here. He's handling all that for me."

There was a long stare between Borders and Ethel, and then he nodded to her and sat down.

"That's the reason we set this up in this way," Ethel said. She took a deep breath and sighed. "Forster Sloan is the problem."

"Ridiculous. If it's about the business, Forster must be here." Mrs. de Vries stood and gathered herself. "He'll be back from his physical therapist shortly and then we can talk about it. Of course, you're welcome to stay until then. I'll just organize some coffee for us. We must discuss the December Swan Lake production, Ethel."

I cleared my throat. "Mr. Sloan is not at the physical therapist."

She blinked. "But it's his weekly appointment."

"He hasn't been attending physical therapy sessions on Thursday evenings." I pulled my files out of the briefcase. I'd had an hour to study Tullah's notes and be briefed by her, but this felt frighteningly unprepared. And I couldn't sugar coat the next bit. "But that's not completely relevant to the purpose of this meeting. Please sit, Mrs. de Vries." I waited while she did reluctantly, casting glances back and forth between me and the others in the room. "I'm a private investigator and I was hired by your minority shareholders, represented here by Mrs. Harriman, to investigate worrying trends in your business. I'm sorry to say it, but your company is on the brink of bankruptcy, and the investigations following that will reveal a pattern of illegal trading that you, as owner, will ultimately be responsible for."

She sat back down abruptly. "That can't be. The business is doing so well. We tripled profits—"

"Mr. Sloan tripled profits last year," I interrupted. "A clever way to ensure that no one asked questions this year." I turned. "Mr. Borders, you can't respond directly to me about the company's finances, but, for Mrs. de Vries' benefit, could you confirm that the various Auradamas accounts which held between one and two million in operating funds all last year are now holding insufficient for the wages at the end of the month?"

Borders stirred uncomfortably. It wasn't just the issue of confidentiality. In his own way, he'd been as taken in by Sloan as Mrs. de Vries. And he should have talked to her, rather than Sloan. He nodded.

"And you presumably queried this?" I asked.

"I raised it at a meeting," Borders said carefully.

Over lunch, I thought, and gestured for him to continue.

"Forster said he was preparing for a very large investment in stock that would allow another 5% off the margin. The same thing as he did last year, but bigger. He asked the bank to cover this month's operating costs at the firm."

"See," Mrs. de Vries said. "This is all a ridiculous misunderstanding."

"Last year," I asked Borders, "did Mr. Sloan move any money out of the accounts prior to the bulk purchases?"

"No."

"So." I motioned with my hands. "Last year the firm had money, then it had stock, and some money left over. And this year, the firm has no money and almost no stock. All that money has been moved to where exactly?"

"Well, I understand he's speculating on exchange rates. Placing the money in China or India over the last few months would have increased his acquisition ability by at least 10%."

Borders' careful choice of words showed he didn't know if Sloan had actually done any exchange speculation at all.

"Can I cut through that banker-speak and confirm that the complete limit of your knowledge is that he's moved the money offshore?"

Borders nodded, his face coloring.

"To an account in the Caymans."

Borders twitched. I knew things I certainly shouldn't have, thanks to Matt.

Right now, Borders would be wondering who else knew.

"It allows flexibility that, for example, London wouldn't," he said defensively.

"It does. For example, flexibility to buy diamonds from somewhere other than de Beers."

"Forster would never do that!" Mrs. de Vries said. "He knows about de Beers' rules. He'd never risk the company for a bit of short-term gain. That would be crazy."

"It would be crazy if he intended to stick with it."

"No! I refuse to listen to this."

"Suzannah, please," Ethel said. "There's not much time. Listen to what she has to say. As a favor to me."

"The total amount we're taking about, Mr. Borders?"

Borders was rattled. All his reservations about confidentiality to Auradamas' shareholders went right out the window if he'd assisted in the importation of illegal diamonds. I still had a problem with Mrs. de Vries, but Borders was on my side now.

He squinted. "About five million."

"And if he agreed to a joint business venture with Mr. Okawa at Hayashi Securities, for example, how much could he raise?"

Borders licked his lips. I knew from Jen that he'd been introducing Okawa around the circuit in Denver. I had no idea whether Sloan had raised any money from Hayashi Securities, but I was absolutely sure he'd raised as much as he'd been able to, from as many investment companies as he could without attracting notice.

"They might match him dollar for dollar, but they'd never put it down up front."

"So maybe only seven million dollars cash with an up-front loan of a couple of million. And if you went onto the market with that and bought legitimately sourced diamonds, that's twelve million or more in retail value." I paused. "But if you convert that cash into conflict diamonds, you'd end up nearer twenty million in retail value. Someone with the right contacts could move those on without trace and at no more than 20% off. Say sixteen million. That's a sizeable amount. A tempting amount."

Mrs. de Vries' lips were a thin, angry line. Anger was fine. One way or the other, she was going to be angry today. I just needed to keep her thinking instead of reacting.

"Are you accusing him of stealing? Why would he do this?" she said.

"Why does anyone steal?" Ethel replied, trying to add her weight to our argument.

"Because it's the only way to get something they don't have, and that doesn't apply to Forster."

I saw a look of triumph mixed with the anger in her face, and I knew with an awful certainty what she was going to say next.

"This isn't the way I wanted to announce it, and obviously, you don't approve of him, but we're going to be married, Ethel. We've agreed on a spring wedding." She actually sat back. "You've made some mistakes, but of course, I understand you had my interests at heart. Thank goodness Forster wasn't here. It would have upset him so much. He hates it when he feels he isn't accepted for what he is."

Ethel was speechless. I had to plow on.

"Mrs. de Vries, your business has a small stock of diamonds remaining from last year's bulk purchases."

"Yes, some of the smaller diamonds. What's that got to do with it?"

"I understand these are kept in safe storage. Would you do me the favor of calling any member of your staff and asking where that safe storage is?"

"Ethel, this is getting intolerable. Why should I do that? Anyway, Forster handles all the business side of things."

"And your personal diamonds, Mrs. de Vries? I understand you have a stunning set of necklace and earrings."

She went pale, her hand unconsciously going to her throat. "There was a problem, with the house insurance," she stuttered. "Forster put them in the storage with the firm's stock."

I could feel her resistance being undermined by doubt. "Where?" I insisted.

She didn't know, but I'd pushed too much. She stood up, trembling.

"I'll ask him when he comes home and clear this all up. Now, I would like you all to leave."

"How sure are you that he's coming home?" I knew he was, but I really needed her to start questioning what she knew about him. "There's this, for instance." I held out a printout of a one-way ticket to Panama.

"That proves nothing," she snapped, glancing at it. "It's not for today and it's not even in his name."

I decided I liked Suzannah de Vries. Beneath the apparent timidity, she was nobody's fool, make that *almost* nobody's fool, and there was an inner core of strength. She'd certainly need it when the full implications of what had happened hit her.

But the more I liked her, the harder I had to hit her now.

"It's his name. His real one." The next piece I handed over had a printout from his driver's license and ID, under his real name and with his photo. Then another paper, a copy of the docking bill for his yacht, berthed at the Flamenco Island Marina in Panama Bay.

"But..."

Time to get cruel. "Do you know where he is now?"

"His physical therapy...every Thursday, for his leg."

"Suzannah," Ethel said softly, picking up the cordless phone from its base and bringing it over. "Please call them. Just to check."

"He doesn't like me checking on him..." She stopped when she realized what that sounded like. She dialed clumsily. Her eyes were misted, but she refused to cry. She turned her back on us as if that kept it more private.

"Hello? Yes, this is Mrs. de Vries. My partner..." she stumbled, "is booked in for some treatment. His name is Forster Sloan. I need to speak to him."

There was a heavy silence.

"Thank you," she mumbled. "Some mistake then."

She ended the call, standing very straight and still. "He's not there. Maybe I made a mistake. I could have forgotten he told me he was going to the club instead." Her voice trailed away and she turned. "He's not there either, is he?"

Mrs. Harrison shook her head and took the phone back.

"You know where he is, don't you?" Mrs. de Vries said to me. She was angry again, a very tightly controlled anger. "It's like lawyers in court, isn't it? They never ask a question unless they know the answer. You wouldn't have had me call unless you knew where he was."

I nodded.

From the briefcase I pulled out one of Victor's tricked-out laptop systems. It was an ordinary laptop with a roaming internet connection, and on the other end of that connection was Bud with a camera, outside a house less than ten minutes' drive away.

The screen cleared. It was dominated by the image from the camera, currently pointing at the dashboard.

"You hear me, Bud?"

"I hear you, Ms. Farrell."

"Date, please."

Bud lifted a copy of today's Denver Post in front of the camera. The lens blurred and then focused on the lead story and date.

"Target, please."

The camera swiveled to look out the window. Mrs. de Vries' bright yellow Ferrari was parked in front of a modest townhouse that looked onto Barnum Park. On a clear day in winter you'd be able to see all the way to the downtown skyscrapers. This was the same place the Ferrari had been for an hour after work yesterday. And every Thursday evening, according to the neighbor.

"Leave it there, Bud."

In truth, if it could have been done without anyone losing, I'd have just left Sloan and this woman to get on with it. Despite the sour taste from learning what had been going on, when I'd seen Tullah's report, I'd laughed out loud.

Sloan had hooked up with a con woman. Maybe he knew he was being played and was just going along with it for entertainment. After all, the ticket to Panama had been for one person. But Tullah's synopsis of Sloan's girlfriend was impressive, in its own way. I'd pay money to see who ended up screwing whom, but we didn't have that luxury.

"Call his cell, please, Mrs. de Vries. He'll have it switched to silent, but he'll probably spot it. Leave a message. Say that Mr. Borders has come over and needs to talk to him."

Ethel looked nervous. "Won't that alert him? He might run."

I gave a small smile. "He'll still come back here first. He has to."

Mrs. de Vries left the message. Her voice was steady and calm. I liked her even more.

Tullah made us coffee and brought it in.

We sat. Ethel started to talk about the ballet production Mrs. de Vries had mentioned, but it was one of those disjointed conversations and everyone's eyes kept flicking back to the camera image on the laptop.

Five minutes later, it showed Sloan coming out of the house. There was a glimpse of a woman in the doorway behind him, but he hurried down the steps to the Ferrari. No need for a cane, then. I strangled my demon before it made a comment about how miraculous the effect of a good massage was.

I froze the best shot from the clip on the screen.

"Bud, back to guard duty, please."

He signed off.

Mrs. de Vries stood and stared out the back window into the gardens without speaking. We left her alone.

After a couple of minutes, Tullah touched her earplug and nodded to me. Jofranka had reported from outside. Within seconds, the Ferrari pulled onto the drive.

I watched from the window as Sloan struggled out of the low-slung car, waving his cane around and then using it to help him walk to the door. It was a very good limp.

He glanced at my Audi with Jofranka sitting there, but ignored her. The front door of the house barely closed behind him and she was out of the Audi and into the Ferrari like an eel, thanks to a clever little device which recorded the car key's lock control radio signal and played it back.

I left her to it, and turned in time to catch Sloan's entrance to the living room.

"Scott, Ethel. Pleased to see you, of course." He limped toward Mrs. de Vries, one arm held out to sweep her into an embrace. "What's happened?"

She moved away from him. Already alerted by the unexpected situation, he understood immediately that we knew something about what he had been doing. His question was how much, and which part of his deception.

His eyes traversed the room. Hesitated at the laptop with the picture of him leaving the house in Barnum and then passed on as if it were nothing. I had to give it to him, he was cool. He was already thinking of how to hold onto something on his way out.

I hadn't realized how much I'd come to use the Athanate and Were senses. I listened to his heartbeats, I tasted the chemistry of his blood in the air he breathed out, the sweat that evaporated off him.

His heartbeat hadn't risen. Not one beat. He really was an ice-cold operator.

Without really meaning to, I reached out with eukori.

It was like putting my hand in a bucket of freezing, slimy mud. His eukori slithered through my fingers and trailed away—an absence of humanity, a negation.

I shuddered. He had no connections, no feelings, no commitment to anything or anyone, other than himself.

He didn't bother to try and lie his way out of it. If he'd had longer, I believed he might have tried, just for fun. But he had a plane to catch tomorrow.

"I'll leave. Of course, I expect the full Auradamas termination package to be honored."

He turned, taking car keys from his pocket.

"In my Ferrari—no, I don't think so." Mrs. de Vries' voice was sharp as a blade.

"Didn't expect it for a moment. I was just giving them back to you," he said calmly. "I'll take my car and free up your garage space. I'll send someone to pick up my clothes."

He placed the keys with exaggerated care on a side table and strode to the hallway, where there was a door to the parking garage. He left the cane leaning against the side table, a prop no longer required.

"Aren't you going to stop him?" Ethel whispered.

I let a little smile show, and waved for them to follow him.

He looked irritated that we were following him, and startled when he saw that Jofranka had the garage door open and his Lexus SUV up on jacks.

"Who are you? What the hell do you think you're doing?"

For the first time, his heart rate rose and my guess was looking better every moment. Seeing Jofranka confirmed it.

Her face was professionally blank, but she just oozed satisfaction.

"This is my assistant, Jofranka," I said. "She's an excellent mechanic and we thought we'd just give your car a quick check. After all, you've been working on it a lot recently. Wouldn't want a problem down the road."

He didn't even recognize her as the woman who'd given him his office massage. "You keep your hands off my car!"

He moved forward threateningly.

Oh, please, please. Just throw one little punch.

"Bit late, sir," Jofranka said cheerfully, entirely unconcerned by his actions. "Still, the good news is I located the problem with the exhaust." She gestured.

Sloan's heart rate peaked. Behind Jofranka, the exhaust was resting against the wall.

"It's blocked, is all," she said, tapping it with a wrench. "And these modifications," she ran her finger down a seam in the body of the exhaust, "they're not standard. Someone's messed with it."

He lunged. I grabbed his arm, jerking him to a stop.

Jofranka slid a screwdriver blade in behind the seam and levered it up. There was a little resistance and then a whole access panel popped open. Inside were small packages wrapped in what I guessed was heat-resistant material.

"The safe storage for your necklace and the Auradamas stock, unless I'm mistaken," I said.

Sloan wrenched away. I let him go and he ran out of the garage.

"Aren't you going to stop him?" Mrs. Harriman asked.

I nodded towards Tullah. She pulled a small box from her pocket and held it up. It looked like a smartphone.

"It's a GPS tracker. I seem to have accidentally bugged him," she said. "There's a Detective Jennings waiting out there with a list of questions about some email correspondence with people in the Caymans, Zimbabwe and the Congo. I'll make sure they meet."

She and Jofranka left and the garage door slid down behind them.

"They'll want to inspect this car as well," I said.

"And the accounts," Mrs. de Vries said quietly.

"I'll do everything I can to help, Suzannah," Ethel said.

"I've been such a fool," she murmured. "God, that's a corny line."

"And it's wrong," I said. "I can explain, or do you want us to leave now?"

"No. I want to listen…while it's so fresh in my mind. Therapy, if you like. Come." She led us back to the living room, her spine stiffening with every step. I really liked her.

Seated again, she looked expectantly at me.

I knew what she wanted. She wanted me to shake this around in her head until it made sense. Until she could understand how an intelligent woman like herself could have been so completely taken in.

And I could do it. Ops 4-10 had needed us to be able to work behind enemy lines. Not long-term or deep cover, but to be able to pass, to hide in plain sight. To disengage the connections we naturally formed with society and become something more like what Sloan was. I wasn't an expert, but I remembered the Ben-Haim lectures.

"Let me demonstrate something first. It'll only take a minute. Stand up." She got to her feet and I pulled her forward until our faces were about a foot apart. "Look at me. Not just anywhere, right in my eyes."

"Are you going to hypnotize me or something?"

I laughed. "No."

She tried and failed as I stared blankly at her. Any drill sergeant could do this. Any recruit would tell you it's because sergeants aren't really human.

After a minute, I smiled gently.

"Uncomfortable, isn't it?"

"Yes."

I let her sit down again.

"Sloan wouldn't have had a problem. You find it uncomfortable because you've been raised in a society where that doesn't happen with strangers. No one writes the rules, but the rules are there. You absorb them from society. You don't stare into a stranger's face, you don't lie, you don't cheat, you don't steal. Now, people break the rules all the time, but there's a cost. You feel bad, your body gets stressed. But not people like Sloan."

Mrs. de Vries was clever enough to see where this was going. "But these people, they're freaks, frighteningly intelligent and so on."

"Hannibal Lecter?" I laughed. "No, there's a lot of things that Hollywood gets wrong. Sociopaths came in all types. The one thing that is common to them all is the absence of the connections that bind us into society. And the scary thing is, even the ones that are just moderately intelligent catch on to that. They put up a front, and we, the rest of humanity, fool ourselves. Because the sociopath looks as if he follows the rules, we think he's normal. But he isn't. He doesn't feel the restraints we do. He has no conscience. The rules do not exist for him."

My own voice seemed to be coming from a distance away.

"We're blind to them. Because they seem normal, we deceive ourselves. We can't actually believe they're abnormal. We deny the evidence of our eyes and the logic of our minds. We invent reasons to explain away their aberrant behavior when it occurs because we can't believe they would do that. And that's because we wouldn't do it. They exploit that. They find that it lets them get away with almost anything for a minimal outlay of faking it occasionally."

Was I repeating myself? I felt as if I'd gone around and around in circles about this. Not circles. A spiral. I was traveling a spiral down to an end. I stared out the window without seeing anything.

"Amber? Are you okay?" Ethel came over and touched my arm. "You've gone all pale."

Yeah, I probably had.

I cursed my brain for being so painfully slow. Strands of thoughts were looming up out of my subconscious and colliding with a measured inevitability, like huge ships in fog.

The Denver pack couldn't find the rogue Were. They were looking for a stranger and there were no strangers in town.

Werewolves can't lie to their alpha. Their whole werewolf society is based on absolute truths like that. Truths they take at face value, assumptions that are wired into their conscious minds so they don't challenge them.

The sociopath succeeds in human society because that society depends on assumptions and signals. The sociopath ignores the rules, learns the signals. They lie with their whole body, and their complete lack of conscience allows them to say whatever they want so convincingly that ordinary people simply believe them.

What if you took a sociopath and made them Were?

He or she would be able to say whatever served their purposes. Could they learn to control the subconscious signals that told the alpha they were telling the truth?

Gut feelings exploded through me. *Yes.*

I *knew* the rogue was right here, in the Denver pack all along. Laughing at us stumbling around without any idea of what was happening. Watching them. Watching me. Brain squirming with madness behind cold, calculating eyes.

Chapter 36

FRIDAY

It's a bad night, that's all. I interview every Were I've met. We laugh and joke. Then I ask them if they're the rogue and they tug at the skin at the side of their head. Rubber facemasks slip off. Underneath, their expressions are as empty as corpses'. After I dream of Alex, I wake up and go to the bathroom.

The light is like pale yellow piss. I look tired in the mirror. Go figure. My skin looks unhealthy. I try to massage some life into my cheeks, but my face splits open and the corpse beneath stares blankly out at me from eyeless sockets.

After *that*, I did wake up, and went to the study to prepare for meeting the bounty hunters and Silas. It was still a rush job. Time seemed to be slipping through my fingers.

There was a message from Ingram; he wanted a call. I forwarded it to Julie to handle. I just couldn't keep any more plates spinning. Whatever was going down at the Ops 4 base, I couldn't let it distract me from what I had to deal with urgently here in Denver. I had to organize the hunters to find the remnants of House Matlal and their Blood slaves, and they had to find them in a matter of days.

I'd tell them they were looking for evidence of the rogue as well, but that was going to be my job. My gut feeling had only gotten stronger overnight. The rogue was one of the Denver pack.

And Silas was going to be there at the meeting.

∞ ∞ ∞ ∞ ∞

They arrived on time, and at 9 a.m. we sat down in a meeting room at the Oxford Hotel. The location was Bian's sense of humor; it was reputed to be the hotel with the most paranormal activity in Denver.

Verano and Gray had taken an immense and personal dislike to each other on sight, which hadn't gotten better overnight. Silas, for his part, distrusted them both as outsider Were on his territory. If I allowed any of them time to let their feelings get in the way of their tasks, I'd end up letting everyone down. So I planned to make them work too hard to be able to spare time for rivalries.

I started the meeting by getting them to describe how they normally worked, so I could double that. It also gave me the chance to watch them closely as they spoke. What common themes could I see in this group of Were? Would I be able to notice a difference in the rogue? A tiny slip that gave him, or her, away?

Verano went first. With his sunglasses off, he had the palest green eyes I'd ever seen. I'd drunk iced lime juice that was warmer and darker. He spoke calmly and slowly. If I hadn't known better, I would have voted him the man least likely to be a werewolf.

His pack had some military-type procedures and decent equipment, including a comms system I could patch into the colonel's TacNet system. He seemed to be able to control his dislike of both Gray and Silas on the surface, though neither of them were fooled. It was strange, as if he were speaking with two different voices at the same time. Still, it was a decent start.

Silas went next.

At six-ten and broad with it, the man was already intimidating. He shaved his head and kept his lean, dark face impassive. His thick woolen jacket was the color of old blood and bulked him up even more. He radiated hostility.

I'd given my opinion of the Denver pack organization, so his animosity toward me wasn't a surprise. And I was justified. As he went on to describe it, the pack had no standard equipment and no familiarity with procedures. They'd tried coordinating their searches with cell phones and a map back at Coykuti. No wonder they hadn't found anything. But there were a lot of them and I needed them.

I held off getting Gray to talk when Silas finished, and concentrated instead on a plan that split up the Verano and Denver packs. The Verano pack were able to slot neatly into six-hour shift schedules, around the clock. The Denver pack's search had to be carried out with constraints imposed by their normal lives. We ended up with about double the number of two-man teams as the Verano were able to put on the ground, but with shorter shifts. The Veranos were being paid for it, so I wasn't going to take any complaints.

Bian had promised equipment from House Altau stores for the pack, including suitable comms, body armor and firearms. Silas didn't like thinking the pack would owe Altau, but he couldn't argue it wasn't necessary.

The Verano and Denver packs were responsible for their own scheduling and search procedures, but all potential contacts had to be escalated. Bian and I would share that job.

Which left me with Nick Gray.

"And what, precisely, are you going to do?" Verano sneered.

Gray smiled. "It's a bounty. I'm getting paid on results, not how pretty I do it. Forget all the procedures. Just give me an area to hunt and numbers to call."

"What if you miss some?" I said.

"I won't."

Confident to the point of arrogance. But if his file from the Dakota House was telling the truth, the arrogance was justified. I hoped so.

I gave out contact numbers and emphasized again that we weren't paying them to kill. The Matlal Were were the Denver pack's concern and the Athanate were Altau's. Anything else was my decision.

Finally, Correia had handed over a list of Matlal names during our secret meeting at Haven. Bian had matched most of them to faces, which she'd printed out in flash cards so they could be used on the street to ask people.

I passed the copies out.

Verano put his into a neat pile, making sure the edges of the flash cards lined up. Silas glanced at a few. Gray started to shuffle through them, sorting into male and female. The top card on the female side was the one face familiar to me. The silver-haired woman who'd been handing me my ass the night Larry and I had been attacked in Cheesman Park, before the FBI arrived. She was one of Matlal's elite Athanate team.

"Someone you know?" I asked.

"No," he said.

"Hunch?"

"Maybe." His stare was flat and uninformative.

I'd take that up with him later. If he had hunches, he was going to have to learn to share with me.

I knew that cut both ways. I wasn't sharing my hunch about the rogue with them.

The briefing was over. Verano and Gray took the opportunity to leave quickly.

Silas waited until the door closed behind them before standing.

I stayed seated. *Ha! Ippon! Point to me.*

He loomed over the table.

"The rogue is our concern." His eyes stayed on me, as if he were measuring me, while he fastened the one-sided toggles on his jacket. "I need to know any developments. Any time, day or night."

He pulled a business card from his pocket and slid it across to me.

And why else might that be, Silas?

"Anything yet?" he said.

"I have nothing to share with you at this time."

He stared at me, but I'd had lots of practice and I wasn't going to back down.

I was sure he suspected I was holding back. It didn't feel right, but I was going with my gut feeling and I had to keep the pretense up in front of Silas. He was a suspect. Him and any of the Denver pack who were big in their wolf form.

He rumbled, deep in his chest, then the moment was gone and he strode to the door.

"Ricky, Ursula and me," he said, from the doorway. "Keep us informed."

I scratched my head. We *had* been talking about the rogue. Why did I feel there was a completely different conversation going on at the same time? And what would a conversation with a sociopathic Were feel like?

I gathered my notes and left. For real progress with the rogue, I needed to talk to Felix, alone. Soon.

Oh, joy.

Chapter 37

Back at Manassah, the colonel stopped me on the way to the study.

A day's rest had done a lot to restore him, but he still looked pale.

"How's Vera?" I asked.

"Asleep again, but she seems fine." He shook his head. "It's incredible. If I hadn't seen it with my own eyes."

I smiled, remembering my own astonishment at Jen's recovery.

"We have you to thank as well," he went on. "If you hadn't gotten us out…"

I waved it off. "I'm sure I owed you my life a hundred times in 4-10."

He snorted.

"Have you thought any more about working for the Altau?"

He and Vera weren't safe while Petersen was still at large. The FBI was moving, and I was sure Ingram moved quicker than most, but it'd take too long. Haven would provide safety from Petersen and I was convinced there was a job there that he'd find worthwhile. And, in my opinion, Altau needed him.

"It's a hell of a commitment," he said. "I need to discuss it with Vera when she's up and ready."

He'd understood. Skylur needed a particular type of military strategist, and the colonel was the best there was. But Skylur needed security as well. The colonel couldn't do this job for a few years and retire. Not with his memories intact, and erasing that level of memories would effectively destroy his mind.

"I spoke to Bian and Pia," he said. "I understand Altau would expect us to be kin." There was a blip in his pulse as he said that. He had the same reaction as José—an instinctive fear. I suspected it wasn't the biting itself, but the fear of losing part of yourself, becoming a sort of slave. And he'd be worried about whose kin they were expected to be. I sympathized, but I guess I was coming at it from the other side.

"It's a problem for you," I said.

He nodded.

It felt wrong to try and persuade him, but without a trained private army to counter Basilikos, Altau were in trouble. Their security issues wouldn't mean anything if they were overrun. They needed the colonel more than they needed him and Vera to be kin.

"I can't make the decision for you, and you've talked to Athanate who know much more about it than I do." I rocked on my heels, thinking. "The best I can do is to try and get you in front of Skylur without a commitment either way. But I think he'll offer you a place to stay for a while regardless. That's got to be worth it."

I could taste the relief in him.

"I'll go with what you say," he said. "I owe you, after all."

Julie came in, looking pleased.

"Just finished talking with Agent Ingram," she said. "The Ops 4 base was closed down last night. Important thing—no casualties." She ran her fingers through her hair. "You were right about the planes. They'd been wired to blow up. Thank God you thought of it and Ingram managed to get everything grounded yesterday. The bad news is Ops 4-16 were gone and the records and backups were destroyed."

The colonel smiled. I suspected the Nagas hadn't found all the records.

"Just came out to tell you. I've got to get back on the phone," Julie said. "Ingram's letting me talk to Keith."

She trotted off, leaving me with another worry. Would she stay when Keith got out?

The colonel went off to look in on Vera, and I went to the study to get my team working on the rogue case.

∞ ∞ ∞ ∞ ∞

Jen was working in her study upstairs, so David joined us—Melissa, Tullah, Jofranka and me.

The study looked more like an incident room now, and that was what I was calling it. The maps of Denver had color-coded pins for the important case locations. The pinboards had photos and the whiteboards had lists. Every inch of the walls was covered.

I'd never been a detective, never done a briefing on a case like this. But I had been a team leader in Ops 4-10, and I'd gotten good at sensing my team's state of mind. This team was fidgety and dismayed. The volume of data was daunting and none of it hung together—it all looked random.

"I've had my first hunch about this case," I said. They all went still. I gave them the short version—the rogue was a sociopathic werewolf in the Denver pack, hiding in plain sight.

"Now that in itself doesn't get us any closer. But what I want today is a brainstorm session," I said. "There are no dumb suggestions. What I'm looking for is patterns in all this that we can match against information about the pack."

No one wanted to go first, but I was expecting that and just leaped in.

"First off; no one's ever reported seeing an abduction. What does that tell us?"

"That maybe they didn't look like abductions?" Tullah said. "Like, the victims went willingly, without struggling. They trusted the person."

"Or it looked like something normal, that people expect to see," Jofranka said. "Like people just getting into a car. Or a couple of guys in coveralls carrying a box."

"Or the witnesses don't trust the police," said Melissa.

Melissa took a pen and wrote '+/- trust' and 'regular behavior' on a whiteboard.

"Where did the known victims come from?" I said.

"Refuges, trailer parks, cheap accommodation, SRO hotels," Tullah said. "Some of them were living on the street. No indication of struggle ever found, so it's likely they were killed elsewhere."

"If we have three locations—abduction, murder and dump, then they must have been transported in a vehicle which didn't attract any attention under different circumstances." David went to the map with the location of the bodies.

If there was any pattern to be seen, it was simply that the dump sites were outside of Denver and were out of the way.

"People downtown getting into a taxi or a van wouldn't be noticed," David said. "But how would you get a van up here?" David pointed at one body location with no roads marked nearby.

"The killer could carry the body," Tullah said.

David measured the distance from the nearest road. "Twenty minutes if you could go straight from the road. Say thirty minutes at a guess. Carrying a body? Too risky."

"Pull up a satellite map on the computer," suggested Melissa.

Tullah swung the screen around, zoomed in and flicked between the road map and the satellite image for the area. There was a trail visible, unmarked on the road map, to within about twenty yards of the body. Close enough for it to be quick to dump the body, far enough that it wouldn't be seen.

David peered at the satellite image. "Not a van. You'd need an SUV or an ATV to get up there."

"ATV with a body strapped to the back? No. So, it could be an SUV of some kind that doesn't attract attention downtown but is strong enough to get up a trail like that. Or two different vehicles, one for the abduction and one for the dump."

"He's fanatically careful about forensic evidence," Melissa said. "Two vehicles is twice the risk." She shrugged. "But there was a van at Wash Park, so somewhere there's an SUV."

"What about the murder site?" I said. "Are any of the body dumps also the murder site?"

"Possibly," Melissa said. "These weren't the best-investigated cases, and for most of them, a lot of time had passed before the bodies were found."

It was frustrating. I understood the pressures on the PD, but just a few more hours spent on any of these murders at the time might provide the clue that cracked the case.

"He has a base somewhere," Jofranka said. "The place where he kills them?" She looked queasy, and I was going to have to talk to her afterwards. She had to be in on these sessions, but there was no way I was letting her get involved outside.

"With a garage for two vehicles, maybe," David said. "A closed garage where he can clean the evidence off."

"His home?" Jofranka again.

Tullah made a face. "Doesn't feel right, somehow. This sort of fanatical care? I'd say a building that can't be traced back to him."

"An industrial unit? A ranch outside the city? Isolated? Somewhere private or well soundproofed," David said.

"Or a house with a basement." Jofranka was determined to keep contributing.

"Interesting." Melissa wrote down a summary of the location options.

I nodded. Nothing as soundproofed as underground.

We were making progress, but we were inching forward. There was nothing to stop him from killing again while we puzzled our way through the clues. The murder at Wash Park was fresh and had to be full of evidence, but Griffith had clamped down heavy security on all details.

Melissa said the rogue's actions were a gesture at the police and that meant he was leaving.

My gut feeling said he might be, but he wanted something first. What was it? More deaths?

If we were going to be able to prevent him, let alone catch him, we had to move faster and smarter. These clues were things that were evident. The FBI would have them too. What did we have that was different?

I turned to Melissa's list of missing women. She'd pinned up photos next to their names and home addresses.

Tullah saw me staring.

"What?" she said.

"Something about them," I said. "They're some kind of group. They share something."

David came over and looked at them. "They're at the other end," he said.

I frowned at him till he went on. "Look." He started pointing. "Jewelry, hairdos, makeup, branded clothing. The opposite end of society from the victims."

He was right. It wasn't what was niggling at me, but it did make a clear distinction between the known victims and the potential victims. But one of the things that could mean was just that the rogue realized there would be more investigation on the second group and had hidden their bodies better.

"Imagine them together," I said to everyone. "What are they doing? Where are they?"

"On vacation somewhere. Sailing. Y'know, fancy yacht where someone else does the work."

"Expensive shopping."

"Golf club social event."

"Opera."

"Doing some hobby that costs a lot."

I rubbed my face. All good, but not what I was feeling about them. "What cars did they drive and where did they buy them from? What clubs did they go to? Do they have second homes? Where? What stores do they shop at? What are those expensive hobbies?"

Tullah and Jofranka scribbled notes.

"Why them?" I went on. "These are high-risk targets. What might he get? Where are the bodies?"

"Risk might be its own reward," Melissa said. "And disposal? If he's in the pack, what are the chances he can dump the bodies into one of the fertilizer factories without anyone else even realizing?"

"I don't understand about the risk," Jofranka said, blushing.

"If he's responsible for all of these," Melissa said, "he needs to kill on a regular basis as a kind of sick fix. But the thrill of killing is different from the thrill of getting away with it. These ones," she indicated the original list of victims, "they go back six years. These women, if they're victims as well, started only a couple of years ago. Just killing is no longer enough. The risk profile is escalating. He needs both kinds of thrill now."

"Culminating in Wash Park?" I said.

"No. That's a clean break. I still say that's his farewell." Melissa made a few more notes on the boards. "Some of that information you were asking about is in the files I brought. I've copied them to the computers here."

I stood back and looked at the board. There was something we were all missing about this group that pulled them together, something I felt from looking at them, but it remained outside of my reach.

"You said at the beginning that we needed to match any pattern against information about the pack," Tullah said. "When will we get that information?"

"As soon as I can get it." I was going to have to persuade Felix.

Tullah and Jofranka started running through Melissa's computer files while I stared at the photos.

"I have a contact we have to go see," Melissa said. "A guy called Clayton. Used to be a detective. He worked on these cases."

The name rang a bell, and not in a good way.

"Okay, we could—"

Pia came in. "Urgent call for you," she said, handing over a landline. "Bian."

"Round-eye? I've been speaking to Skylur and Naryn about the colonel. I gave them the proposal you made, about him running a covert Athanate army. Naryn's totally bought in."

"Good." I hoped it was good. I got the impression Naryn would want exactly the commitment that the colonel wasn't ready to give.

"Yeah." Bian's tone told me I was right to be worried. "You need to bring them in now."

"But Vera's still recovering."

"I know. Naryn said she'll be in better hands here at Haven than there. I'm sorry. They've made some time in their schedule and we're all just going to have to fit in."

Chapter 38

The colonel and his wife had already been warned by Pia, and it wasn't as if they had much to pack. We were on the road in five minutes, most of that taken with Vera thanking me again and apologizing for all the fuss she'd caused, as if it had been her fault.

"Will I meet Ms. Trang today?" she asked as we drove out.

"Probably."

I could tell she was worried about that—the effect that Bian might have on her. Bian's scent still clung to her.

I pulled over short of the highway, and took out the two blindfolds Pia had given me.

"Sorry," I said.

The colonel laughed and put Vera's on.

"It won't make a blind bit of difference," she said with a smile. "I'm going to sleep anyway."

I tied his and we set off again. In fact, both of them slept until we turned into the gates at Haven. I wished I felt as relaxed as they did.

∞ ∞ ∞ ∞ ∞

Bian met us at the main door.

"House Farrell." She nodded to me. "Colonel and Mrs. Laine, welcome to Haven."

We were being formal, so she kissed necks with me. She shook hands with them.

Vera kept hold of her hand. "We both wanted to take this opportunity to thank you." She looked at me as well. "Whatever happens now. To thank both of you and your colleagues as well. And my personal thanks to you, Ms. Trang, for saving my life." She stopped. "That sounds so awful."

"It's Bian, and I'm glad I was able to." Bian shed her formality and hugged Vera. "Your recovery is thanks enough," she whispered and then she broke away, and was all formality again. She touched her tiny Haven earpiece.

"I apologize. We're a bit rushed today. Please, follow me."

She took us along to the small library where I'd met Diana the previous week. I was relieved Skylur wasn't insisting on the spooky dungeon treatment.

He was waiting there with Naryn.

"Colonel Laine, Mrs. Laine. Welcome." He shook their hands and waved us to seats.

Bian served us coffee from the sideboard, then went and leaned against a bookshelf.

Naryn was sitting to one side and watching silently, as if he were weighing us all.

I tried to ignore Naryn and to see Skylur with fresh eyes, like the colonel and Vera would.

He wasn't imposing, at a glance, the leader of the Panethus Athanate. You'd hardly notice him in a crowd. His hair was dark, cut short and neat over regular features. His skin was lightly tanned. His clothes were casual but too well fitted for store-bought.

It wasn't till he turned his eyes on you that you started to re-evaluate. They were a cold, hard blue. Once they caught you, it was as if a cold corridor opened between minds. Maybe when I'd first met him in the dungeon, he'd chosen that location so I couldn't actually see his eyes?

My elethesine spiked and my senses sharpened. Everyone in the room was suddenly much more in focus. The image that came to mind was a spider web, and through that web I knew that the colonel's heart rate had risen, and so had Vera's.

No prizes for guessing which of us were the spiders and which the flies.

"House Farrell has put a proposal to us," Skylur said. In one sentence he'd somehow managed to convey the relationship between me and Altau, and the gravity of the situation.

Skylur made a steeple of his fingers. The colonel sat back and crossed his legs. He wasn't fooling any of the Athanate in the room, and he knew it, but I was still impressed he managed to look relaxed.

"You're familiar with the situation between the two main factions, Panethus and Basilikos?"

The colonel nodded.

"The last hundred years of political fighting has resulted in a win for Panethus. We believe that may cause Basilikos to escalate their armed aggression from minor attacks in disputed areas to major attacks anywhere in the world they feel they can. It's House Farrell's opinion that Basilikos have an advantage in military capability. The potential inclusion of Ops 4-16 in Basilikos ranks can only make any disparity worse."

Skylur paused to take a sip of coffee.

"By worse, I don't mean just for Panethus, I mean for humankind as well."

He let that sink in before continuing. I'd briefed the colonel about the differences between the two Athanate types. He'd be in no doubt of the effect of having Basilikos run unchecked.

"To win against Basilikos, we can't just beat them. It would be a disaster for us to win the armed struggle and yet reveal ourselves to the human world prematurely. So we must beat them covertly, with an army of experienced soldiers and leaders who are experts in this covert way of fighting. Now fate has handed me exactly such a leader," Skylur said. "You appreciate I can hardly just let you go?"

I wanted to say something, but the colonel beat me to it. "You must be careful, Mr. Altau," he said. "It's all too easy to become what you fight."

Skylur smiled thinly. "Call me Skylur," he said.

"Jari," replied the colonel.

"Sun Tzu thought it was necessary to become the enemy," Naryn said quietly. I shivered and wondered if he'd intended it to sound as if he'd spoken with Chinese generals in 500 BC.

The colonel had shown he wouldn't be pushed around. In an ordinary interview, that would have been good. I was worried how serious Skylur was when he said he couldn't let the colonel go. He had the power to compel people, but surely it wouldn't work for something as complex as running their army.

"If I'm being offered a job, what are the terms?" the colonel said.

Skylur let the silence build. I knew that there would have to be conditions attached. The colonel knew it too. I could smell his worry.

It was Naryn who answered, and he focused on that worry. "This work would be for an indefinite period." He got up and strolled to a side cabinet, where he picked up a small statue of an eagle. "Which leads us to questions of your status within this House. The Athanate have survived among humanity by following a set of rules called the Hidden Path, symbolized by this." He held up the statue. "The eagle blindfold, unable to see the path we follow. It has kept us safe for thousands of years. One principle of the Hidden Path is that there are three types of people within the Athanate domain, and *only* three—the Athanate themselves, Aspirants to become Athanate, and those humans bound to the Athanate as kin."

I cleared my throat and they all swiveled to look at me. "Things change. Emergence challenges the Hidden Path. Definitions have to become looser. They already have for me. I'm Athanate, and yet I'm Were as well."

That got the frostiest of smiles from Skylur.

And Adept. When are you going to get around to telling them that?

Quiet, Tara.

Their own political structures had the concept of looser and tighter bonds between Houses; they should be able to transfer that to the bonds within a House. I wanted them to concentrate on what they couldn't avoid—humans finding out about them, and how they dealt with that in the future.

"If you proceed down the path of Emergence," I continued, "you will have to learn how to cooperate with humans who are not bound as kin. What better place to start?"

"Looser definitions," Skylur said, "do not mean looser consequences. Jari, I sense your fear of the Athanate, our culture and structures. In this, you are so like your former sergeant when she first came to Haven." He smiled at me. "Amber, describe your position now."

The bastard. I knew exactly what he wanted.

"I am Athanate." A simple statement that was the start of the oath of allegiance I'd given at the Assembly. Words have a power all of their own. These rang deep in me. "I am House Farrell, and responsible for my House to the Athanate. That responsibility is channeled through House Altau, whose mantle this is. I have made an oath to him, on my Blood. I am completely aware that, as I am responsible to him, he is responsible to the Athanate as a whole. Because of that, everything, my life and my House, are at his disposal."

I swallowed. It was one thing to say that in the Assembly in front of Athanate witnesses, and something completely different to say it in front of the colonel and his wife. He looked pale. Vera sent me a look of sympathy.

"For Athanate purposes, you are Athanate," Naryn said. "As for looser definitions, I consider you an experiment in process, and I advise against starting any more experiments while the first goes on."

I bit my tongue to stop my demon from making things worse. Altau needed the colonel. Compelling him or making him kin against his wishes were hardly the right way to proceed. I was sure if Diana were here, the argument would be over already, but she wasn't. And if Naryn had been with Skylur so long, his opinion would carry more weight than mine. I needed an argument, not an opinion. The point about my being an exception was a good one, but between Skylur and Naryn, they'd shot it down.

The colonel and Vera knew it.

"If you weren't here, colonel, what would you be thinking of doing?" Bian asked.

She'd cleverly defused some of the tension.

"I think it's safe to assume that the government won't allow groups like Ops 4 to exist in the future," he replied, bitterness in his tone. "Redeployment of command staff would be highly contentious."

He shrugged, hiding the pain. "When that sort of political wind is blowing, even the big trees bend. Years of service and successes won't count."

"You're saying you're out of a job," Naryn cut in.

"Or possibly I'd be offered a job running weekend training camps for reserve assistant cooks. My commitment isn't to one military group or another, it's to doing something that I'm skilled at which makes a difference."

"Basilikos certainly would make a difference, and they'd love to have you," Bian said casually. "They're probably better set up as well."

The flare of the colonel's anger didn't get past the eyes, but every Athanate in the room felt it. Just as Bian intended.

Thank you, Bian.

She put up her hand. "Not intended seriously, Colonel. I didn't mean to be insulting."

I ignored the byplay and focused on Skylur. I saw the subtle change in his eyes, I felt the even subtler changes in his marque.

Naryn and Bian shifted positions noiselessly. They'd felt it too.

The colonel's instinctive, bone-deep hatred for Basilikos and all it stood for was like a binding. Not to Altau, but to their cause. Was it enough?

But Naryn wasn't finished. "The general without the troops isn't much use. Where would we find the troops? We don't have the time to recruit and train them."

"Don't need to train them," I said, "if you recruit our old unit, Ops 4-10."

That interested them. Skylur tilted his head. Naryn's eyes narrowed thoughtfully.

"I haven't spoken to them, and I'm not the person to do it," I said.

Recruiting would be the colonel's job, maybe helped by Julie, and Keith when he got out. If the administration decided the Ops 4 were a liability they wanted to disown, I had the feeling that would include discharging everyone. If Altau were up for it, I'd bet the majority of Ops 4-10 would come and work for them, once they learned the real situation with Basilikos.

They all already knew about Athanate, and a talk from the colonel would lay out the scenario. They wouldn't be based at Haven. They wouldn't even need to be kin, though Naryn might disagree again.

Skylur broke the silence. "House Farrell is obligated to me. This is an Athanate obligation, and that means her entire House is required to behave exactly as if they were any other, standard Athanate House, comprised of Athanate, Aspirant and kin. In return, I behave the same way to them." He tapped his steepled fingers against the end of his nose. "You can arrive at a status within House Farrell that you are both comfortable with."

Naryn looked to interrupt, but Skylur held his hand up and continued, speaking slowly.

"*But…*you must be aware of the liabilities and responsibilities this carries with it under Athanate law. If, for example, the colonel were to breach security, or act against Altau, or Panethus, or not act against Basilikos, then it is the responsibility of House Farrell to remedy that. Failing that, or in the case that remedy is impossible, the entire House is liable to me and the lives of all would be forfeit."

He sat forward, his eyes locking on me and then the colonel.

"Amber, Jari, are you both completely clear on this?"

My life, and the life of everyone I declared to be in my House, would depend on the colonel's loyalty. If he were kin, the binding would ensure this. If we agreed he wasn't going to be kin, I was dependent on his word. I might have to kill him. Skylur might have the whole House killed.

We needed the colonel. Not just me and Altau—all of Panethus needed the colonel. Which meant I needed to take this risk.

"I understand," I said, sounding half strangled. The colonel just nodded. He'd gone as pale as I felt.

"Take it as read that the ordinary package will exceed what could be expected in an equivalent role for the army. You would be seconded from House Farrell to live and work here. Your ability to come and go would be the responsibility of your House under the obligations I've explained. At your choice, you could enjoy kin benefits from Altau without further commitment."

Naryn's brow furrowed.

Skylur ignored him, his eyes fixed on the colonel and me. "Given that, are you willing to commit to us?"

The colonel and Vera looked at me. I read the apprehension in his eyes about the effect of his decision on me and my House. But did I trust the colonel? Of course. Sweat chilling my brow, I nodded.

He and Vera looked silently at each other, before he turned to Skylur. "I am," he said.

At that moment, my cell beeped an incoming message—*V team*—*Target acquired.*

Verano's team. The bounty hunters had found something already. There was no way I was going to let this descend into a scrabble.

Skylur waved me out.

Chapter 39

The TacNet headset whispered with messages as I flicked through onto the command channel, heading into the city.

"V1, this is Charlie," I said. "Update."

"Charlie, this is V2. V1 en route. We are at Zuni 3. We have positive sign. Mixed multiple. We have a perimeter this side of the river with two teams and a reserve. We are undetected, but unable to contain should they move. Request instructions."

Zuni 3 was the grid reading. It was a small industrial area between the interstate and the river. It was much closer in to the city than I had hoped for. Not a pedestrian shopping area, but enough offices and factories around that there would be witnesses and bystanders.

Mixed multiple just meant there was more than one marque detectable. Not even Were noses could count the number of people in a building.

"V2, fall back as far as you can without breaking surveillance. Do not engage. Await reinforcement and further instructions. Charlie out."

I keyed in the Denver pack frequency.

"Sierra or Uniform, this is Charlie," I said. Silas or Ursula.

"Ursula," she said. "Drop the military bullshit."

I huffed. Amateur hour.

"Okay *Ursula*, I need everyone available at Zuni and 13th. Verano teams have got mixed multiple."

I checked the map as I spoke.

"Mixed?" she said.

"Yeah. I think the Matlal Were might just be hosting some Confederation guests. That gives us a tactical problem. We can't afford to give the Confederation an excuse—"

"I'm not stupid."

"Good. Then you'll get forty people, split into four teams on the east side of the river. You'll put another team on the west side, just across the rail bridge. You'll do it within fifteen minutes. And you'll wait for my instructions. Out."

It wasn't a minor point I'd been trying to make. Any deaths on the Matlal Were side could be justified. They were trespassing, and their purpose was clear.

But Confederation Were casualties, even though they didn't have permission to be in Denver, were a problem for the pack—the Confederation could use it as an excuse to push into Denver.

And casualties on our side would be another problem.

Bian came through on the control channel. She'd stayed behind at the meeting with the colonel, but it sounded as if that'd ended.

"Not forgetting to invite me, are you?" she said sweetly.

"You have the information, Pussycat. See you there."

The Matlal Were hadn't picked this place as carefully as the Oaxaca diner up in Swansea. Sure, there were the same sort of escape routes—railroad tracks, running trails along the Platte, a freeway not far away, but there were too many people around. They must've wanted to impress the Confederation with how deep into Denver they could operate. Mistake for them; we'd caught them. Headache for me; with people around, it was going to be nearly impossible to contain this.

And I had volunteered for this? Had I learned nothing in the army?

Fifteen minutes later and the headache hadn't magically gone away. I had a solution no one was going to like. Hell, I didn't like it.

The Denver pack was in place. I was in a Verano SUV, peering down to where an orphaned spur of 13th Street stuttered out to nothing just before the Platte river. Cinderblock buildings and lockups leaned against each other like they were tired. Tattered square-pane windows looked down onto the street or were blank-eyed where they'd been boarded up. Faded graffiti struggled with cheap whitewash that scabbed the walls. A solitary air-conditioning unit hung halfway off a wall where a truck had sideswiped it. Wires swung overhead and trailed down across the fronts of buildings. The smell of a small brewery behind me stole across the road.

I wished for just two squads of Ops 4-10. One would be through the roof and the other through the door, noisily or silently, but expertly. It would be over in two minutes.

Instead, I had enthusiastic but untrained Denver werewolves and a bunch of professional bounty hunters of unknown capabilities.

But sitting there wishing wasn't going to change that.

"Verano teams," I said into the TacNet system, "maintain position. Engagement rules are now red three. Confirm."

The two patrols and one reserve team dutifully read back the statuses. They were now authorized to use their silenced weapons on anyone escaping. They were the safety net.

I got out of the Verano SUV.

"Denver teams one, two and three. Commence infiltration at rear on my mark. Silently. Confirm wearing markers."

The team leaders answered, excitement building in their voices. They were wearing luminous road workers' safety vests. Those hid the Kevlar vests underneath, which would keep them from being accidentally shot by Verano. I hoped.

Bian hadn't gotten here yet, but I couldn't wait.

"Denver four, you drive your van down the road right behind me."

I started walking and I could hear the sound of their tires creeping on the road.

"If they attack me, Denver four, your job is to alert the other teams and bottle them in the building. And make sure that van is blocking the view."

I was more nervous than I should be, repeating instructions I'd already gone through with them. Back in Ops 4-10 days, my teams hit hard, left the scene and didn't come back. I couldn't do that with the pack in my home town. And I couldn't alert the police or let bystanders get too curious about what was going on.

All of which meant it came down to me.

"Denver one, two, three—go, go, go." Three teams began working on boarded-over windows at the back and I hammered on the door, hidden from the rest of the street by the van behind me.

One possible reaction was a gutful of shotgun pellets through the door, but I didn't want to dwell on that. No time now anyway.

The door opened a crack and slammed shut again.

Message delivered.

I got out of the way, but no blast came through.

There were noises inside, a shimmer of the Call from the Denver pack, then the TacNet hissed. "It's Ursula," she said. "They tried the back. Three of them down."

"Hold position."

I took another deep breath, stood in front of the door and knocked again. The scent of Matlal and other Were mingled with the acrid smells from gunfire and fear slipping out of the house.

The door opened a fraction.

The same sort of messages that reached my nose would be reaching whoever was behind the door. Denver pack and Athanate. They'd be thinking they were trapped in a building and not only surrounded by Were, but Athanate as well.

The weak point of my plan was that was a very different message for the two different groups inside. The Matlal Were would probably think they had nothing to lose. Shooting me would be a good first step. The Confederation, however, might see a way out with talking.

More noise inside—a struggle and shouting. The two groups had seen they had a conflict of interest.

It took every ounce of control not to haul the HK out and lead a charge. They'd be distracted. It was the ideal time for an assault, but that wasn't my plan.

Top is behind my shoulder, standing at parade rest. Tall as a tower, dark face unreadable.

"You going in, soldier?"

"No, Top."

"Why not?"

"No idea of building layout or enemy numbers. No idea how good my team is. Absolute requirement to keep it covert."

"Good answer, soldier. Good answer."

I smiled sadly.

The door opened enough for me to see a face. Beneath it, a barrel pointed at me. I sniffed and slowly folded my arms. It'd slow me down if things went south, but I'd be dead anyway, and until I was dead I was going to keep sending messages. I sniffed again. Despite the gun pointed at me, this was the person I wanted to see.

"Well, well, the Confederation sneaks back in again," I said. It was a guess, but a safe one.

"Who the hell are you?"

He'd be sensing the Athanate marque and the Denver Were marque from the team behind me. A confusing smell, but I was hoping he would concentrate on the main point. It wasn't just Were here.

"House Farrell, affiliate of Altau and tasked with cleaning the area of undesirables...and the uninvited."

"Since when do Altau get involved in Were politics?" he snarled.

"Since it's in our back yard. And that's a big back yard now. Have you any idea the shit you're in? No, stupid question, of course you don't."

His face remained carefully blank, but the pause told me I'd rattled him.

"Now, we've already told you, politely, that we don't support you moving in on Denver." Well, I hoped Skylur had been polite. "And still you come back."

"It's Were business."

"It's not when you're dealing with slaves from an Athanate House that not even Basilikos recognize any more."

"They aren't tied to Matlal anymore."

"You know that because they told you?" I laughed. "But you better hope that's true, because by that slender thread hangs your whole federation."

He blinked. His eyes slid past me to the van behind. The panel was open just enough for him to see and sense the waiting Were. The Call was muted, like a distant trumpet, but if I could feel it, so could he. The Confederation had to have achieved a lot of what it had by negotiation, not aggression. They'd have people who thought on their feet, and they'd have sent someone like that down here to assess.

He still hesitated, so I pushed again.

"That's right, Mr. Confederation. Athanate and Were working together. Just think of that, all the way up in your little Rocky Mountain federation. Altau has claimed all of North America. Any Houses not willing to swear allegiance are leaving. As far as you're concerned, from now on, Athanate means Altau, and Altau will work with local packs. Whether they work with the Confederation depends on exactly how much you can credibly deny supporting our enemies."

No, Skylur hadn't just died and assigned me control over Altau diplomatic strategy, but I'd carefully not committed Altau to anything. The threat was all there by implication.

His ongoing silence and jittery eyes confirmed he understood the problem. The worst outcome, if he believed my threat, was that the Confederation could suffer attacks from neighboring packs supported by Altau. Or even attacks from Altau Houses in their own established territories. The best outcome was their expansion had just come to a crashing halt—and history was littered with the corpses of empires that had stopped expanding and succumbed to internal problems.

He licked his lips. "You're not Altau. You're bluffing."

He wasn't sure, but he'd go along with whatever I said. The alternative was the deaths of every Confederation Were in the building. He was a realist; he'd already written off the Matlal Were. All he was trying to do now was gauge from my responses exactly how much of a problem the Confederation was in.

For me, my marque senses told me that had just become academic. My stomach tensed as I counted the approaching footsteps.

"Is she, Iversen?" Bian said from behind me. "What are you going to bet on that? The whole Confederation? I thought we'd made our position clear when you came calling."

"Diakon," he said quietly, and I could see the scenarios re-running through his head.

"You were just leaving?" Bian said.

"Maybe I should stay while the rest of them go," he replied. "The situation seems to have changed. It's probably a good idea for me to talk to you again. To ensure understanding."

No lack of balls then. As if balls made a difference. Fragile, sensitive things in my experience.

"All of you?" Bian said.

His eyes flicked to me and the van behind me, then returned to Bian.

I guessed he still had a problem. Maybe the team he'd brought down from the Confederation was outnumbered by the Matlal Were in the building. I'd heard the struggle inside between the Confederation and Matlal. Since he was still alive, most likely it had ended in a standoff. He was now wondering whether the offer still stood for him and his team to get out if we then had to go get the Matlal Were.

"All of them," I said quickly, before my better judgment could back out of it.

He jerked back to face me.

"You'll take the Matlal Were out of Denver and return with them to Confederation territory." I could feel the Denver pack stir all around me, the unhappy, growling variant of the Call. From Bian, silence. "How you deal with them, and any impact it has on any Athanate, or any pack outside of your territory, will affect how Altau deal with you in the future."

The TacNet was still on. I heard Ursula's indrawn breath. Her reaction was key. She was Larimer's lieutenant here, not me.

"Ursula?" I said into the mike.

Seconds ticked by. Despite the cold air, sweat gleamed on Iversen's brow. His gun hadn't moved an inch. I wondered morbidly just how much damage I could survive as an Athanate.

Then Ursula came back. "Yes," she said. Tense, not quite a snarl.

Iversen looked back to Bian.

She shrugged. "What she says."

∞ ∞ ∞ ∞ ∞

The Confederation had come down in a little eighteen-seat coach with 'Happy Mountain Tours' written down the side alongside a grinning wolf cub emblem. Cute.

The Matlal Were had drug gang SUVs.

We arranged for their vehicles to be brought around and watched them load up, mixing the two groups between the four vehicles.

One of the Verano team had a camera, and every face that came out of the building got captured. The Confederation looked confident and alert—too much for my liking. The Matlal looked like they were in the last chance saloon. Maybe they were.

I stopped a Matlal Were. "Where are the rest of them?"

His head was already down and he didn't want to look at me.

"They're going wild. They went off. We don't know where."

I grabbed his jaw and lifted his face. His eyes slid from side to side and sweat beaded on his skin.

"Look at me."

He managed to look at my chin.

"How many?"

"Six," he said hoarsely.

"And you claim you don't know where. How were you going to square that with the Confederation? Claim to be a pack in residence leaving rogues to run free?"

He jerked his head side to side.

"Where?"

"Trailer park, top end of Commerce, near the aggregate depot."

I squeezed harder. "And the Athanate?"

"Don't know. Straight up." He was shaking. His hands came up, but he didn't dare touch me. "No lies. They don't mix, man."

I let him go and wiped my hand on my jeans.

Once they'd loaded, we let them drive off in convoy, with a couple of Denver pack SUVs following to make sure no one got lost.

I had the Verano team leader call in the cleanup crew. There were four bodies to dispose of—three killed by Ursula's teams at the back and one from the struggle between Confederation and Matlal inside the building.

I wondered what the Confederation would do with them now. They'd been considering doing a deal with them as a rival Denver pack, so they had to believe they hadn't been driven crazy by Matlal. Would they give them a territory inside their own? Seed them out to existing packs? Kill them?

Not my immediate concern.

"Denver one and two." I spoke into the TacNet mike. "Check the building's clear of anything else and then return to previous assignments. Verano patrol, continue searching your patch, and well done on calling this one. Denver three and Verano reserve, go check the trailer park in Commerce City. Open mike when you get there. Break. Ricky, you on?"

"Got that," Ricky replied quickly. "I'm in Arvada. On my way to rendezvous with team three and Verano reserve in Commerce."

Team three went at a flat run, picking up the Verano guys without complaint.

Worked in the army, worked here.

No matter how much they distrusted each other, even a little action together fixed things. I wondered if Verano would be upset about it. I had the feeling he wanted his pack to keep aloof.

The other teams didn't like their orders. They wanted to go kick Matlal ass or go party, not return to patrol. Tough. We had a whole city to search and there was no guarantee our information was any good. They trailed out once they finished checking, their equipment hidden in gym bags. Grumpy, but not overtly hostile to me. I'd take that.

Last out of the building was Ursula. She loomed over me, eyes narrowed.

"I've called it in," she said. "Felix wants your report. In person."

She climbed into the van and they took off.

Well, the good part of that was I'd never have a better chance to talk to him alone.

"Felix can go howl at the moon," Bian murmured in my ear. "You've got bigger problems. Skylur's been called away to LA, and what you gotta worry about, Round-eye, is what the frigging hell you're gonna say to Naryn about committing Altau to a position on Were politics."

Chapter 40

I sat in the study at Manassah that evening.

Hiding away, said Tara.

A tactical regrouping.

I'd called Felix and simply said I would visit Coykuti tomorrow. And I wanted to talk to him alone.

"Make it early," he'd grunted and ended the call.

That was going to be fun, persuading him that there was such a thing as a sociopathic Were and then that he had to give me a list of pack members. No point stressing about how difficult it would be; it just had to be done.

Naryn was going to call me in when he was ready to bite my head off.

But not tonight. No, tonight I had Pia's kin visiting and with Jen's agreement, I'd invited Tullah and Jofranka. That was enough to get me nervous.

Then I'd returned to find Alex and Jen having a steaming argument, of all things, about which of them should pay for the truck that I'd blown up rescuing Jen at Longmont. It was Alex's truck. It was Jen's rescue. Insurance didn't want to know because it hadn't been where it was supposed to be, or some such bullshit.

I'd tried intervening, and they'd both shouted at me.

How could my kin be so wonderful and so awful at the same time?

Their arguing was actually painful, so I'd taken the coward's way out and hidden in the study.

And sitting here, I had started second-guessing everything I'd done over the last couple of days. Not helpful.

I tried concentrating on the rogue incident boards instead.

Melissa's information now covered the maps like a multicolored spider's web. The web reached out and connected to victim photos. The one on the far right was Barbara Green. It was an old army photo. She was in camo, a forage cap on her head and her hair pulled back underneath it. Her rifle was slung across her chest, pointing down. Her square, competent hands rested casually on the rifle's butt and she was half smiling, but her eyes were already shadowed. They seemed to be accusing me of not trying hard enough.

The panel on the far left was for Melissa's list of potential victims, people who had disappeared without trace. I was still sure there was some similarity in their photos, something that would make everything else fall into place.

I knelt in front of the panel.

All women. Attractive. Slim, curvy, blondes, brunettes, redheads, tall, short; no physical typecasting from what I could see. Hairdos, jewelry and upscale clothes; wealthy. In their thirties. Healthy-ish. Tan at the swimming pool, diet and aerobics, tennis and golf club sort of healthy.

Tullah had listed facts about them. Clubs: no overlap. Work: none of them really. Second homes all over the place. All of them had marital problems or were separated. Some of them had disappeared before, only to return. Lots of things in common without being something that bound them together.

I sat back on my heels and tried to imagine them all meeting at some glitzy function, but all I could think of was a sort of catty preening— neurotically comparing houses, cars, vacations and maybe the performance of the gardener in bed. Quietly, desperately unhappy. Or maybe that was just what the rest of us thought, jealously watching them in their privileged lifestyles.

Like I could talk, living here in Manassah.

Was Melissa right? Had the rogue shifted his attention to these high-risk victims for the thrill of it? To show that he could get away with it?

Or was I being completely distracted, and these weren't rogue victims?

I heard the door open behind me and sensed Tullah, alone.

"Where's Jo?" I said.

"She's coming."

"She knows who's going to be here?"

"Yup."

"How is she about us?"

"Cool. She knew there was something. It was almost as if it was the missing piece that completed the jigsaw for her. She was nervy at first and she's not going to forget it, but it's not something that's really on her mind. And she understands the stakes about keeping it secret."

She sat down.

"She's moved out as well."

I looked up sharply. "What about her brothers? She can't leave them with her father."

"No, she hasn't. We've all moved into the rooms above the Kwan with one of Pa's aunties. The kids love her and I don't think her father's actually realized yet."

That was a good result all around. At last, some good news.

"Alex and Jen stopped arguing yet?" I asked.

"Nope." Tullah smiled.

Jofranka called and Tullah went to meet her at the door.

It was time for people to start arriving. I couldn't do anything more tonight. There was some hard work to come on this case, but we'd gotten a start.

And yes, I should listen to my own lectures sometimes; being a PI was hard work. Maybe I should have taken Mom's advice about going back into accounting...

Oh, my God! Mom.

I switched on my old cell, the one that Mom called. Only about a thousand missed calls and texts, and only three quarters of them from Mom. She'd been back all week and I hadn't even called.

I was so dead.

Holding my head in my hand, I called her on one of my burn phones.

"Amber, what on earth has happened?"

"Hi, Mom. I'm sorry. Nothing has happened."

I could hear Tullah and Jofranka talking outside in the hall, but the silence on the line seemed even louder.

"Well, lots has happened," I said, speaking quietly. "But I just can't tell anyone about it. It's been busy."

"I understand you're busy, Amber, but not even a call? Surely you could spare enough time to come around for coffee?"

"No! I mean, Mom, this is really not a good time to meet. There are dangerous people out there who are looking for me. I can't risk coming to your house."

"Amber, what is this? You're scaring me. Why aren't the police doing something?"

"It's gotten beyond the police. You know there was an arrest on your street a couple of days ago. Two guys in a van?"

"Yes, but—"

"Those guys were waiting to see if I showed up there, and the people doing the arresting were the FBI."

"This is ridiculous, Amber. Why are you whispering? Look, where are you? I think I should come and see you."

"No, Mom. I can't tell you."

Alex opened the door and looked in. I waved him in and mimed closing the door. He'd given me an idea.

"Is this something to do with, well, your personal life?"

It was and it wasn't. I just couldn't tell her without making it even more confusing. But I had a plan.

"Look, I told you Alex wanted to meet you to record the Arapaho stories you used to tell us."

"Well, yes," she said hesitantly.

"What if we all meet at Alex's house on Sunday afternoon? You, me, Alex and Kath."

If I kept it brief, I could divert one of the pack's teams to provide security and make sure there were no Nagas in the neighborhood.

"I guess that would be wonderful." She sounded unsure. Probably about Kath.

Alex nodded, so I gave the address. "Please get Kath to bring along the necklace I asked about. Remember, Speaks-to-Wolves' necklace you loaned her?"

"I'll ask."

"Thanks. It's important. I love you, Mom."

"I love you, too. Bye."

I ended the call and leaned against Alex.

"Family is difficult," he said with a tight smile. "You were talking about the necklace you think was used in the Were changing ceremony?"

"That's the one. And once I have it, all I've got to do is find an Adept who remembers the ceremony and who I can persuade to do it or teach me and…"

I stopped. I really didn't know what it would take or whether it was possible. Olivia was one of the Were that hadn't managed to change and I'd promised I'd help her. I'd used the Athanate oath 'on my Blood', and that, I guessed, made it a kind of binding.

I sighed. "What else did you and Jen find to argue about?"

"Why you're staying here, for instance."

"Because Felix said I can't stay with you."

"And this is such a pleasant place."

"Yeah." I put my arms around him and squeezed. The strongbox rattled a bit, but stayed closed. I buried my face in his shoulder. "It feels like home, here. I know that's not fair, and I've never tried staying at your home. It just does."

He hugged me back, as carefully as if I were bruised.

"What's the real problem between you and Jen?" I said. "Besides the obvious."

"It's her attitude toward anyone in business who doesn't run it like she does the Kingslund Group. I'm a 'dilettante', I'm not serious about business, I'm a waste of space."

"Hmm. So much for what you think her problem is. Takes two to argue. What about your attitude toward her?"

"She's privileged. All her so-called business acumen is just capitalizing on a position she was born into."

"You're both wrong."

"No, she's wrong and I have an arguable, considered opinion."

"You are full of—"

"I gotta go make some calls," he said. "This *dilettante* has a business to run."

I snorted and let him go.

∞ ∞ ∞ ∞ ∞

I walked to the living room to find Jen.

"Casual?" I said. For me, that was my working clothes, jeans and T, which made up most of my wardrobe.

"Casual," Jen confirmed. She was wearing tight leather pants. It looked as if she'd had her legs covered with thick, glossy paint. Her blouse was a square loose smock in cream with a wide neckline that fell off one shoulder. The sort of thing that looks like a shapeless tent on the hanger and wonderful on someone like Jen.

I didn't have time to comment.

Pia had arrived, and her kin, part of my House, followed her through the door.

"Amber, may I present my kin," she said proudly.

"Irene Rhodes kin-Shirazi," the first said shyly. Irene was darker than Jofranka by no more than a dash of creamer held back, but very different. Her hair was a burnished bronze, cut short and styled in ringlets that framed her open face, with a single lock spiraling down over a wide forehead.

I made the Athanate bow. "Honor to you, Irene kin-Shirazi, and twice welcome." That was as much as formality dictated, but I wanted to set a precedent and kissed her on both cheeks, following Jen's style. She shared Pia's scent and that meant she had traces of mine as well.

House, said my Athanate with a thrill.

Kissing cheeks also gave me a couple of seconds to catch up with my surprise at the other two.

I understood why David was concerned.

Redheaded twins. And, gods above, they were an attractive pair.

"Well, hello, boys," the demon in my throat purred, without the slightest acknowledgement to Athanate formalities or the color that rose in my cheeks.

Chapter 41

Whatever else had gone on, Jen was the perfect hostess.

We had dinner in the formal dining room, which I would have thought would be almost scary, but she'd gotten Carmen to cook a succession of small dishes. Everyone moved around the table.

It was a little awkward, but everyone seemed to be getting along and relaxing. Except me.

In my mind, my Athanate House would be the same thing as my Were pack and my Adept community. So in addition to these people here tonight, there would be the colonel and Vera, Mary and Liu, and Olivia. Maybe Matt. If Julie stayed, maybe Keith.

How could I keep these people in this room safe, let alone if I expanded the House? How big was too big and how fast was too fast to grow?

What would Skylur and Felix think about it?

Melissa definitely was shy, but she and David were talking earnestly now. Jofranka and Tullah had ganged up with Irene and were giving Alex a hard time about something, stabbing him on his chest with their fingers to make their points. The redheaded twins, Gary and Leon, were chatting to Julie. Jen and Pia were laughing about something.

Why did I feel so clumsy?

Some of it was unfamiliarity. As House, I would be expected to share Blood with David and Pia, but the position also meant I would have rights to their kin. All of them had made it plain that they looked forward to being bitten by me. I wasn't ready for that yet, by a long way. The thought of biting Jen and Alex was exciting, but actually drinking Blood? Still had the *eww* factor for me.

The others—Melissa, Julie and Jofranka—I felt they were looking at me, wondering if I wanted to bite them.

And Tullah's spirit guide wanted me to bite her.

All on top of a snowballing weight of responsibility for my House, which I still had no idea how I'd run or finance. Or even where we'd live long term. We couldn't all live in Manassah.

No wonder I was being awkward.

I was also bone-tired. When we finished dessert and returned to the living room, I slumped on the sofa.

"Hey! Slumber party," Tullah said, to laughter.

I didn't care. I wasn't going to be able to sleep, the nightmares would wake me, but damn, it felt so comfortable. The party was going fine without me. Some kind soul turned the lighting down and lit the fire.

I grabbed Alex and Jen.

"I want you two here with me. And I will not have you arguing."

I guess being tired and drinking a few glasses of wine made me fierce. They were meek as kittens as they sat on either side of me. A few token glares may have been exchanged, but wine and warmth worked its magic.

I gathered a reluctant hand from both of them and hugged them to my chest.

Conversation fell to murmurs. Someone stripped the guest rooms of mattresses and pillows and scattered them around.

Must remember to get them to tidy up tomorrow.

Jen had been so laid back, but I was feeling guilty, between yawns.

Pia's face floated past, grinning like a cat. Comforters appeared. I sank into a sea of contentment, my Athanate pheromones probably swamping everyone.

A nightmare made the strongbox creak, and I felt hands from both sides silence it, pressing it down. Down.

∞ ∞ ∞ ∞ ∞

I am a creature of night and shadows. The day has long folded back. Edges become soft and blurred, walls insubstantial as mist. Souls glow. These, this warm cluster, that is me, many in one. A House. A pulse of Athanate pleasure. Yessss.

Hana lies in my lap, twitching, deeply asleep.

I look up and, with no more than a stretch, see through the veil of walls, to the quiet patter of the guards' minds, bored but alert.

If that far, how much further?

The night is smoky with the haze of a million minds, like candles in the dark. Somewhere out there, I seek one that burns with malevolence, leaking poison fumes.

If we could just reach, could we not see?

"You do not have the strength." The dragon's voice calls me back. "Welcome, House Farrell."

"Kaothos, you damn lizard. Am I always dreaming when we talk?"

"What is dreaming?" The sizzling of dragon laughter. "Walls are dreams."

Her scaled body lies inside and outside the room, passing through walls. It is bigger than before.

"I'm not talking to you without Tullah," I say.

"Wise," says a voice I recognize. My great-grandmother, Speaks-to-Wolves, in her wolf form, pads into the room from the darkness. "Or at least wiser than you were, cub." She sniffs Hana's unresponsive body gently and turns to Kaothos. "Wake your host, Shaper-of-Flames."

"I prefer Kaothos," she says, but Tullah stirs and rubs her eyes.

"Oh, freaking hell!" she says. "What is this? Spirit Skype?"

"This is a time for careful decisions," Speaks-to-Wolves says. "And a time for apologies."

Kaothos lays her head alongside Tullah.

"It is. I have damaged you, House Farrell, and your spirit guide. Hana sleeps. She will recover."

"And me?"

"I do not know. The path of energy through you may take away your ability to use energy for yourself. I did not know this. I am sorry."

"And?" Speaks-to-Wolves says.

"And I may have damaged more. Your key for the energy is anger. You keep that hidden inside you. A secure place. I reached for it. I was clumsy. I may have made this place less secure."

She's talking about the strongbox, about where I imprison all those things that would make me weak, make me lose control.

"I may be able to fix it," she says.

I hold up both hands. "Enough."

Tullah's mouth is set, deeply unhappy.

"You must accept boundaries," Speaks-to-Wolves says to Kaothos. "You must accept training and guidance."

"The community?" Tullah asks.

Speaks-to-Wolves lowers her head in confirmation. Or threat.

Kaothos' great lids sweep down and up. "I will." The Athanate stirs in me, hugely pleased. Kaothos' great eye fixes on me. "Does that mean that we will have the Athanate Blood that will empower us?"

"Maybe. In time," Speaks-to-Wolves says.

"How can you be so sure you can control the Blood?" I ask.

"Little Hana kept you from turning for two years," Kaothos replied. "I am much stronger and better suited."

Speaks-to-Wolves nudges me. "Later, granddaughter. You have too much to do. Rest."

They become thinner, translucent reversed, the darkness showing through.

"How better suited?" I say. "How do you know?"

"What is the name of mankind's greatest vampire myth?" Kaothos asks.

"Dracula."

Kaothos gives her sizzling laughter as she fades away. "The name means 'son of the dragon'," she whispers.

Chapter 42

SATURDAY

I'd always found Coykuti Ranch spooky. The way the pines seemed to reach down from the mountain behind it. The screen of maple and cottonwood that shielded the main house from view. The quiet. It wasn't silence; the wind coming down the mountain whispered words on its cold breath.

Traces of morning mist trickled down from the pines as if a huge beast slept beneath their dark cover.

I shivered. Last night's dream conversations included, I had enough to worry about without getting over-imaginative.

I'd nicknamed the farm worker Leatherface when I'd first come here, in keeping with the horror-movie setting. He was leaning against the door of the nearest farm building, watching me get out of the car.

The house felt empty, so I walked over to him.

"I'm here to see Felix," I said.

Well, doh!

He reached behind the door and pulled out a shotgun. Nothing fancy, an old under-and-over Remington. Good for bird. More than adequate for a hybrid that didn't fall in with the pack's rules and way of doing things. He rested it on his shoulder and headed around the buildings, and took the dirt track up the slope behind the house with me trailing after him.

There were more maples and cottonwood dotted around here too, but they stopped about halfway between the back of the house and the start of the pines.

Leatherface stepped off the path and gestured up to the right with a lift of his chin.

Okay. He wanted me to walk on, with my back to him and his shotgun.

Was it a test, or had Felix had enough? I could imagine him saying—*don't shoot her in the house and get blood all over everything. Take her out back.*

I stared at Leatherface.

His face betrayed nothing, but I could sense he knew exactly what I was thinking. Was there a sniff of wolfish amusement leaking from him?

I walked where he'd indicated, my back muscles tensing. As if that would do any good.

The ground to the right flattened out, which formed a little hollow, hidden from the house and the track. There were conifers here too. Not the dark pines of the slopes above, but small, tended yew trees. They were grown to form the shape of a crescent moon, tall ones at the back, tapering down to knee-high bushes at the tips of the two horns. Their green foliage was lightened by crimson berries.

Inside the barrier of yew, there was a neat border of flowers. Indian blanket razzled with cheerful red-orange-yellow flowers waving in the breeze. Scarlet leadwort echoed the berries in the branches above them.

And inside the enfolding arms of somber yew and bright flowers, Felix Larimer stood silently in front of three weathered gravestones.

I joined him. His senses would have alerted him that I was nearing long before, but he made no sign to acknowledge me. His deep-set eyes were fastened on the middle grave and one dark lock of his swept-back hair had escaped to arc over his forehead.

I felt I had intruded on a private ceremony, but Leatherface had sent me up here and Felix had been expecting me.

The stone was blank and old, but not crusted with lichen. It was swept clean regularly, probably as frequently as this little cemetery was tended.

I knelt down, glancing back to see if he objected. When he didn't, I trailed fingers over the worn front, feeling out the letters.

Candace Lis Larimer

Beneath that were dates.

Aug 30 1822 – Oct 3 1853 – Jan 5 1918

Born. Turned? Died.

Beloved wife of Felix and mother of Vincent

Vincent's grave was on the right. He'd been born before his mother changed of course, and he'd died on the same day in 1918.

On the left, the headstone was newer. I could make out the lettering without touch.

Donna Helene Larimer

Jun 1 1931 – Jul 8 1958

Beloved wife of Felix

"She couldn't change," he said. His voice was hushed, as if it had picked up the soughing of the wind in the pines. "She died right here, trying."

"And your first wife and son?"

"Killed by Athanate."

Oh, shit.

"Not Altau," he added as an afterthought. "Basilikos. Now you've met my whole family; my sister gave you a lift into town the other day, and that's my nephew back there."

Leatherface was propping up a cottonwood, hugging the shotgun angled over his shoulder. Not close to us, but wolf hearing is good.

"I need to talk to you, Felix. Without anyone else hearing."

"About yesterday?"

"Some."

He grunted, and turned.

I got up and followed him. He took the track up into the pines. Leatherface was still behind us.

"You know, the Celts called yew the tree of life," he said, as the slope steepened. "And yet the wood made longbows and the berries are poison. I never figured that out."

"What made you choose them for the cemetery then?"

"Candy loved them. They don't grow too well up here, or there'd be more."

We walked in silence awhile. I didn't want to start talking about the possibilities of a sociopathic werewolf with Leatherface in hearing distance, but neither was I comfortable not talking.

"Where does the track lead?" I asked.

"There's a cabin at the top of the mountain. Old hangout for the pack when we ran here. Only Doc Noble uses it now. We're not going that far."

A minute later we left the trail and made our way through the woods.

Great. Even better place to kill me, deep in the woods.

Although there was no track, I got the sense that Felix came here often. He moved through the trees like a ghost.

Slowly the noise of a stream grew until we emerged from the thick covering pines.

Felix sat on a rock and motioned me to sit across from him.

Leatherface could see us, but he wouldn't be able to hear unless he came right alongside our position.

I looked back as he emerged from the pines, still cradling the gun.

"Is he necessary?"

Felix shrugged. "Silas' insistence. He's right that I can't look both ways at once. There have been three attempts to kill me this year." He smiled frostily. "Down from five last year."

"Who?"

He shrugged again. "Confederation? Kansas Plains pack? Crescent Lake? This is prime werewolf territory."

He looked tired, almost resigned, and I wondered how long he and the Denver pack had been a target for others. Year after year, that would grind anyone down.

"Thank you for coming out here," I said.

He nodded.

"I don't want to make things even more difficult—"

"But you will," he interrupted. "It's what you do, even if you don't mean to."

I bowed my head, refusing to get angry. He deserved that, at least.

I managed a weak smile. "I'm sorry," I said.

His mouth twitched. Any more of this and we'd be best pals.

"I made a decision yesterday to spare the Matlal Were," I said. "Seemed the best choice at the time. I realize it may not seem that way to you."

Felix laughed. It was a pleasant laugh, quiet and deep, from his belly.

"It may surprise you," he said, "but I do think about things. Sure, when Ursula called, I had the same knee jerk reaction she did: Why didn't you kill the bastards? Are you trying to sabotage us?"

He stopped to pick up a stone and hurl it accurately at a crow on the opposite side of the stream. It flew off, cawing insults back at us. Leatherface tracked it with his shotgun, but let it go.

He brushed his hands on his jeans. "But you made the right call. We ended up with no injuries to the pack. A lead on the rest of the Matlal Were. The Confederation handed a ticking bomb and sitting there crapping themselves over the nightmare of thousands of Athanate hunting them down on every side. Not bad."

I wasn't sure how to deal with this calmer Felix. It wrong-footed me.

A different crow came riding the air current down the path of the stream. Felix reached for another stone, but the bird banked high and disappeared over the tops of the pines.

"Why do you chase the crows away?"

"Ask the Adepts."

I bit down on the retort my demon came up with and tried a more gentle approach.

"I'm getting a lot of runaround from one group to the next. It means I'm always less informed than I should be. Could you just tell me?"

He leaned his elbows on his knees. "That mind-leeching stuff Athanate do..." he hesitated, probably remembering he was talking to one of those mind-leeching Athanate. "Some Adepts can do that sort of thing too, but a bit different. They can see through animals' eyes, listen with their ears. They like crows for it."

That was so cool. And disturbing.

"I've met with Adepts and I can't—"

"I'm sure you've met some of the locals, and I'm sure they're very pleasant people, but Adepts have no territories." Something of his wolf reaction to that trickled through to me and made me shudder. "There may be Adepts in Denver who have nothing to do with the local covens. Adepts who work for whoever pays them. You wonder how what we do is known by the rogue?" He waved at where the crows had gone. "That's one possible way."

Maybe. I wasn't discounting it, but was it more likely than a rogue in the pack?

I took a breath to launch into my theory, but he hadn't finished.

"What's happening at the trailer park?"

I clamped down on my impatience. "The rest of the Matlal weren't there and they didn't show last night, but it's their marque all right; we're sure that's their base. I pulled the teams back. I don't want to risk spooking them."

"So how are we going to keep a watch?"

"Maybe we should have an Adept who can see through a crow's eyes," I said. "But since we don't, I put a couple of my own team in this morning. They're not Athanate or Were, so the Matlal won't sense them."

Felix's eyes came back to me thoughtfully. Not Athanate or Were. He might make the assumption that Tullah and Jofranka were Adepts, and he'd be half right. When they handed over to the next watch, Tullah was going to put in one of those masking spells, at which point, the pack would know about her. Mary had given the go-ahead, so I let it pass.

"They're connected in to my comms network. Any sign and we'll know. Meantime, the search goes on in the planned way. We're not just looking for Matlal Were," I reminded him.

Felix was still watching me.

"Who's coordinating while you're here?"

"Bian."

His fingers dug into his thighs. He'd already known she was my alternate on this. He didn't like Altau coordinating his pack, but he'd agreed to it.

"Altau," he grunted. "What about the threat you made to the Confederation? Altau working with us. Is this for real?"

"I was careful how I said it."

Felix's lip curled a touch. Were didn't like double talk.

"I believe in it and I'll push for it. But I'm going to have to go and explain it to Naryn after we're done here. Or even before we're done." I pulled my Altau cell and looked at the screen, but it was still blank. On Bian's advice, I was waiting on a summons from Naryn.

He grunted. "Well then, what did you want to talk to me about?"

"It's about the rogue. Who he or she might be."

"And the reason this has to be secret?"

"It could be anyone. Even him." I jerked my head at Leatherface.

Felix looked to see if I was serious and gave a half laugh.

I preferred him angry rather than amused and dismissive, but that might come soon enough.

"You think it's not a Were because of the increase in size, the lack of Call, the lack of marque," I said.

He nodded. "And the length of time. A rogue escalates much quicker than your list of victims has been accumulating. The rogue spends too much time in the wolf, and the wolf is mad. The madness bleeds back into the human. It would be noticeable. He couldn't hide that." He juggled a stone from hand to hand. "The bites? Well, as your little spy pointed out, anyone could make a device that mimics a bite. And the pattern of bites is not what you'd expect from a rogue attack."

"But you don't think it's a human?"

"This level of ability to escape detection? No. I think it's an Adept using his powers somehow. Maybe even being paid by the Confederation to destabilize us."

"It doesn't seem like a very effective destabilization tactic. You didn't even notice it happening until I told you about it." Felix didn't like me pointing that out. "You'd think those alleged Adepts would have moved on to a different plan long before now," I went on. "No. I think it's a Were. But not a rogue in the usual sense."

"What other 'sense' is there?" Felix turned to look directly at me. His face didn't change, but there was the wolf, just under the skin.

And I was trying to convince a werewolf who was over a hundred and fifty years old that there were things about Were psychology he hadn't considered.

"Felix, have you ever heard of a sociopath becoming a werewolf?"

His eyes went flat and golden, but then he turned away and looked over the stream for a long time.

"No," he said finally. "But we don't become, we're made. Who would have done that?"

"Who would know?" I countered. I'd been doing some research. "Among humans, they might be as much as 4% of the population, but most people would never believe that. Part of the deal we make with society is that the rules become subconscious. But that means when we come across someone who behaves completely outside the rules, we can't believe it. We refuse to believe it."

"So, you're saying we could have a sociopathic werewolf in the pack. Someone who's learned how to lie convincingly, even to me."

He'd understood immediately where I was going with it. Did that mean he thought it was possible? His face gave no sign either way, but the tone of his voice wasn't encouraging.

"I'm saying it's a possibility I have to investigate."

"What about the growth in size?"

"Could be measurement error, considering the level of decomposition in some of those bodies. Or, the growth could be coming from an increase in dominance."

"I'd notice an increase in dominance." Felix smiled thinly.

"Maybe. And maybe not, if the sociopath didn't want you to." I sighed. "I know it sounds crazy, I know I'm talking to a long-established alpha, but I've studied this."

Not quite a lie, but certainly fudging the truth. I'd had a little training in the army and I'd read some articles in preparation for talking to him. I wanted to see if I could lie to Felix, and if he could tell I was doing it.

So far, no reaction, so I pushed it further. "In fact," I went on, "I have a diploma from an online college."

Complete lie. But if he sensed it, Felix made no sign.

I picked up a stone and threw it at another crow who was looking to land. *The pack can't lie to the alpha.* So did this mean I wasn't pack? Or just that I was a stronger alpha than Felix? I'd never felt anything for Felix that resembled what I thought a Were should feel for their alpha.

"I'm not promising anything," he said, "but what do you want from me?"

"A list of members of the pack."

"What would you do with it?"

"Cross check against known and potential victims. Places of work, addresses, club memberships. Standard investigative work. Unless it turns up something more significant. Then what we do depends on what we've found."

"You realize the damage you're doing to the pack? The damage you will do if you're right?"

"I'm not trying to damage the pack, and what I might do is nothing compared to what would happen if the rogue is caught by the FBI."

He stood and looked thoughtfully at the stream for a minute.

"Do you feel Were?" he said. His voice was neutral, just asking the question, but the weight of the feeling behind it was intense.

"I feel part Were," I replied.

He shook his head. It felt like I'd misunderstood, or answered the wrong question. "Think about being a Were for a moment. What does it feel like?"

I tried. I closed my eyes. The memory that popped into my head was before Alex had infused me. It was from the evening after I'd first been up to Bitter Hooks. I'd wanted to go back up there and run naked through the pine forests, howling at the moon. I smiled. Maybe I would, one day soon.

"Cool." As soon as I said it, the word seemed too light, but just as I'd felt I'd gotten the last answer wrong, Felix seemed pleased with my response this time.

"Let's get back," he said finally.

We walked into the woods again, Leatherface trailing behind.

I found the little cemetery preying on my mind and I was never one for subtle. "Can I ask why you never remarried?"

He frowned, concentrating on the uneven ground we were crossing. "No suitable female alphas in Denver. Has to be an alpha for the pack. Got offers from outside, but I trust 'em like I trust snake spit."

"That's rough." It hadn't occurred to me before. As alpha, he'd be bound by consideration for the pack in a choice as fundamental as who he could marry.

He cast a sideways glance at me. Was he able to sense what I felt, even if he couldn't tell if I was lying? Did that seem strange to him?

"What's our position with the pack at the moment?" I said to cover. "Alex and me?"

He scowled.

"The pack is disturbed. That's one reason why I agreed to go along with this hunt the way you're running it; you're keeping them occupied. Unfortunately, you're also acting like an alpha. You realize that you and Alex get their attention? Especially together."

"Not what we want—"

"What you and I want on a personal level isn't important to the pack."

I stopped him with a hand on his arm.

"Felix, I know you're not my alpha." I felt awful, as if it were some kind of betrayal. But it needed saying. "Never have been. But I will do everything I can to keep your pack stable."

"And what if the only way to keep it stable is to take over?"

"I don't want it. Neither does Alex."

He shook his head. "You just haven't tasted it yet. Like I said, the pack pushes things in certain ways."

"I can hardly understand what you want. When you start talking about what the pack wants, I feel like it's a different language. One I can't speak."

"You're right there." He loomed over me. "It's not simple and easy like you want it to be. When you hunted up in Commerce, you felt the Call?"

"Yeah."

He grunted. "That's the language you need to learn. I can't explain it with words, but let's try this; have you given an Athanate oath yet, 'on my Blood'?"

"I have."

"Felt it, didn't you? Just like you feel Skylur's right to be head of Altau. His right to receive your loyalty."

"Yes."

"The House is held together by bonds. The Athanate to each other and the House, the kin to the Athanate. You share Blood. With the Blood comes the marque. For outsiders, that makes the House distinct. For insiders, it's what binds it together. The marque requires the members of a House to act for the good of the House."

I shivered. This was close what Vega Martine had said to me before the Assembly, trying to stop me from allying myself with Altau—*the marque knows about need*. I rejected her argument that made us simply pawns of the marque. The marque existed because of us, not the other way around. But my counter-argument was more faith than logic.

"That's like the Call. The pack is held together by bonds, and the Call is how we feel it. The Call requires us all to act for the good of the pack."

He turned abruptly on his heel and walked off. I had to jog to catch up.

"Alexander's an alpha, whether he wants it or not. I've managed to ignore the tension caused by him being in the pack, but I can't ignore the pair of you. From the point of view of the pack, it's like a challenge that I'm refusing. The Call will demand a resolution. If it doesn't come from me, then from the others."

We came out from the pines and continued down towards the ranch house.

I stopped him again. I was having enough trouble making sure I understood without having to trot alongside him.

"So, even though we're not challenging, you're saying either you deal with it as if we are, or someone inside the pack will challenge you. And then they'll deal with it."

"If they win."

"If they lose?"

"Another, and another. But it won't come to that. The Confederation would be in here taking advantage long before that. They'd just scoop the whole pack up under a new alpha, or split it into a couple of packs, north and south. And they'd make it work. They might split the territory. They'd lose half the pack in fights, but what would they care?"

His face was bleak, and the cold, hard reality of what he was saying chilled me.

"No alternatives?"

"There are. Here's one; you leave Denver, with or without Alex."

He might not be able to tell I was lying, but he could read the instinctive, angry rejection that flared up in me.

He nodded, as if he'd expected exactly that.

The sun had been up long enough to take the chill off the air, but the breeze whispering out from the pines was still cold as a mountain spring.

Felix's eyes flickered off to the left; the little cemetery enfolded in its green arms, the yew trees that spoke of life and not death.

Something wounded passed behind his eyes. He reached and took my hand between his.

My breath caught in my throat.

"Or you could marry me, Amber."

Crap! Not what I was expecting.

I didn't trust my voice, but I could see he knew my answer from his eyes.

After a moment more, he dropped my hand and started walking again.

I stood still in shock for a minute longer. Nothing had changed. The same breeze flowed down the mountain, the same flowers nodded in the beautiful little cemetery. It felt like something had been looking at me, and I hadn't noticed until now, when it stopped.

A large bird, a hawk probably, passed overhead, making the sun blink, before he turned and soared down the valley, barely moving his wings.

Leatherface walked past, slowly, not looking at me.

I followed Felix into the ranch house and found him in his den, staring out the window.

"What makes it impossible for us to be a separate pack in Denver?" I said.

"I don't know," he replied. "But you risk everything trying to persuade the whole pack to accept you in their domain."

He held up a USB.

"This is a list of the pack," he said, turning to loom over me again. "You swear it would not be used to harm the pack?"

"I swear." That didn't work; it sounded flat. I lifted my head and looked him in the eye, alpha to alpha. "I swear, on my Blood, I will not use this to harm the pack in any way."

A ripple passed over his face and the wolf stared out at me.

I could feel my own wolf stir in response.

"We walked a mile today." His voice was low, almost a growl. "Not in each other's shoes, but still, we have a better understanding, you and I. None of which will make any difference if it comes to it, and the Call presses us to fight. We will both do what we have to. But if you misuse this information, I will hunt you down and kill you."

"I understand," I said, my voice husky.

The USB dropped into my hand.

Leatherface was waiting outside the front door, the shotgun still resting against his shoulder. I headed down the steps and he matched pace with me, wordlessly, kinda like an escort. Was he seeing me off the premises?

At the car, he nudged the tire with his foot.

"City tire," he said. His voice was creaky as old pine in a wind. He squinted northwards. "Big snow coming."

"Thanks...uh, no one's told me your name."

"Duane."

"Okay, thanks Duane, I'll put winter tires on." It was too early for snow, but yeah, winter is coming. Where had I heard that?

He nodded. "This weekend." He turned and walked back up to the farm buildings.

Chapter 43

"You sure about this?"

Melissa had persuaded me that this might yield a vital lead. I liked the look of the bar about as much as I liked the thought of kissing a rabid dog. It was a step above drinking in an alley from a bottle in a paper bag, but only one step. It was in northwest Denver, between where the quiet residential areas stopped and the sleek commercial zone started, and it was neither quiet nor sleek. The solid iron frames over the windows gave away the locals' favorite after-hours hobbies.

Melissa peered around nervously, then back at me. She seemed to take comfort from my presence.

"I'm sure the address is right," she said. "And it's the right name."

"Hmm. Okay, let's do it. Stick close."

We stepped inside, and Melissa stumbled as her eyes tried to adjust to the gloom.

I saw people as warm bodies, surrounded by a haze. Good enough; I didn't want to stand there looking out of place, so I moved forward, my hand on Melissa's back.

The place smelled of stale beer. That was good; there were no Were or Athanate marques. All I had to look out for were Nagas and random jerks.

The central bar and the pool table were lit, but the rest of the room was in shadow.

A couple of men tried halfhearted comments as we made our way to the bar, but this was a serious drinking place, even at midday. I ignored them and they went back to talking to their glasses.

I saw a biker sporting his gang colors, the eagle and capital A of the Sons of Silence, but he was here with his girl and probably just scouting. The disappearance of so many ZK bikers had probably left a bit of a vacuum in bars like this, and gangs would be putting out feelers.

Clayton, former Detective in the Denver PD, was sitting about halfway down the bar, head in his hands. A folded newspaper was at his elbow, but he wasn't reading now. He was staring deep into his rotgut. There were no answers there, but to be fair, there wouldn't have been answers in a glass of water either. And from the look of him, I wasn't sure how interested he was in finding answers anymore. We'd probably wasted our time coming here.

I let Melissa past and took a better look at the other men in the bar. No one set off any alarms, but a couple of them were staring at us with enough interest that they rated designations. Okay. Batshit 1 and Batshit 2.

Clayton sensed Melissa and his head twisted around. His eyes narrowed.

"Owen," he said after a pause. "You look different."

At least he wasn't incomprehensible drunk.

"You always did say the nicest things," Melissa said.

"Yeah. What I shoulda said was you gotta great new hairdo and how good it makes you look and shit like that." He took a shot of his drink. "Truth is, you look older."

"Truth is, you look worse than I do, Clayton."

He laughed. The sort of breathy laugh that doesn't take too much effort. "You're right. I look like shit." His head tilted and he looked at me from beneath heavy lids. "Who's GI Jane here?"

I smiled and leaned against the bar. He was still sharp enough to spot that. Maybe not time wasted.

"Farrell's a PI," Melissa said. "I'm working with her."

The bartender wanted us to drink something. I wasn't as tough as I once was; I doubted I could stomach what they called rum here anymore. Not after sampling Jen's drinks. They had Pabst on tap, but instead I got a couple of bottles of Fat Tire beer for us to chew on.

Clayton was frowning at his drink. "Farrell. Farrell. Heard something."

"People come and talk?" Melissa was interested. She meant people from the force.

He nodded. "Time to time. Old cases. New scuttlebutt. Always was a good listener. Got nothing much else to do now."

I stuck the neck of the bottle in my mouth before my demon said something about destructive self-pity. I hadn't been there; it wasn't my place to judge.

"So what brings a forensics star and a yellow ribbon PI to talk to me?"

He knew. Through the bleary eyes and the fog of drink gleamed a hard, calculating mind. In the way of these things, that clever mind twisted back on itself. We weren't his drinking buddies and we weren't down here to shoot the breeze. It followed we wanted to talk about an old case, and in his mind there could be no other case than the one that had sunk him. His very own Moby Dick.

"Your last case."

"Figures," he said. "You want to talk about what I got nothing to say about."

"Come on, Clayton. Loosen up," I said. "We're not Internal Affairs. We're not here to hash over the fallout. We want to talk about the case."

Melissa had briefed me as much as she could.

Clayton had been highly rated in the PD, until he'd gotten his teeth into the same line of questioning as Melissa. Over the course of a couple of years, he'd squeezed in extra work on a number of unsolved murders among the poorest section of the Denver community: the homeless, the institutionalized. He'd managed to overcome suspicions and had interviewed dozens of people that the original investigating officers hadn't had time for.

It was regarded as a harmless eccentricity. It raised the profile of the PD in a section of society where it was needed. No one complained, except possibly his wife.

Then, out of the blue, a prostitute he'd interviewed had accused him of rape. It was credible enough, but it depended almost entirely on the woman's testimony. And the day before it was due to be heard, she'd disappeared.

He'd claimed that he must have gotten close to someone who knew the truth behind the murders, and that he'd been framed because of it. His contacts in the community refused to talk to him anymore. The department had reinstated him, but not everyone bought his story. He ignored orders about which cases to work on. He ignored pleas from his wife and remaining friends to get back on track. He obsessed about the murders and the supposed conspiracy to derail his investigation.

'Delusional' got entered into his psych report, and finally lost him his badge.

And his wife divorced him.

"You can't talk one without the other," he said. "That's what IA wanted to do."

"I'm betting, if the person who framed you was on your list of suspects, you had a hunch about who it might be." Melissa took a sip of her beer. "Why isn't there anything about that in the report?"

"Because you don't do that without proof, and I couldn't get the proof." She'd managed to needle him enough for him to sit up and glare at her. But I liked him a lot more after hearing that.

"You didn't even talk to your partner about it?" I asked.

"My 'partner' wasn't talking to me. The bastards gagged him. Said he might have to be a witness against me." He slumped forward again with a muttered "Ah, shit."

I leaned across the bar. "There's a new angle you haven't heard about."

I thought for a moment we'd lost him, but his head tilted up enough for me to see a frown deepen the creases of his forehead.

"What?"

"Melissa's been suspended for following in your footsteps."

He raised his head to look at her. "Idiot," he mumbled.

"If we can get her back, we can get you back," I said.

He shook his head. "Oh, I don't doubt you'd try." He was frowning again. "Farrell. Yes, that was it. They didn't get to suspend you, did they? Didn't get the chance."

"Not relevant," I said.

"I never make snap decisions about relevance. Bit twitchy about it, are you?" He laughed. "This is getting like a club for former employees of the law."

I'd just about reached the end of my patience, but Melissa sat alongside him and gave him the rundown on what she'd looked at and why. He kept his head down, but he nodded now and then, between drinks. Whatever he said, he was still interested.

I got us all another round to stop the bartender from hassling us.

He didn't say anything when she finished, but she'd gotten him thinking about it again. It wasn't for long though.

"You tell me something, Farrell." He took a swallow of his rotgut. "All that talk about military experiments gone wrong. You one? You leap tall buildings? Bend metal bars with your bare hands?"

"I'm not a military experiment. If I were, they'd keep a better hold of me."

"Heh! That they would. But I recall now, you went into that building alone, against three guys with shotguns. They're dead and you didn't get a scratch. Don't look like Supergirl."

"I'm not Supergirl, either." I leaned closer again. I had his attention, held his eyes. "The truth is even stranger than that. But the problem with knowing that truth about me is you can't do anything with it. We can do things with your truth, maybe even nail the killer that no one else believes in."

Clayton's eyes lost their focus. For a second, I was worried that he was about to pass out, even though he didn't seem that drunk. But it wasn't that. He was seeing things.

"Oh, they believe all right," he whispered. "Some of them. But a case with a profile like that and no end in sight? They don't want that."

Okay, so he had a beef against the police and the city. It wasn't surprising, but it wasn't going to get us any further in a hurry.

"So your evidence wasn't good enough to close the case?"

"Would've got it," he said angrily. "I was that close. Just a little longer. That's what they didn't believe. That's when they pulled my badge."

I edged in past Melissa, so I was right in his face, eyeball to eyeball.

"Close to who?"

"Trail's cold," he said.

He stank of rotgut. He was leaking it like an old wooden barrel, his staves loosened from too many knocks, his hoops rusted and eaten away by the acid inside him. His breath, his sweat, his clothes—the rotgut permeated everything about him. But deep inside all of that…

"Come on," I coaxed him. His knowledge was like a splinter embedded in his head. It just needed teasing out. "You can tell me. You trust me. You know—"

"Amber. *Amber!* "

I blinked. Melissa's hand was tugging at my arm.

Crap. What the hell was I doing?

Clayton was sitting there like I'd hit him. His mouth was open and his eyes glazed.

I'd just been halfway to compelling him. Was it justified?

No.

I stood back and folded my arms to hide the shiver. Looked anywhere but at Clayton.

We didn't need Clayton. Like he said, his trail was cold. And I didn't need to do it this way, because if I started, where would I be when I stopped?

"We'd better go," I said.

Clayton kept giving his head little shakes as Melissa and I left.

Chapter 44

I dropped Melissa back at Manassah and headed out to the area I had assigned to Nick Gray—South Platte and West Evans.

I wanted to check on him, both his strange marque and his method of searching.

I figured if he was that good, he might find me before I found him. I wasn't going to spend the afternoon chasing him, but a half hour would be interesting. Then I'd call him.

It didn't take a half hour.

He called me on my cell.

"You wanting to meet?"

"Yeah. Coffee break."

He snorted. "Back across the river. Corner of South Broadway and Washbrook. Clipper Café."

He was already there when I went in.

I collected a mocha and a fruit salad for lunch, and a tiny slice of walnut cake, before joining him at the table.

He was drinking espresso. The fresh-ground coffee smells tamped down his unusual marque, but if he'd chosen this place to hide it from me, he'd miscalculated.

"Looks like you've already solved the Matlal Were problem," he said.

"There are still six missing."

The waitress interrupted us with an all-day breakfast for him.

"They'll either return to the place you've got staked out or they'll be gone," he said, once she was out of hearing.

"Gone? Where?"

He tilted his head towards the west and the Rockies. "Running."

"Freaking ace. Rogue werewolves in the mountains?"

He frowned as if I'd disappointed him. "What did the Matlal Were say about the missing ones? Their exact words?"

I had to think about it. "They said they were going wild."

"Not rogue, then. Going to the wolf, they call it in the north. Not wanting to change back."

"Well, that's all right then. Just six wolves the size of freaking ponies lurking in the mountains."

He smiled thinly. "There are ways to deal with that. But not Verano's way."

He didn't like Verano, but this was something more.

"What do you mean?"

"Verano would simply want to hunt them with rifles."

"And you?"

"There are places in the north where they could just be wolves. I'd be willing to transport them."

"Whoa. Slow down here." I shook my head. "We're working for the Denver pack. That's not what they want. And remember, these guys were working for Matlal."

"Both of which didn't stop you from saving the lives of those you sent off with the Confederation."

"It was a gut feeling," I said. "Dumb luck it turned out okay."

"I don't think luck had anything to do with it, and gut feelings need to be listened to."

"I didn't come here to get your validation," I snapped. I was being an ass, but he was making me uncomfortable. Why had I done it that way? Yes, it'd kept it all quiet, which an all-out firefight wouldn't have. But something more: I wasn't happy with the thought that they all had an automatic death sentence hanging over them just for being in a pack that had been taken over by Matlal.

Maybe passing them to the Confederation had just avoided responsibility for killing them. I wasn't happy with that either.

He was watching me closely. Time to get on the front foot.

"What I came down here for was to find out a bit more about you. How a Were ends up solo, and with such an interesting marque."

He grinned. "Yeah, I understand it's something special, isn't it?" Something shimmered in his marque, quickly hidden. I couldn't put my finger on what made his marque so unusual. The scent was lighter than the Denver pack, but that wasn't it. The telergic part, the eukori, didn't give me an image like Alex, or Felix for that matter. Gray's was like his name, gray. It was closed, as if it hid something. I wondered what his wolf looked like.

"And talking of unusual," he jabbed his fork at me, "can't recall ever coming across an Athanate-Were-Adept before."

The casual way he said it hit me. The Were and Athanate knew I was a hybrid, but only Adepts had been able to see that I had a claim to be Adept as well. And here he was, talking as if it were only slightly out of the ordinary.

"I don't think that's relevant at the moment," I said.

He tilted his head. "Yeah, maybe not. On either side. We need to concentrate on the Matlal Athanate and the rogue."

"For now." I was not letting him off the hook, but he had a point.

He finished his brunch and pushed the plate aside.

"What about the Athanate we find?" he asked. "You going to kill them all?"

"That's Bian's decision."

"That's avoiding responsibility."

It stung. I hadn't been happy with this at all, but who the hell was he to point it out to me? Anger sparked like a faulty engine. The strongbox creaked and I shuddered as I pushed it closed. I couldn't afford to lose it here.

His dark eyes were on me, and I felt they missed nothing of my inner struggle, but his face stayed expressionless.

"What if there are one or two who're trying to get away from Basilikos? Is it just easier to kill them all?" He wasn't going to put this aside.

"It's not a matter of being easy."

Images of Larry surfaced. He'd been part of House Romero and compelled to work with Matlal. And he'd saved my life at the cost of his own. How would I have felt if he'd been grouped together with the rest of them?

"So you'd contemplate judging it on an individual basis?"

"Yes. No! I can't make that decision. I have to defer to Altau." I couldn't afford to piss off Bian the way I'd managed with Naryn.

"Defer to Bian?" Gray asked.

"Yes. Look," I said, "you're a bounty hunter. Why are you concerned with this?"

He ignored that. "What would you and Bian judge to deserve death?"

"If they've gone rogue," I said. "If they're actively working against Altau. Harming innocent bystanders. Feeding on their toru."

"Or marai," he said quietly. "True Basilikos make no distinction between the toru they keep as Blood slaves, and the marai, the rest of the population."

I acknowledged the point. "Why are you so concerned?" I asked him again.

"Because I'm not a bounty hunter in the way Verano is. I find paranormals, I even kill them sometimes, but I don't enjoy it. For those I don't kill, I care what happens to them afterwards. Like you do."

The waitress came and refilled our coffee.

Did he know something about Larry? I hadn't told anyone, had I?

"Tell me," he said.

I wanted to. I wanted someone else to know what Larry had done and how he'd died. To stand witness with me. To share the weight of the memory.

What the hell?

I dug my heels in. I'd explain it to Diana, along with everything else. Not to the first apparently sympathetic ear that came along.

I cleared my throat. "Which leaves us the rogue."

He raised his eyebrows. He'd been expecting me to talk. "Which leaves us with the rogue," he echoed.

There was something about the way he said the word rogue. "You have something to say about that too?"

"Not a werewolf. Or not just a werewolf." He ran a hand over his face. "I can feel him out there, and whatever he is doesn't feel like any other Were I've come across."

I leaned over the table.

"Not just a werewolf, eh? Who does that make me think of? Tell me, Mr. Gray, what are you and exactly how are you doing your searches?"

"You'll tell me what you were thinking of when we spoke about Basilikos Athanate. I'll tell you how I work. We'll both keep each other's secret."

His voice was flat, uninflected. He hadn't asked a question, he'd simply stated the terms.

Why should I trust him? My gut said I already did. Why? Was he messing with my head?

My cell buzzed. Altau's switchboard.

Naryn. At the worst possible moment.

"I gotta take this outside," I said. "Don't go."

I walked out.

"Yes?"

"It's me, not Naryn chasing you."

"Hi, Bian. That's a relief. Sort of."

She laughed.

"It must be your lucky day, but only today. Skylur's still in LA, but the exchange of prisoners with Basilikos had to go ahead, so Naryn's in New York and he won't be back until tomorrow. He wants you here at 4 p.m."

"This is lucky?"

"He gets more time to calm down, and Skylur might be back."

"Okay, lucky. Have you got time for me to check a few things with you?"

There were noises in the background that got cut off as Bian closed a door.

"Go ahead."

"Athanate in Denver: All the Houses that were here for the Assembly are gone, and all Altau are out at Haven?"

"Yes to both."

"Then in Denver itself, there's me, David and Pia, and possibly some Matlal Athanate."

"As far as I know. What's up?"

"Y'know, Adepts say they can sense Athanate?"

"Yeah, but not the likes of little chicks like you and me."

"Skylur, Diana, maybe Naryn?"

"Yeah. All three."

"None of the Matlal Athanate are close to that, are they? Alice Emerson would have told you if they were, and you wouldn't have me chasing them."

"Yeah. Why?"

"Gray's implying he can sense the rogue. He's not getting it mixed up with some major-league Athanate, so I've got to assume there's something to it. What the freaking hell is he? And what is he sensing?"

There was a silence from the other end.

"I don't know, Round-eye. As far as the Dakota House is concerned, he's a Were. I'll ask Alice if there's some Adept ritual he could have picked up that would help him sense marques remotely. Alice can't pick them out at any great distance, or we'd use that somehow. Hold on." I could hear her speak to someone else in Athanate. She seemed as busy as ever—of course with Naryn and Skylur gone, she'd be running the show at Haven. "Sorry, I should have done a bit more checking before taking him on. Is there a specific problem?"

"I don't know. Not on the rogue maybe. On the Matlal Athanate, he's saying that we should take them as individual cases, and maybe not kill all of them."

"I understand the point, Amber, but we don't have the resources."

I didn't like that. It didn't seem right. But this wasn't the time to lose friends at Haven. I kept quiet.

"Gotta go. Talk later," she said.

"Bye."

Back in the café, the table was empty. There was a slip of paper under my coffee mug with 'talk tomorrow' scrawled on it.

"Your boyfriend's gone," the waitress said sympathetically. "Did pay the bill though. Puts you way ahead of me, hon."

∞ ∞ ∞ ∞ ∞

"Hello?" Mary answered her cell cautiously. I was still using different cells to call people. I had no idea what resources the Nagas and the Matlal Athanate might have, but I didn't want any chance of them chasing me down through my cell calls.

"Mary, hi, it's Amber. I have a question."

"Only one?" she said and laughed. "Go on."

"When we met at the Café Vienne, a couple of weeks ago, you remember you spoke about sensing other users of the energy in Denver. You said it was like people on a trampoline, you can feel big users."

"Yeah, yeah. Not a very good image, but it'll do."

"You can tell the difference between types?"

"Between Adepts and others. Where are you going with this?"

"Can you still feel the other types in Denver?"

"Yes, from time to time. Less than when we spoke."

"What if they're outside of Denver?"

"I only sense up to five miles or so. Why?"

"Mary, there are no major-league Athanate in Denver at the moment. If you're sensing something now, you know it's not Adept and we know it's not Athanate. Where does that leave us?"

Her voice was slow and thoughtful. "A Were who's gone beyond just using the energy intuitively." She paused. "Is this anything to do with the person who broke into your car?"

"Yes."

"What's going on, Amber?"

All the paranormal communities were trying to hide their secrets from each other. I was sick of it and beyond being tactful.

"There's a rogue Were in Denver. Been here a while. The Were are trying to tell me it isn't Were. Athanate say it can't be Athanate. I'm sure you'll tell me it can't be an Adept. All I have is a growing body count, and a guy who says he's a Were *and* that he can sense the rogue."

"Oh."

I could almost hear the wheels turning.

"We'll need to talk about this, Mary. I gotta ask this guy a few more questions first. When I can find him again."

I ended the call. I had to go. I was late again.

Chapter 45

Doc Noble was waiting outside Alex's house for our first session.

I'd refused a list of other places. I didn't want to go to his office. That felt a little too much like I was admitting I was crazy. And I really didn't want anyone else in Manassah. I couldn't say why I got such a reaction from the thought. I was happy for Bian to visit, and Tullah, and Olivia. I hadn't had much of a problem with Ricky. I just didn't want any more of the Denver pack there.

What did that say about me and the pack?

He'd been insistent on meeting, even with everything else going on. If it were purely about keeping me sane while the hunt went on, maybe I'd have refused. But the rogue was a Were. I needed to understand the Were to make sure no clue slipped by me.

And on the pack side, maybe I'd get more insight into why I was such a problem for them—not just the issue with Felix and being alpha, but the territoriality and everything that went with it.

Doc was pacing in front of the door and talking on his cell. A frown creased his forehead, but he was talking calmly and firmly. A telephone consultation, maybe. He waved me on and held up his free hand with fingers outstretched. Five minutes, I guessed. Or some Trekky greeting I hadn't caught up on.

I went in and made coffee. Mistake. When he bustled in, he practically tore it from my hands.

"No; it's a stimulant."

"But it's one of my major food groups."

"Heat it up afterwards," he said.

I felt the wolf growl inside me. Noble felt it too, and it made him pause.

"Sorry," I muttered, and pushed it all back down.

He recovered and took the cup back to the kitchen. I turned on my heel and went to the living room.

We sat in recliners opposite each other. There was a sofa, but I wasn't going to lie down and he didn't insist. He did get me to tilt mine back while he sat upright, scribbling in his notebook.

"This is a session purely to form a basis for progressing," he said. "I don't want to get into anything stressful or private, but I don't know what might constitute that for you, so please keep directing me. I will ask only general questions about how you feel about being Athanate and Were. In turn, ask me questions about the pack or what it means to be a Were and I will answer as fully as I can. I shall not attempt to hypnotize you, but I will from time to time suggest relaxation. Maybe we should start there. Tell me the things you have done to relax."

I cringed and we were away. Once I had persuaded him I was relaxed, I was allowed to ask a question. Just as he was trying to get me to open up, I was trying it with him, so the first one had to be something he was expecting. And it was vital to me.

"So how do you control changing to wolf?"

"The first few times, you'll find it frightening. Like the wolf is clawing to get out. The wolf is scared as well, so you emerge into wolf form in an excited state. This is where having the pack around you helps. You will sense them—"

"Like the Call?"

"Exactly. The Call will calm you, bring you into the pack gently. Then, when you're accustomed to changing, and don't need the pack so much, you'll find a little mental routine that works for you. Many of the pack close their eyes and imagine their wolves running. Then they imagine flying behind them, closer and closer. They describe it as similar to a water slide, a falling sensation, then the sharp level out and suddenly shooting forward, into the wolf."

"That's it?"

"Unless you fight against the change. Then, it's back to the wolf tearing its way out."

"And what about getting back to human?"

"Again, the first few times you may panic and it's as if the human is tearing itself out of the wolf. You'll get over this. The common little mental trick a lot of the pack use is to imagine standing and stretching up. It becomes that easy."

"What if the pack aren't around to help when you change? You must have had that experience."

I could hear him stir uncomfortably in his chair and there was a pause before he answered. "Personally, I had a blackout, probably brought on by the stress and fear. You will at least know what is happening, so that may not apply."

"Okay, so make sure I'm away from people if I get into that situation."

"Hmm."

"Does anyone ever become locked in the wolf? Go wild?"

"Yes. I speculate that it is voluntary. That they simply do not wish to return. But it would be a little difficult to get answers at that stage."

I snorted. "Any from the Denver pack?"

"Not to my knowledge."

I was supposed to be pumping him for knowledge about the pack, but this personal stuff was too interesting to stop while he was answering.

"What about while you're in wolf form? What does it feel like?"

"Dreamlike. Different things are vivid and important when you're wolf; like a dream, they make sense to you while you dream. It's all very immediate."

"Like a child? The past and the future are blurry and the present is very focused?"

"Exactly! Is this something from the Athanate side you can describe for me?"

The eagerness in his voice was kinda sweet. He was a small, academic sort of guy who'd wandered by accident into a pack full of jocks. He said the crucial characteristic of the Were was enthusiasm, and I guessed that pursuit of knowledge was where he found an outlet for his.

"A little," I said. "Remember, I haven't progressed to full-on biting and drinking Blood. I found I feel slightly disconnected from everything, but very aware and focused. Things feel like they happen in slow motion. There isn't any ritual about the fangs as far as I can see. At first, it was just a sort of ache in the jaw. Now there's a definite thrill and my jaw feels different. I can only describe it as feeling loose."

I could hear the hurried scratch of his pen on his notepad.

"An anticipation of pleasure?"

"Yeah." With my recliner laid back, I hoped he couldn't see me blush.

"Do other factors in your life influence the Athanate?"

This felt too close for comfort.

"Everything," I said shortly.

"Leading to loss of control?"

Much, much too close. "It might." I stirred uncomfortably and I guessed he saw that, but he kept on.

"Now, I understand you felt the Call, so you have progressed on the Were side even if you haven't changed. What about the two together? How do they affect each other? Does the more established Athanate control the Were?"

"If anything, they set each other off," I said. "But I feel I understand the Athanate more. I guess I might be more able to control that rather than the Were."

Enough.

I pulled the recliner upright. "But I still don't understand the *why* about wolves."

A flicker of irritation passed over his face, followed by a rueful smile. "Well, we better feed your curiosity first, otherwise I'm not going to get you to relax at all. What do you mean?"

"Sorry, Doc. Look, the scientists at the army base had a long look at me, and they're sure the active parts of the Athanate 'Blood' are proteins, linked together in strings."

"Like prions?" he said.

Of course a doctor would know the terminology.

"Yes, in fact, that's what they call them. Part of the reason humans haven't discovered Athanate before is that prions have been so difficult to isolate and analyze."

He shrugged. "It's possible. I still don't follow how you get from there to 'the why about wolves'."

"Ah. Okay, here's the link—the instrument they designed to measure prions in my body also detects similar proteins, and it says the active parts of werewolf blood are prions as well."

Doc Noble went still. "That is…fascinating," he said thoughtfully.

"Bear with me. I can understand that prions in Athanate evolve, in exactly the same way humans evolved. The fittest—which means the ones that increased the chances of producing more of the same—they increased while other variants died out. So, Athanate today are the combinations of human and prion that are best at perpetuating Athanate. They keep themselves secret, because the Athanate that thought being open was a good thing were more likely to be killed by humans. And they bond with humans that provide Blood, because that's the best way to ensure they can remain hidden—"

"I understand evolutionary theory, Amber," he said patiently. "Even in this context. I'll agree that the Athanate represent a form that has evolved to survive and prosper in its niche."

"Right." I wondered at the sense of taking his valuable time up with my half-baked theories, but I'd come this far. "Then werewolves should show some similar evolutionary benefit. But I can't see it. And I can't see the mechanism."

"Werewolves have a pack structure," he said. "Social animals succeed where solitary animals have difficulty. That applies to the paranormal as well."

"Yeah, but why pick wolves? Why not lions? Why are there solitary werebears and weretigers? If I was a werebear I wouldn't go rogue, so why do I go rogue if I'm a werewolf and I leave a pack?"

"That I can't answer."

"Even more basic. How does a prion know anything about a wolf? Or a tiger? An animal is a complex organism and very different structurally. How do the prions know what to change the host body into?"

"How it all started, I don't know, but the wolf part of the DNA is part of the infusion, and the percentage difference between human DNA and wolf DNA is smaller than you may think. Twenty-five percent of the sequences are identical and the remainder derive differences from patterns rather than the constituents."

Never for one moment when I dropped out of school had I thought I would need PhD-level biology to understand things going on in my body.

A million questions clamored to be asked.

"What are DNA tests on a werewolf going to show? What are the FBI looking at now?" I asked. The tests that they must have done on the victims of the rogue at Wash Park would be in front of Griffith by now.

"The human DNA masks the wolf. It's still a human. An odd human, but not so odd that it will be casually discovered. If they become suspicious and reexamine it…" He shrugged and glanced at his watch. "I can see you need some general answers before we can get into the specifics. Trust me, I look forward to working with you in the future to discover the reasons behind everything you've mentioned, maybe even to find improvements and synergies." He cleared his throat. "However, my first task is to make sure that you're around for that, and in a state where you can contribute to the process. That means I have to keep you sane and functioning. I have to understand what's going on inside you." He frowned. "This has been…interesting, but not enormously useful for those goals. I can't allow this. We have a tough schedule."

"I'm sorry, it's like I overdosed on caffeine. Actually having someone answer questions has been different. Even if you couldn't answer them all, it's a start."

He hummed. "Still, next time I must insist on quiet and relaxation."

"I understand."

"Tomorrow?"

"There's a rogue to catch."

"How well will you do trying that, if you turn rogue in the meantime?"

"Not well, but how likely—"

"Very likely. You've confirmed my suspicions that your Were side influences the Athanate. All you need is one episode, one small thing that sets your Were off, and either you'll be coping with it, or you'll leave your Athanate to work it out." He peered at me. "Is this a sensible course of action?"

"No," I admitted.

"I will bring some suppressants." He held up his hand at my knee-jerk reaction. "Very mild, and probably very brief in their action, given your Athanate metabolism."

I wanted this like a hole in the head, but I'd wasted our time today. I needed him to get inside my head and help me. I nodded reluctantly.

"Good. I'll also try some more definitive hypnotic suggestions. These will work extremely gently, and for a limited time, but they will improve the speed at which we can arrive at some actions."

"I understand," I said. Crap. I didn't think I was going to do well with drugs or hypnotism, but I needed to try. I could feel the wolf stirring, but like the man said, we had a schedule to keep.

Chapter 46

I returned to a Manassah in chaos.

Jofranka's bicycle was propped up next to the front door. All the potted plants had been moved out of the way. Inside, the chairs in the hallway were covered in coats and jackets. It was a good thing no one ever used them to sit down on. And the rest of the hallway was packed with Melissa's CSI equipment. How the hell had it all fit in her small apartment?

I could hear Tullah and Jofranka talking to Matt and Melissa in the study. I'd let them finish and find me. Hopefully, I wouldn't be going out again tonight. Instead, I went to the living room and found Jen lounging on the sofa with a glass of brandy.

"Sorry about the mess," I said.

"Oh, the mess. S'okay. I have a solution." She waved her glass in the air.

"Brandy is the solution?"

She giggled. "Shut up and pour yourself a rum. Next door is the solution."

"How many brandies is that?"

"Why, are you going to play catch-up?"

"Can't." I touched the TacNet headset lying around my neck.

She pouted.

I got my rum and put it, along with the TacNet system, on a small table within easy reach.

Jen leaned against me with a sigh as soon as I sat down.

"Bad day?" I said, resting my cheek against the top of her head.

"Bad day at work. Not bad now. But…"

"Hmm?"

"I have to go to New York. The PR office there has some personnel problems."

"When?"

"Monday, early. We should be back late Tuesday."

"Okay. I'll need to arrange—"

"Nothing. Julie and Pia have done it already. Those women are stars." She sat up and swiveled her legs around on the sofa. "Bian's agreed to let a couple of her guys escort us to the airport. Tom and Paul?"

We couldn't do better than that for an escort. Those guys were top drawer, even if I had once taken them *and* two of their buddies out singlehandedly. "Okay. Who's going to New York?"

"Julie, of course, and Pia."

I took a sip of rum and let it tingle over my tongue. If Julie arranged this, it would all make sense and be safe. I just had to keep asking questions to confirm that.

"Pia's riding shotgun with Julie?"

"Ah, no. Pia's coming to work. Julie's providing security on the plane and then she contacted an old Ops 4-10 colleague in New York who does close protection. There'll be a team waiting for us."

Okay, I guessed I could let go of the security issue.

"Pia's going there to work?"

"Well, I couldn't have them sitting idly in my office. Neither of them have jobs, and—"

"Wait! *Them?*"

"Yes." Jen was enjoying herself. "The boy wonder is the best thing that's ever happened to my finance department. He not only understands all their jargon better than they do themselves, he understands it well enough to give it back to me in plain English."

"David?"

"Of course David! I needed a new Chief Financial Officer, after I fired Bernard. And somehow I can't see David stabbing me in the back like Bernard did."

I had always said that David was one of the smartest men I knew, and he'd proven himself to others. Why not Jen? It wasn't that I was disputing it, more that it all seemed so sudden.

"And Pia?"

"My new Human Resources Director." She laughed and ran her fingers back through her hair. "You have to admit, it's a hell of a benefit to have an Athanate running my HR. Let's see those bastards in New York try lying to her."

I felt as if the ship had left without me. It was ridiculous to say I should be controlling all these things, and yet it felt as if I'd lost control of them now.

"Honey, it just makes sense at the moment," Jen said. "If it doesn't at some point in the future, then we change it."

"And why is next door the solution?"

"Overflow. The neighbors have been trying to sell that place and it's a steal."

"But you shouldn't have to fix everything for me..."

"It isn't me fixing things for you. It's all of us fixing things for all of us. Each doing what we're good at." She tucked her legs underneath her and leaned toward me with the over-serious look of one too many brandies before dinner. "Like you charging in and rescuing me at Longmont."

"Hold on, Jen. You can't use that as justification for all the things you're trying to do: paying for the truck that was destroyed, employing David and Pia, buying a house next door." The house next door was a freaking mansion, for heaven's sake. This was getting out of control.

"Why not? I'm employing David and Pia to do jobs that need doing, so leave them out of it. And you, for that matter. You're still my firm's security consultant. Best man for the job." She giggled.

"Well, the rest of it."

"But I want to."

"That's no reason—"

"It is. It's a very good reason. Honey, everyone wants to be the heroine. You did that at Longmont—"

"You can't count that. You were kidnapped to get at me, so it was my fault, all of what happened. And that sort of mission is what I was trained for; the kind of unpleasant thing I have an aptitude for. Like I said before, I'm not a nice person."

She snorted. "Well, I have an aptitude for making money. That doesn't make me a nice person either. But it does give me what I need to make a difference now." She got up on her knees and pushed me back on the sofa so she could loom over me. "You were my heroine. Why won't you let me be yours?"

I swallowed. Between the tightness in my chest and the Athanate zing she was giving me, I had difficulty speaking. "You are already," I managed to say.

"Good. That's settled then," she purred and stretched, putting her empty glass down on the table.

Little Athanate pulses were throbbing along my jaw and straight down into my belly.

"Whoa, Jen."

"Hmm?"

"I'm getting fang warnings."

"And you promised this Diana person you'd wait. I know." She settled back on her heels with a sigh, and some of the pressure eased on me.

"It's not just that. It could be dangerous."

"Nothing you'd do would harm me. I just know."

No, she thought she knew. Our hearts had fallen into sync as soon as I sat down. We did it unconsciously now. The tentative touch of eukori followed just as naturally, without effort.

"I couldn't bear it if I did hurt you," I said.

I could feel that was only bittersweet to her.

"What?" I asked.

"I know we have to be careful, but you can't blame me for wanting more, honey." She sighed in frustration. "It's just you're so damned...strong. I've never met a less needy person."

"Huh?" I frowned.

"You like Manassah?" she said, holding her hands up to take in everything. "Clean and spacious. Comfortable beds, big, hot baths. Yes?"

"Of course, yes."

"But you can live out of the back of your car. Hell, you can live in the mountains. You can sleep in a cave and scrub up in glacier runoff. You can make your own fires out of pine cones and patience. And food. You like Carmen's cooking, but I bet you can live off bugs that you find under the bark of dead trees. You don't *need* any of this."

Yeah. I could do that, all of it. I guessed it was my fault for telling her about the survival courses that Ops 4-10 had put us through. But I still wasn't getting what she was driving at.

"You don't need any of it," she repeated. "But there's one thing you will need. Blood."

"But it's not like that—"

"I know. Really, I know. I'm being stupid, but gods, the kick I get from thinking you'll actually need something from me." She laughed and wiped a tear away. "Talk about my self-confidence taking a hit."

I pulled her around until she and I were curled up together like puppies.

"Me too," I said. "Because I do need you, even without the Blood."

Our eukori tangled.

"Like I need air," I whispered, and we both felt the rush of warmth through our bodies.

She kissed my neck. "Your Athanate happy-time pheromones are kicking in."

I smiled. "I wonder why." I leaned back and looked down at her. "You're not scared about being bitten at all?"

"Believe me, I've become an expert. I've talked to Irene and the twins, and Mykayla as well, just after Bian fed from her. Scared? Hell, no. Can't wait."

"You don't feel that's strange at all?" I said. "Not that it's something I've done with some kind of mind voodoo?"

She snorted. "You persuading me to change? Ha! Boot's on the other foot."

"What?"

"Thanks to Pia, I've also become something of an expert on what you've been going through in crusis. It's like a half-controlled mental breakdown. And while you were in this vulnerable state, you fell into my evil clutches. Mwa ha ha ha. I took advantage of you. I changed you. I'm the one who's done the voodoo."

"Ridiculous." I tried not to laugh.

"Only as ridiculous as you claiming you've done something to me. We both want things we might never have thought we wanted before we met."

"Hmm." I happily lost myself in her blue, blue eyes.

And David came in. "There you are. You wanted to see the analysis of the New York operation as soon as I was done."

Jen squeezed her eyes tight shut and clenched her jaw.

"Yes," she ground out.

"Boy wonder," I murmured.

"Boy blunder," she hissed and got up.

"Oh, and they taste like shit," I said.

"Huh?" She frowned.

"The bugs you find under the bark of dead trees. They taste like shit."

She laughed, tossing her golden hair back and trailing fingers over my cheek.

"I'll be back," she said, her eyes heavy with promise as she followed David out the door, passing Melissa and Tullah coming in.

"Did we disturb you?" Tullah said, eyes wide and innocent.

"Yes, I am disturbed. What?"

They sat down.

"We thought you'd want an update on today's searches," Melissa said.

"I do." I took a sip of my rum, and put my professional face on.

"Right." Tullah arranged the files in front of her. "Matt managed to get regional downloads from the national criminal databases, including recent searches based in Colorado."

I shuddered. Hacking the FBI. I didn't want to know how. "I hope this was well disguised."

"Yeah. The advantage should be there are no triggers on the servers that will tell Griffith who we're looking at or why. If he knows anything, it'll just be that there's been a leak of data."

That was one way of describing it.

"And it's just *full* of interesting hits," Melissa said. She picked up a printout and passed it to me. "We were talking about the rogue having access to a place in Denver registered under a different name. Well, one of the searches Griffith's team has been doing is to find ghosts."

"Ghosts?"

"People who have standard data on them, then nothing, or minimal data. Exactly the sort of search that threw your name up as an anomaly. You had plenty of data until you left school, then you joined the army and there's effectively no data on you for ten years." She wriggled with pleasure. "It's a fascinating search. It has all the missing women on my potential victim list, for example. Now, I put in some new filters on the list from stuff Matt was able to find. Home ownership in Denver, with the home still registered and taxes paid. No record of the house being rented out. No record of other people claiming to live at the house. Surprisingly large number of people."

"And then," Tullah interrupted, "we linked that with a list of houses that are known to have basements. After what Jo said about noise."

"Must still be a lot of matches," I said.

"No. There aren't many basements in Denver because of the soil type."

"And then the final filter I put on was for ease of access," Melissa said.

"How'd you mean?"

"Gated communities, for instance." Melissa handed over a single sheet of paper with about thirty addresses on it. "Obviously there are some huge assumptions in all of this, but we thought you'd want to treat these as a priority list for a check."

"I do." I passed my eyes over the list, but nothing leaped out. "So, you're saying the original owner of one of these houses may be a victim of the rogue. They've gone missing, but no one's followed up. The rogue has killed them and is using the ghost house, making sure bills are being paid and so on."

They nodded.

"Okay, I'll get them checked." I'd done enough PI work to know the first ideas usually came up blank, but I got a tingle from this. It felt right somehow. "What else?"

Melissa glanced at Tullah and sat back.

Interesting.

"We cross-checked everyone on the pack list with everything we could think of about the victims and potential victims." Tullah nervously tidied the file in front of her. "There aren't that many, but there are a lot considering that it should be a random selection."

"And they are?"

She cleared her throat. "Alex, for one."

I laughed. "Not the rogue, but what did you find?"

"Alex's company does deliveries to a lot of the hostels many of these people passed through. And Barbara Green did some casual work for the company last summer."

"Okay, it's something. But he's not the rogue. Neither is Ricky, nor Olivia. They were with me the night my clothes were stolen, remember?"

Melissa shifted her position. "Just as a theory, there could be two of them."

"You were telling me that one is statistically very unlikely, so two would be even more."

Tullah and Melissa glanced at each other and Tullah moved to the next sheet of paper.

Of course, Alex had left the restaurant for a short while that evening, saying he had to make a business call. Enough time to get to my car. But if my kin were the rogue, my world was going to come crashing down around me. I couldn't believe it.

"Larimer is a trustee for one of the charities that runs some of the hostels."

I nodded.

"Silas Falkner and Kyle Larsen live close to a couple of the hostels. They both do volunteer work in the area; the sort of work that would bring them into contact with these people."

I grunted. I didn't know Larsen. Silas, well—he seemed all too obvious as a candidate. But that was the rogue all over—hiding in plain sight.

"Ursula Tennyson."

"What about her?"

"She's a veterinarian, and she may have attended livestock for six of the missing women. Four of them kept horses for their own riding and another two had dude ranches. All six used Tennyson's business at some time. Now the business employs a couple of contract veterinarians, so it's not definite, but it's possible she met all six." Tullah handed me a file for Ursula with details of the six women, including copies of their photos.

A female rogue? Ricky and Alex had said there wasn't any gender bias in rogues.

"I'll ask her and see what response I get."

"She also has a criminal record," Melissa said. "She beat some guy senseless in a bar."

I looked at the sheet they'd printed. The details were scant and I could think of all sorts of good reasons for hitting guys in bars, but I'd check that as well.

Tullah handed me the last file. "The rest. Anyone with any criminal record. A scattering of assault, solicitation, DUI, minor misdemeanors."

I raised my brows. They'd turned up a lot of possibilities in a short time.

I was about to get myself another rum when the TacNet squawked.

"Charlie, this is V2. Sighting at trailer park. Looks like five of them. Need to wrap this up."

"V2, hold off, I say again, hold off."

One missing?

I grabbed the files, my gun and my jacket, and ran to the car.

Chapter 47

Inside the trailer, it was a like a scene from hell, side-lit with a single weak bulb.

The Matlal Were had been cornered inside and overwhelmed. Their bodies were hardly recognizable. They'd been big men, but the sheer ferocity of the attack and the choking weight of death seemed to have crushed them down into disconnected bags of torn meat and broken bone. The walls of the trailer were sprayed with arterial blood. The stench was gut-turning.

One had tried escaping through the window. His body had been dumped with the rest and cardboard was hastily taped over the hole. The trailer was at the back of the lot. There was a neighboring trailer occupied, and a couple who'd gotten curious were being held in there.

It was an absolute disaster.

And both Gray and Verano were here, their argument about to go supersonic.

They both outweighed me, but there was no time to think. I charged in between them. The cramped quarters gave me a small advantage. Verano fell back over a broken table, sprawling into the ruins.

Before he could get up or his team could respond, Ursula shouldered her way in, tipping the balance my way. I hoped.

I grabbed Gray's jacket.

"There's nothing you can do here. Get out."

The anger flaring in his eyes died down. I did the only thing I could think of and pulled out the list of ghost houses.

"These are top priority. I want them checked tonight for any sign of a marque or any suspicious activity. Go."

He hadn't helped here, but this carnage was caused by Verano's team.

Their leader was picking himself out of the wreckage of the table.

I helped him up by grabbing his jacket and lifting.

"What the hell did you think you were doing? I said to hold off."

Behind me I felt his pack edging forward, but I wasn't go to achieve anything by backing down now. Verano's eyes were still that icy green, but flecked with orange and yellow. I guessed that in another minute, he and Gray would have fought. What was wrong with them? Couldn't they see beyond the fallout we already had to deal with?

"They were going to go back out. We might have lost them. Why are you and Gray," he spat the name, "so bothered?"

"It's not up to you to wonder why. You're hired to do exactly as I told you, nothing more. I told you to hold off."

"They shifted. We had to."

"They shifted because you came swarming in here. What did you expect them to do?"

He didn't have an answer to that. His team had come in spoiling for a fight, otherwise they'd never have shucked and shifted quickly enough. And he was smart enough to know I knew that.

I was gambling on him being more interested in keeping his livelihood than playing dominance games with me. As far as he knew, I represented the only Athanate client in all of North America. He didn't dare fight me.

I won. I could see it in his body position.

"Get out," I said. "Get back to patrol and do not, I repeat, do not engage. You're there to find and report."

His head ducked a fraction. Stiff-necked bastard.

I let him gather his team and move.

"Is there someone from your team in the next trailer?" I asked Ursula.

She nodded. "Clean-up crew's coming too."

"Not going to be good enough," I muttered, and dug my cell out.

I left the trailer. I preferred the bitter cold to the smell inside.

"Bian?"

"Round-eye. What's up?" She could tell something was happening just from my voice. I really was barely holding it together.

"Five of the Matlal Were have been killed at the trailer park. The pack's clean-up crew are just about to get here, but there's a problem."

"Witnesses." She got it immediately. "Oh, shit."

"Yeah. Does your clean-up crew have someone who could handle a memory blanking?"

"Normally we would, but we're running on empty here. Crap. I can't even leave Haven. Amber, this is a bitch, but you're going to have to bring them in."

"For you?"

"Err...no. Naryn got back a few minutes ago."

"Shit."

"Yeah. Sorry, it's going to be another reason for him to be pissed, but he's the best we've got in the short term, and it's much better to do it quickly."

"I'll be there as soon as I can."

I ended the call and turned to see Ursula directing the pack's clean-up crew.

They drove unmarked green vans, and under the bulky parkas, they were wearing blue coveralls.

I walked up behind her. "Are these only used for clean-up?" I asked, pointing at the vans.

She looked down at me. In the darkness, her face was unreadable. "No. Sometimes they use them to ship fertilizer. I've used them to transport animals. Everyone in the pack can use them. Even just as moving vans."

"Who looks after them? Who books them in and out?"

"They move around. Mostly they're parked at one of the factories. We need them, we just call around till we find them. We don't keep sign-out sheets. We aren't Athanate. Why all the questions?"

"I'm going to have to find out who's had these out in the last week, but right now, I need two things at the same time. First, I need the couple in the next trailer to be tied up so they can't move, blindfolded and put in the back of my car. Can you get the pack to do that?"

"Where are you taking them?" she asked.

"To the Altau, to get their memory of tonight blanked."

She grunted and walked over to the second trailer. Instructions passed on, she returned.

"So, what else?"

"Let's get in my car, out of the wind."

We climbed in and I put the interior light on. Ursula had deep-set eyes and they were shadowed as she watched me pull out the file of missing women.

"I want you to go through these and tell me if you know any of them."

She sat unmoving. She wasn't stupid. "You think the rogue's one of us? Me?"

"Ursula, honestly, I don't know what to think. Everyone's giving me a different angle."

"But Felix has spoken to every member of the pack. It's not us. We can't lie to him."

"Everybody keeps telling me that. Just like they told me that Athanate and Were don't cross infuse."

She sat for a minute more, just looking at me.

Her team brought the couple out. They dropped the back seat flat and hog-tied them in the back of the car, then tossed a blanket over them. The pair looked groggy; they weren't even struggling.

I bit my lip. They hadn't done anything to deserve this.

"S'okay," one of the team said. "We've given them some of the booze from their trailer and some downers. Standard practice. They're out of it, is all."

When I turned back, Ursula was looking at the file. I'd intended to ask her the questions Tullah had set up for me, but I had to get the witnesses to Haven asap. I'd have to settle for seeing her reactions to these photos.

"This one." She lifted the sheet out and put it to one side. By the time she'd gone through she'd taken out five of the six that Tullah had said had some connection to her business.

She closed the file and went back to the five.

"This one owns a dude ranch. Her manager called me to look at one of their riding horses that had a problem. She was there, but I didn't speak to her."

"What was the problem?" It wasn't that I was interested, I wanted a feel for Ursula's reaction.

"Just basic bad treatment. People have no idea. Horses aren't rental cars." She pointed at the others. "These also keep horses, but privately. There were the usual problems. Underuse. Overfeeding. Poorly fitted shoes. It's not my normal business, but they called, and you don't turn it down."

I was watching her as she looked through the photos. There was nothing to suggest they were anything other than casual business acquaintances. Her heart rate had risen when we started, but it didn't vary while she answered.

Unless Ursula was a sociopath, and didn't have normal reactions.

I tried reaching with eukori, but either it wasn't working on demand, or she was blank. How had I done it with Sloan at Mrs. de Vries' house? I hadn't even tried—it'd just happened.

"Is there anything you can think of that these women have in common?"

"Aside from being one-time clients of mine?" Her mouth twisted. "Not really." She shuffled through them again thoughtfully and sighed. "I assume I'd be speaking ill of the dead here?"

"I don't know. It's possible. Officially they're missing. What?"

"They're all proof of that old cliché," Ursula said as she opened the car door and got out.

"Which one?"

"You can't buy happiness." She closed the door and walked back to the trailer.

Chapter 48

At Haven, Tom met me at the front door. The couple, deeply asleep, were lifted from my car and carried carefully away. Tom guided me back to the familiar little library.

"Naryn will come and see you when he's finished," he said. "We'll do what we can, but I have to warn you, dealing with Basilikos at the exchange hasn't put him in the best of moods."

"It went as planned, though?"

"Eventually."

After he'd left, I browsed the books. They were old-fashioned hardbacks, a strange mix of classics in many languages and books I'd never heard of. Some were in scripts that I didn't recognize, others in leather bindings that smelled like exotic travel is supposed to smell like. I'd travelled to exotic places with the army and I had different perceptions on that.

Half an hour later, Naryn came in, alone. His mood boiled through the room like a winter storm front.

I gave it my best diplomatic effort. "Diakon," I said, and dipped my head.

"House Farrell."

We sat at the table next to the dark French windows that led to the gardens.

"Are the couple okay?" I asked.

"They're asleep and drunk. They're being taken back now and they'll wake some time tomorrow with hangovers and no memory of this evening, beyond things they'll think they dreamed about, like wild dogs fighting."

"Thank you, on behalf of the pack, and from me personally."

I couldn't say he was being pleasant, but he was being entirely too controlled for my liking. He stared at me. I stared back and waited him out.

"Farrell, you're not acting in the interests of Altau," he said. "Even when you make considered decisions, they're biased with concerns that aren't relevant to Panethus. Your levels of impulsiveness are a fraction away from the behavior of Aspirants undergoing crusis mania, or rogue Athanate for that matter. I'm willing to countenance that your efforts to fight this may have been heroic, but the fact remains that you're being driven by the Were changes to your body. Skylur has been willing to risk this and leave you out in the community without support, but I'm not. I'm going to bring you in to Haven and put you under supervision while you work out the balance between Athanate and Were."

"Have you any—" I started.

"Stop," he said. "You're brought into a sensitive meeting with the leadership of Basilikos and you practically go rogue during the conversation, with all the fallout that would have had for the Assembly and Skylur's position in it. Then you're given control of a hugely expensive search for remnants of House Matlal, on the sole basis that you've made an oath to the Denver pack. An oath you had to make, I would point out, because you were unable to provide sufficient security for your kin. In the course of the search you've managed to make a commitment for all of Altau, every house in North America, to work with Were. Now you've botched a takedown of the Matlal Were and we've had to clean up after you."

"That's complete bullshit," I said.

My heart was in my mouth. At the meeting with Correia, I'd seen Naryn and Skylur easily balance a squad of Correia's security. This wasn't someone I could push around, but if I let him push me around, I had little doubt I'd end up locked in the basement here. I couldn't take that; not personally, and not given my commitments. It would drive me insane. Probably literally.

He'd gone still as a snake.

He was waiting for me, and it was verbal judo—the next person to speak was the one who'd blinked in this confrontation. But that doesn't always work, if you press your attack.

"I was in that meeting, *without* any warning, for a specific purpose. Skylur wanted my reactions to be extreme. The more extreme, the better for his purposes. He's had plenty of time to take me up on it if he didn't like the reaction I gave. It worked. And as for going rogue, I didn't. Close doesn't count."

I was warming up to my rant. He felt the initiative slipping away and started to speak; I bulldozed ahead.

"If you want to dispute that, I want to hear it from Skylur. As for the cost of the hunt for Matlal, it's hardly my fault that there are so few Altau in Denver that you have to resort to hiring in bounty hunters. And I haven't botched anything. The hunters ignored my instructions."

"You committed the Altau. A commitment we can't maintain. We're overextended."

"What would you have done? Storm the place and shoot everyone in the middle of the day? And why is this a commitment? The Confederation is sneaking around Denver and you're not bothered, but I send them back with a threat and it's like I've robbed your bank. Why can't Altau make alliances with Were? Allies increase your strength, they don't diminish it."

He stood up and leaned over the table. "We don't trust them."

"And so they don't trust you. Where does that get us? Nowhere." I tried to hold back, but it all slipped away from me. I was matching him, leaning over the table and shouting. "How can I cooperate with the pack here in Denver to everyone's benefit and ignore that opportunity in the rest of the country? If you refuse to see anything but the worst outcomes, you might as well pack up now."

"There are no good outcomes from this," he shouted back. "We can't commit to alliances with Were. We can't get involved in their struggles. We are overextended as it is. One solid blow by Basilikos and we'll lose allies. Even if that doesn't happen, the proposal to ally with the Were will lose Panethus allies."

"Panethus is supposed to be about Emergence. Are you proposing we accidentally forget to mention Were when we talk to the government? If we go ahead, we've got to go ahead with all the groups."

"So House Farrell has developed its own agenda and the rest of us have to follow along."

He was so thick-headed. Or not. I realized he might be goading me into making some kind of statement that would justify him taking the action he'd already decided on.

Calm down.

"No." I sat back down, trying to slow my racing heart. I folded my arms. "Skylur leads, but he has to lead. On all fronts. We don't have time for anything else."

"This is worse than rogue behavior. A rogue acts on instinct, but it's as if you planned to create problems." He shook his head. "I can't possibly allow you to be out there creating more problems for us."

Shit. He's going to put me in a cell.

"You can appeal to Skylur if you want, but as of this moment—"

The door burst open.

"Ah! There you are, Naryn! I've been looking all over for you."

The man who came through the door was beyond unusual. His marque proclaimed him Athanate. It didn't just precede him, it struck me forcefully, as noticeable as Skylur's was subtle, and as powerful. Much more powerful than Naryn's.

Even more singular was his appearance. The rejuvenating effects of the Blood kept all of us looking no older than me. I'd seen no gray-haired Athanates, but this man's hair was black flecked with gray, swept back on his head like raven's wings. His eyes were black stones, his skin the pale tan of latte coffee, and his features were refined, almost delicate.

I wonder how many have been fooled by that?

Bian slipped in behind him, quiet as a shadow.

"House Tarez." Naryn choked his anger down and gave a half bow.

Tarez. The House that Skylur had exchanged his priceless Hidden Path statue for, the one with affiliations that underpinned the farthest ranges of Panethus.

I started to introduce myself, but Tarez brushed it aside.

"And this is, of course, the lady I have been hearing so much about. House Farrell! Thrice welcome!"

His arms spread wide and swept me into an embrace.

I kept my wits about me enough to kiss necks on both sides. Unlike some of the Athanate I'd met at the reception, his kisses felt as if he meant them. I couldn't help but smile.

In my nose, his marque was sharp and dry. It made me think of the dreams that the wind brings in the cold, high places.

"Tarez..." Naryn seemed to have mislaid his eloquence.

"What?"

"This is not an appropriate time. I'm discussing problems that House Farrell has caused us."

"A fine? Ha! Charge it to me. I declare my firm affiliations with House Farrell."

"But—"

"Could I do less? She was offered and accepted as a Blood price for my freedom."

"She was never offered," Naryn said. "It was a ploy." He'd known that, of course. Maybe even Bian had too. I'd been the only one on our side to come into that meeting blind.

Tarez turned to me, his eyebrows raised. "Did you know it was a ploy, that you weren't being offered?"

"No," I replied. "I had no idea what was going on."

"Did you complain and refuse?"

"No."

"Why?"

"Because…" Why hadn't I yelled and screamed and refused? "Because I am affiliated to Altau. I swore an oath." My mouth felt dry. "It was within what was expected of me."

"An oath that is entirely reciprocal," Tarez noted. "And did you remember this oath as you went about whatever business has caused the Diakon such discomfort?"

"Yes, I did."

I did. I was arrogant enough to think I saw things that were for the benefit of Altau, even if someone like Naryn said they weren't.

"You truly believe whatever you have done is in the interests of Altau."

"I do."

I could feel the rake of his eukori across my mind and shivered.

"On the matter of association," Bian said, standing with her hands held behind her, "Skylur himself precipitated this. He said at the Assembly that he had an association with the Denver pack—"

"His exact words, Bian?" Tarez asked.

"He said the Denver pack was an ally."

"Did the Truth Sensors point out a lie?"

"I believe the Assembly was distracted by Skylur's announcement of Emergence as the major policy going forward."

Tarez laughed heartily. "He's not lost his sense of timing, and it has fallen to House Farrell to make his words true, then."

He turned to me.

"May I call you Amber?"

"Yes," I said. "Of course."

"Unfortunately, when I was born, names were rationed to one name per person, so you must sound formal and call me Tarez. Well, Amber, House Tarez is being sent to Los Angeles, for our sins—or maybe, for all the difficulties we have caused Altau. But there will always be a welcome there for you. Now, forgive me, I need Naryn to bring me up to date on all the strategy before I relieve Skylur there." He gripped my shoulder lightly. "I will look for you in LA. Tread carefully."

He grabbed Naryn and almost dragged him out.

I sank back down into my chair and blew air at the ceiling.

"Thank you, Bian."

"I don't know what you mean."

"You created that *accidental* meeting." I made quote signs in the air.

"I couldn't influence someone like Tarez. And whatever you think he came in for, that offer of affiliation is not to be treated lightly."

"Hmm. Understood."

"Don't get comfortable, Round-eye. I've just had a very interesting conversation with Alice and now that you're here, and you're free, we need to act straight away."

I sat up. "I thought you wanted to chuck Alice overboard."

Bian's mouth twisted.

"Maybe I still do, but between the two of you, you've given me an opening that Skylur asked me to work toward."

"You've lost me."

"You wanted to know if Alice had any contacts with Adepts in the Empire of Heaven?"

"Yeah," I said slowly. Mary and Liu wanted to connect with Adepts in China and ask them how to base a community around a dragon spirit guide. Kinda essential advice, if we didn't want to learn by making mistakes. If we hadn't already.

"I'm supposed to open a dialogue with the Empire in preparation for discussions between Skylur and the Emperor."

"Okay, you've got the number, presumably. So, call them."

She snorted.

"They're prickly at the best of times, and talking to the Empire is like Kirithia, the Game of Dominion." She waved her hands. "That's the Athanate version of chess between multiple players. You never, *ever* open a discussion with what you want to talk about. Not the first play, not the second, maybe not even the third."

"Unless you bluff."

"Maybe. I'm not that good a player. So, I want to open with something else. Something like what you and Alice want—to talk to their Adepts—not what Skylur wants."

"I'm not sure about this."

The problem was that Mary and Liu would say that this was confidential Adept business. It was all right to go through the Athanate channels to get to the Chinese Adepts, but I had a suspicion Bian would want to know exactly what was behind it.

"I'm not sure," I said again.

Bian slunk around the table and arranged herself over the back of my chair. I was getting pretty good at handling this. Breathe evenly. She couldn't embarrass me into doing what she wanted. No way. Not even—

"You said blank check, baby," she whispered against my neck. "And this is such a little thing."

I had said that. I owed her.

"Wait, didn't you call on that?" I asked.

"Not for the full amount. Come on," Bian said. Grabbing my hand, she led me down the hallway toward the other end of the house.

In the entrance hall, she picked up a house phone and dialed a number.

"Alice? We're on," she said and put it back.

I was looking up at the blank spot above the main house corridor. The spot where the huge eagle had spread its wings. The room looked unbalanced without it. I hoped that didn't say anything about the state of Panethus.

She saw where I was looking. "It's gone. Time to move on." She grabbed me again and pulled me onward.

Bian and Alice. Things were moving too quickly for me. Everything seemed to be sliding out of my control. Should I stop this now? Call Mary, despite the late hour, and clear it with her?

I was still debating when we turned a corner and I saw Alice already waiting for us at the end of the corridor.

Bian entered a seven-digit code into a keypad on the wall and then leaned into an iris scanner.

A metal door slid aside, just as my cell phone buzzed in my pocket.

"Turn it off," Alice said. "No signal in this room anyway."

I looked at the name as I obeyed. Melissa. What on earth was she calling me for at this hour? It was nearly midnight. I'd call her back once we'd finished.

The door closed behind us. We were in a dark, windowless room with a huge screen on one side and a conference table in front of it with chairs.

Under instruction from Bian, we quickly moved the table and chairs and knelt in the empty space, Bian in the middle.

The conference system came up and showed us as we would appear. Bian looked at the clocks on the wall. Exactly midnight. It was 3 p.m. in Beijing. She dialed a number.

The screen cleared to show an empty white pavilion with fine gauze curtains screening out the background.

"Come on," muttered Bian. "Don't brush us off."

A Chinese man walked to the middle of the pavilion, his eyes downcast, the model of humility. He was dressed in dark brown pants and a white, long-sleeved shirt with an open neck. His feet were in sandals. His hair was short and neatly parted.

Bian straightened her back.

This guy? This was the Diakon of the biggest independent Athanate group in the world?

Then Bian bowed and held it. Right down, head-on-the-floor bow.

Alice and I glanced nervously at each other and followed suit.

"*Garheem*," he said.

Athanate for hello, for semi-formal meetings. Pia was teaching me some standby words.

Bian sat up and Alice and I followed again. The guy was kneeling in the same position as us. I'd had my head on the floor, so I didn't know if he'd bowed back. Somehow I doubted it.

Bian spoke in Athanate and the man's eyes turned first to Alice and then to me, with interest.

I was starting to worry that I'd need to do everything through an interpreter, but after what I assumed were introductions and polite, formal questions, Bian said something short and stopped.

"Yes, it is acceptable to speak in English," he said. "Greetings, House Farrell, Adept Emerson. My name is Xun Huang, and I am Diakon of the Empire of Heaven."

"Greetings, Xun Huang," I said, and tried a short bow with just my head.

"I understand from Diakon Trang that you have a request to make of me." He smiled. "I am most interested."

I wasn't sure if that was a good thing, or just politeness.

"We are honored, Diakon Huang," Alice said.

I guessed he'd said he would listen to us, and Alice had said thank you. This diplomatic language was tricky stuff.

"We would ask a favor of you," Alice went on. "That you allow us to communicate with Adept communities in the Empire."

"I am most sure they would enjoy such contact." He rocked back a little on his heels. "You understand that, here in the Empire, the community is more unitary than elsewhere."

Well then, we could learn lots from you.

Alice and Xun played verbal ping-pong for a few minutes. Xun explained that Adept communities in the Empire were organized along the same lines as Houses, with the oaths and loyalties under the Athanate structure, but it was always accepted that Adepts had interests of their own.

It looked as if this was going to be relatively easy. I sat back on my heels and kept my smile in place.

"I understand the general academic interest of Adepts to communicate and compare their cultures," Xun said, nodding to Alice, before looking at Bian. "I always welcome contact from Panethus, and I hope to continue discussions another time with you, Diakon Trang, especially on the matters of our southern Houses."

He meant Vietnam and the countries of the Indochina peninsula. I could feel Bian's satisfaction. I could see that this might be the sort of contact that Skylur wanted her to develop with the Empire, as a first or second step, so that Skylur could then casually introduce what he really wanted to talk about.

"And House Farrell, about whom we have heard so much." He turned finally to me, and I tensed. "I am fascinated to meet you, even in this manner. I am even more fascinated to hear why you want to talk to Adepts in the Empire."

"It's more that friends of mine, who are Adepts, want to talk."

It was as if I could see beneath his face; the surface remained polite and interested, but beneath that, he was starting to switch off. I concentrated on breathing evenly. I couldn't let this slip away. Tullah, Mary and Liu were depending on me.

Trust and Jump. Oh, boy.

"The topic that most interests them are the Adept communities built around dragon spirit guides."

Bian didn't move, but I sensed the shock ringing through her marque. Alice's nose flared and her eyes widened.

Xun remained motionless, courteously attentive. The screen showing him might have frozen, except for the idle flapping of one of the curtains behind him.

Then his eyes flicked to one side.

"Ah. Excuse me. I am called away. My most sincere apologies. I remain fascinated by this discussion and I look forward to meeting your friends and talking many more times with you all, and listening with such interest to your conversations with our Adepts."

Bian did the bowing thing, which was diplomacy. I did it, and it was more to cover my face.

Damn. Have I done the right thing? What the hell just happened?

The screen had faded to gray when I came back up. Alice's face wasn't far off the same color.

Bian got up, as slinky as a leopard, and led us out.

Automatically, I turned my cell back on. Messages from Melissa.

Neither Bian nor Alice said a word, but they were both staring at me.

"What? What did we just do in there?" I said.

It was Alice who answered. "We've woken the sleeping dragon."

Chapter 49

SUNDAY

It was freezing outside, and Bian's team had taken my car to drop the couple back at their trailer. Bian had already disappeared with Alice, taking quietly and quickly in Athanate.

I called Melissa.

"Melissa? What's up? Where are you?"

"I'm at Clayton's home. He called me to come see him. Amber, he's dead. I mean, someone killed him."

"Shit! Get *out* of there. Where's your car?"

"Uhh. Right outside."

"Stay on the line. Get into your car now."

"But I should—"

"Listen to me! This isn't a police crime scene. You don't have backup. Whoever killed Clayton could be watching. Probably is. Now get out."

I'd gotten through to her. I could hear her car door open and close and the sound of the locks engaging.

"Okay. I'm in my car." Her voice was much quieter, but she was in control.

"Drive away. Use the hands-free and stay on the line. I'm coming."

I heard the car start in the background.

"But shouldn't I just get back?" she said.

"I'm working on the assumption you're going to be followed, so no."

Breathing came a little easier as I heard her pulling away.

This could be a random murder. Clayton had made enemies—all the people he'd put in jail, for a start. But I didn't believe in coincidences.

"Where are you?"

"Just turned onto Grand View."

"Anyone pull out behind you?"

"I'm not sure. There's another car just coming out now. It'll be a couple of cars back."

Exactly where a tail would want to be. "Type?"

"It's a Chrysler sedan. Dark."

"You get a plate?"

"Too far."

"Okay, concentrate on the driving. Take the bypass down to the interstate. Nice and steady."

I grabbed a passing Altau.

"I need a car, urgently. Life or death."

"Ahh, the parking garage, House." He pointed me at a door. "Through there, down a level. Most of the cars will have the keys on a board next to the elevator. Should I call security?"

"Get a message to Bian." I held up my cell. "I'm talking someone through evading a tail. I'll try and call her."

"Got it," he said, and was heading for the house phone as I ran down the stairs.

I burst into the parking garage. Right across from me was a yellow-edged board with keys hanging on it. I sprinted across and grabbed the first one, pressed the key fob.

An Audi, the twin of mine, flashed its lights.

I got in and checked the gas. Plenty. It'd have to do. I hoped the owner didn't need it soon.

"Still there, Melissa?"

"Yes, just coming to the junction."

"Get on I-70 westbound toward Grand Junction. I'm going offline for a second while I get this cell connected."

"The Chrysler's still there," she said. She sounded frightened now. My gut said she needed to be.

Connecting the cell was easy and the motor that I started was *not* the twin of the one in mine. I'd been lucky in my choice—this was the same model, but the complete sports package. Someone's favorite. I'd have to be careful, if I got the chance.

"...now that weather front," said the radio, "is just starting to push down along the Rockies, but it's okay, folks, we might just see some dusting on the mountains..."

I turned it off. Duane-Leatherface had gotten it wrong.

On the gravel drive I left a ten-second summary voicemail for Bian on her cell, and then I hit the speed dial to get back to Melissa as I headed out the gates.

"Any change?"

"No."

"Keep it completely normal. You know the Cabrini turnoff?"

"To the shrine in the hills? Yeah. I come off on US 40 and turn up the hill."

"You should be there in fifteen minutes; take that whether you can see anyone behind you or not. There's a gas station on the way. I'll be waiting there, and you drive past without stopping."

"Yes, Amber."

She was subdued, but working with me. I could handle that.

∞ ∞ ∞ ∞ ∞

I got to the gas station and sat there with the engine idling. I checked the HK and made sure there was nothing loose in the cabin. I didn't know how this was going to go, but it was always best to be careful when I had time.

The way it was kept suggested this wasn't a pool car. Out of curiosity, I checked the glove compartment.

Crap. Double, triple, quadruple crap.

Out of all the cars in the garage, I had to pick Naryn's.

"Coming off onto 40."

Less than five minutes away. There was nothing I could do about my appalling bad luck in choice of cars. At rock bottom, I couldn't be in any worse position with him anyway. I put it out of my mind.

"They still there?"

"I think so. There's a dark Chrysler about fifty yards behind me. I can't be sure it's the same one."

And I couldn't be sure who was in the car. But at this hour, behind her all the way from Arvada?

Melissa drove past, and I put on my blinker to pull out, waiting like a good little driver until the Chrysler went past as well. My headlights picked out two figures. I got the impression of a man in the passenger seat and a woman driving. The man was looking my way, but it was too dark for him to see me. He turned away rather than look at my headlights, but the glimpse of him side-on was enough for me.

Melissa had picked up a couple of Nagas. I'd busted that guy out of Ops 4-10 at induction.

I pulled out behind them. We were the only three cars on the road.

"Melissa, I'm going to take them out, but I'll need your help."

"Okay." She sounded nervous.

"What you have to do is very straightforward. Drive normally until the turnoff to the shrine. Don't put your blinker on. Leave it till the last possible moment to turn, and then go up that hill as fast as you can without crashing. Did you do the evasive driving course at the PD?"

"Yeah."

"Any good?"

"Yes!"

"Then you'll be fine. These guys aren't racing drivers and they don't know I'm here. That's two huge points in our favor. Leave the line open and I'll tell you when to come back down."

"If there's a problem…"

"Get to the shrine. There's some kind of accommodation there. Get inside and call Bian. She'll be here quicker than the police."

"Okay. I see the turnoff."

She did exactly as I had asked. Her brake lights flared and her car twisted around the hairpin bend and shot up the road to the shrine.

The Nagas had left enough space between them and Melissa. As soon as Melissa hit the brakes, they'd known what was happening and that they'd been spotted. So far, so good. Their really clever move would have been to wave it off and call in the reinforcements that had to be converging. There was no way out from the road up to the shine.

They didn't take that option. The Chrysler skidded around the bend and tore after Melissa. Their bigger engine would outpace Melissa on the straightaway. Unfortunately for them, this road was anything but straight.

I killed the lights and followed, the Audi snarling. With its hard suspension and four-wheel drive, it gripped the road like a demon. Almost fun, if Melissa hadn't been in danger.

"They're catching me," Melissa yelled.

"Concentrate on driving."

The Nagas didn't check the rearview mirror, they didn't look back. They were completely focused on overtaking her. Mission blinkers, we used to call it in 4-10.

On the third switchback, a left-hander with Melissa taking the inside line, they drifted wide, the weight of their car losing them traction, but right in close behind her. I gunned the Audi at the small gap between them, aiming for the driver and switching on my headlights.

Then she looked back.

She did what anyone would have done with two tons of screaming metal appearing out of nowhere and seemingly intent on ramming right through her door—she jerked the wheel right, swung her car away. The Audi helped her on her way.

There was a small ditch followed by a raised bank beyond the road. The Chrysler lurched into the air and seemed to hang there, rolling slowly as the nose floated down. Then it hit a rock and twisted viciously with a neck-snapping flick. I was out of my car and running toward the crash before it'd finished happening.

The first moments were critical. Even if they weren't seriously injured, a crash like that is disorienting, but those two had the same training I did and probably more weapons. If I let them recover, I was in trouble.

The Chrysler settled on its roof. The far door got kicked open. Passenger door; the man was coming out. The first lick of flame fell from the engine compartment.

I bent low as I ran. I couldn't see through the air bags to the other side of the cabin, but there was no movement on this side. Twenty yards away and I came back upright, leading with the HK.

He wasn't using the car as cover, so he was thinking clearly. Cover that was about to blow up wasn't good cover. He was limping backwards, a shotgun waving in my general direction, and a gym bag gripped in his left hand.

It took a moment to realize he couldn't see me in the darkness.

I couldn't kill him like that.

"Put the shotgun down," I yelled.

He fired at the sound of my voice, and too freaking close. And the fire was catching now. If he couldn't see me, he would soon.

I stopped running and put a round through his right leg. The impact buckled it under him, pitching him down into the dirt.

He didn't try and crawl. He ignored the wound, scuttling around till he presented the smallest target to the direction of my shot. With his elbows on the ground, the shotgun was steadier than it had been.

With a sudden whoosh, the car was burning. Now he could see me.

He fired again and I rolled to the side, coming up with my arms extended and braced. Both hands gripped the butt of the HK, steadying it. In the time it took him to jack another cartridge, a single round from the HK through his forehead ended it.

I ran over and took the gym bag. If it had been important enough he'd tried to protect it, I wanted to know what was inside. I shoved the shotgun in and took off for the road.

Melissa's car skidded to a halt at the corner and she got halfway out before I pushed her back.

"You weren't supposed to come back down," I growled at her. "I'll turn. Follow me down. There'll be others coming."

I threw the gym bag in the trunk and looked at the scene.

Damn. Damn. Couldn't leave it like that. A body with a gunshot head wound and residue on his hands. The media would be all over it. At least removing him would slow things down and make it less newsworthy.

I ran back and picked the man's body up. He weighed over two hundred pounds and I felt every pound jarring my knees as I trotted back with him draped over my shoulders. But I'd carried bigger for Ops 4-10. He leaked all over me, of course. I was going to need another change of clothes.

Melissa had seen what I was doing and jogged over carrying something she'd taken from her trunk—a body bag. Trust a CSI.

We slid him into my car, neatly bagged, and set off.

At every turn I expected to see cars full of Nagas coming up at us, but we made it to the main road without meeting anyone. Just yards away, the interstate traffic ran by, oblivious to what had been happening. We turned and tracked alongside it for a mile before we could join and disappear into the anonymous crowd.

I called Bian.

"You still alive, Round-eye?"

"Yeah. Thanks. D'you know any all-night Audi repair shops?"

She snorted. "Don't tell me you bent Naryn's car."

"Just a headlight and a bit of crumple zone."

"Drop it off and run, Round-eye. Seriously, he'll be irritated, but it's nothing on the rest of the problems he thinks you're causing. Oh, and that blank check, it's just picked up another digit." Her voice got all breathy. "You will be working this off with me a *long* time."

"Uh. Yeah. There's also a body in the trunk. Can your cleanup crew handle it?"

She sighed. "Anyone I know?"

"A Naga."

"What the hell?" Leopard Bian disappeared and the Diakon got back into full swing. "Where was this? I thought this was something to do with Melissa?"

"My question exactly. Meet us at the gates."

Chapter 50

We got to Haven and the guards directed me down into the underground parking garage where Bian was waiting.

The damage to Naryn's car looked worse under the lights, but Bian scarcely glanced at it.

We hauled the body bag and the gym bag out onto the ground and unzipped them.

The gym bag had Clayton's journals and notebooks in it.

Melissa started to flick through the notebooks while Bian inspected the dead Naga.

"He called me and said he had something he wanted to show us," Melissa said. "It sounded important, and I couldn't get through to you, so I went." She passed an arm across her face. "He was old-school. Kept a notebook for every case and a journal. So, theoretically, somewhere in here are his case notes from his investigation of the rogue."

Melissa and I split the pile between us and started to go through them.

"When he called you, did he say specifically that he would show us his notes?"

Melissa frowned. "No. Just that he wanted to tell us about the case. Something about the information he wasn't even allowed to put onto the PD computers."

I put another journal aside. It was from years ago. Some of the journals had pages that were going brittle and yellow. I moved all those into the reject pile.

Bian hissed. "Never just one thing, Round-eye."

I joined her. "What've you got?"

She'd stripped back the man's shirt and wiped the blood off his neck.

Midway down the left side of his throat were two old wounds, about an inch and a half apart. Athanate fang marks.

"The colonel told us he was afraid there was contact between Petersen and Matlal." Bian checked the right side of the neck and ran a finger over older scars that might have been fang marks as well. "So the odds always were that they'd find each other in Denver. But killing this detective and staking out his place? His only connection with you is his investigation into the rogue."

"Is there anything else you know that could possibly have attracted their attention, Melissa?"

She shook her head.

"Then we have the rogue cooperating with the Matlal and Nagas," I said. "Just wonderful."

"But why would they?" Bian frowned.

I got up and leaned against the car, smearing more blood and mud on it.

"Nagas are here for me, Julie and the colonel. The rogue sent a message to me with the murder in Wash Park, either keep away or he's coming for me. The Matlal…"

"…have you to thank for their House being destroyed." Bian said. "And you're leading a search for them."

I shrugged. "Okay. They all have it in for me. Then *how*? We can't find the rogue. How would the Nagas? Or Matlal?"

"What about the other way around?" Melissa said. "The rogue finds the Matlal, persuades them to help with whatever he wants, and they get the Nagas involved. As for finding the Matlal, maybe he's just been looking longer than we have."

Bian and Melissa stared at me. It felt odd, as if it were half a solution. What if the rogue had only been looking for a link to Basilikos? The rogue wanted to live somewhere else? Have the protection of a group who didn't care how sick he was?

"Well, then, we step it all up. Find the rogue or the Matlal, and we might unravel the whole thing in one shot."

I raised an eyebrow at Melissa.

"Great plan, but we've struck out here," she said. "There's nothing in these journals, they're too old."

I slid down the side of the car and sat in a frustrated heap on the ground.

"You said he was meticulous in keeping notebooks and journals," I said. "That has to mean the recent ones are missing."

"Maybe the Nagas kept them separately?"

"The guy took the time to grab this gym bag as he was getting out of a car that was about to blow. No. He thought this was it."

"So the missing notes will be back at his home."

Or in some lock-up somewhere. I caught the demon before that came out.

I sighed. "The trail starts back at his home in Arvada. And it's too late to go to bed. Come on, Melissa."

Bian scowled and touched my arm.

"Your security is becoming an issue, Round-eye. I can't keep ignoring it." She was looking at Melissa, who was trying to shrink behind me.

"Melissa is House Farrell."

"Is she? No bites. No bond. First Julie turned up at Haven, now Melissa. Even if I did ignore it, Naryn gets gate reports and he's going to ask, believe me."

"It's in process. We're Panethus, Bian, it's got to be voluntary on both sides."

"Deal with it, or I'll have to." Her eyes had gone all glittery and I could feel her fangs just ready to manifest.

Melissa was trembling, and it wasn't the cold that was reaching down into the garage.

I put an arm around her and glared at Bian. I understood the problem, but this wasn't getting us closer to the solution. If anything, I thought it was making it less likely.

"Ah, mmm..." Melissa stuttered. "Maybe David?"

Where did that come from?

"See." Bian smiled, showing no fangs. "Progress."

My Athanate growled silently. Time to get out of here.

Looking around, I saw my car was back, but there was a problem with that.

"Can I borrow another car, Bian? The Matlal know my car, and Diana's Jeep."

She had a closer look at Naryn's and rejected it. The damage would attract attention. She walked back to the board where all the keys were stored.

"You are kinda hard on cars. Hmm. I know!" She pulled a set of keys off and tossed them to me. "It won't matter if you crash the Hill Bitch."

"The what?"

She pointed down at the far end.

In the gloomy recesses, almost too tall for the garage, sat a modified Jeep Wrangler on supersize tires. It looked dirty, but as we got closer, that turned out to be hundreds of scrapes and scratches in its dark blue paintwork. It had a bare cabin, five point seat harnesses and a roll bar. Stick shift. No heater or entertainment console. Just a double helping of attitude.

"Fine," I said. Not the discreet transport I needed as a PI; in fact, totally inappropriate, but beggars can't be choosers. "At least I'll be following Duane's advice."

"Felix's nephew?" Bian asked. "What did he say?"

"He said to get better snow tires this weekend."

Bian laughed. "You got 'em."

Chapter 51

Clayton had a repo single-wide, tucked in between a couple of old cinderblocks and tight against the railroad tracks. It was a handy two blocks from his bar.

We'd left Melissa's car on the main drag and she was sitting very still in my passenger seat, nervously checking to either side and behind us. There was no one there at the moment. The street was quiet, dark and cold. It was even colder in the spartan cabin of the Hill Bitch.

We slipped on latex gloves and booties while we waited.

"Okay, let's go," I said, after ten minutes of scanning the area without seeing anything suspicious.

We got out quietly and walked to the trailer's door, Melissa behind me.

"I didn't lock it," Melissa whispered.

The place felt empty.

I checked the safety on the HK and stood to one side as I opened it. Much good that would have done if there'd been Nagas inside. High velocity rounds would go right through the walls, the person outside and probably into the next trailer.

It was dark inside and the stench of death drifted out.

"You leave the light on?" I murmured.

She shook her head. Tidy girl.

"Wait."

I went in low and quick, HK sweeping back and forth, eyes struggling to see into the blackness. Silence. Nothing to see, even in the infrared, other than a blur on the floor which I assumed was Clayton.

"Come in."

I stepped carefully over his body. I wanted to give him more respect than that, but there simply wasn't time. I had to assume one of the Nagas would think to come back here to check.

Clayton's home was about twelve feet by forty. On my right was the living room, with a cooking and eating area that was supposed to open out onto a covered porch. The porch had all but rotted away.

I crossed to the opposite end and checked the bedroom and shower. Nothing.

Melissa closed all the cheap curtains and switched on the light.

It wasn't bad. I'd lived in a smaller apartment when I'd been at Mrs. Desiarto's in Aurora.

And despite his slide into the bottle, Clayton had kept it clean. He'd probably kept it tidy too, but the Nagas had torn the place apart. Not a single box or drawer was left whole. Everything had been opened and smashed.

Clayton wasn't at the very bottom of the debris.

I swallowed. He'd been alive when they'd started. If I had a look, I suspected I'd find he'd been tortured. There'd be no way a drunken old man would have stood up to it, but from the amount of debris that was on top of him, they'd gone on searching after he died. Did that mean he'd died without telling them?

Melissa cleared his body and started inspecting him.

"We're not doing a police investigation, Melissa," I said. "We're looking for a hiding place for his missing notes. We can't take long."

"Sorry," she said.

"I think we may be out of luck anyway." I gestured at the devastation. "That's about everywhere there is to hide something, all in pieces on the floor."

"Maybe."

She walked the perimeter, stepping over the trash and looking at every wall, every corner.

I looked at the ceiling for suspicious bulges, but other than some small water stains around the vents, there was nothing.

"He wouldn't want to keep a storage locker," Melissa said. "He'd have something here."

"Wishing won't make it so." I really hoped there wasn't a storage locker. A key is way harder to find than a notepad.

"He was bitter," she said, thinking out loud the way I did occasionally. "He was sure there'd been something to his investigation. Something he was going to uncover. He would know the rogue had framed him and then murdered the prostitute to weaken his credibility even more..."

She slowed.

"Why would he think that was the end of it?" I finished her thought. "He was expecting to be killed?"

"Yeah. You and I might say the rogue had done enough, and could just leave him, but for Clayton this was personal. He believed he was going to be killed as soon as the rogue felt it was safe enough to move on him."

"And he was right," I pointed out. No wonder he'd started drinking. "However the rogue found out, Clayton gets killed the same night he wants to talk to you."

"Or he was tortured into making that call." She started pacing. "That's not important. What I'm saying is he expected to be killed and he would want to leave something that the killer wouldn't find, but the police would."

"Hmm. Okay. That might be why he was eager to keep up his old contacts, so that however he was killed, however it was arranged for him to die, it'd be looked into deeper."

The death of a policeman always got more attention.

"Yes." Melissa turned the light off. "He'd be expecting CSI to look at this place. He'd want them to find his notes."

"In the dark?"

"No." She pulled a flashlight out of her pocket and flicked it on. "Under UV."

The trailer filled with neon blue. The area around Clayton's body was black where his blood absorbed all the light. I could see the dark flecks of blood extending out across the floor, and black patches on some of the broken furniture they'd used to hit him with.

And at the ends of the curtain rod above the window to the porch, two large, dark X shapes. They were older, with soft edges. Not his blood, but whatever he'd used, he'd done a good job.

The hollow rod broke easily. Inside were the loose-leaf remains of notebooks.

And the TacNet, switched to silent and worn like a necklace, was pulsing against my throat.

"Farrell, you there?"

"Gray?"

"Yeah. Got a hit on that list you gave me. You better get here."

Chapter 52

We arrived at the place we'd agreed to meet, just inside Denver's upscale suburb of Glenmore Hills Village, only half a mile from Suzannah de Vries' house. Mary, roused out of bed in the middle of the night, had barely said a word on the trip. There was no sign of Nick or his Harley at the roadside.

"He doesn't know this car," I said, opening the door. At least it wasn't any colder outside than in.

"He's here," Mary said quietly. "Watching."

"You can sense him?"

"This one? Yes, when he's close. He can sense me, too." She sighed. "I never thought…You do make me mix with strange types, Amber."

I opened my mouth to question that when Gray appeared out of the shadows by the road.

How did I not see him?

He cast a thoughtful eye over Mary, but all he said was: "Take the second right," as he climbed in alongside Melissa, behind me.

Mary spoke to him, the words fast and low. It wasn't Arapaho and I doubted she spoke Chippewa. That'd make it one of the old plains trader tongues. Gray answered, slower than Mary.

I turned where he'd said, and he broke off long enough to tell me to look out for the spruce trees.

"Turn in and stop at the gate," he said, when I found the wall with blue spruce looming above it.

We were facing an iron gate between two brick pillars. Through the gate I could see a drive snaking toward a house that was mostly hidden by more spruce, with a scattering of cherry and mimosa. It was very expensive, very private.

I had been searching my memory for the details associated with the house. The man who had lived here was an eccentric recluse. Tullah had marked him as borderline for inclusion in the list. Bills were paid, food and goods occasionally delivered. No car. No taxis. Unless he walked to the stores and bought food with cash, there was just too little of everything.

The house certainly would fit the needs of the rogue. It was isolated from the neighbors by its trees, not to the extent a ranch would have been, but enough that no one would notice what went on in here.

Gray got out.

"There's an alarm," he said. "Wait here."

He walked to the right-hand pillar and leaped up, suddenly catlike. From the top he looked carefully at the ground below and then jumped silently down. All I could see in the night was a blur of warmth heading toward the house.

I blew warm air into my cupped hands.

"You found a lot to talk about," I said to Mary.

"Uh. He's very polite for a skinwalker," she replied.

My mouth worked soundlessly for a couple of seconds. "As in, like the stories? He can change to any animal?"

Mary snorted. "I doubt it, but the stories say several different animals. He's a sort of Were, with a big dose of Adept. I never thought I'd meet one." She shook her head. "Huh! I didn't think there were any left."

That set another cascade of thoughts off in my mind, but the one that came to the surface was: "Could the rogue be a skinwalker too?"

"No. I'd have felt that." She looked out the window. "I think. But this house Gray found—he's right. One of the Denver pack has been here."

The gates opened silently. Gray reappeared beside them and waved us in.

I stopped next to him.

"You're a man of surprising talents, Mr. Gray. Are you sure the house is empty?"

"Ask her," he said, indicating Mary, who nodded. "Go on and park in front." He stood on the running board while we drove the loop to the house.

The house was as expensive as the setting suggested, but to me it was a haphazard pile of boxes, without any true design. Still, the exterior was as well-maintained as the grounds. Those had been some of the bills that were paid.

Melissa and I handed out gloves and booties, then Gray let us in through the front door and turned on lights. I guess he had to be completely sure in his own mind that the place was empty. I glanced at the doorframe in passing. It hadn't been forced. Surprising talents indeed. I'd have to get him to teach me how to do that.

We stood in a hallway. There'd been no bills for interior cleaning and it showed. The place smelled musty. I could tell why Gray had thought we'd be in no danger coming in.

I opened doors at random to see a variety of rooms with dust thick on the furniture. If anyone lived here, they didn't use the ground floor.

"Garage and basement," I said. If the rogue used this place, he'd want to drive into a garage and have access directly to the basement from it. Not that there was much chance of anyone seeing him, but it would fit better with him being fanatically cautious.

"Basement," Mary echoed. Her voice was hoarse. She didn't look well.

Gray touched her arm. I expected her to flinch or snap at him, but something had happened between them in the few minutes of our drive.

Melissa had picked a door that looked as if it was the way to the basement. It wasn't the original wooden door. It was out of place and ugly, a steel door with no handle and no keyhole. We pushed, but it didn't budge.

"Sealed," I said. "We need to break into the garage and go from there."

Gray led us out and around the side. He knelt in front of the garage doors briefly, then left them and found a side door. The lock was rusted, but in a couple of minutes he was forcing the door open against the sound of squealing hinges right out of a horror movie.

Hints of werewolf marque drifted out with dry, dusty air. And the suggestion of spells, a scent like the sea, a scratchy shiver on my skin.

It was a three-car garage. Two spaces were empty and the third had a green Ford F-250 with tires like the Hill Bitch outside. Same green as the ranger vans.

Melissa peered in the car's window. "This wouldn't have trouble reaching those body dump sites. Want me to check for signs of bodies inside?"

I shook my head. "I bet it'll be too clean for anything we can do in a hurry." I pointed at the equipment racked up against the back wall: power sprays and chemical cleaners, and a stack of brand-new brushes and sponges. Use once and dispose of. Ultra-cautious.

"We need to see the basement," I said.

There was a door on the opposite side from where we'd come in. Gray picked the lock and it opened onto a small landing and a set of steps going down into darkness.

Mary and Gray both looked unwell now. Whatever it was didn't seem to affect me as badly. I was getting the itchy skin effect of spells, but nothing worse. I left them to gather themselves in the garage and went down the stairs, flicking the light on as I did. I held the HK out in front, but my instincts told me there was nothing alive down there.

I heard Melissa's footsteps following me.

Halfway down there was another landing and a branch going back up to the steel door that would open into the house. I ignored it.

There was a sharp smell of bleach. Underneath that: mixed Were, and blood, and days-old death.

The steps came out into a basement that was a simple rectangle, about twenty feet by fifty, with bare concrete floor and walls. All along the walls, at intervals of six feet and about three feet up from the floor, solid steel bolts were set into the concrete. They had hoops as thick as my thumb.

At the far end, the body of a Were slumped in chains—strange, adjustable shackles fastened around his neck and stomach and fixed to the wall bolts.

The chains held him in a half-standing position, in a sick parody of a broken puppet. His flesh was ripped everywhere, strips of skin and muscle hanging from him. He'd died in an orgy of violence.

"The missing Matlal." I breathed through my mouth, but the marque, even in death, was still clear.

Melissa went to him. I stood in the middle and turned around and around, trying to comprehend the mind that did this.

The whole thing, except for the body, was obsessively tidy.

Water pipes ran down in a corner. Next to them, there was a pump and a power spray and brushes, just like the garage above. Coiled electrical cords. A row of electrical sockets. A stack of trash bags. Chains and ropes in neat piles. Power tools. Toolbox. Rack of knives.

Methodical. Orderly. Precise.

And at the other end, a body torn and abused beyond belief. A violent, bloody contrast.

"He was killed right here and then left," Melissa said. Her voice shook a little, but her gray eyes were clear as she looked at the equipment. "I have some DNA samples from the wounds. We might be able to match with suspects, if the rogue was careless." She held up her sample kit. "It looks like this guy was tortured first."

"Maybe that's how the rogue got the information about how to contact Petersen," I said, swallowing hard. "Got to step back from the detail. What's it telling you?" I pointed at the two ends of the room.

She cleared her throat. "It's the same attitude as he showed at Wash Park. He's finished here. He's gone."

"Something's happened," I said.

She nodded. "Or will happen."

I heard slow steps on the stairs, and went and stood in front of the body. I'd wanted Mary along to see if there was any reading she could make on the house, any spells she could sense that would give me a clue. I hadn't thought I'd have to confront her with this. My itchy sensations increased, and I felt the strongbox groan. Something about all this was making a horrible resonance inside me.

Gray came into the basement first, leading Mary by the hand.

Her eyes turned away from the body. I doubted it was the death itself that disturbed her, but the manner. Maybe that left an awful echo in this room.

"If you're finished, leave us for a while, please," Gray whispered.

I nodded, secretly immensely relieved. "We'll have a quick search through the rest of the house."

We climbed back out of the pit, and every step seemed to ease a little more pressure off me. I was nowhere near Mary's capabilities, but something in that basement had weighed on me. Something about the terror of the people who'd been held captive there. Was that how it was in a Basilikos House, with their toru? I shuddered.

The rest of the house was a blank: cold, empty rooms and dust over everything.

Melissa and I returned to wait in the car. It was freezing, but I preferred that to getting anywhere near that basement again.

Melissa was clutching Clayton's notes. She'd been reading them while we drove here.

"Anything?" I asked.

"There's a lot there, and some of it just sounds like Clayton ranting. But there's a list of people he talked to, and a list he was going to talk to."

Her voice was uncertain.

"Anyone from the pack?"

"Yeah. He talked to Silas Falkner, Kyle Larsen, Ursula Tennyson and Dr. Noble. Larimer was down to be interviewed next, right at the time Clayton had his badge pulled." She coughed. "A couple of other people and then, after that, was Alex."

I scrubbed my hands tiredly across my face. That was a lot of the pack. How had Clayton come across them?

"Alex is out," I muttered. "Even though he had the opportunity to steal my clothes. I just know him at a level where he couldn't hide this. Larimer's out; alphas' mental health feeds down into the pack, like that bloodthirsty bastard Verano. The doctor's simply too small. Ursula and Silas are plenty big enough and they're on my list. Larsen, I have no idea. I'll have to find him today and talk to him."

Melissa scribbled contact details for the list onto a piece of paper and passed it over.

"You know the rest of them," she said, "but I'll text you a photo of Kyle Larsen when I'm back in front of a computer."

"What was Clayton's reasoning for the people on his list?" I asked. "Did he give any indications?"

"He's blank on means and motive. It's gotta be opportunity."

Opportunity. And we were talking about the known victims, not the potential list with the wealthy women. Silas and Larsen did volunteer work in that community. What opportunity had Clayton spotted for Doc Noble and Ursula? I should have questioned Ursula more when I had the chance.

The eastern sky was lightening; we had to go.

Crap.

I needed to go back to the basement and bring them up.

They were back to back in the middle of the floor, eyes closed, slowly stepping around in a circle. A wash of prickles ran over me, as if my skin had suddenly dried and tightened in the sun.

Mary held up one hand.

Her eyes opened and I felt a tremor like an aftershock pass through me. Nothing else stirred.

She sighed and moved away from Gray. The sensations eased. My other senses took over and the marque, the smell of dead Were and dried blood returned. The feeling of wolf abruptly rolled over me.

Mary drifted past.

"It's time to go. We have to talk, Amber."

All very well, but I couldn't talk. She hadn't noticed, but I had clamped my teeth together. I wanted to hunt and kill. Blood was speaking to me. Saliva filled my mouth. My limbs trembled. Frantic scratching inside.

And Gray's hand rested on my shoulder.

"My grandfather always spoke to me with wisdom," he murmured. "And so one day I told him what I feared most in all the world: that I had not one, but two wolves in me. One bright with joy and running in the woods. The other dark and twisted with hate, who lurked in the shadows of the mind. 'It is so with all of us,' he said, 'even me.' 'Then what must I do, grandfather?' I asked, and he replied, 'feed only the one you wish to grow.'"

I closed my eyes. I remembered back to when I thought I only had turning Athanate to worry about, before I'd met Alex and been cross-infused. I remembered imagining running naked through the pathless woods up at Bitter Hooks and singing to the moon, in the cold, clean air.

The horrors of the basement didn't go away, but they didn't press so hard on me anymore.

"Not just a wolf, though, are you, Gray?" I whispered hoarsely.

"No. Bear and cougar too," he said quietly.

Damn, that was so cool. Not what I'd been asking, but cool anyway.

I turned and followed him up the stairs.

"What will you do about this house?" he said when we emerged, as if nothing had happened.

"Call it in." My mind was clear again.

"Not worth a stakeout?"

"No," I said. "The rogue never intended to come back. Even if he did, you turned off the alarm."

"Huh?"

"I bet he's set it up so turning the alarm off sent a signal to him. He wouldn't be coming back here. And anyway, he's planning on leaving soon."

Was that what he wanted the Nagas for? A ticket out of the US? In exchange for what? Handing me over?

"Gut instinct?" Gray said.

I nodded. "What did you two find in the basement?" I asked as we climbed into the Hill Bitch.

"You're in great danger, Amber," Mary answered, resting her head in her hands. "This one's so powerful, so evil."

"The dead Were was nothing to do with what that room was used for," Gray said. "There was a ritual practiced there, many times."

"A working, a twisted working of the energy," Mary said. "To take, to give nothing back. Not an Adept working."

"Not entirely." Gray cut across her.

"A working of bits and pieces," Mary said. "All embellished like a crazy patchwork. As if the caster worked from hints and experiments. Like the working on your car. This is the same one."

"Those experiments…" I said.

"On people," Gray replied, his face grim.

"To take what?"

"The essence of a person," Mary said. "It's not clear what it's doing or how, but I think the intention is to steal abilities. But it's like the caster— it's insane. It takes everything: abilities, flesh, bone, everything."

"The bodies! The damage done to them," Melissa said. "A spell like this would cut through bone without leaving a mark?"

Gray nodded.

Mary lifted her face and looked at me. "This was a Were. However he managed to get started, he has built his abilities by stealing from people who access the energy." She wiped her cheek. "I could feel him in Denver; I knew he was twisting energy and I knew he had to be Athanate. Because that's what Athanate are—evil. Everyone knew that. I looked away. This is my fault."

"No," Gray said. "You aren't evil. This isn't your fault."

"It is. All that is needed for evil to prosper, is for good people to do nothing. I did nothing. I share the blame."

"Surely the victims aren't all Adepts?" I said. "You would have known."

Mary shook her head.

"No," Gray answered for her. "Not Adepts exactly." He thought for a moment. "There's a task that Adepts must sometimes do," he said. "You've been told that everyone has a little access to the energy?"

"Yeah."

"Some people can develop their ability without spirit guides, without the safety net of the Adept community. Sometimes, Adept communities adopt them. With most, it's safer just to lock down their abilities. That doesn't destroy their ability, just prevents them from using it."

"But why?"

"Because the type of person we're talking about is on a fine line at the edge of sanity. For this small group, the same thing in their mental makeup that makes them borderline insane also enables them to develop their access to the energy. It would be very dangerous to leave them."

I was angry. I didn't know how it could be changed without making it worse, but the thought of treating people like this was plain wrong. And then abandoning them into the human community where a predator like the rogue could discover them…

"This is why he's so interested in you, Amber."

"What? But my Adept abilities are nothing."

"No, not that," Mary said. "He's absorbed the Adept abilities he wants. He may have even tried to absorb Athanate before and failed. But you're unique. You've found a balance between Were and Athanate. That's what he wants from you."

Chapter 53

I laid my head back on the seat and listened to Agent Ingram's cell ringing. Any second now, his voicemail would cut in. I didn't want to talk to his voicemail, but if I left a message, I could claim I'd done my duty, couldn't I?

I closed my eyes.

The Hill Bitch was just as cold, but I'd picked up an old ski jacket from Liu when I'd dropped Mary off. Melissa was safe back at Manassah. I was warm. Bliss.

"Yes?"

I jumped.

"Ah…Agent Ingram?"

"Ms. Farrell. I do say, I am most pleased to hear from you."

"Yeah, hold onto that. Are you back in Denver?"

"I am. Are you coming in to talk now?"

"No. Sorry. But I have some intelligence for you. There was a crash out on the Cabrini road off US40 late last night. It's my belief that the driver belonged to Ops 4-16. Seems like there's a lot in Denver at the moment."

"Looking for Colonel Laine?"

"Among others."

He went ominously quiet for a couple of beats. "My level of discretion about how and what I report doesn't extend to the army's fourteen-million-dollar gunships being blown out the sky, or a battalion of special forces running amok in Denver."

"I hear you, Ingram. Me, the Alversons, the colonel, you and your boss. It'll be good to talk. Soon as you put 4-16 away."

"Ms. Farrell—"

"I'm in a hurry. I have something more specific to the other investigation the FBI seems to be running in Denver, but it overlaps with 4-16. Will you be taking charge of the combined investigation?"

"No. I appreciate your concerns on the matter," he said, "but I do need to bring my colleague into this conversation." The sound muffled for a few moments.

He was calling Griffith in. I had been sure he would have to. I didn't want to talk to the man, but it felt wrong to hide what had happened last night.

"Yes, ma'am." The sound had changed. I was on a speakerphone.

"Who's there?" I asked.

"Agent Griffith, Ms. Farrell."

"Okay." *Here goes nothing.* "My intelligence is that a string of murders has been committed in Denver by one person. Many of these had a signature of damage to the thighbone of the victim. The victims came largely from itinerant or homeless people and I understand little investigation was ever done to connect these cases."

"Culminating in the murder of Barbara Green," Griffith said. "Wearing your clothes and in your old house."

"That may have been the last," I said. "There was one detective who investigated—"

"Clayton," Griffith interrupted.

Yes, Agent Griffith, you are right on top of this investigation. Now shut up.

"My intelligence suggests he was killed at his home last night."

There were some muffled background noises, and I let them run with it for a while. Griffith was probably sending a car out to Arvada.

"Are you saying that the detective was on the right track and he has been killed by whoever killed the others?" Ingram again.

"In a manner of speaking. I believe the detective was killed on the orders of the murderer he nearly caught three years ago. But here's where it gets weird. I believe he was killed by Ops 4-16."

"The woman at the Cabrini crash?"

"Yes."

"This all ties back into the military?" Ingram asked.

"I can't say. My intel simply suggests that the woman and a male accomplice who were at the murder scene were members of Ops 4-16. And there's one other item. I believe the killer used a house in Glenmore Hills." I gave them the address, and there were more background sounds.

Griffith came back on.

"Where's Melissa Owen?" he said.

"She's safe," I said. "And she has nothing to add to this conversation at the moment."

"Ms. Farrell, you've been very careful how you've phrased all this 'intelligence', and I'm going to find out how you came by it. In the meantime, I remind you, if I catch you or Owen at any crime scenes, I will arrest you for impeding my investigation."

"I hear you." I cut the call and scrubbed my face with my hands, stifling a yawn.

I had more important things to do than swap insults with him.

I had a session booked with Noble. He wanted to get inside my head. I needed things from him that would help me catch the rogue. One little clue that would unlock the puzzle. The trouble was, I didn't know what that clue was, and the only way to find it was to subject myself to Noble's well-meaning questioning.

Chapter 54

Something fundamental. Something very important. I have to pick it out from this jumble of images. Nick Gray, wolf, bear, cougar. Dead Matlal Were, hanging on the wall. Silas, Ursula, Kyle. Mary. Where did the trail of unhappy women lead? How far am I from the rogue? Sick fascination; the thought of feeding on fear.

Feed. Which wolf do I feed? Can I tell them apart in the night?

Diana's hand gripping my neck.

Time is running out. Time!

My head banged on the steering wheel and I sat bolt upright, panic rippling down my skin.

I was parked.

It was all right. I was safe. Not on the roads. Not about to swerve across the interstate and crush someone under the monster tires.

I must have dozed for a second. Or two.

What time was it?

What the freaking hell time was it?

I never carried a watch unless I needed to time something to the second. My dad had trained me to keep time in my head. I hadn't lost track since…

Since I'd been in Obs—strapped to a gurney, a medical experiment to study.

Sweat stood out on my forehead.

I was sitting in the Hill Bitch, parked across from Dr. Noble's office. I had no memory of how I'd gotten there.

What had I been thinking of all that time?

Colonel Laine, up close in my face, tracking my symptoms for the Obs unit. "Blackouts?"

"No, sir."

Liar. But he can't tell. He's not my alpha.

I got out of the car.

There was a tremor in my hands.

What the hell was happening to me?

People have attention lapses all the time.

Not like this.

A drugstore sign had the time on it, and I was late. I remembered something now. I'd called and asked for a later appointment with Noble and it was only available at his office. Now I was late anyway.

Other than last Friday night, sandwiched so happily between Jen and Alex, I hadn't had a decent night's sleep since the Assembly.

"Four days awake and you start hallucinating," says Ben-Haim. *"As an interrogator, this can be your friend. As a prisoner, not so much."*

It might be that—too little sleep. It might be the Athanate crusis returning, pulled back by my Were infusion. Or the Were and Athanate fighting. I needed help, and I didn't know who to trust. Bian didn't trust Alice. Alice said not to trust anyone but Diana. Diana wasn't here. Skylur wasn't here. Noble had been helpful, but he was pack first, whatever he said about patient confidentiality. If he thought I was flaky, he'd tell Felix, and that would escalate the issues that Felix was trying to keep us both from having to confront.

Bian. Something I'd forgotten to do with Bian.

I slapped my head and lifted the TacNet from around my neck.

"Bian, you there?"

"I am, Round-eye. I thought you were going to pull a treble shift."

I snorted weakly. "No, just late handing over is all. I'm going in to see Doc Noble and then I'll be at Alex's if you need me."

"Yeah, well, you know my opinion of the doctor. Come talk to Alice and me. It'll be a lot better for you."

"Maybe so, but Doc knows a bit more about the Were."

"I hope you know what you're doing. I really don't think I'd want that quack messing with my head." She huffed. "Anyway, I got the hunt coordination till tomorrow. Get some rest, Amber. You're still healing from last week."

"I will. Thanks, bye."

I cut the comms link and tossed the TacNet in the back of the truck.

I *would* prefer to be talking to her and Alice, but I was here now. I crossed the road and went into the office.

Doc Noble's receptionist was too bright and perky for someone who was working on Sunday. She was about forty—a pale-skinned brunette, sensibly and formally dressed. I figured the makeup would have taken an hour by itself.

"Oh, I'm always here when Dr. Noble is working," she said, when I commented. "He makes such a commitment to so many, I can only try and do my part to help."

I strangled the little demon in my throat. The way she said his name gave away how she felt. I wondered if the doctor reciprocated. But then, who was I to comment on other people's love lives?

"You *are* a little late, Ms. Farrell." She wriggled on her seat. "I've had to shuffle one of his telephone consultations. It shouldn't be too much longer. Can I make you some coffee?"

Given Doc's reaction last time, I turned it down.

I'd fall asleep if I sat, so instead, I looked at his certificates and testimonial photographs.

They took up the whole wall, except for a couple of spaces where ones had been removed.

Why?

I caught myself with a snort. *Paranoid, much?*

The wall was impressive. He did a lot more than his private work here.

I'd known he worked at the Psychiatric Center in Centennial; we'd met for lunch not far from there. Centennial was famous for treating addictions and 'deprogramming'—curing people with obsessive/compulsive psychoses or victims of cult programming.

By the look of it, he also worked at the discreetly named Aurora Regional Center, which was essentially a lifer prison for the criminally insane. Max, they called it on the street.

And the Denver Free Psychiatric Outreach Association.

And—

"Amber, come in, please."

I followed him into his office. There wasn't a black couch. In fact, we sat pretty much as we had at Alex's house, with me rocked back on a recliner. Doc's chair was cleverly small so he didn't look so lost in it.

"I had hoped to find you more relaxed today," he said.

I barked out a laugh.

"Doc, I've barely slept. I've been out fighting. Been all but buried by Were and Athanate politics. Found a hideout house with a torture dungeon. Had to fend off the FBI. And I haven't even had coffee today."

"Well, let's get away from what's happening outside and concentrate on what's happening inside. I'll start by giving you the mild sedatives I told you about—"

"Sorry, Doc. I just can't." I pulled the recliner back up. "I can't even lie back. I'll go to sleep and drool on your pretty chair."

He was pissed, and I couldn't blame him.

"Look, I promise I will next time," I said. "I can't slow down. I know I'm messing you around, but I can't spend time talking about my childhood while there's a rogue out there. I just feel that things are too critical."

"You're right, the next few days *are* critical—they're critical to you. There's no point in running around Denver like a zombie. You'd be a danger to yourself and others. We have to get you to a state where you can operate to your full potential."

I rubbed my eyes, which didn't seem to help much. Time to change tack. "What causes blackouts, Doc?"

His eyes narrowed. "For humans, momentary interruption of blood supply to the brain, electrical failure, or psychogenic causes like extreme stress."

"And for Athanate, you can add crusis, which is, I guess, paranormal psychogenic stress. What about Were? The same? Is it normal to have blackouts?"

"No. For the Were, the blackout represents time spent in a mental state as a wolf that is incomprehensible to the human side. Time spent fully wolf."

"But it could also just be a human reaction to lack of sleep?"

He tilted his head. "Possibly."

I couldn't be going wolf, not while I was driving.

"I'm just stupid tired," I said. "Falling asleep for seconds at a time."

"Well, relax for a few minutes before you rush off again." He picked up his notepad. "Let's see what we can salvage from this session."

Crap. But he'd answered a question for me. I pushed the recliner halfway. As long as I kept talking, I guessed I had a chance of staying awake.

"Hmm. Family is important to mental health." He chewed his lip. "You say you're not getting along well with your mother and sister. Let's start by expanding on that a little."

I had Mom and Kath visiting at Alex's later. I'd find out how broken it was then. Would Kath come along? Would she want an explanation before she handed over the necklace? What would she do when I couldn't tell her? And how bad would that look to Mom?

I tried to put that out of my mind and answer the question.

"My sister's the problem." I couldn't help but give away my feelings in my voice. "There's a bunch of reasons, some of which might be the stuff you came up with last time. Anyway, she doesn't believe anything about me. I can't tell her anything about what I've really done or what I am. So, she makes up things; says I've been living as a whore, I'm a drug addict, I've been brainwashed by a cult or whatever comes into her mind. The trouble is, as far as my Mom's concerned, Kath's there for her at the moment, and I'm not."

"I see." His pen scratched quietly. "What about the pack as a family? Does it feel like that?"

"Felix as Dad? No." I laughed.

"What about you as the father-figure? You have the alpha tendencies. You took over the role of provider after your father's death. You were in command of a team in the army. You are a House in the Athanate structure. Do you feel comfortable as the team leader rather than the team player?"

I wriggled. Was he saying I couldn't be in the pack? I was too alpha? "I'm adaptable," I hedged.

"How did this adaptability manifest in the police? I understand there was an incident at the end of your time there where you acted alone."

"A young girl, Emily Schumacher, was abducted by three rogue Athanate. I was on the scene, I could smell them. I understood what the stakes were. The SWAT team were too slow and they didn't know what they were dealing with. I had to act. There wasn't an option to adapt to working with others."

"You had to take responsibility for a kidnapped child? Is this a recurring theme?"

"No. I knew her. And it was the only thing I could do. Can we talk about something else?"

"The Athanate build a family around themselves of necessity, but it is structured, with roles and tasks. The pack much less so. Does the structure feel important to you?"

I frowned and closed my eyes. This felt less irritating.

"No, not really. It's family, even if there are bits missing. I mean, as a paranormal, I'm not going to have children. I'm not broody or anything, but I know there'll be a time when I regret it."

"A daughter would be important for you?"

I smiled to myself, imagining Emily as a daughter. "Yes."

"Not a father or mother figure?"

It was so comfortable sitting back with my eyes closed, but I'd have to go soon. I couldn't be late.

What had he just asked? Father and mother figures?

"Huh. Skylur and Diana, I guess. It's not quite like that."

Where the hell was Diana? Why hadn't she been in contact? I sat back up, the bubble of comfort broken, and the wolf starting to stir inside me.

Doc looked up. His pen stopped scratching. He looked in a much better mood than when we started.

"That was good! A moment there where you actually relaxed. Maybe in the next session, we can work it up to a minute or two."

I guessed he was just joking, but my wolf felt my space had been invaded. I growled.

"We're out of time," he said. "Next session will be better. We can discuss control issues."

Interesting. Noble might be small, but his importance to the pack gave him enough status that he was able to push back at me.

I got up and stretched, refusing to let the wolf out. Everything else filtered back in. I had duties.

"Doc, I need to ask some questions."

He shrugged and glanced at his watch. "Okay. You have five minutes."

"A detective came to see you three years ago. Although he didn't realize it, he was working on the rogue case."

"Yes. Detective...Clayton. I remember."

"He's dead now. I'm trying to piece together his investigation. What did he want?"

Noble raised his brows at the news and then shrugged again. "He was asking about some patients who came into the Free Outreach sessions. Trying to determine their last known movements. Other members of the pack got called on as well. Silas and Kyle, I know. Felix, I think. Clayton was very interested in anyone who worked down in those communities. He was desperate to fit facts to theories."

"But why did he concentrate on you? Surely there are dozens of doctors down there?"

"Ha! There are four or five of us on a really good day. I got volunteered, I suppose. The others, they don't like my approach."

"Why?"

"I don't believe in institutionalizing people, or putting them on prescriptive therapy, when there is no assurance of continuation, either from funding or commitment. Episodic treatment is more damaging than leaving well enough alone."

"Wow." I raised my brows. "A doctor who doesn't prescribe."

"Under those circumstances, no. Of course, I recommend returning to the center frequently and talking to one of the doctors there. Simply talking in a group or one to one. Socialization is far more potent in the long term than dulling the senses or making people dependent."

We'd moved swiftly to an area I couldn't argue one way or the other, and we were both silent while we walked through the office. The receptionist smiled and I was impressed all over again by that wall of photos and certificates.

He opened the door and ushered me through. I was surprised that he was seeing me out. Surely he didn't do that for every patient?

"You think Clayton was on to something?" Noble asked once we were in the lobby.

"I think he got close enough that it was worth murdering him as soon as he started talking to me."

"Oh, my God." He shook his head sadly and thrust his hands into his pockets. The lobby was cold and he was definitely not dressed for stepping outside.

"They say snow," he said, looking out the front. "Your car's not far?"

"Just around the corner," I said. I wanted no one to know what I was driving. "I'm borrowing something bigger to fit in with the pack."

He chuckled. "Size isn't everything."

"No, of course not. But everyone in the pack drives something oversized. I guess it might be difficult to contain all that Were enthusiasm you talk about in a small car."

Sitting in the Hill Bitch at a drive-through ten minutes later, cuddling a coffee, I called Felix before I lost my courage.

"...so, we have DNA from the basement, and our own CSI agent, with equipment," I said, winding up a report of last night. "This may be chance to prove if it's a member of the pack."

"You want DNA from the whole pack?"

"Yes." There was an ominous silence. I cringed. I had known this wasn't going to go down well. If only there had been time to explain it face to face. That would have been better. Maybe. That or fatal.

"It happens that I can help," he said.

"Err...great."

"Doc took blood samples from everyone a year or so ago. We should still have them. But..."

That was like two punches in the stomach, one after another.

"Yes?" I said.

"But we will raise this at a pack meeting first. You need to convince them."

He didn't wait to hear what the demon in my throat had to say about that.

"I have to go now," he said, and the call ended.

Well, that was potentially huge, but I wasn't going to do the happy dance just yet. And I didn't want to stop looking for solutions in other ways. Lots of things could go wrong or be inconclusive. This wasn't standard human DNA we were talking about.

I called Melissa.

"Yes, boss?"

Tullah's joke was catching. First Julie, now Melissa. It served as a prompt that I'd have to put them on the payroll. Or rather, get Tullah to do it.

"Very funny. Good news: the pack may have a DNA database for you to check against the stuff you got from Glenmore Hills."

"Excellent!"

"*If* he was careless. Meanwhile, slave, check the missing women's files."

"Hold on a second. Okay, ready."

"I don't want to stereotype, but wealthy, unhappy women go to therapists, don't they?"

"Yeah. Gods, you're right, they do look the type, don't they? Stereotypes are us." I gave her a minute querying the data.

"No, Amber. Most of them did, but there's no common factor. They went to different doctors all over town."

That would have been too simple.

"Okay, leave that. Do an internet search on Dr. Theodore Noble, please. I want to know all the places he works."

"Easy." There was a clatter of keys in the background, then she started through the list.

His private practice, the Psychiatric Center, the Aurora Regional Center, the Denver Free Psychiatric Outreach Association.

And the Denver VA Medical Center. The Post Traumatic Stress Disorder Faculty.

"Thanks, Melissa. Later." I ended the call.

There could be a hundred reasons that his wall of certificates and endorsements had a couple missing. And no certainty that the missing ones would be from the VA Medical Center. Where Barbara Green might have been treated.

I finished the coffee and swung the Hill Bitch out onto the road.

So that was what therapy was like.

You go in thinking one thing and come out thinking another.

I'd lost normal a long, long way back, I guessed, but I caught myself thinking: Is it normal to have a suspicion that your dapper, urbane therapist is secretly a deranged, sociopathic serial killer?

No. I was just too tired to think straight. It was physically impossible. Maybe I'd have the DNA database soon, and it would all become easy.

Chapter 55

Not trusting my memory, I mentally went through everything with the deliberate, fumbling care of a drunk as I drove to Alex's.

Bian was coordinating the rogue hunt until tomorrow now. I flipped the sound on the TacNet and listened to a couple of standard reports as team leaders declared an area searched. They'd come find me if they needed me.

Tullah was at the Kwan, discussing the outcome of our request to talk to Adepts in the Empire of Heaven with Mary and Liu. I hadn't received any angry calls about revealing Tullah's secret, and I was more than happy to let that sleeping dragon lie for the moment.

Melissa was safe at Manassah, trying to decode Clayton's notes and warming up her DNA analysis machine.

Jen, David, Pia and Julie were downtown. Julie had called to say they were going in to use the office conference system. Some problem had come up in the New York subsidiary.

Alex was waiting at his house, where Mom and Kath were due to arrive in thirty minutes.

I couldn't shake the feeling that I was missing something as the Hill Bitch snarled through the traffic, scaring other cars out of the way. Something I'd almost reached when I'd fallen asleep in front of Noble's office.

Maybe all I needed was a good night's rest.

No chance.

I pulled up outside Alex's and I knew there was something wrong immediately. One of the cleanup crew's green vans was standing there.

Silas was coming down the path. Alex and Ricky were just emerging from the house, supporting another big man in blue overalls. I recognized Kyle Larsen from the photo Melissa had sent me. Olivia was coming out behind them.

Larsen was a mess. His legs didn't seem to be working. His eyes were glazed.

Olivia was in tears.

Had the pack found the rogue and started summary justice?

"What's going on?" I said as I ran up the steps.

Silas blocked me like tall, dark wall. "This isn't for you."

"It freaking is until I know what's going on. I want to ask him some questions. You as well."

I tried to get around him, but his big arms just swung out and stopped me. He pushed me off the path. They were past and Kyle was in the van before I got free.

"Alex?"

He looked past me and just shook his head. I couldn't believe it.

"Damn it, no. What are you doing?" I yelled.

Alex grabbed me.

"Have we come at a bad time?" Mom's voice.

Yes, you could say that. Mom and Kath had arrived behind me.

"Right with you, Mrs. Farrell." Alex tried to hide that he was holding me. He nearly got his ankle broken for his efforts.

Silas turned as he got in the van. "We can't talk about this now," he said quietly to me, his eyes flicking to my family. "It's not outsiders' business."

Ricky leaned out the window as they pulled away and called, "We need you there with us, Alex."

My mouth opened, but Alex was shaking his head at me.

"I am so sorry, Mrs. Farrell." He held his hand out. "Won't you please come in?"

I was trembling with anger. Not just at the pack for whatever it was they'd done, including brushing me aside, but at Alex. How could he do this?

Mom sensed the tension. She used what she'd always used when I was angry; she talked.

They got the house tour. The split level, the kitchen, with its very, very sturdy railing above the hall, the bedroom, Kath's eyes slyly looking for signs that I lived there, the airy study, and back down to his living room with its big timber beams and Native American bookshelves.

The old photo of Hope—Alex's girlfriend who'd died from her inability to change—had been removed from the bookcase. Even that irritated me, as if she were mine as well. I wanted it back. The stupidity of that calmed me down a little. I was still seething at him for not explaining what had gone on, and having pack business at his house when my Mom was due, but I'd smile and talk for the moment. Now was not the time for a fight.

We sat down for coffee and conversation in the living room.

"What a lovely house, Alex, thank you," Mom said.

"Very bachelor," Kath said brightly.

I ground my teeth. Kath was just fishing to see where I was living. Mom was probably measuring the rooms for the engagement party.

"Your last call was so strange, Amber. Is everything all right?"

She didn't want to come right out and ask about the FBI. And no, everything wasn't all right. And I'd forgotten to organize some kind of a guard today, to make sure there weren't any Nagas around.

Did I need to? I'd started to sound paranoid to myself.

"Things are complicated," I said, "but I'm fine."

"You look tired," Kath said.

"Are you sleeping well?" Mom asked.

No. I'd barely been able to sleep since the Assembly, except for the night I'd persuaded Jen and Alex to be my bookends on the sofa. None of which I could discuss with Mom. Especially the last. "Fine," I said again.

Mom gave it a rest. "These are Arapaho as well?" She pointed at the rugs Alex used as throws on the sofa.

They were, and Alex carried them to the window to show Mom the workmanship.

Kath zeroed in on me like a barracuda. "Why haven't you been calling Mom?" She spoke quietly. "Do you know how upset she's been?"

"And how much of the upset has been caused by you spreading lies to our friends?"

"I may have been mistaken in some things, but you've got to admit, you've been acting more and more strangely lately."

"*Mistaken?* Kath, you make up shit like that and all you can say is you're *mistaken?*"

"Are you doing anything with those anger management issues?"

My demon got off the leash. "Yeah, I'm seeing a therapist. What are you doing about your chronic lying?"

Alex had been explaining his project of collecting the oral traditions of the Arapaho and Cheyenne. Mom had just came up with one of the little stories that Speaks-to-Wolves had taught her. She recited it just like I remembered it from my bedtimes—half in English, half Arapaho.

It drew me out of my argument with Kath, and the sound of the tale, the rhythm of the Arapaho shut me up and carried me back to happy times.

Alex dragged her up to his study to get it recorded.

My eyes came back to find Kath staring at me, and the happy times evaporated.

"You brought the necklace, right?" I said.

"Jesus, enough already with the small talk, hey?" She scowled at me. "No, I didn't."

I clamped down on my temper. "It's important."

"Why is it so frigging important? It's not to me. It's not to Mom. It's important for you, for some reason you won't bother to tell us, so everyone has to jump around because Amber wants a necklace. It's not even yours."

"It is. It goes to the eldest."

"Oh, for fuck's sake. That old trash. Why's a stupid, old bead necklace so important anyway?"

"You can see what this 'trash' means to people like Alex. It's important as part of our cultural history. It's a genuine find. Alex thinks it may have been used in sacred rituals." Kath was looking as if I was speaking a different language. "You clearly can't understand, so it's not worth trying to explain."

"Is this some kind of cult you're mixed up in? What did that guy in the van mean—'outsiders' business'? For God's sake, what have you got yourself into that you can't tell us?"

"Forget it, Kath. I'll come to your place after we're finished here and pick it up."

"No. Why should I let you? Why the hell should I hand it over just because you want it?"

Because it was my only lead on the puzzle of finding a way to help the Were who couldn't change. Because it might be something that helped keep Olivia alive, and I'd promised, on my Blood, to do everything I could.

The anger was boiling up in me now. I could feel Were and Athanate stir inside. This was Were business, but I needed a cool head. An Athanate head. I stood up.

"Because I want it," I said. Cool, cool head. Beneath the raging tangle of emotions on top of her mind, I touched the quiet below. I rested a hand on her shoulder. "That's all you need to know."

Her heart rate slowed, her breathing deepened and her eyes blurred.

"Because I tell you," I said. So calm.

"Because you tell me," she whispered, her voice indistinct, soft, pliable, like her mind.

My wishes were symbols, hard-edged and heavy, like Chinese characters cut from thick metal. They floated down and pressed themselves into her mind, pushing her wishes aside. I could make her do anything. Not that I would. But to get her to stop spreading rumors. Maybe even to find out what lay behind all the negativity toward me that seemed to be powering all her actions. First, the necklace.

My hand was knocked away from her and I was spun around.

What happened?

I was looking up at Alex. He was angry, as pale as his ceiling. Mom was at the top of the stairs looking bewildered.

"Stop it!" he hissed.

The link with Kath wasn't broken. Why should I stop? I was only fixing something that was her fault anyway.

But my kin. My kin was angry at me.

Why?

Everything seemed so slow. I looked down at Kath. She was staring at me, open-mouthed. It was wrong. It was all wrong.

With an almost physical clunk, the connection was broken.

Kath pitched forward on her seat, frowning.

What had I done?

"Excuse us," Alex said, grabbing my arm and marching me out the front door.

My Were and Athanate lashed out in me, making me stagger. I was horrified and yet I couldn't face that. Instead, the anger that Kath had caused boiled straight back up at the worst possible target. Alex.

"I will not let you compel her," he hissed.

"Who are you to tell me what to do?" My mouth just ran away with it. "Don't you see all the shit I have to wade through? What harm is there—"

"Everything." He shook me. "You justify it for something like this, and what's next? Who's next?"

I broke his grip and pushed him away. "But Olivia—"

"I know better than you what Olivia needs, believe me."

Our eukori touched. Not in the gentle way we had before. This was pain, like a branding iron. I could see through Alex's eyes. Hope screaming, tearing with her nails at her flesh, bloody foam bubbling out of her mouth and nose, yet her words so clear. *Kill me*, she had screamed, *please kill me*. Like Olivia, she hadn't been able to change. A Were who couldn't change, died from it. Horribly.

That was the wrong thing to show me.

Couldn't he see? I had sworn an oath on my Blood to help Olivia, to protect her from that fate. I couldn't do it. My oath pushed me to behaving like a Basilikos. No way around.

My strongbox groaned open.

"We'll find another way," he said. He reached to hold me again.

"Don't touch me," I screamed. "Get away from me. Get away."

Kin!

Pack!

I couldn't stand it. I turned and ran.

Mom came out of the house. There was more shouting. Fading away. Run. Run. Don't think. Run.

Chapter 56

People write whole books on what you think about when you're running. I didn't think. With my Were and Athanate-enhanced body, I could run from one side of the city to the other and back again. Thinking wasn't required.

Maybe that was what saved me.

I didn't know how long I ran or what direction I took. Some remote corner of my mind worked, and when I collapsed onto my knees, it was in front of the door to the Kwan.

My eyes cleared, and for the second time, I saw a closure notice on their door.

Classes canceled due to weather.

Call and check before coming.

Keep warm folks!

It *was* cold. My body was able to run for a long time, but the laws of physics being what they were, I'd generated a lot of heat. As soon as I stopped, steam billowed off my skin like a fog.

If I stayed out here someone would call the fire department. My hands wouldn't work. They felt like paws. The wolf was clawing her way into my head. I fell against the door, felt the tingle of their Adept alarm as it opened.

"Amber!" Mary and Tullah were rushing forward.

I couldn't talk. They laid me out on exercise mats; sweat was pouring off me.

Blackness. Then cold packs; freaking, freezing cold packs. That woke me up.

Liu was sponging my head.

"Sorry," I muttered. "Got to get up." The words ran into each other.

Mary pushed me back. It took all of one finger.

Tullah knelt over me, talking to Bian on my cell.

"Listen to me, Amber. Listen to me," Tullah said. She gripped my shoulder.

It sounded as if she were talking from the other end of an empty, echoing hall.

"It's all right, you're safe now. We'll stay with you. This is just an Athanate reaction. Nothing to worry about now. Nod if you can hear me."

Whole body shivers ran down me. My skin rippled. My jaws pulsed and I felt my Athanate fangs. Not an Athanate reaction. I tried to nod anyway, but it was probably lost in the rest of the shaking.

"You should have been resting this week. The injuries from Longmont, what Kaothos did, the fight with Matlal. You should have spent the week in bed."

I tried to laugh. Or cry. I wasn't sure which.

"No. Can't sleep," I croaked. "Nightmares."

There was more hushed, urgent conversation.

Tullah leaning over me again.

She was crying. Why was she crying?

Something about Kaothos. I could feel her in my head.

"Hello, lizard."

"Hush. Listen."

She understands the strongbox. She can't fix what's going wrong in my head, but she can fix the strongbox. Close it back down. Make me sleep.

"Do you want to seal it, Amber Farrell?"

"Yes."

And I feel the weight of her in my mind. Pressing down on the maelstrom of the strongbox.

"Just so long as you keep it closed," she says.

Then: "Sleep." But I only hear her start the word.

Chapter 57

It seemed like days later when I woke. Everything felt kind of muzzy, then as it came back, I panicked, thinking everyone would be wondering where I was. Or worse, they'd know and they would forever be looking at me with sympathy.

Poor girl. Had a terrible breakdown.

Or even worse, the meltdown would happen again.

It was dark outside. They'd moved me to a foam mattress and covered me with a comforter. I had no idea of the time.

Tullah sat beside me and calmed me down. With Kaothos' help, I'd slept deeply, but only for a few hours. No one else knew anything about what had happened. No one was trying to find out where I was.

I felt numb, disconnected. I needed to get back. After an hour or so, Mary finally agreed.

They drove me down to Wash Park, but Alex's house was empty.

What had I done? I stood outside wanting to cry and not daring to, in case Mary hauled me back to her home. Wonderful as it was, I couldn't.

After making me promise I would rest, they let me drive the Hill Bitch the few blocks back to Manassah, but followed until I got there.

I waved goodbye and they disappeared into the darkness as the gates opened.

Shadows cloaked the Spanish portico. The usual scents of lavender and hibiscus had been frozen out.

I was still thinking slowly. It wasn't until I stopped the car that I noticed the number of guards walking around outside. Was it time for a handover? Too early.

And they were in uniform.

My heart skipped several beats before I recognized the faces.

"Good evening, Ms. Farrell," the nearest one greeted me. One of Victor's men. And the uniforms were not really military.

"Evening. Are you changing shifts?"

"No, ma'am. Ms. Kingslund ordered everyone out of the house. Ms. Alverson said we had to double up on the perimeter."

"Fine, I guess." Don't buy a dog and bark. Don't second-guess Julie's security arrangements. "Does 'everyone out' include me?"

"I don't think so."

"Out where?" I asked as I climbed the steps.

"Just next door," he said. "The new building. Should I alert them?" He touched his comms gear.

I looked back from the porch. "Tell them I'm here, is all. Nice uniforms, by the way."

"Yes, ma'am. Ms. Kingslund insisted and we kinda like them."

"Oh. Okay."

I opened the door and stepped hesitantly inside.

Manassah was still. I realized it hadn't been for some time. No wonder Jen had thrown a fit and sent everyone out. I felt more than a pang of guilt. Planting my oddball House at Manassah without invitation had been taking advantage of Jen. And I'd been blind to it, rushing in and out as if I owned the place.

I winced. I'd apologize. If I got a chance.

The hall was bare of evidence of the invasion. No bags and coats. No forest of boots. And just cleaned, so the floor gleamed.

I put my borrowed jacket on the empty rack, took off my boots and tiptoed into the living room.

"Hello?"

Silence. Not even a murmur from the kitchen.

As I stood there, a different type of fear grew in me, nameless and formless, like a black fog filling my body. I might have lost one kin today through my own stupidity. Please not two.

I walked down the hallway to the bedrooms, my heart thudding painfully in my throat.

The door to my suite was open. I never left it open.

Inside, the bed was stripped bare. The walk-in closets were open and completely empty.

I could understand. The guard outside was wrong. I wasn't welcome any more. My clothes would be waiting for me next door. No doubt, neatly and efficiently folded by Jen's maids.

And really, it was all my fault. Jen had been patient beyond belief with me, but she was only human. I'd screwed this up with her, like I'd screwed it up with Alex. My fault.

She was probably in her bedroom. No doubt enjoying the silence after her house had been emptied of the noise and hassle of uninvited guests.

If I was careful, I could probably make it back out without disturbing her. Thank God I'd taken my boots off. Later, we would meet again and be polite while I found some way to pay her back for everything she'd done for me.

I'd need to find a way to remove the kin bond, if I hadn't destroyed it already. Was that possible?

And the house next door. Hell, how was I even going to start paying for that?

But it was all right. Much better for Jen. I was a freaking liability as a…as a friend, let alone anything else. Really, it was fine.

My Athanate lashed to and fro, but I wasn't going to do anything to make it worse.

I turned and stumbled blindly back to the door of the suite. Not *my* suite any more. The guest suite, and I wasn't even a guest.

"There you are!"

I jerked to a halt, only just managing not to run her down.

"I need you to decide." She grabbed my arm and dragged me into her room. "After all," she said, "it's your stuff."

She had me standing open-mouthed in front of her walk-in closets. Bigger than the guest suite of course. Much bigger. The size of a small apartment.

"Now, I like the matching suits at one end and the mix and match at the other," she said, waving at one side. "I couldn't work out your method from your closet. Do you arrange by color? It's so difficult to assess when you don't have enough to go on."

"I don't have a method anymore," I mumbled.

"Well, they must have in the army."

"They eased up on that. Mostly, it needed to be clean and neat."

"Bet you had your own system, though?"

"Uniforms on the left," I said. It came back to me. "Formal dress uniform leftmost, then BDU, cleaned, bagged. Civilian clothes on the right. Most formal rightmost."

"Most formal, hey? What was that?"

"A plain dark dress and jacket."

"Wow." She giggled. "That formal."

A lock of golden hair had escaped her casual bun, and she thoughtfully wound it back with the rest.

She'd moved my clothes in here, and all that implied. She'd gone down to Lisa's and brought back my green ball gown, slotting it in next to the gold dress I'd worn to the reception. My jeans, all three pairs of them, were hung together, and my shirts next to them. A scarlet kimono, the twin to the one Jen wore now, hung by itself. There was a lot of space between things. A lot. More space than things, in fact. The open drawers alongside held my underwear, also looking plain and lonely.

"How did you get it all in?" I started, and then I saw a pile of her clothes to one side.

"I got rid of things I don't wear any more. And it's not as if I'm short of things to wear." She waved it off. "This has been a great excuse. I moved your toothbrush, too. I guess you don't go much for makeup and creams."

"No," I said.

Jen walked past me and pirouetted in the middle of the bedroom, her arms spread wide. Showing off her room.

I'd seen inside her room before. Security checks.

And the rest, said Tara.

Dreams. Just dreams.

But to stop and look at it was different.

All the wall lighting was soft and bounced off the ceiling. A single snake-head lamp stood to one side for reading in bed. The bed itself was Olympic-sized, covered in a bright, silky comforter and scattered with pillows and cushions. The carpet underfoot was a field of cream. Huge bay windows looked out on dark gardens, but unlike the guest suite, the view would be down to the Country Club. The half-open door to her bathroom gave a glimpse of an ornate marble altar to cleanliness.

It was like the most luxurious bedroom suite from the ritziest magazine I'd never expected to see in real life. And I was being invited to stay.

She pulled the blinds and came back to me.

"Well?"

"Jen, it's beautiful, but—"

"But nothing. I've been spinning my wheels. Time to get a grip." She demonstrated by slipping her arms around me.

The way we fit together hadn't changed. A sense of completeness stole through me. My Athanate purred and the feeling of lazy anticipation bubbled up again.

Oh yes!

Our hearts settled into sync, as if we practiced this. No fuss. No urgency. No pressure, other than the gentle crush of our arms.

And the insistent hammering in my head.

"It's too dangerous, Jen. I'm not in control. I had a complete meltdown this afternoon. I don't know what I'll do."

I tried to move away, but she didn't let go and we danced awkwardly back until I thumped against the full length mirror set between the two halves of her closet.

There was something hanging there. I could feel the slick fabric against my neck.

"And what on earth is this?"

She eased her hold to allow me to turn around to see what she was pointing at.

"It's my batsuit and brake," I said.

"Your *what*?"

"For jumping out of planes. It's the name we gave it in Ops 4-10. It's for VHALO. Vectored High Altitude Low Opening parachute jumps. The brake is the parachute. You jump out of the aircraft when it's very high and far from your drop zone, so the aircraft noise doesn't give you away. You use the batsuit like a base jumper," I babbled, lifting the arms and showing the tough, stretchy fabric between the arms and the body, and between the legs. "Squirrel would be a better name than bat, because you don't fly, you just sort of control the angle and direction of your fall. It's fun. We always said it was almost as good..." I stumbled to a halt.

"Ahh," said Jen, grinning. "And what's that?"

Her fingers brushed the letters I'd inked on the breast.

TaJ.

They'd had me take it off, but it had always found its way back.

"Sort of a motto. Completely against regs." I rubbed at it, but it would take more than that to erase it. "I probably shouldn't have the suit at all."

"Hmm. You have a history of not doing what you're told," she said.

I turned back. Mistake. Once I started looking into those blue eyes, I couldn't look away.

"And 'TaJ', that wouldn't be 'Trust and Jump', would it?" Her breath trailed phantom fingers over my cheek.

"You know damn well what it stands for. I've told you before," I said and swallowed. "I never meant it like that."

"Like what? Like 'trust me and I'll jump you?'"

I laughed. More a surprised bark than a laugh. "Yeah. But seriously, listen to me. I trust you, Jen. It's me I don't trust."

"I know. But I also know that you wouldn't hurt me. That includes all of you. You have to trust me to trust you," she whispered.

Kin!

Something Pia had said. *The desire of kin is sacred to me.*

Jen's lips brushed mine.

Oh, my God. Oh, my God. Oh, my God.

Oh, shut up, said Tara.

Jen's lips were so soft. I just melted into the kiss, like falling free.

"No!" I panicked and jerked back. My mouth ached for the touch of hers again, and my heart was trying to break a rib or two. I didn't let go of her.

"Hmm." She reached to her left, into her half of the hanging space, bringing out a black silk scarf. "Let's try this. Hold still."

She wound it around my head, blindfolding me.

With my sight gone, everything else sharpened. I could hear the twinned thud of our hearts. The unsteady ebb and flow of our breath. The scent of Jen; it made me think of jasmine and sea-salt. The warmth of her, through her thin kimono and my cotton shirt.

And the touch of our auras, the eukori. Mysterious. Beguiling. Lapping and merging at the edges, sending me flickering, disconcerting images of how my body felt to Jen.

Not calming me at all, but I was no longer panicking.

"Wow," Jen breathed. "The blindfold works for horses, wasn't sure it'd work for you."

I laughed nervously again. "You get mares to have sex with each other this way?"

She giggled. "Don't be silly. Mares sometimes need something to calm them when the stallion's new. But the principle's the same."

Her fingers touched my cheek, gently guiding me back into the kiss and I was flying again. Our tongues twisted languidly around each other.

This time, she broke it, but slowly.

I sighed. It was the sound of doubts finally trickling out of me. "Never done that before."

"Well, long overdue." She stepped back and took my hand, pulling me lightly. "And time for you to come out of the closet."

I started laughing and she caught it.

For a minute or two we couldn't do anything else. Then she tugged my hand.

I walked forwards blindly, trusting her to guide me. It was strange, to hand over responsibility and simply follow. I felt light. Calm and excited at the same time. Eager and relaxed.

It was still a shock when her fingers began tugging at my shirt buttons. A pleasant shock, echoed in the depths of my belly. My hands came up to help, but she pushed them back down again.

Then her hand slipped inside, pushing the shirt away, circling back to caress my breast as my shirt slid down my back.

I gasped and Jen's mouth closed over mine. My nipples were painfully sensitive to her gentle touch.

Another couple of tugs. The rasp of the zipper, my legs began to tremble as she eased the rest of my clothes off me. Her kimono floated down to the floor.

I was completely blind, completely naked and completely loving it.

A couple of steps and she was pushing me back onto the bed.

It was soft as feathers beneath me, but not as soft as Jen's skin against my mouth. I reached to pull her down on me.

"Oh, no, no, no," she said, pressing me back with a hand in the middle of my chest. "This is my show."

She grabbed my wrists and stretched my arms over my head, pinned them there.

"God, you look amazing." Her voice was rough with desire.

"So do you."

"You can't see me."

"Don't need to."

We kissed again. She held herself off me, refusing to touch me anywhere else until my whole body felt like one endless hot zone, desperate to be kissed or stroked, anything.

She paused. "How much self-control do you think you have?" she murmured.

I laughed, releasing some of the growing tension that had me struggling for breath. "I'm lying here on your bed, blindfold, stark naked and begging you to make love to me. How much do you think?"

"Hmm. Well, here's your test." She leaned over me; her lips grazed mine, swung away. Her breath tickled my chin, down my neck, sending goosebumps rippling over my chest. She let me go. "Keep your hands up there, whatever I do."

She roamed over me, holding herself just apart, touching me with nothing but her breath and the warmth of her body floating above me. I could sense exactly where she was. I groaned and arched my body, but she was merciless. The best I could manage was a fleeting hint like the kiss of a ghost or a dream of fingers that vanished with daybreak.

Exquisite, unending torture.

My hands knotted in the sheets and my jaw clamped in frustration, and at the very point I could bear it no longer, her clever tongue found me and I exploded, screaming, the velvet darkness of the blindfold filling with such sweet light.

∞ ∞ ∞ ∞ ∞

It was still deep night. We'd slept and woken many times together. When finally I woke and she slept on, I moved to the living room, unable to get back to sleep and not wanting to disturb her.

Despite the broken sleep, I was feeling happy and peaceful. Fulfilled.

Kin. Purr.

I heard her footsteps.

"I'm here," I said, sitting up on the sofa.

The situation was reversed from last night. I could see in this light, and she was blind. I went across and captured her, led her back to the sofa.

"Everything okay?" A hint of concern hid under the casual question.

"Of course. I woke up and couldn't get back to sleep. I didn't want to disturb you."

"Oh."

I pulled her under the blanket and we tangled comfortably together, a patchwork of flesh and silk kimono.

"Is everything really okay?" she asked again.

"Depends what you mean. If you mean I had sex with another woman for the first time and is it okay? No. It's not okay." I hugged her closer. "If you mean did making love to you turn me inside out and fill my veins with champagne and make me want to do it over and over again, forever, then the answer to all that is, hell, yes."

"Oh."

"Hmm. *Oh.* Oh, what have you done to me?"

The kimonos parted as I wrestled us around until I had her pinned under me.

We'd swapped roles all night, sometimes with every kiss. I bossed her, knowing deep down that I'd enjoy being bossed next time. I'd never felt so relaxed.

So very relaxed, I barely noticed until my fangs manifested and grazed her cheek.

Her gasp was like a slap across the face. I tried to wrench myself away, but she wouldn't let me go. Her hand snaked out and fumbled with the lamp. For a minute I thought she was going to hit me with it but she just switched it on.

I had my hand in front of my mouth.

"No," she said, pulling it away. "Show me."

The tickle of fear and excitement from her teased me. The fangs stayed, for all my willing them to disappear.

It wasn't the sickening emotion of terror. She was a little scared and a little eager. She reached up and ran her tongue along a fang. I nearly came right then and there.

"Wow," she whispered. "Pia did say they were a hot zone."

I was trembling, in fear of what I might do to her and the urgent desire to do it. Our emotions mirrored each other.

"Shh." She left my throbbing fangs alone and hushed me. Her arms encircled me, drawing me back down into her embrace. "We both want this. You know I do, you can feel it, but we can wait. I understand."

The fever drained from me, pushed back out by a lazy, sensuous satisfaction. My Athanate took rain checks when they were written like this. The fangs disappeared.

Our bodies stirred languorously together.

I gently urged her higher and higher. Pia was right, Jen's pleasure was sacred to me.

And at the very moment she reached the peak, I pressed my lips to her ear and whispered. Then watched as the storm of her climax boiled through her.

And whether it was the words themselves, for words have power, or the bond we shared, I could not stop myself from joining her.

Chapter 58

MONDAY

Monday morning hadn't even dawned.

Jen had to make the 6 a.m. flight to New York. We'd gotten up early and dressed, close, sharing space, everything feeling strangely awkward and pleasantly familiar at the same time.

I'd made the coffee and Jen was wheeling her overnight case into the living room when the rest of the crew trooped in.

Pia's face immediately lit up. Julie, equally quickly, adopted Sergeant face number 3—'I offer no opinion on events I know to have just happened'. David, such a smart man, hampered in this only by the wrong set of chromosomes, smiled in slight bewilderment at the Athanate contentment pheromones that had to be rolling off me.

Jen didn't give them time to make more of it.

"David, I need the New York projections taken forward to account for the opening prices in London and I need them now."

He handed over a USB with a quiet smile. "I'm back in Fort Collins today," he said. "I'm going to need another day or so to unravel their system."

"That's fine. Getting it right is what counts at the moment."

"Tom's outside," Julie said. "He wants to go now. They've upgraded the snowfall forecast twice in the last hour, and he's worried about getting back."

"The flight's okay?" Jen asked.

"I just checked, we're on. Not sure about the return."

"We'll worry about that when it's time."

She gave me a last hug and whispered in my ear. "Nothing will keep me away, but you really must stop looking like the cat who found her way into the dairy."

"Whose fault is that?" I murmured and she laughed as she moved away, trailing fingers down my arm.

My fangs pulsed with pleasure, but I could already feel her absence like a physical pain.

Paul came in and helped with the luggage.

"Be careful," I said to Julie.

She smiled tightly. She looked down at her boots, the scatter of snow on them melting over the hallway's clean floors. "Yeah. Boss, y'know," she said, "after Keith gets out, if you're still having difficulty finding your ass with both hands, we'd be okay to help out. If you—"

"I'd love to have both of you on board," I said, and I meant it. Julie being shy was a new one on me.

She nodded her thanks and quickly followed the rest of them out, her security persona slipping back on like a jacket.

Tom and Paul had come in two SUVs, but they were alone. It was an escort, but it was the barest minimum. Altau was stretched every which way.

I stood and waved goodbye from the portico. The snow was falling steadily now.

One of the guards I recognized walked past. He was wearing an outdoor coat, but I could see the new uniform underneath.

"Hey, Steve."

"Morning, Ms. Farrell."

In the light of the portico, I could see the uniforms were just good quality, regular clothes with patch pockets and the look of hard-wearing material. His coat was part of it, and it had a new logo. Steve brushed the snow off when he saw me looking.

Gayle Security, it said. And underneath that, *Part of the Kingslund Group.*

I burst out laughing. She wasn't ever going to miss an opportunity. And proved time and again, that when she did move, she moved decisively. On all fronts.

"Neat, huh?" he said.

"Yeah, really neat." But we were talking about something a bit different.

Steve had something else to say. He banged the toes of his boots on the ground to clear the snow and stalled. "Not really my position to speak, Ms. Farrell, but I know all of us here," he jerked his head to indicate the rest of the guards, "all of us really appreciate the package Ms. Kingslund put in for Zimmerman's and Reynolds' families. Really appreciate it."

I nodded. "Thank you," I said quietly. "I'll make sure she knows."

Back inside, Manassah had returned to calmness. Not the silence of last night; I could hear Carmen was in the kitchen.

I went back into the living room and sat on the sofa, running a disbelieving hand over the cushions.

Maybe this really could work. However I did it, I'd get Alex back. I'd build my House around me and I'd build bridges with Mom, whatever it took. If I could do that, I could face anything. Sure, I'd come out a bit different, but I'd fix the things I could and live with the rest.

I'd deal with Skylur and Naryn. I'd deal with Felix.

And as for the Nagas, the Matlal and the rogue?

We had them. The Nagas' mugshots would all be on FBI wanted posters soon. Between the pack and the bounty hunters, we'd track down the Matlal Athanate. We'd nail the rogue with science as soon as Melissa's DNA machine started spitting out the numbers or whatever it did.

With a sigh, I put the coffee down and turned on the TacNet and my cell. Time to stop being goofy and get back into the real world. Alex first.

But the TacNet squealed with an emergency contact.

"Bian? Talk to me."

What had happened while I was off?

"Amber, are you okay? Tullah was upset—"

"Yeah, yeah, fine. Just over-exerted, like you said. Why the emergency call?"

"Do you know what's happening with the pack?"

"No. What?" Was this a problem I'd caused? Please, no.

"They're gone."

"What do you mean, gone?"

"They signed off half an hour ago, and I can't get any of them on the comms. I spoke to Verano and Gray, so it's not equipment. It's not a major problem for the search—I've just closed it down because of the weather. But I don't like them bailing out without giving us a reason. If they're going to work with us, we have to be able to count on them."

"Okay, I'll check it out."

"Talk to me when you know."

I ended the call and flicked the messages on my cell to find anything from Alex. Nothing.

I called his cell number. Then work. Then Olivia. Then Felix. I got voicemails.

Shit.

This wasn't anything to do with Alex and me. There was something big going on. Larsen? Was he the rogue? Why hadn't they just told me that?

I slung on my HK holster and Liu's borrowed ski jacket.

Where to go?

I didn't want to head out all the way to Coykuti, especially if the snow was predicted to get worse. Bitter Hooks, where the pack ran? Just as bad. Alex's house was a couple of minutes away, but I doubted I'd find anything there.

I lifted my cell to call Tullah and saw the top message I'd flicked past, looking for one from Alex. It was from Melissa. Only half an hour old.

Got it. Come to Mayne's on Ridou Road.

Damn it. She was supposed to be next door, safe.

What the hell had gotten her out? What was 'it' that she'd gotten?

I didn't like this.

Chapter 59

I couldn't get through to Melissa, and I'd had to find Ridou Road on the internet. It was a dead end, a short, curved road tucked into the shadow of the huge cloverleaf interchange made by Colfax and I25.

The whole thing felt wrong.

I pulled off on the other side of the cloverleaf, and left the Hill Bitch in one of the Mile High Stadium's overflow parking lots. From there I trotted around until I could just about make out Ridou Road snaking beneath the overpass columns. I checked the HK was snug and safe under my jacket and called José. I got lucky; he was in early.

"I'm hating this," I said, after explaining the bare bones. "She's not answering. Can you trace where she last used her cell?"

I could hear him swearing under his breath at the computer system.

"Damn," he said eventually. "Cell's turned off, but the text was sent from down near where you are."

From where I stood, I could see beneath the overpasses across the width of the interchange. The tail end of Ridou had a couple of shabby businesses running out of squat cinderblock buildings. Graffiti writhed across the sides of their walls like bizarre jungle vegetation. Further away, the road took a bend around an auto scrap yard; a high chain link fence sectioned it off, with stubby towers made of crashed cars blocking a clear view of anything beyond. There were at least two more buildings there, presumably one of them Mayne's, whatever that was. Not far beyond lay the edge of the University campus.

A few cars and trucks were parked along the road. Most of them were no more than one short step better than the wrecks in the compound. I couldn't see anyone moving around.

It practically shrieked *trap*. Question was, whose?

"Hold on there," José said. "I'll send Edmunds to you with a SWAT team. I'm going to check her apartment. There was a call from there earlier."

While my cell had been turned off. I swore quietly.

He ended the call and I went back to looking.

No roads passed under the interchange between the campus and Ridou, but an unprotected railroad track curved through. I walked along it till I was under the overpass and had a better view.

I tried to put my worry about Melissa aside. If she was being held here, I'd find her, but I needed to stay alive and free.

So, if I wanted to set up an ambush here, what would I do?

What were the parameters?

Whoever this was, they'd want to keep it quiet and quick.

For a kill, a sniper. Very efficient and a small footprint. But there were no vantage points from this end of Ridou. The cinderblock buildings were single-story and in clear sight. No sniper in his right mind would climb up and trust a wobbling, rusting pile of scrap metal from the compound.

For a capture, a trap in the building itself. That needed a bigger team, more planning. They had to keep it out of sight and it would be difficult to escape. I was *not* going into Mayne's without backup.

For either a kill or a capture, lookouts. And if it were me, I wouldn't make any assumption about which way the target would approach.

Crap.

I stopped concentrating on one direction and took a slow walk around the overpass pillar.

Two people walking across the campus parking lot, heading this way. Maybe nothing, maybe the one was talking to a friend on a cell phone. Maybe not.

Two more, glimpsed through the interchange, coming from the other way.

I walked away from them, away from Ridou, towards the central tangle of the overpasses.

They started to jog and I went to flat-out sprint, crossing the railroad track and hurdling the short fences.

Shit. How many of them, and where were they?

A trap in Mayne's. Sweepers on all approaches. Twenty Nagas? It'd have to be that many. They'd be spread out around the intersection. I was heading right into the middle of them, but at least I wasn't where they'd prepared something.

How quickly would the SWAT team get here?

There was a brick building in front of me, squat as if it were crouched beneath the overpasses. A factory. Corrugated sheet metal production. All this passed in a blur as I dodged down the side and took the invitation of an open window.

From the hallway I landed in, I moved into the noisy main factory. There was no one around. I turned the lights off and it went dark. Good. I'd need every advantage I could get, and then some.

I didn't want to use the gun unless I had to. I had no silencer and a limited number of bullets.

And there had to be workers somewhere in the building, even if I couldn't see them. I didn't want them caught in the crossfire.

The Nagas would kill them without blinking.

I texted José in the dark.

Trap. 20+. Armed. Special forces. Extreme caution. Backup++. Quickly.

How long? Twenty minutes, maybe, for the first of them to arrive. I needed to survive for twenty minutes.

Too long.

I slipped through the darkness. Great shadowy hulks of automated pressing machines screeched and banged. Rollers turned, and sheets of metal clanged along rolling lines to more machines that stacked them up into pallet loads.

Workers would have to come move those soon.

I couldn't hear them through the din, but in the darkness I could almost feel the Nagas come into the factory.

They'd move cautiously. They'd know there would be a time limit, but this was a small factory and there were a lot of them. I had minutes.

There was an electrical panel on the wall. And a fire alarm. I had to get the workers out of the building or the Nagas would kill them.

I hit the alarm. I pulled the panel open and gave thanks. Good, solid, industrial fuses, not rocker switches. I yanked them all and hurled them into the deepest, darkest corners of the room. The machines stopped. The alarm continued yelling. It had to work from a different electrical connection, maybe a battery somewhere.

Still, no lights coming back on for a while, boys. Find me in the dark.

But it'd slowed me down. I heard doors opening, feet running, commands grunted. I'd run out of time.

Behind the main machine room was another corridor. Offices with desks and chairs. A locker room with rolled-up blankets in the corner. All empty. Too early for the day shift to come in. And a dead end. Nowhere to go, no way back.

Shit!

I could hold them off for a few minutes with the HK, but if I'd put this team together, they'd have grenades. A couple down this corridor would end it.

Up!

But the ceiling held nothing.

No hiding spaces. Not in the ceiling, not in the offices, not in the locker room. I was trapped. I'd lost the advantage by hiding in a building. Stupid.

Deal with it. What have I got? What can I do in the next sixty seconds?

Something I really didn't want to do, because I couldn't predict what would happen. If anything.

Always create surprise. Surprise doubles your forces.

Well, Top, this'll sure surprise the hell out of them, especially if it doesn't work.

I shucked my clothes and flung them into a locker, hiding my HK beneath them.

I spread the blankets in a corner. Oh, the irony. One of the day workers must leave his dog in here on the blankets. They stank.

The alarm cut off. They'd have to be in the factory to do that. Right next door.

Thinking about that's a distraction. Ignore it.

How had Noble described it?

Running.

I sucked the stale, oily air down into my lungs and tried to taste the sweet pine breezes of Bitter Hooks.

The strongbox groaned. I had to ignore it. Sweat popped out on my skin, as if I were really running through the woods. My head felt light. My skin felt wrong. I wanted to tear it off.

Fly behind her. See what your wolf sees. Flickering shadows of trees whip past. Sense what she senses.

Distant sweet call. Far away.

Closer. Closer. Falling.

Not the sweet pine. The smell of metals, harsh and cold. Oil. Dust. Fumes from the interstate traffic. Not the gentle sigh of wind, but the rumble of trucks. Cold, hard concrete under my feet. The staccato beat of boots outside. Now or never.

Sudden slamming.

Ow! Shit! What the hell?

All wrong. Crouched.

Have to hide, have to. Want to kill. Threat. Protect my pack. Melissa is pack. Kill!

No! Hide!

I turn and curl on blankets. Stupid dog smell. Not dog. Wolf. Threat, coming into the room. Want to kill. Killing breath shaking in my throat, slipping through my teeth.

Sounds. Meanings. Important.

Harsh voices. Excitement. Confusion.

"Clear."

"Clear."

"Clear."

Lights. Flashlights shining.

"Can't be. Where the fuck's she gone?"

"Nothing here but a big mutt, Sarge."

"Get out here. Russell, you're backstop. Wait here, cover these rooms. The rest of you, next block."

I want to kill. I don't want to have to cower like a dog.

Squawking.

"Shit. Scout says SWAT in ten. Move. Move. Out in five. You don't make it, you're on your own."

Boots not thudding like before. More shuffling now. Puzzled. Angry. Excitement gone. Moving away. Quieter.

I want to kill.

His face was pale and blank with shock, his eyes staring at the ceiling. I couldn't see what color they were. That was strange, because I knew his name. He was called Russell. He was the backstop. He was dead. His throat was destroyed, chewed through to the spine.

Then I realized that I had bits of his flesh in my mouth.

I vomited all over him.

Cold. Cold. Shivering.

Stomach empty, still heaving.

I'd gone wolf. And I couldn't control it.

I wiped myself down on the dirty blankets and dressed, hands shaking badly.

I had to get outside. What had they done to Melissa? What would I find at Mayne's?

Ops 4-16 was gone. Their operation timer had hit the end and they'd just left. No one checked on Russell. Anyone who hadn't made the call had to fend for themselves. But he hadn't been prepared for me.

I could still taste his flesh. I would never get rid of that.

I pitched over, dry heaving again.

The front doors were open, allowing the snow to swirl into the building. I stumbled outside.

And stopped.

The SWAT team was in place.

I raised my hands, laced them on my head. "I'm Amber Farrell. I made the call to Captain Morales to bring you guys in."

"Keep your hands up there." The voice came from my left. "Walk forward."

They guided me between two SWAT vans, and were about to cuff and search when Lieutenant Edmunds came running up.

"I got it, guys, I got it. I know her."

They backed off and he leaned in close. "Anything in there?" he asked quietly.

"One dead. I upchucked on him," I said, my stomach churning. "The rest got some kind of warning. Someone watching the depot, I think. They're gone."

He turned to the squad commander.

"There's one body in the building. We think the others have gone. Check it carefully. I'll be with Morales."

"You got it, Lieutenant."

He took my arm and started pulling.

"No, I need to check the building they set up as the trap. Melissa—"

"No time. José's orders. Straight to her apartment."

We trotted to a waiting squad car and I'd barely got my butt on the seat when he took off, relying on the lights and sirens to keep the road clear.

"I'm sorry, I don't know." He shook his head before I could even ask the question. "He just said to get there quick."

Chapter 60

We arrived at Melissa's apartment in Glendale and I ignored the elevator to sprint up the stairs.

The door was open. José had heard me on the stairs and he was standing just inside.

"Amber." He tried to slow me down, tried to block the way.

I shoved him aside.

The place was barely touched. Tables and chairs were in their places. Pictures sat square on the walls. Everything screaming that it was all right. Nothing to be concerned about. Everything was normal.

Except it wasn't.

An empty bowl was lying on the floor. The sofa blocked my view, but beyond it, I could see feet on the carpet, and the dread that had gripped me since I saw the text that morning became the sickening, white-hot pain of certainty.

I slowed. I didn't want to see this, and I had to.

I could hear Edmunds at the door behind me. Sirens outside. Muted traffic sounds. A whole world that just kept going on outside this apartment, without caring or noticing.

Another step.

Her feet had been bound together. One shoe had come off and sat there as if at any second she'd slip her foot back into it. It was her sensible working shoe, dark-colored and low-heeled. A little scuff on the toe.

Her hands had been bound behind her back.

She was wearing her gray pants and a red shirt.

Except it wasn't a red shirt. It was white, soaked in blood.

A shiny spoon from the kitchen had fallen onto the carpet, distracting me for one last second from her face, and then it all rushed in on me.

Her eyes had been gouged out with the spoon. Then she'd been stabbed, if you could call it that. She'd been subjected to a prolonged, frenzied assault with a knife.

"…evidence of almost uncontrollable rage…" I could hear her measured description of the rogue's handiwork as if she were standing beside me. "…140 stab wounds…"

I knelt at the edge of the carpet. I was hyperventilating, dizzy.

I forced myself to look at her face, and another voice came back to me: "…or I'll rip those eyes out myself…." The voice calm, as if it would be no big thing to carry out his threat.

Silas!

A bitter despair and a gut-twisting anger swept through me.

It fell into place. We were getting too close. Maybe Ursula had called him and told him I was asking questions about Clayton. He'd needed a distraction, and Larsen just fit the bill.

The Larsen I'd seen wasn't the rogue. His bewildered terror at what was happening had been too...human.

And I'd let it happen. They'd hauled him away to some kind of trial, with Larsen of course claiming innocence. But I'd laid the groundwork to ignore that. A sociopath could say anything convincingly. Silas must have produced some manufactured evidence. The pack had probably taken Larsen to Bitter Hooks and extracted their revenge this morning. That'd be where they were.

And Silas had managed to divert here first, to lure Melissa out and kill her.

My friend. My House.

Tears streamed down my face.

On my Blood, I would not rest until I tore him apart, strip by bloody strip. I wanted him screaming his life out under at my hands.

If I could.

The strongbox had been loosened. The wolf wanted out again.

I was shaking violently with the effort of holding it together. I couldn't even stand up.

As if it were happening to someone else, I heard voices behind me.

Griffith.

"I warned you, Farrell," he said. "You have the right to remain silent..."

I clenched my teeth together. The shaking would not stop. I wanted to kill him and anyone else who got in my way. Kill and kill and kill, until I got to Silas, and then kill him too.

I was shaking so badly, they had trouble putting the cuffs on.

They were shouting at each other. José, Edmunds, Griffith. It washed over me.

I could hear, but I couldn't listen. If I let go for one instant, for one tiny second, I would change right in front of them and kill them all.

Chapter 61

They'd injected me with something. The shaking had stopped. The tears had stopped. Only the anger was left. It was a sullen, formless blanket over everything, pressing down on me, crushing my heart.

Melissa.

I was so tired.

I was at the CBI in one of the interview rooms. I slumped in a chair and waited for Griffith to come back.

He wasn't far away.

There was an argument right outside the door.

I frowned. They'd been arguing around me like wasps since I'd been arrested, but there were some new voices now.

"I don't care if you're her lawyer. Farrell is being held under the Patriot Act. I don't need to allow her access to representation yet." That was Griffith.

"How the hell are you trying to swing that, Griffith? This is gross abuse of process. You can't hide behind federal indemnity." Morales.

"I don't actually have to tell you, but I have a military assault rifle with her fingerprints on it."

"Now, we're getting somewhere. Thank you, Agent Griffith. So, this assault rifle. What is it, a Kalishnikov?" Who was that? He had to be a lawyer, because he knew the answer to the question he was asking. Someone from Jen's lawyers? No, the voice was familiar. Who the hell did I know who was a lawyer? Apart from Kath, who would probably have been cheering Griffith on.

"You arresting everyone who owns a rifle?" Morales said.

"No." Griffith said. "No to both."

"So? What is it? What type of rifle are we talking here?"

"An FN Special Operations Combat Assault Rifle."

"Ah. One of our own," the lawyer said. "I see. Someone has been providing weapons to the enemy. Well that certainly is a major felony, putting our own weapons in the hands of terrorists. Now, this rifle, would you happen to have the details on it? Serial number? Provenance? How did it get into the hands of a terrorist? And back again?"

"What are you insinuating?"

"That maybe it never got into the hands of terrorists. That it was actually a weapon signed out of FBI stores by one Agent Griffith."

There was a crashing silence.

"So, what is it, Agent Griffith? I believe the FBI keep good records. What are we going to see if we subpoena them and drag you in front of a judge? You signed it out and it was never out of your possession, but mysteriously has the fingerprints of a terrorist on it, or you signed it out, it was then in the possession of a terrorist and now it's back in your possession? What would go down better with the judge?"

Ingram. Agent Ingram must have tipped off my knight in shining armor.

Bless your big Texan heart.

But who was my knight? Not something I'd ever thought to say about a lawyer.

"How the fuck—" Griffith choked.

"I think that's entirely secondary to the central issue of the credibility of your assertion about Ms. Farrell." The lawyer was warming up nicely. I'd thank him as well as Ingram.

I stood up and walked to the door. Every step seemed to take a huge effort, but just moving helped. The door was locked of course, but I banged hard on it.

"Keep it down, I'm trying to sleep in here," my throat demon said before I could catch it.

Surprisingly, the door was opened. Agent Ingram stood there.

In the corridor, Griffith was pale as milk and I guessed he was trying hard to backpedal his way out of a difficult spot without appearing to.

Morales reached my side and peered into my eyes.

"Jesus! What have they dosed you with?"

I swayed and shrugged. Whatever, it was wearing off. It had given me the opportunity to get the strongbox closed again, so I wasn't complaining, as long as I got out of here now.

The shock was the lawyer.

Taylor. Taylor Tyson, Kath's fiancé.

What the hell was he doing here, arguing my case?

"Taylor?" I said.

"We'll just be a moment, Amber. I'm sure Agent Griffith has become aware that there's been a mistake made about the grounds for holding you without representation. I believe we'll deal with the charge of interfering with an FBI investigation quite easily."

Ingram muttered something in Griffith's ear, and whatever it was, it worked. Ingram began shepherding us down the corridor to the lobby.

"I do believe we need further discussion with you this afternoon, Captain Morales, but I think Ms. Farrell has had a difficult time and she should be escorted home. Mr. Tyson, would you oblige?"

"Yes."

Huh? I looked at Taylor. His answer had come out wrong for some reason. I guessed it didn't matter. If I could just get out of here, I'd be able to find my own way home. Maybe I could call up a bit of Athanate and burn the sedative off. Then again, I didn't want to try anything, Athanate or Were, at the moment. Shelve that idea.

"We do need to talk again, Ms. Farrell," Ingram said. "Please don't wander away from Denver."

"It'll be a pleasure," I said, feeling warm and fuzzy toward him. "I'll call."

I got my jacket back, and given the snow flying outside the windows, I'd need it.

Taylor took my HK and a bag of my possessions.

Fine, for now. Just get me out of here.

More shocks in the lobby.

"Kath?" I blinked hard, but she was still there. Not a drug-induced hallucination. I couldn't understand what was going on, but she was there for me. That meant something. "Thank you."

"You're my sister," she said as she pulled me through the doors into the biting cold. "I'll stand by you, whatever."

Damn that wind. Damn the drugs. Couldn't see straight. Everything moist and blurry.

The storm had settled in over Denver with a vengeance. Snow was falling heavily.

"Light dusting over high ground," I quoted, stumbling. "They got that wrong."

Taylor took my arm and helped me walk quicker.

Kath's car was parked next to a paramedic van. A couple of orderlies came out, shivering and hugging themselves, hiding their hands from the cold.

"It's okay," I said, my lips still feeling numb, so I had to talk slowly. "It's just a sedative. It'll work its way through. Don't need anything."

Can't have medics looking at me. Colonel Laine's rules. Don't work for the army any more. Still, probably a good rule.

"It's for your own good, Amber."

"Huh?"

"I won't let any cult take my sister away from me."

I understood the words, but nothing was making sense. I was still trying to process that and I barely registered the sharp jab in my arm.

What the fuck!

I tried reaching for anger, but there was nothing. Inside me, it was as woolly as the snow all around us.

The world was tilting slowly upwards.

"Straight to the center," Kath was saying.

"We understood there'd been a change—"

"Listen, you're working for me. I'm giving you instructions which you will follow to the letter if you don't want your ass sued off. If he needs to move her later, that's fine, he can talk to me. Not now. Not in this weather. Straight to the center."

"You got it, lady."

And everything went soft and white and blank.

Chapter 62

Lights. Noises. Warm and cold at the same time. Cold air on my naked skin. There's a foul taste in my mouth and my head feels like it's stuffed with cotton.

I couldn't see anything. I tried to sit up, but nothing worked, like one of those nightmares where you don't have control over your body.

That was okay. If it was a nightmare, I'd wake up soon, wouldn't I?

Instructor Ben-Haim is sitting beside me.

Is this part of a dream?

"Farrell. You're in med. You're experiencing what it's like to be injected with some of the substances commonly used in interrogation. There is no training we can give you, just familiarity. Can you hear me?"

My mouth won't move. I can't reply. I want to tell him I already know this feeling.

He goes on as if I have answered him. "You're feeling confusion. Disinhibition. Delirium. Hallucinations. You can't trust your senses. Turn inward. Remember who you are."

I remembered this. I remembered crying. I remembered being sure Dad had sat next to my gurney. Like I had sat next to his bed.

I remembered wanting to tell Dad everything and knowing I couldn't. Because he wasn't real. He was the enemy.

This wasn't happening. This was a memory. A memory of a hallucination. Ben-Haim wasn't here. Dad had never been there.

"Subject recovering consciousness at 10:43," someone said.

The voice was flat and emotionless; it triggered an avalanche of memories. This *was* a nightmare. A nightmare about Obs.

My stomach heaved, but there was nothing to come up. I felt a tube in my throat. The name came to me from military med courses: endotracheal tube. What had happened to me?

"Clear the room." Another voice, speaking with authority.

Not from Obs! I knew the voice, but there was something in my ears, distorting the sounds.

I felt another injection in my arm. Or was that just the memory of one before?

I couldn't see. I tried getting up again. Nothing. Then I tried lifting just one hand, but I still couldn't move. I was strapped down. Chest, wrist, hip, thigh, ankle.

NO! NO! NO!

I heard a sound like an old-fashioned kettle boiling on the stove; the thin sound of muffled screaming. I realized it was me. I forced myself to stop, tried to make words instead.

I couldn't even speak. My face was held in some sort of webbing. It ran across my mouth. Metal clamped my jaws.

That sobbing. That sobbing couldn't be me.

I was sick with fear.

Another memory avalanche churned up images that had been locked away. Screaming at the touch of cold metal plates against my head. The foul taste of plastic in my mouth, choking my screams. A sense of utter hopelessness as the first warning prickles began to stab at my temples.

This couldn't be happening to me again.

My body was shuddering violently.

Ben-Haim debriefing us. Asking us about the vulnerabilities we felt under chemical interrogation.

"I felt compliant. Eager to please," someone says.

"Compliant. Eager. And this without effort on my part," Ben-Haim replies. "In the hands of an experienced interrogator, under the effects of these chemicals, compliance will become the prisoner's sole reason for existence. He or she will burn with desire to help. The interrogator will become God."

He looks around the silent room. "Not a good position to be in," he says with his customary understatement.

My mind went blank again.

What had I been thinking about?

Petersen! The name was like an electric shock. Somehow Petersen must have persuaded Kath to help kidnap me. How? *Why?*

The room was very quiet.

It's always been quiet. A long time. I'm still in Obs. I've been here forever. It was all a dream. I never got away. I never will.

"Amber."

I jerked in surprise, stiffening against the restraints. The whisper was very quiet, very close to my ear. A hand pressed on my shoulder. Warm. Comforting.

"It's Alex. I've come to help you escape."

Blinding tears of relief flooded out of my eyes. I wanted to say his name at least, but I couldn't speak and my body shook in frustration.

"Shhh! Not a sound. They'll hear us." His hand massaged my shoulder. "Shhh."

I tried to calm down. Alex was here. I was safe. He wouldn't let anything happen to me.

"Better," he whispered. "Listen to me. This is very important."

I listened. It felt as if my whole body was listening. I wanted to hear him more than anything else in the world. I wanted to hear his voice clearly, without all the distortion in my ears. This was important. My kin.

I cried; but I cried silently so I could hear him.

"You're all dosed up. I want to free you, but I can't until I know you won't go berserk. It's very dangerous at this stage. While you haven't changed yet. Can't have you going wolf while we sneak out."

His hand continued to massage me gently. Yes, I was full of drugs. I had to relax.

But I had changed, hadn't I? I wanted to tell him, but I couldn't speak.

"Listen, you do everything right and we'll get out of here."

I would. I would do whatever he said. Kin. His desires were sacred to me. The rest wasn't important.

"Concentrate on my voice. Nothing else matters. Just my voice. The voice you want to hear."

He was right. Nothing else mattered.

"I can't set you free until you're steady enough that I can trust you."

I wouldn't do anything. He could trust me.

"Try not to be sick."

He pulled the endotracheal tube out. My stomach tried one last heave, but I stopped it.

See, I can do it.

"That's good."

I felt warmth, despite the cold. He was pleased with me. That was so important.

"You mustn't call out."

I wouldn't. I wouldn't.

He eased the strap across my mouth. The metal fixings released my jaws and then his hand went across to my other shoulder, massaged that as well.

"I need to you to trust me. Do you trust me?"

"Yes," I whispered. My throat was so sore. My own voice sounded strange as well, echoing in my head.

"Good." His hand came up to my face and tugged back the blindfold.

The room was flooded with bright, colorless light. A screen surrounded us, like the ones they put around a hospital bed.

Alex was bending over me, his finger on his lips. My eyes were still blurred by stupid tears. I wanted him to hold me. I wanted him to tell me that I hadn't messed up with him. That it would be all right. He'd get me out of here, he'd save me.

"Shhh. Everything's fine. You trust me."

I nodded, as much as the webbing would allow.

"You have to show me I can trust you, too."

Both his hands moved to my shoulders. They were warm against my skin, almost hot. I was so cold.

"In addition to the psychoactive effects, Benzilate will reduce your ability to control body temperature," Ben-Haim says. *"Recognizing purely physical effects like that will give you a connection to reality. An anchor."*

Benzilate? Had I been given an interrogation drug?

It wasn't important. Alex was here. I had to trust him.

His hands moved lower.

I gasped.

"Shhh. I have to know I can trust you. You understand that. Just relax. You're feeling so good. Don't worry about anything else."

His hands ran over my breasts, squeezed the nipples.

Wrong!

But how could it be? It was Alex.

"Disinhibition doesn't mean you'll do things you don't want to do. Just things it may not be appropriate to do." Ben-Haim leans forward and the sunlight falls across his face, making distracting patterns, changing the whole shape of it.

That's stupid of me. It's not Ben-Haim at all. It's Alice. How could I have mistaken her?

"Keep away from physical intimacy," she says. *"It lowers your mental barriers."*

No. I'd been safe with Jen. She'd been safe with me. This is Alex! I trust him.

"No aural sex."

A giggle threatens to burst out of me, but I have to stay quiet. My body is not into giggling at all. My back arches with pleasure against the straps. Alex's hand is moving across my belly. Lower. If only he'd free me. It's safe. I want his loving arms around me.

"Relax. Let go of all your concerns."

Bad. Shouldn't. No auras. Alice said no auras. Shouldn't.

Just a peek.

I felt my eukori unfold like a flag in the breeze, floating out toward Alex. Eagerly seeking the warm embrace of his eukori.

Shocking, slimy, slithering, frozen NOTHING.

SHIT!

My body spasmed and went rigid with shock for a second, then I tried to push him away with my eukori. I started twisting and fighting against the straps. There was confusion on his face and suddenly it looked wrong. It was Alex's face, but it moved in a different way. Like a plastic mask. How could I have mistaken it for him?

The scream burst out of me.

I turned inward. I could fight with the telergy. I had to reach that anger that I had hidden. It was buried and locked away. The strongbox was open. I thrust a hand down into the formless nightmares and I started to light up like a flare.

My eukori stopped floating and hardened like an axe to strike.

And the imposter flipped a valve on a stand next to me. The tube stretched down to my arm. I could feel snow mushroom inside me, like a soft cloud, blanketing everything.

The strap was pressed across my mouth again, the metal forced inside, pushing my jaws apart and locking them.

A door opened. "Everything all right, Doctor?" A voice came from the corridor, hesitant, uncertain about intruding. Not willing to come uninvited into the room, let alone pull the curtain back.

I tried to scream again. The endotracheal tube was shoved violently back down my throat.

"Yes. I'm afraid she's quickly moving to a complete mental disintegration. I'm going to have to move her to my facilities and start treatment immediately."

The imposter grinned at me with Alex's face. Completely confident, hidden behind the screen.

"This IV is nearly finished," he spoke calmly to the unseen nurse. "Prepare another one, please. The prescription form is on the side."

"Of course. Ahh…you do know, the weather's getting much worse. They're closing the roads."

"I know. I'll arrange suitable transportation, but I'll need to hurry."

"Okay. I don't have these here, Doctor. I'll need to go down to the pharmacy."

The sound of retreating footsteps was cut off suddenly by the door closing. Through the haze of drugs, I knew it was a solid door. No, not just solid, that wasn't quite right, it was a *secure* door. This place was equipped for violent inmates.

And wherever I got moved to would only be worse.

He leaned forward, the imposter with Alex's face, and whispered in my ear.

"That was stupid. Me, for underestimating your ability and you, for trying to fight. It won't change the outcome. I'll take what I want from you anyway. This was your easy option—just lie there comfortably for a few minutes and let go."

His hand squeezed a breast and flicked the nipple painfully. I wanted to struggle, but my body lay there, unable to move even within the limits of the straps that held me.

"You were enjoying it, weren't you? Well, you won't enjoy it next time. No more than your little spy did. But she had to die. You, I've got to try and keep alive. You're my passport with your friends from the army."

He chuckled. "When I've finished with you, I may let you beg me to keep you instead of handing you over. Do you think you can do that, Amber? It's something for you to think about while you wait. What can you do for me? How are you going to persuade me not to give you to Petersen?"

The door opened behind the curtain, and he put his lips against my ear. "You wait right here for me. I'll be back soon. I'm going to enjoy this so much."

He stood. There was the eye-twisting distortion of his face, just like a Were change, and then Dr. Noble was smiling sadly down at me, his face the picture of professional concern.

He turned and pulled the curtain aside.

"Be extremely careful," he said to the male nurse who'd come in. "No release of restraints. Not even the gag. She once bit someone's finger off."

"Ah, of course. Can I get you to sign the transfer authorization please, Doctor?" He held out a clipboard.

There was a sound of scribbling before Noble went on. "I can't take the time to fill in all this background information. I'll call and explain in detail to the director tomorrow. But I'm going to have to rush tonight to get her moved before the roads close."

"I'll pass that on."

Noble left.

Only it couldn't be Noble, any more than it could be Alex. He couldn't be the rogue. He wasn't anything like big enough to create a wolf that could produce the bite patterns we'd looked at.

Another man came in. He was wearing a security uniform. He and the nurse spoke with their voices low.

"I'm telling you, this isn't standard treatment," said the nurse. "I've never administered this stuff here. And this one, it's too much, for too long. What's he trying to do?"

Blurred at the edge of my vision, I could see their heads bent over the forms.

"He's the doctor," the guard said. "You want to get reprimanded for following his prescription or for not following it?"

"I don't know. I mean, look at that." His finger jabbed at something. "For fuck's sake, she's not a horse."

"Not far from it." The guard laughed. "Freaking physical nutcase. Look at her. Don't get a body like that without serious work. So, maybe she has a super-high metabolism."

"Yeah, and maybe she'll have cardiac arrest when I give her this."

"Hey! Look, buddy, we never had this conversation. I'm just doing my rounds. I see everything is normal in this room. I'm out of here."

"Thanks a bunch," the nurse said as the door closed again.

I struggled to make my brain work. The dosage would be high to overcome my Athanate metabolism. High enough? Whatever was in the IV was working at the moment.

I remembered burning off the effects of alcohol. I'd been wandering drunk through an alley, and had been threatened by a gang. Elethesine, the Athanate equivalent of adrenaline, had pumped me up and I'd sobered up in seconds. I needed elethesine now. I needed to get these drugs out of my system.

Diana had said anger was my key. But I couldn't reach the anger.

No. Not quite right. She'd said anger was my key to my telergy, my paranormal mental capabilities.

I needed something else. I wasn't like Bian, who could turn it on and off when she wanted. I needed help. I needed a trigger.

Was there just one key? Only anger?

No. I'd stirred the Athanate up without anger.

Alex. Jen. Think about kin.

I squeezed my eyes shut.

Those eyes. Jen's depthless blue. Alex's brightening to gold as the wolf stirred in him.

Their voices. My kin's voices.

Alex teasing when I said I wanted to bite him. "Yeah, and? Knock yourself out, vamp."

The feel of Jen's tongue on my fang. "We both want this."

My fangs throbbed. I didn't push it back down, I welcomed it. The pleasure ran through my body. I didn't feel so heavy. The drugs *helped*. They overcame my instinct to suppress it.

I took a full breath, slow and concentrated instead of panting with fear.

And the fog burned off like mist in the desert.

My eyes cleared. My head cleared.

Now, how the freaking hell to get out of the restraints? Houdini, I was not.

You know what you can do, said Tara.

Images flashed through my mind.

The Were in the house at Glenmore Hills. Bound by adjustable shackles around his neck and stomach. Why?

Because it's not worth trying to put shackles on a Were's wrist or ankle.

The alley where I'd been ambushed by the punk street gang; my arm rippling, part-changing to wolf.

I don't dare. I can't control it. I can't go wolf. I can't black out. What if I wake up looking at a dead orderly with his throat torn out? What if I don't wake up at all? What if I turn and betray the existence of paranormals to the rest of the world?

But there was no choice.

I concentrated on my arms, on the feel of rippling.

There was nothing.

The orderly pushed the privacy curtain all the way back out of the way of his cart with a swish.

He seemed startled that I was awake.

Arms. Change.

He bent down and studied the IV drip, his brow wrinkled in puzzlement. He made sure the valve was open and the needle was in my vein. Then he shrugged and turned back to his cart with the replacement drugs.

Arms.

I could see him looking at the drugs and forms again. He shook his head. Took a couple of the ampoules and put them in his pocket.

I couldn't kill him. He wasn't one of the ones who had kidnapped me. He didn't want to give me too much sedative. He was willing to go against a doctor's orders.

But I had to change.

The wolf moved sluggishly in the depths of my mind, confused.

The flesh on my arms felt as if it was bubbling. My fingers felt bigger and softer. I couldn't move my head to look, but I tried to follow it in my mind: the pads forming, the nails hardening, curving into claws. The wrists shrinking.

I pulled. My paws squeezed through the grip of the straps. The shock of that sensation stopped the change with my left hand still only halfway out. I had to clear my mind and start again. Slowly the rippling grew until I felt the changes and pulled my hand clear.

Everything felt so slow and heavy, but the arms went back to being human arms.

Now legs.

Too late; he was turning. He hung the new IV bag on the stand.

I wanted to snatch at him.

Wait, wait.

I lay still until he bent to check the catheter in my arm. Then I grabbed him, twisted him around and held him against me in a choke hold.

He couldn't shout but he sure struggled hard. The restraints worked in my favor. He would've been able to lift me alone, but not with a gurney effectively strapped to my back. He tried desperately to get a loose finger on my hand to pry it open, but I hadn't left any where he could get a grip. I squeezed harder on his neck until I got my message through—stop fighting if you want to breathe.

When his hands stopped scrabbling at mine, I tore the catheter out of my arm.

He fought again as I ripped the Velcro webbing open and pulled the metal jaw braces from my mouth. I just squeezed harder. I didn't want to strangle him, but I couldn't let him get free. The endotracheal tube came out next.

"You keep struggling and I'm gonna break your freaking neck," I croaked.

He stopped. I could imagine him trying to figure the best way out of this. Talk the crazy down? Not while I was choking him. Struggle some more? Same problem.

I eased the pressure a fraction.

"You're sick," he gasped. "We're only trying to help you."

"Yeah. Got that, bozo. Including kidnapping me off the street."

That puzzled him a bit, while I loosened the chest strap.

"My name is Ian."

Oooh. They had him well trained. Make personal contact with your kidnapper. Make them see you as a person. Tell them your name.

"You'll understand I can't really say that I'm pleased to meet you, Ian."

My voice was ragged and still sounded off. There was something in my ears which I'd have to get out when I could spare a hand from more urgent tasks. In the meantime, humor wasn't what he'd expected from a crazy who was intended to be tranked out of her head. That gave me time to work the hip strap loose.

"I'm not crazy," I said. "I've been kidnapped, and all you're doing is helping him."

"That's..." He stopped.

"Yeah. Crazy. I know. You see my problem here?"

I had the chest strap off. The big challenge was going to be getting vertical without giving him an opportunity to get away.

My legs rippled and I stealthily pulled them up and free of the ankle restraints. They changed back.

"Look, I can call the director. We can get this settled right away."

"I think I'd rather get it settled, including the lawsuits for wrongful imprisonment, once I'm outside the building."

"You'll never get out," he blurted without thinking.

"That, Ian, is where you're wrong."

I tensed. He knew enough about the position he was in to think I might be about to kill him. He instinctively tried to get up. I pushed up with him. The straps were loosened enough that I rose with him, still holding his neck.

We surged clear of the gurney. My vision went gray and I had to bite my tongue to keep conscious. The pain helped.

I will not pass out.

Then I trapped his foot, curled him around and slammed him down against the side of the gurney.

While he was getting his breath back, I was tying his hands with the endotracheal extension tubing and then gagging him with metal braces, tied in place with the IV tube.

Stage one. Between adrenaline and elethesine, I probably *was* crazy now, and that wouldn't exactly help me get out of here. I pulled the buzzing earplugs out and sighed with relief.

What next? I didn't want to play the hostage game. Too slow, too many ways for it to go wrong.

Which left impersonation and improvisation.

First things first. I was buck naked.

I stripped Ian's shoes, socks and pants off. He struggled, but it didn't do him any good. I left him his underwear. I wasn't that desperate. None of it fit, but I stuffed latex gloves from the dispenser in the shoes and pinned the blue trousers up with paper clips from his clipboard.

Getting his smock was going to be more of a problem. I had nothing in the way of handy weapons to threaten him with.

I swung him up on the gurney, making sure he could see how easily I moved him. He let me, then fought a bit as he realized I was going to strap him down.

I had to punch him hard, which served as an introduction to the next step.

"Ian, I have no intention of hurting you any more than I have to, but I am getting out of here." I paused while his breathing eased and he got his wind back for a second time. "Now, I'm going to take the tubing off and strap you down. If you think you can take me, half strapped in as you are, then you better be prepared for some serious pain. I could always dose you up with drugs first. Do you hear me?"

He nodded jerkily. His eyes went to the IV bag. I had no idea how I would administer it, but he didn't look as if he liked the idea.

I pulled his smock up and back over his shoulders. He looked frightened, but he didn't try anything while I tightened the chest strap. I got one wrist half fastened in the straps and then removed the endotracheal tube.

The fight seemed to have left him after the last punch. He let me fix him in place and change the tubing restraints for the webbing that had gagged me. Done.

I put the smock on. It smelled of him, but that was the least of my problems. It'd have to do. I took one of the easy release fasteners on the IV drip and used it to tie my hair back.

His glasses had fallen on the floor. I picked them up and perched them on the top of my head. Anything to distract from my appearance. I really wanted one of those facemasks, but there was nothing else in the room, other than a thin blanket which I used to cover him.

I found his pen on the floor and took an empty form from the clipboard.

At the top of the page it stated in bold letters: Aurora Regional Center. Great. I was in the Max, Colorado's most secure institute for the criminally insane.

The patient's name was Crystal Vincent. The signatures were illegible, but apparently I had been committed by a court order.

I kept the forms.

I scrawled 'Problem with restraints—moved patient to E-15 to await transfer' on the back of a spare prescription form and left it on the cart. It might buy me an extra couple of minutes. Anything that might help.

I unlocked the gurney's wheel with a bit of a fumble and patted his cheek as I swiveled it around. "That's a good boy, Ian. Try and look crazy for me."

I hoped he appreciated the irony.

The corridor was wide and yellow and empty.

At the end, there was one of those helpful maps that tell you how to get out of the building in a hurry. Right next to it was the fire alarm itself. It was tempting, but it was a last resort. I would have hated to be responsible for any genuinely insane criminals escaping, and anyway, the security procedures during an alarm would probably make it harder to get out.

The building was laid out in a huge tic-tac-toe shape with a central exercise area. I was on the east corridor. It looked as if the elevators were on the west side, but there were fire escape stairs in the corners.

I needed to do the circuit and see what looked best.

As I came out of the corridor, a nurse passed by. I looked down at my clipboard and pushed.

Don't notice me. Just routine.

I pushed us into the north corridor. Through the doors at the end was the central area. The fire escape stairs had alarms. The elevator it would have to be.

Then where? Somewhere in the building would be a locker room where staff changed. That'd be good to get to. The pocket of the smock held Ian's ID card with a magnetic strip, so I hoped that might get me there and into his locker. Some outdoor clothes and a car would be handy.

I was almost at the door to the west section when someone came through from the other side. Administrator type. He frowned, but held the door open as I waved my ID.

"You shouldn't be moving a patient alone," he said.

"I know," I said humbly. "Debby's gone home sick and the doctor wanted him moved right away."

"And for goodness sake, it's against regs to leave your glasses on your head."

"Yes, sir. Sorry, sir." I folded them and slid them into a pocket.

The man looked down at Ian's wildly distorting face, rolled his eyes and I was through.

There were elevators clustered around a central column, a security station with one sleepy guard, and a staff break room with the lights off.

Time to ditch my prop.

I wheeled the gurney into the break room.

I held up the ampoules he had pocketed where he could see them. "Thanks for that. You're okay. And neither of us is crazy," I said to him. "But only one of us is in restraints. Relax. They'll probably let you out eventually."

I left him in there.

"Just been reamed out for pushing him by myself," I mumbled at the guard. "Gotta get help. He'll be okay in there for a couple of minutes."

The guard grunted, not bothering to look up.

The elevator seemed to take forever to arrive.

When it came, there was no convenient labeling to tell me where to go. It was time for guesswork.

Six options. We were on third. Basement would be cars. First floor should be locker rooms. Maybe second or top would be offices and consulting rooms.

I hit the button for the first floor and hoped. If I could find Ian's locker, maybe he had a car in the basement. We were still a good long way away from Christmas, but hey, I was due for an early present.

The first floor was mixed. There were offices, but there were also locker rooms and showers. That much was good. They were segregated. Not so good.

I barged into the men's locker room as if I belonged. I could always claim I'd gotten distracted.

The place was empty.

I'd gotten lucky on shift times but less so on Ian. I knew which was his locker—his ID had the number printed on it. But inside, his bike helmet and florescent Lycra gear mocked me.

There was another ID for main gate security, which I took, along with his jacket and a chocolate bar.

I left him his glasses.

There was no point hanging around here, especially in the men's locker room. On this level the stairs were open. I ignored the elevators and ran down the steps into the basement.

I was short on planning, but something would occur to me.

Maybe someone had left their keys in their car.

I burst into the empty parking garage, automatic ceiling lights coming on as I moved in.

Where to start looking? Which side felt luckier?

As it turned out, neither side. The silence was shattered by an alarm.

Crap. Time up.

Bollards began to rise out of the floor on the ramp exiting the garage. Beyond them, sheet metal shutters started to come down.

I sprinted forward and rolled under the shutter.

The top of the ramp was half-covered in snow despite the efforts of someone to shovel the worst away. It was falling heavily, and the wind was pushing it up in drifts.

There were lights coming on across the grounds, but between the snow and the dark, I wasn't getting worried yet. Unless I ran straight into a patrol, I had a few minutes more.

I discounted the main entrance. If the alarm hadn't gone off it might have been an easy way out, but not now. I'd get out all right, but I could end up killing someone to do it. The fence would be better.

I ran across the open ground. They'd be able to track the marks I was making in the snow, but I planned to be long gone by then.

Across the perimeter road, the fence was chain link, about ten feet tall, with inward-leaning barbed wire. It looked formidable, but within the first week of training in Ops 4-10, they'd had us climbing worse. My real problem was if there were sensors on it, but I didn't have time to check. I wasn't going to be on it very long anyway.

I was not at my best, and it was slippery underfoot. My leap would have had my old army squad hooting with laughter, but it got me up. I grabbed the angled stanchion used to hold the barbed wire at the top, swung my body up and did a sort of sideways pole-vault over, falling into the unmarked snow outside. Shouts came from the direction of the buildings; they'd found my tracks, but I bet myself none of them could vault the fence and I was certain none of them could keep up with me running for any length of time.

I guessed that was stage two completed. I was feeling *much* better. I needed a shower to scrub the top layer of skin off, but I had to push that aside.

It was time to get away and start settling scores.

Chapter 63

TUESDAY

The Aurora Regional Center was out on the east side of town, hidden away next to Buck airfield.

Rom's garage wasn't that far away, but I wasn't looking for a place to hide, and I didn't want to involve him anyway.

I wanted to confront my sister and then I wanted to chase down the rogue and kill him. Or her. Part of my brain not involved in escape had been kicking scenarios around, puzzling out the problem. Was Noble the rogue? Or had the rogue simply taken on Noble's appearance, the way he had Alex's, in order to get access to the Center? I didn't see how the rogue could be Noble—there was still the issue with the size of the rogue's wolf form. But insane asylums were Noble's territory. If the rogue were someone else, why bother to take me there at all? Why not just take me to his or her hideout? Did he need access to drugs? Or was it to implicate Noble?

The rogue had fooled me too many times. I could no longer trust anything I thought I knew.

It was a little after midnight, so officially Tuesday morning. It was dark, and even near streetlights, I could barely see twenty yards in the heavy snow. I could have had every policeman in the city looking for me and still walked along the roads without worry. Or without worry of capture. Freezing to death was a problem.

The wind was howling down from the north, whipping snow horizontally. And thanks to the forecast failure, the road crews had obviously been overwhelmed and the roads were quickly becoming blocked. Good for escaping mental prisoners.

It was only a dozen miles to my sister's house, and I wanted to make sure the drugs had worked themselves out of my body. So I found Mississippi Avenue—long, straight, wide, heading in exactly the right direction and practically empty of cars. With lots of side roads and paths off it, just in case.

I started running.

Even with the snow, and wearing shoes that were too big for me, I still reckoned I'd be there in a couple of hours, maybe less. My sister was going to get a very early morning wakeup.

Well over an hour later I passed Garland Park, visible only because of the tennis court fencing that stood out from the banks of snow. The snowfall had gotten heavier and the wind stronger. My ETA was creeping up all the time, but on the other side of the park, I scrambled down onto the Cherry Creek running trail and felt I was on the home straight.

The sheer amount of snow had slowed me some, but the sunken running track was slightly sheltered and easier going.

The cold was fine. Running at that pace for that length of time would have overheated my body if it were warmer.

The trail took a detour around the Country Club. I ignored the deviation; I jumped the fences and ran straight across the silent golf course.

On the other side, I didn't bother getting back on the trail. Emerson Street was only a block away, made strange by the huge mounds along the sides of the road that were buried cars. The snow had drifted up against the trees lining the sidewalk, and I slowed to a trot, breaking fresh tracks down the middle of the road.

I knew where Kath lived, but I'd never been invited there. It was Taylor's house, a pretty little bungalow on a pretty, tree-lined street. Not where she wanted her sister visiting.

After a block, I had to wade through the sidewalks to check a house number, and when I got back to the road, an SUV was inching its way slowly from the far end. I snatched myself back from the beam of the headlights, but the driver didn't seem to have noticed me.

I cursed and moved cautiously along the sidewalk.

The SUV stopped roughly where I anticipated Taylor's house was.

Crap. I hid and watched, but I was cooling down too quickly to wait around long. My hands and feet had gone from cold and painful to numb.

There were no streetlights in that stretch, but a porch light came on and showed me a tall man, bulky in a ski jacket, checking house numbers just like I had.

My heart stopped. It was Alex.

Or it looked like Alex.

Whether I made a sound, or he sensed me some other way, his head turned.

"Amber?" he said.

Suddenly, he was running toward me, forcing the deep snow aside.

"Stop!" I yelled. "Stay back. Just stay back."

He did, coming to an abrupt halt. It was like his hands didn't want to stop. He held his arms out to me.

"It's me," he said.

I edged backwards.

"Amber, what happened?"

"Just stay there!" I said. Speaking hurt. My head swirled with nightmares of the rogue looking like Alex; I could feel his hands on my skin, his breath on my face. My empty stomach churned again.

Was this him?

He'd stopped when I'd yelled.

It had to be Alex. It had to be.

Wishing wouldn't make it so.

It was too far for the eukori to reach. I knew too little about the Call.

I couldn't think of anything else. "What did we talk about during our first dance?" I croaked.

"Nothing," he said immediately. "It was too amazing to say anything."

Tears were suddenly freezing on my cheeks.

I took one stumbling step to him and he closed the distance, sweeping me up in his arms, his eukori breaking over me like a beautiful, dark wave.

"What happened?" he said again. "I thought I'd lost you."

"Melissa's dead." The grief and anger swept over me again. "Killed by the rogue. I got arrested by Griffith. Then I was sprung by my sister and her boyfriend. But they handed me over to some paramedics who knocked me out. Woke up in Aurora Regional Center." I buried my face against his neck. "The rogue was there. Alex, he can shape-shift faces."

"What?"

"When I woke up, he was there. He looked like you."

Alex was stunned to silence by that.

"What are you doing here?" I asked.

"Bian's special phone she gave you? She can track it. You sister must have left it turned on till they got home."

Someone else came out of Alex's SUV. In the weak porch light I recognized Olivia.

"What happened with you guys yesterday?"

"Time for that later," he said, looking around at Kath's front door.

"Yeah." I let go of him. Concentrate. I had business here. "How are we going to get in? Break a window?"

He smiled. "Nah. If it comes to it, I have a key for the front door." He reached under his coat and pulled out a crowbar. "But we should just try knocking first."

"Why? She—"

Olivia slipped in next to me and she and Alex hugged me.

"I can't believe she knew what was going to happen," Olivia said. "Please, take a moment. You don't want to do anything you'll regret."

"She's not the rogue. If he can do something like change faces, imagine what he could have done to persuade her that you needed to be hospitalized," Alex said.

They were right and I hated it. I had a wheeling ball of anger inside me that wanted to lash out violently. Kath was here; that didn't mean I should go berserk. She hadn't killed Melissa. She probably didn't realize what the hell was going on.

Calm.

"We'll back you, whatever," Olivia whispered.

The wolf was too close. If I went in there out of control like that, it would have gotten bloody. Kath was a stupid, spiteful bitch, but she didn't deserve to die for it. My anger subsided reluctantly.

"Okay," I said finally. "Thanks, guys. Let's find out what we can."

Alex pounded on the door and leaned on the bell.

Five minutes later, when a confused and sleepy Taylor saw me outside, he opened the door.

"What's going on?" he mumbled.

I shoved him out of the way and Alex and Olivia followed me inside.

I left him to Alex and stormed through the house. In the bedroom I tore Kath's bathrobe off the hook and threw it at her.

"Get up," I yelled.

"Amber," Kath gasped. "What…"

"Surprised? You thought I was safely locked up in an insane asylum?"

I dragged her into the living room, where Taylor was already sitting nervously, watched by a looming Alex. He didn't want me to run amok, but he was two hundred pounds of pissed werewolf and he kinda looked it.

"Wait, we can explain," Taylor said, holding his hands up.

"And I'm going to listen. But you can listen first." I got the crumpled forms out of my pocket. They were the worse for wear, but still readable. "Whatever shit you thought you were doing, you were wrong." I slammed the forms down on the coffee table in front of them.

"Who's this?" Taylor said. The name on the forms was Crystal Vincent.

"That's me. Didn't you know? Committed to the detention wing of the Aurora Center like an insane criminal under another name. Signed off for a transfer." I jabbed the next form. "Destination unknown. Overdosed on sedatives, barbiturates and hallucinogenics."

I leaned over and glared at them until they wilted, and when I spoke again, it was almost a whisper. "All, presumably, set in motion when you signed me off on a court order as mentally incapable."

"We...no...not that," Kath stuttered. "He said—"

"I can explain the institute," Taylor said in a shaky voice.

"I'm listening."

Taylor licked his lips and glanced worriedly at Alex, who was looking more angry by the second.

"Dr. Noble showed us video evidence of your last breakdown—"

"My *what*? No, go back. Start at the beginning."

"Dr. Noble came to me," Kath said. "You said you'd been to see him. He told me he'd been treating you, but he said he was very concerned after your recent sessions."

The wolf began to pace inside me again. I felt my lips pulling back.

Alex put a hand on my arm.

Calm.

I took a breath, concentrated on getting my neck muscles relaxed. A shiver passed through Alex and Olivia. I realized they'd been keyed up as if they were wired into me.

We'll back you, whatever.

Shit. If I went berserk and killed Kath and Taylor, they'd help. I swallowed. It was a hell of a responsibility to carry, but actually realizing I was carrying it helped.

Calm.

"He said he wanted you in the hospital for evaluation and stabilization, but he was worried about your reaction," Kath said. "He wanted my help to get you in."

"He wanted you to trick me. Have me injected with anesthetics and kidnapped off the street." Saying it like that made it hurt all over again. "Why, Kath? Why would you do this, even if you thought it was legitimate?"

"You're out of control," she said. "At Alex's house you—"

"At Alex's house I did what? I yelled at you?" I was angry again, this time at myself. I had been out of control last time we'd met, but she didn't know that.

"You..." Her eyes slipped to and fro between me and Alex. "You scared me. And Alex said you were doing something. He told you to stop. Then you just blew up and ran away."

It was a long way from justification. It sounded thin and she knew it.

Taylor fidgeted and came to her rescue. "Dr. Noble showed us the video."

"What video?"

"He said it was from your time in the special forces—" Kath said.

"Oh. And because *he* says I was in the army, now you believe it." That was sweet.

"He had other evidence, some other pictures of you with your unit, before your accident."

"And what accident is this supposed to be?"

"The head trauma," Kath said. She couldn't meet my eyes. "The reason you had to leave the army."

"Apart from the fact that I was in a special forces unit, that is complete bullshit, end to end."

"But why would he do this?"

"Because I'm investigating him!"

They looked wide-eyed at me.

I paused. I couldn't explain the paranormal aspects to them. "Dr. Noble, or someone passing himself off as Dr. Noble, is a suspect in a string of murders. He knows I'm on to him. What better way of protecting himself than getting me labeled insane?" I jabbed the forms again. "Or filled with the kind of drugs so I go insane anyway."

"But that's ridiculous."

"Like me being in a special forces unit is ridiculous? So ridiculous that you told our family friends that I'd spent the time as a whore? How's that looking now, Kath?"

My fists bunched. If I couldn't take it out on them, I wanted to start breaking furniture.

"Or like claiming to be a security consultant for Kingslund Group is ridiculous? Until you see me on the news rescuing Kingslund employees and jumping off a building down in Meridian. What did you think? I was having a manic episode? I was being chased by paranoid delusions?

"You can't believe anything I say, but this guy comes along with a story that I need hospitalization and the pair of you swallowed it whole."

"He seemed believable. He had proof of what he said. You just expect me to believe what you say!"

"And why shouldn't you? Have I lied?"

Taylor's hand crept over Kath's to pull her back.

"The video," he said, clearing his throat. "It is clearly you. It was...alarming. I said that was why you had to be assessed in a secure facility. In case there was a regression. I didn't want us to be liable..."

"Where the hell did Noble say he got all this from?" Alex asked.

"Amber's army doctors, of course," Taylor said.

There was a moment of silence. Petersen and Noble. Or Petersen and the rogue masquerading as Noble.

"How 'alarming' was this video?" I asked. "What does it show?"

"A group of orderlies trying to sedate you." Taylor licked his lips nervously. "He said you put three of them in the hospital. The video backs that up."

"Neat trick while I was suffering from head trauma," I said. I couldn't remember it. Something that had happened in Obs that my mind had just closed over. "What was the rest of the bullshit about cults while I was getting kidnapped, or did you make that up yourself?"

"He said you'd gotten in with a cult and they were messing with your head. He said that he'd helped you make an exceptional recovery before that, but it was all being undone," Kath said. Her eyes slid back to Alex. "We just wanted you well again."

Crap, her voice actually caught when she said that. The sound stabbed me in the gut.

"Why, Kath?" I'd heard what they said, but there was something deeper behind this, something painful.

I waited until she lifted her head. Her eyes came up. They were red from crying. Everybody else went quiet and distant as I focused on her.

"I just wanted my big sister back," she said. Tears streaked her cheeks. "You went *away*, Amber. You *left* us. You never came back." Her head dropped. She drew her legs up and hugged them. "I know you're standing here. You and Mom can't understand what I'm saying. But you never came back, not like I remember. I'm always scared around you. You don't talk about anything. You act weird all the time."

Taylor put his arm around her and glared at me.

They'd been stupid to fall for Noble's lies, but it's what sociopaths are good at—making people believe them. They'd been callous to just leave me to be driven off to an asylum, but they'd have wondered what good they could have done by trailing along.

I had to get out of here before I started making any more excuses for them. Just being here was setting my wolf off, and I could feel the Athanate stirring as well. Since Kaothos had closed it, I'd had to open the strongbox a couple of times. And she'd warned me about loosening the lock. I didn't want it opening again here.

Calm.

"You've got my things," I said.

"In the second bedroom," Taylor said.

I found a plastic bag that had been tossed on the bed. It had my HK and shoulder holster, a couple of cell phones, including Bian's encrypting one, my billfold wallet, my credit card and my keys. It looked pathetic somehow.

I took the chance to breathe deeply for a while before returning to the living room.

"Give me a minute here please, guys," I said, looking at Alex.

Olivia had come down from whatever I'd been using to pull her along with me. Now she was nervous about leaving me with them, but Alex nodded and guided her out. His trust was like a shield around me. I couldn't abuse it.

Safety-minded Taylor had unloaded the bullets from the magazine. I sat opposite them and began to methodically load them back in.

I could feel the fear swirling off them, and the siren song of Basilikos stirred in the depths of my mind. I shoved it down and concentrated on slipping the bullets back in. The sound of them racking in was loud over the background of the wind.

"Where's that necklace?" I said quietly. "Great-grandma's necklace."

"How can you think of something like that now?" Taylor said.

"Because, like I said, it's important." I slammed the magazine back in the HK, making them both flinch.

"I don't know," Kath said.

"You're lying," I said. I knew it, and she could see I knew it.

"I lost it," she tried. Her eyes were growing wider and more desperate.

"You're still lying."

"I threw it away!" Her voice was a reedy shriek. "It was just a stupid bead necklace. Are you satisfied now?"

I let her squirm for a minute.

"You're not lying anymore. But I'm not satisfied at all."

This would just be another example of my craziness as far as they were concerned. And yet it was hugely important. Olivia's life might depend on it.

It was the wrong time to take it further now. I felt the wolf as if she had expanded inside me, a frisson that seeped down my limbs until my hands and feet tingled. I wasn't finished here but I had to go, and I couldn't afford any more distractions.

"If I hadn't escaped, I'd be dead, or as good as. Think about that. I can't tell you what I'm doing at the moment. Maybe, sometime, I will be able to. It's dangerous. Meantime, just leave me alone. Don't even talk about me." I holstered the HK and stood up. "And keep the hell out of my way."

"Just go," Taylor said defiantly.

I stared at him until he lowered his eyes.

I paused in their open doorway, and looked back. The cold wind trailed in ribbons of snow across their floor.

"I had a little sister once," I said. "I loved her with all my heart."

Chapter 64

We drew away from the house, Alex steering the SUV carefully down toward Speer Boulevard, where the snow had been cleared. I felt too tired and sickened to want to talk.

The necklace was gone. I'd made an oath to help Olivia. I couldn't even think how to tell her that my best lead had vanished into a dump somewhere, let alone what I was going to do about it.

Alex broke the silence.

"Tell me what happened," he said, slowing the SUV gently as we came to the end of the road.

The difficulty he was having driving got my head working again.

"Make for the stadium parking lot," I said. "I want to pick up the truck."

The Hill Bitch might be cold to drive, but she'd laugh at the snow.

"Got it." He turned north onto Speer. Snowplows had been out here and the way was easier, although the snow was already drifting back across the road.

I gave them the short version, but there was no way of hiding the effect it had on me. At the end, reliving the terror of being helpless and imprisoned set my Athanate off. I had to stop every few sentences to calm myself down.

"Noble," Alex said, his voice tight with anger. "I can't believe it. I'll…"

I put my hand on his arm, trying to short-circuit both his rage and my memories.

"We need to be sure," I said. "We're only going to get one chance at this. Melissa was right; one of the first things she said to me was that he's leaving. All the years of hiding have been thrown aside. He's left clues because it doesn't matter anymore. But that's not the same as telling us who he is. Or she is."

"But you saw him."

"I saw Noble. I saw you, too. And think about why Melissa would leave the house? Maybe she got a call and thought she saw José outside. Maybe I saw Noble's face only because the rogue needed to use that to move around in the prison. What if he, or she, showed up at Noble's house earlier looking like me, killed him and took all his IDs?"

"He knew things that you'd talked about with Noble."

"Maybe the rogue tortured that information out of him."

"Shit!" He hit the wheel with his hand. "It's a freaking nightmare. How the hell are we supposed to prove anything?"

"If we get close enough, I can tell from the eukori." I shuddered. "I won't forget that feeling."

He was shaking his head, but I pressed on. I felt as if my investigation had been blown apart, but I had the one strong gut feeling on this—that it was one of the pack. I needed to know what had been going on.

"Alex, what's happened to the pack? What were you doing to Larsen?"

"We were up at Bitter Hooks. It's his trial," Alex said quietly.

"But he's not the rogue," I said. "We've got to call and stop it."

"No, not that." Alex ran a hand over his face, looking tired. "Larsen can't change. His wolf never comes through. But the wolf keeps trying more and more. We call that the trial, when someone who can't change is forced by the wolf to make the last attempt."

I'd gotten it completely wrong. Larsen was like Alex's old girlfriend, Hope. Condemned to die by the transformation they couldn't complete, their last minutes a torture as the body fought to change to wolf, and failed. The same thing that would eventually happen to Olivia unless I found some way to help her. I thought I'd been so close to the necklace. If I'd gotten it, maybe I would have been able to help Kyle.

The anger that boiled through me was useless. I had to let it go. I couldn't mention the necklace to Alex with Olivia in the back. She was keeping it quiet, but I could feel her. Like the snow had blown into my sister's house, gray strands of grief weaved around me in the car from both of them. The Call or eukori? I didn't know. Olivia wasn't supposed to be able to use the Call until she changed, but I had.

Focus.

"Was Silas there?" I said.

Alex looked at me, sensing the emotions without realizing their cause. "Yes, from the start. Still is. They're still there."

Silas wasn't the rogue.

And how come Alex and Olivia weren't there? This was supposed to be for the whole pack. They'd left that for me?

Focus.

"Who was missing?"

"Noble." Alex's tone told me he'd made his decision, but I waited. "Ursula," he said. "Neither of them are answering their cells."

Ursula.

She was big enough to be the wolf that made those bites. And on the other evidence, she knew the women from Melissa's list of potential victims.

Or Noble. He wasn't big enough as a wolf, but he'd probably came into contact with all the known victims. And he might have tried to mislead me about knowing Barbara Green.

Could Ursula masquerade as Noble? As a veterinarian, she had some medical knowledge. But she was so much bigger than Noble. Had he looked taller than normal in the center? I hadn't been able to see clearly, trussed up on the gurney.

Or was it both of them? Some kind of sick sadistic relationship?

If it was more than one, why not suspect Silas again? But that path spiraled down to suspecting all of them.

Something taunted me from the edge of my memory. I'd heard or seen something important and I'd ignored it.

"Where do they live?"

"Noble's got a townhouse down in Parker, and Ursula has an apartment in Arvada."

Opposite ends of Denver. Which first?

Alex interrupted my chain of thought. "Bian will have tried calling Jen as well. You'd better call both of them."

"In a minute."

My hand was still on his arm. We weren't linked through eukori, but I still sensed a turmoil in him and I sensed it wasn't about what had happened to me. There was something he was hiding from me about us, the pack and Larsen's trial, something deep.

"Pull over and tell me what else is going on."

We eased off the cleared street and stopped in front of a closed coffee shop.

"Aren't you supposed to be with the rest of the pack?" I asked.

"When Bian called, I couldn't ignore it. I had to come looking for you." He looked away, studying the front of the coffee shop. "I had to leave Kyle."

There were echoes of his grief over Hope in there as well. I bit my lip, glad he'd come for me and sorry for the pain it'd caused him.

"That must have gone down well with Felix," I said, feeling clumsy.

Alex didn't answer.

Crap.

Felix and Alex must have argued over this.

I knelt on the seat, grabbed his jacket and twisted him around to look at me.

"Alex, you can't do this. You'll be thrown out."

"Too late. I already have been." He shook his head.

"What? Alex, this is crazy," I yelled. "They're your pack. You love being in the pack. You've earned your position; you can be excused for one slip. Both of you. You have to go back to Felix."

"It's not about a rule. It's not even about not being there for Kyle. It's about wanting, no, it's *needing* to be with you more than I need the pack, more than I've ever needed anything else. It's about choosing. It's about a commitment." He stopped for a moment, his eyes staring, seeming lost, looking anywhere but at me. "An absolute commitment."

"Olivia?" I wanted her to talk some sense into him.

Olivia was almost whining. She leaned forward to touch my arm carefully.

What the hell was happening?

"I can't go back," Alex said.

"Why?" I shook him, and for a second I thought I'd shaken sense into him. But his eyes flared gold and anger fired up through him.

"Because you're my alpha!" he shouted.

Utter silence. My mouth moved wordlessly.

There was a wrench inside me, as if a dislocation that I hadn't been aware of had been suddenly reset. All the talk before of being a pack had felt good. It'd just been talk. My House was not my pack. It was nothing like it.

Naming me as his alpha *made* us a pack.

I felt like I'd been gut-punched.

I'd come to love the Athanate and I loved being Athanate, belonging to that vast structure with its huge arrays of loyalties and obligations. I was a little scared of it as well, feeling the complexity of the structure respond to me. I loved being House Farrell and sensing my House around me.

But that wasn't pack.

Pack was a big old V8 spinning up inside me. It was a sense of power building, a bonfire catching. It was liquid fire in my limbs and the roar of the crowd shaking the stands.

I wanted to scream and shout.

I hugged Alex to me. Olivia reached from the back seat, ran her face along my arm. Her eyes were down and her breath keened in her throat. I pulled her roughly into the hug.

Emotions churned through us. Kyle. Melissa. Being strapped down on the gurney. Being unable to change. But also Jen and Alex, joy and making love, pride and elation.

Like a river after the rapids, the seethe of emotions calmed slowly into a gentle euphoria. We floated. We'd just officially formed a pack. And as I thought that, I felt our Call: smaller, sweeter, more intense, more focused than the Denver pack. *Our* Call.

Reality came crashing back.

"We are so screwed."

Alex snorted. "You think?" But the crazy jubilation leaked between us and it bubbled out in nervous laughter. We were behaving like a group of teens, completely caught up in the moment and ignoring the consequences of our actions.

We couldn't take the time this deserved. Even Felix and the huge problems this caused with him would have to wait.

I kissed them and let them go. I'd probably half-throttled Olivia, reaching over the backrests. No wonder the Were went for bigger cars. We needed the extra room.

Then I sat back down and pointed at the road. Time to get back on track.

My pack.

I preened.

I turned my cell back on. Jen was first of course.

But I didn't get a chance to dial before the cell beeped. José. He'd have been able to put a monitor on my cell. That he was still sitting there waiting in the early hours of the morning made me feel a little better.

"Amber?" he said.

"I'm fine now, José." That didn't satisfy him and I had to recount what had happened again. I didn't reveal Noble's part yet, and I had to call him off from arresting my sister. Not that she'd done anything actually illegal, but I appreciated his support.

He told me that as soon as the snow allowed it, there would be a team down at the Aurora Center trying to find out how on earth they'd accepted someone under a false name. By the time they got that far, they'd be hearing Noble's name. I had however much time that was to come up with a story that would hide the paranormal aspects of the case.

I'd finished as we entered the stadium parking lot. It was a field of white with no more than a few bumps down at the end, where the cars were parked.

"José, I gotta go. One quick question, if you're getting info on the search from the FBI."

"Oh, we got it, Amber. Seems like there's been a sudden change over there. We have a feed to at least some of their notes, courtesy of Agent Ingram, and a request for information sharing. What're you looking for?"

I was staring at the Hill Bitch as she emerged from the snow. Alex had left me inside his SUV and dug into the mounds until he found her.

"The house at Glenmore Hills. What do they say about vehicles in the garage?"

"Garage was empty," José said after a moment.

That was what I was afraid of.

"Okay. You have some information to feed back to them. The killer is mobile and driving a field-green Ford F-250 with huge tires." I squeezed my eyes shut and pulled the license from the depths of my brain.

"You sure?"

"The truck was in the garage, and now it isn't."

We left it there and I called Jen, feeling guilty as I watched Alex and Olivia trying to unfreeze the manual locks to get in my truck.

Jen answered immediately. She hadn't slept and once she heard the even shorter version of the story, she was all for suing Kath, Taylor, the Aurora Center, the FBI and probably the city of Denver before I calmed her down.

She'd be back that evening. I promised I would be fine and we'd talk through everything before we ended the call.

I needed to talk to Bian as well, but that would wait a few minutes. Alex had gotten the Hill Bitch open and I went over there.

I'd gotten a ticket, naturally. Only the snow had saved me from being towed.

"It might need a jump start," Alex said.

I sneered theatrically and twisted the key in the ignition. The Hill Bitch coughed and shook like a wet dog before settling down to her customary snarl. It was going to take more than being buried in snow to faze her.

Unfortunately, I hadn't treated her like I treated my car, as an extension of my personal space with spare shoes and clothes in the trunk.

"Okay, I guess back to Manassah," I said. "I need to change."

As I spoke, I turned the TacNet headset back on.

The emergency communication alert squealed.

"Farrell, where the hell have you been? I need you here urgently."

"Gray, the hunt is supposed to be stood down."

"It's not that."

He gave me an address uptown and killed the connection without answering any more of my questions.

Chapter 65

"The problem is that fucking cowboy." The guy screaming at me was one of Verano's pack, and he'd pissed me off before he'd even finished the sentence. The irony of calling Gray a cowboy just spiced it up. The man was pointing up at the second floor of the building from where we stood at the base, next to a door that Gray had apparently been able to open and close behind him. Also apparently without setting the alarm off. I needed to talk to this guy.

Alex growled softly behind me, unhappy at the shouting.

"Where's Verano?" I said quietly, forcing them to lower their voices.

The man himself emerged around the side of the building. He'd ditched the fashion designer outfit. He and his pack were wearing everyday work clothes with bulky parkas and snow boots. I wondered what weapons they had beneath those parkas.

"I wondered if you'd show up," he said.

"You just wondered rather than calling me?"

He shrugged casually. "It would have been premature until we caught him."

"Caught him at what?"

"While we were out searching, Gray's been talking to the Matlal Athanate."

"Is that so?" I'd had a feeling that was what this was about. "And you know this how?"

"We spotted him with her. One of the Matlal Athanate."

"You just happened to spot him," I said. "Hell, that's lucky." I had no idea where this was going, but I trusted Gray much more than I trusted Verano. And Gray had called me here.

"So? We were following him," Verano said. "It didn't impact on our job."

Verano's pack was milling around behind him. The man himself maintained a calm face, but I could feel the Verano Call, seething like marsh gas.

His animosity was feeding into the Call and affecting the whole pack. Couldn't he sense what he was doing? How had he gotten such a recommendation from the Athanate on the Eastern Seaboard?

"And talking to one is talking to them all?"

He ignored my jibe. "Why are you on his side?"

"I'm not, but I'd like to hear what he has to say first, not judge him guilty immediately."

"You're claiming we're lying?"

A ripple passed through his pack, and I felt their Call. It was angry. It felt unbalanced, as if it was the sort of anger that was just looking for an excuse, any excuse, to blow.

"No. But I'm sure you don't know the whole truth. That's what I intend to find. In the meantime, I'm pissed you've been acting on your own without informing me."

Verano grunted. "Well, you can ask them yourself now. She's in there with him."

I looked up at the building and its neighbors. Standard office buildings, packed in too close together. I thought about what I would do.

"She may have gone in, but I doubt she stayed long," I said to Verano. "I think you've been suckered."

That was stupid of me, given how worked up the whole Verano pack was about this, but I'd had enough of talking to him.

I flicked the TacNet. "Gray, let me in."

"Just you," he said.

"Just me." I held the door and turned to Verano. "Back off."

He walked back to join his pack. They fell into a hushed conversation and my trust of them found a new low.

The electronic lock on the door clicked open.

"Alex, watch them, please. Call me on the TacNet if there's a problem."

"Will do." His voice got quieter. "I don't trust Verano either."

"Yeah, but how much of that is because of my attitude? Are you picking that up from me? Like his pack is wired into his attitude toward Gray?"

He shook his head. "Packs shouldn't react like that unless he encourages them. I'm not just channeling everything you think."

"Good." I caught myself brushing against him unconsciously, and tried to focus. "What are you carrying?" I'd seen him load up from his SUV before Olivia took it. I'd arranged for her to stay with Tullah and her family for safety at the moment.

He held his jacket half open, letting me see one of the ugly P90s he must have borrowed from David or Pia.

"Be careful." Alex let the door close behind me and leaned against it, somehow managing to look both tense and relaxed.

I was standing in a lobby. The streetlights outside barely shone through the smoked glass windows, but I could see the location of the stairwell from the illuminated exit signs. I made my way up, mostly by feel, to the second floor. I was aware that Gray was watching me when I started on the stairs, just as I was aware when he left me to it. Presumably to check that no one was creeping up another way.

The second floor was spookily lit by computer screens, all displaying the company's pale green log-in screen and making the room seem like it was underwater. Movable chest-high partitions created dozens of Dilbert cubicles on my left, leaving a corridor ahead down to a set of double doors.

Gray was a shadow standing against the doors.

I felt the sigh of air currents as he let them close and turned toward me. There was no sign of anyone else, as I suspected. A lingering marque teased my memory. Matlal, yes, but not only that. Still, the Matlal woman had been here and she was now long gone. But he'd waited for me. Interesting.

"Consorting with the enemy, Gray?" I said. "Didn't think to keep me posted?"

"She's not the enemy. I think you understand."

"Why?"

"Because of Larry Dixon."

Larry's name still hurt, but I kept my face blank.

"He wasn't Basilikos," I said. "He wasn't even really House Matlal. He was House Romero, acting under compulsion."

"I know."

So, we'd both met someone from House Matlal, and I'd been slower to report Larry to Bian than he'd been to report this to me. But that wasn't at the forefront of my mind.

"If she knows about Larry because she was one of those that tortured and killed him, then I'm not dealing, Gray."

"I didn't think you would." He opened the doors a crack and listened again. "She wasn't involved. You know her, by the way."

"Huh?"

"You met her at Cheesman Park."

"The platinum blonde. Kick-ass martial arts."

"The same. She wants out, like Larry did."

I huffed. "She's been compelled? She's House Romero?" He could push that Larry button once too often.

"No." He was quiet for a moment. "I won't argue her case for her, Farrell, but I'm asking you to talk to her."

Okay. She was here to trade. What would she want, other than not to be killed? Could I promise even that? Clearly, she was Basilikos and all that went with that. Blood slaves. Feeding on fear.

I would have been happier if I could have simply said no, to have said that Basilikos were beyond the pale. But who was I to point fingers?

I tried to think like Bian would.

"What's she got to trade?" I asked.

"Locations of others, including the toru."

It was a good gambit. Toru were an emotional issue all right, and the option of clearing the rest out quickly would go down well with Bian.

"And her own toru?"

"Basilikos don't own toru privately, toru are owned by the House. She isn't using toru. More than that, you'll have to discuss with her."

"Why did she come to you?"

"She didn't. I found her."

Interesting. We had a long talk coming up, Gray and I.

"Okay. It's enough to talk to her, but I can't promise that Altau will accept her."

He shook his head in the darkness. "She's not appealing to House Altau. She wants to join House Farrell."

Crap.

"Freaking hell, Gray. I'm *not* the person she wants to ask for asylum." The thought of what Naryn would make of this sent shudders through me.

Gray opened his mouth to answer and Alex's voice came through the TacNet.

"Amber! I think they've split up. Some of them drove away, but I think four have gone around the side. Do you want me to come up with you?"

"No. Make sure the others don't come back."

"I got it."

I turned to Gray, but he was already responding. He was listening again through the double doors.

When I moved to join him, he shook his head and pointed at a spot about fifteen yards from the door. He stood to one side, moving surprisingly lightly for a big man.

I understood. I was the distraction. Not the most comfortable thought. I had twelve rounds in my magazine, which was plenty in theory, but things can get difficult in a firefight with paranormals. Verano couldn't be pushing to kill me, though. Surely not? How would he explain that to Bian?

Easy enough to explain it to Naryn.

Gray slipped out of his clothes, stood against the wall and closed his eyes.

I wasn't getting an eyeful, but he seemed unconcerned anyway. From the way his head bobbed slightly, he might have been listening to his favorite music.

My ears strained to catch the Veranos approaching. They'd calmed down from the over-excited idiocy outside, but I caught a sense of them, their Call, quiet as a breeze slipping through pine woods, a feeling of fierce focus, of being pared down.

I swallowed hard. Whatever Verano had intended when he started, he'd lost control now. What I could sense approaching was a four-man killing machine. Or four-wolf, to be more accurate.

My skin tingled with currents. Gray was calling on the energy and some of it was being leeched through me, even though I was fifteen yards away.

Let him do his thing. Concentrate on yours.

I braced and raised the HK. Safety off.

Single shots to wound. Preserve ammunition. Remember there are more of them outside. Keep the shots away from Gray.

Crap, the rest of the Verano pack would go berserk when they knew what was happening in here. I had to warn Alex.

My hair began to float with the force of the energy that Gray was pulling, a witch-wind that stirred and flowed around me.

I caught the scent of Verano. They were here. There was no time to warn Alex.

They didn't try anything subtle. They gathered behind the door and then they rushed me—four streaks of pale silver death hurtling through the doorway.

It all went slow. I started with the leftmost, furthest from Gray. Tap. Single shot. Difficult to aim for a non-vital spot on a charging wolf. That might be fatal.

One down, three left, eleven rounds.

No time. They'd reach me. I moved, getting ready to roll with the force of their impact. I'd go down but they wouldn't be able to stop me from firing again. I swung the HK to aim at number two.

I didn't make it.

As the fastest wolf hit me, there was a scream from where Gray had been standing and a shadow streaked out and hammered into the two remaining. All of us tumbled onto the floor. I had no idea where Gray was in this free-for-all, so I didn't want to shoot again, but I slammed the butt of the HK into my attacker's skull until his jaws opened and I ripped my left arm out.

I jumped to my feet in time to see a huge cougar hurl one of the wolves into the partitioning, breaking it. The second wolf just backed down with its tail between its legs. A pack could overpower a cougar, but no wolf in its right mind would go one-on-one against the claws and jaws.

Gray screamed again, showcasing his impressive teeth. He was so cool.

I sensed that last wolf was Verano. With him cowed, the fight evaporated from his pack.

I stepped up, the HK pointed at Verano and my voice working on automatic.

"You change back, take your pals and get your pack the freaking hell out of this city, or so help me, we're going to kill you," I shouted. I hoped I was getting through to Gray as much as the Veranos. I wanted the Verano pack and their sick alpha out of Denver before they started something else, and I'd prefer to do it without having the deaths of the pack on my conscience. This was Verano's fault, not his pack.

The two standing changed back, and kept their eyes down as they limped carefully toward their comrades. Only Verano was uninjured, but the other three could walk. The change made their wounds worse, but there didn't seem to be anything life-threatening.

Gray's cougar took a slow step back, giving them room.

I made my way around him to the double doors. Their clothes and guns were on the other side. I gathered the guns. They dressed and I watched them slink away, trembling, toward a second set of stairs.

When they'd gone, I went back in and confronted the monstrous cougar. His eyes stared smugly at me. He was over four feet at the shoulder. Must weigh in at over two hundred and fifty.

Damn. How the hell?

"Kitty," I said, and he blinked at me. "Change back and get dressed now." I was proud my voice remained level. Pretty much.

"Alex, we're okay, we're coming down," I said into the TacNet and pulled my cell out.

I had to ignore Gray's pulling energy again. It made me dizzy, but not as dizzy as what I'd just realized.

I shook my head. I needed to get a team together to answer a question that could nail the rogue, and the snow would make it impossible for them to move through the city.

But there was more than one way to skin the cat, with apologies to present company.

I dialed Matt's cell, hoping for a miracle. He answered sleepily after a minute.

"Matt," I said. "Sorry. Is there any way I can get into Jen's conference facility right now? I'd need you to talk me through setting up a conference call, too."

"Yeah, no problem," he said. "As long as you can get to one of the main doors. I'll let you in."

It was still the small hours of the morning. "You're in early. How did you get in to work?" His Harley certainly wouldn't be out today.

"Umm. I saw the weather forecast last night. I stayed here. It's cool. There are emergency rooms for exactly that."

At last, something was working out for me.

"Great. Lucky for me. We'll be there in ten."

Next was Bian. I got her on the TacNet.

"No time to get you up to date, Bian. You and Alice in the Haven conference room in fifteen. I'll send you instructions."

I ignored her questions, ended the call and tried Tullah's number.

Olivia had just reached there in Alex's SUV and they were all still awake.

"You've got your laptop and internet connection?"

"Yeah, sure," she said.

"I want you to set up ready for a conference call in about fifteen minutes. With Mary, please. I'll call again with instructions."

I hung up.

I'd get them in the same virtual room and I'd get answers one way or another. I was sick of being short of information that I needed to know, and if we didn't work fast the rogue would slip away.

Gray was in human form and dressed again. He looked quizzically at me.

"And you." I stabbed my finger at him hard enough to make him flinch. "You're coming with me."

Chapter 66

In contrast to the bright marble lobby of the Kingslund Group headquarters building, where Matt had met us, the conference room was warm and dimly lit.

Matt had gotten used to me. He asked no questions as he explained the operation of the conferencing system. Then, in language that was almost English, he confirmed the electronic security of the conversation and the completeness of the soundproofing of the room itself.

I called Bian and Tullah and let him talk them through making the connections.

Alex, Gray and I sat at one end of a mahogany table the size of a small aircraft carrier and waited as first Bian and then Tullah appeared on the conference screens that took up one whole wall.

Matt smiled to himself as he was leaving. I didn't doubt his overactive mind was constructing theories as to why I was here at this time of the morning talking to these people, and why it was so urgent, but he seemed to prefer guessing to knowing the facts. Thankfully. At some stage, maybe, he might need to know more of what was going on, but I was already far out on a limb with Altau. I didn't want to pull any other unaffiliated humans into this mess.

And it was about to get worse; with Bian were both Alice and Naryn. I'd known Naryn would have to be involved at some point, but I'd hoped to filter this to him through Bian.

Tullah had both Mary and Liu with her.

"Thank you, and my apologies for the hour," I said, getting my tactful bit in early. I was starting to sound like Diana. I took a deep breath. "The reason for the urgency is that I believe we have no more than the rest of this day to catch or kill the rogue."

"Why do you think that?" Naryn asked.

"What can we do to help?" Tullah said at the same time.

"The FBI are right behind him. They have an evidence trail at the house he was using in Glenmore Hills. They'll be on to the Aurora Center and the paramedic team that kidnapped me."

"What?" Bian sat bolt upright. "You were kidnapped?"

I waved it away. "They'll have the name of Dr. Noble this morning." I paused. "The problem is, I don't know that he's the rogue. And if we get it wrong, he'll be gone."

"Where to? And how?" Naryn said.

"Anywhere outside the reach of the FBI. This is a guess, but I think he's come to some deal with Petersen. They've been working together. With the FBI on to him, he's going to need their kind of capability to get out of the country."

"Why would Petersen do that? What's he got that Petersen wants?" Tullah asked.

"It's what he thinks he can get," Mary said. "He's after you, Amber. You're the price for Petersen getting him out."

"But why would Petersen want me? Petersen had some kind of link to Matlal, but Basilikos don't want me, after Skylur's meeting." I didn't want to come out and say we'd been meeting with Correia. I was sure that qualified as an Athanate secret, but Naryn just nodded. He'd gotten the reference.

"Maybe Basilikos weren't entirely truthful about Matlal," he said. "Maybe Matlal, or remnants of Matlal's House, are still active, and they still want you."

"That badly?"

He shrugged.

"So what can we do?" Mary echoed Tullah's question.

"Help me decide who to go after," I said. "I can't chase both of the suspects."

"Who are they?"

"Ursula Tennyson or Dr. Noble."

"Hold on," Bian said. "You said Noble's too small."

"That's where you come in, Mary, Alice." I turned from the screen and pinned Gray where he sat. It wasn't really his fault, but still. "And you."

Gray fidgeted nervously, but waited.

"How much do you weigh?" I asked.

"Two hundred," he said.

"And that cougar you just turned into?"

Naryn and Bian looked startled. Alice and Mary frowned.

Gray fidgeted some more. "Never had a set of scales around at the right time," he hedged.

"Let me guess. About three hundred pounds?"

He shook his head. "Two-seventy-five."

My line of questioning started to make sense to them now.

"Better than a third heavier," I said. "I don't know what the difference is between you and an ordinary Were, but you change using the energy, and end up bigger. My question to the group is this: why can't a Were, who already has some skills with energy, learn that particular skill? Noble is about one-sixty pounds. To produce a wolf as big as Alex's, he only needs another sixty pounds or so."

"No reason at all he couldn't do it, I guess," Gray said. He leaned on his elbows and addressed himself to the others. "You'd call me skinwalker. It's a name that is burdened with bad images, so I prefer to keep that secret and call myself a Were. I *am* a Were, just not fixed to one form."

Naryn and Bian kept their faces carefully blank. I could see them thinking through the possible benefits. I was sorry to have dumped Gray in this situation, but everybody keeping secrets had just jammed the whole process.

"Wait." Mary shifted uncomfortably. "The energy could be used for this. But a working to increase size is a massive use of the energy. That's not the pattern of workings I told you that I sensed." She looked at Gray. "You changed shape twice about half an hour ago?"

He nodded.

"Those I sensed. They're distinctive. The workings I spoke to you about, Amber, those were different. I called them evil, and I meant it."

"I know," I said. I felt nauseous by what I was thinking, but I went on. "What if he were taking that extra bulk from a victim?" I said.

I could hear Noble's voice at our last meeting—what I'd taken as a joke. 'Size isn't everything', he'd said.

He'd been laughing at me the whole time.

"God." Tullah looked sick. "The victims' bodies all had part of them taken. That's what he does. He's found a way to steal not only whatever abilities they have, but their physical bodies as well, using them to increase his size during the change. Then he must shed that when he changes back."

"Yes." Mary put her head in her hand. "That would give off that sort of signature. Spirit hold me, those poor people." She wiped at her cheeks, her voice raw. "They would have had to be alive when it happened."

The missing piece of the puzzle. There was no need to create complicated theories about who else it could be. It was Noble.

The teleconference team had done their job. Now I had to go out and nail Noble.

It was deathly still in the room. The wind wailed mournfully outside.

Chapter 67

Denver was a phantom town, with gaunt, monochrome buildings emerging through the snow and then fading away behind another thick flurry. Streets were buried in wind-whipped dunes as we drove down to Noble's office. The eastern sky was paler gray than overhead, but it looked closer to midnight than 9 a.m.

"Schools and businesses closed, National Guard called out," muttered Gray, staring at his cell.

They were keeping the major roads open, and a few SUVs had ventured out on them. The swirling wind filled the smaller roads with snow, but the Hill Bitch just shrugged it all off. I was more worried that we'd run over someone's submerged car than be unable to keep moving.

We were heading to the offices because Alex had just received a message on his cell, from Ursula—*Noble's office. Now.*

Despite everything that pointed to Noble, I was still uneasy.

Just like Noble, Ursula wasn't a typical werewolf. Then she'd gone missing when the rest of the pack—*Felix's* pack, I amended—were at Bitter Hooks. And like Gray, her eukori was tightly controlled. I'd found out what Gray was hiding. What was Ursula hiding? Why was she calling us to Noble's office? And why wouldn't she answer her cell?

∞ ∞ ∞ ∞ ∞

Alex parked right outside Noble's office, next to a heavy-duty snowmobile. I had wondered how Ursula would be getting around in Denver.

I could see the space around the door had been cleared, and as we got closer, that the door had been forced. The building's power was out. I pulled the HK out and led the way in, Alex right behind me and Gray bringing up the rear.

The lobby was empty, snow sprayed out over the floor like a huge white fan, melting into the carpet. The alarm system was disabled. The door to Noble's suite off the main lobby had been broken as well.

With the power out, Ursula had dragged Noble's desk over to the window, where she was sitting, flicking through paper files. A filing cabinet stood to one side with the lock torn off and a drawer hanging open.

Her black hair was pulled back with a leather cord. She was wearing rough work denim, a big padded jacket and heavy work boots. A pair of filthy gloves lay beside her. In the beam of Alex's flashlight, her face was still red from a night spent in the cold outside. It was also smeared with dirt and creased with her usual unhappy frown.

It occurred to me as we walked in that this was my first meeting with someone from Felix's pack since Alex and I had crossed the boundary and formed our own pack. And not just anyone—one of his senior lieutenants.

Joy.

She looked up as we entered.

"Morning," I said.

Her eyes widened, flicking from me to Alex, and her nose flared.

Oh, crap.

She jumped off the desk, making my heart kick, but there was no aggression in her movement.

After a long drawn-out couple of seconds, I blew out a breath and slid the HK back into the holster. It was the wrong solution to the problem here.

"Challenge?" Ursula's voice was husky.

"No," Alex said immediately. "We don't want to take over from Felix. We want to be our own separate pack."

"In Denver?" The skepticism made Ursula's voice sound even hoarser.

"We know it's going to be difficult," I said.

Her eyes came back to me, widened again, and I felt the shakeouts of pack dynamics twisting my gut. She was sensing I was the alpha.

Her eyes dropped, and went back to Alex. "That must hurt," she whispered, a trace of a smile in her voice.

Alex snorted.

She came back to me. She'd always made me nervous and it wasn't going to get better soon. Being alpha didn't mean being the biggest or the best fighter. Ursula was a lot bigger than me and I instinctively knew I wouldn't get her to underestimate me like some big guys would.

But it was Alex and me. We were an alpha pair. Surely she wouldn't attack both of us.

Except we were an alpha pair intruding on her pack's territory.

"Do we have a problem?" I asked, easing my weight forward and tensing.

"No."

There was more behind that monosyllabic reply than that, but if she wanted to concentrate on the important things today, I'd go with that.

"Good. You called us here. Why?"

"You got me thinking about those women," Ursula said to me, working to get things back on safer ground. "The horse-owning community's pretty close in Denver, and they talk to me. So I started asking questions." She grunted. "That's where I was last night when the storm hit. When…"

She stopped and she and Alex looked at each other.

Alex's hand gave mine a squeeze and then he stepped forward and opened his arms.

They hugged, and I was shocked to see her eyes misted.

"I was getting horses under cover," she whispered. "Saving them seemed more important than watching Kyle die."

He patted her back. "I had to leave, too," he muttered. "They're still there."

"God." Her eyes closed for a moment, then they split and she turned away to retie her hair.

"Anyway." Her usual voice was back when she turned around. "I was out at Pegasus Ranch helping Ellie Bernstein. She knew three of those women, a couple of them quite well." Her voice went rough with anger. "Well enough to know they'd gotten involved with their psychoanalyst."

She waved a hand at the files on the desk. "Guess who?"

I stood next to her and picked up the nearest file. They were the state-required minimum information—basic patient details, overview diagnosis, start of treatment, end of treatment, recorded outcome. Four of the missing women had their files on the desk. All of them had been referred to other therapists under recorded outcome, so Tullah's list showing all the missing women having different therapists was right. But at least four of them had come through here. Too many for coincidence, along with everything else pointing to Noble.

Too easy? My paranoia kicked in.

Ursula felt it. "I can't lie to you," she said.

"Yeah, like Noble can't lie to Felix."

I was in close enough that I had to tilt my head back to look up at her. She smelled pretty much as I'd have expected from her description of her night—horses and sweat. And this near, the woman was intimidating. It wasn't her size; she wasn't that much bigger than Alex. But there was a feeling of power that came off her like smoke. It had the same wild tone of wolf, but it wasn't.

Was she another skinwalker? Was that why her eukori was so tightly bound up?

At the thought of it, I realized my eukori was reaching out to her. I carefully put a hand on her arm and the connection seemed to come into focus.

"What...?"

Whether it was because I'd startled her, or the sorrow over Kyle, her eukori loosened.

Alex pressed in behind me, worried about what I was doing. But this time, I was in control. I wasn't trying to compel her. I just wanted to be absolutely sure.

There were no lies in this woman. What we saw on the desk was what she'd found. She was certainly hiding things, but none of them to do with the rogue.

I pulled back, and felt both Alex and Ursula relax. Eukori wasn't something they controlled as Were, although they instinctively understood its power. Just as I could understand their paranoia about it.

We all stepped back, feeling awkward. To cover it, I brought Ursula swiftly up to date.

"So, he can look like you too," she said. "That's...worrying."

I opened my mouth to answer, and Noble's phone rang.

Not the main office phone, the private line on his desk.

I knew immediately who it was. Combined with what Ursula had just said, I had the first sickening taste of awful premonition.

Chapter 68

Noble had his spider's web set up too well. He would have had his alarm system here alert him as soon as it had been disabled, just the same as he knew exactly when we'd found his hideout in Glenmore Hills, allowing him to get there and take his truck before the FBI arrived. The truck that meant he was as mobile as we were, even with Denver snowbound.

It was more than just a sense of foreboding as I picked the telephone up; I felt physically ill.

"Yes," I said.

"Congratulations, Amber. Your resourcefulness has been entertaining."

"Don't call me that, you sick bastard. What do you want?"

I had José's number on speed dial. I put my cell on the table and started scribbling a message to Alex to get José to track the location of the call.

"Quite simple, really," Noble said. "And you won't even need to track my location. But first, the incentive to cooperate. I have your surrogate daughter, Emily, with me. She's unconscious at the moment. If you insist, I can wake her up."

I had to lean against the table for support. My body felt too weak to contain the anger that was burning inside me. I wanted to let the wolf out and I knew I had to control that. I couldn't afford to lose it now.

I forced my mouth to work. "No. Just tell me what you want."

"As I said, very simple. You for her. No FBI, no police, no Altau. One other person."

His voice was different. Every time he'd spoken to me before last night, he'd used a disguise that was whatever he thought appropriate. That dry, academic therapist didn't exist. The pack colleague trying to help me; that certainly didn't exist. He'd used that voice to make me believe he was trying to help me. His voice now was just cold and arrogant; the voice of a man completely in charge of the situation.

"How do you expect me to believe you'll do that?"

"I'll explain. I'm in the cabin at the top of the mountain behind Coykuti. I have Emily here. Park at the ranch house and walk up. Bring Alex with you. It'll take you a couple of hours to get up here."

"Then what?"

"At the top, I have the snowmobile I used to get up here. Alex and Emily go down on it. By the time they're going down, I will have called Petersen. His troops will arrive and come up the track. They'll have instructions to let the snowmobile past once they get my signal."

"Why would we trust you to let them go?"

"It's not me you're trusting. It's your army colleagues."

Trusting Nagas wasn't going to happen anytime soon.

"And then?"

"I have ten minutes with you before I hand you over to Colonel Petersen. I'm sure you've figured out what I want from you by now. If you prevent me from getting it, then Alex will be stopped and killed and Emily brought back up to see if that changes your mind."

"Or you just kill them anyway, regardless of what I do."

"I can't kill them. I'll be at the top of the mountain. You may not trust your former colleagues, but I don't see that you have any options."

"It seems you're trusting them as well."

"I don't trust them any more than they trust me. I have been careful enough to leave sensitive information about their real command structure in the hands of legal firms who will publish it in the event of my death. I don't expect them to thank me, but provided I pass you alive to them, they will fly me off this mountain in a helicopter and put me down where I tell them to."

He was a fool if he relied on that to keep him alive, but all I wanted was the opportunity to get Emily out. If I could do that, then finding out who was behind Petersen would be good. If I could stay alive.

But I wasn't going to deliver Alex and Emily into Petersen's hands.

"No deal, Noble. You keep Petersen and his troops away. Alex and Emily get off the mountain first. They call me when they're clear, then you have your deal. You'll have as much time as it takes for Petersen to get up to the top. If he's coming by helicopter that wouldn't be long."

The phone went silent for a long few seconds before he spoke again. "All right."

Way too easy. Not that I expected anything else. While I was trying to think how to trap him, all he was thinking of was how to get me onto the mountain. I didn't trust him to keep any deals any more than I trusted Petersen. He'd already worked through the options and this was just another one he was ready for.

"No weapons," he said. "You know I have Adept abilities, and one of them is the working to detect metals. You come up that track carrying metal and the girl dies."

Bluff, surely. I wished I had Mary at my side.

"Okay," I said. I had no option but to go along at the moment.

"One other thing. Petersen has the same military comms system you do. Don't assume your encryption is secure. Don't use it." He paused. "Now, you know as much as you need to. You have till 3 p.m. to get up here. No excuses. If you're not here, she dies at one minute past three." He cut the connection.

I stood there, the dead phone dangling in my hand.

Noble was a walking dead man, one way or the other. If I didn't kill him, the Nagas would. Petersen's boss in the administration would be too exposed as the FBI investigation went on. The threat he held over them was bullshit. Whoever it was would be on a flight somewhere right now. I had the idea that Petersen's real bosses were Basilikos anyway.

What Petersen and his Nagas wanted was me, alive. After Noble. My flesh crawled.

I wasn't going to make it easy for him, but provided I got Emily and Alex away, he could take his best shot.

Chapter 69

It was beautiful now. The storm had blown through and the sun was out.

That was a freaking disaster. We'd been counting on the cover of falling snow.

I emerged from the tree line and started on the final section up to the cabin. The air was cold, but sweet and crisp. It punched right down into my lungs. I'd have been loving it, if I wasn't walking alone up the mountain behind Coykuti Ranch, with the prospect of handing myself over to a psychopathic rogue on the slim chance of freeing Emily.

I didn't know if it was the situation, or whether I'd changed, but Coykuti and the mountain felt different. As if the place was on my side. Part of my territory, though Felix might have something to say about that. It was like Bitter Hooks now—a place I wanted to come. If I could.

My boots crunched in the snow, following the tracks of Noble's snowmobile where I could still make them out. I carried a backpack, but no weapons. Mary had been unsure about the self-taught ability of Noble to detect metals, but there was enough to go wrong with our plans without adding to the dangers.

Complex plans are fragile and vulnerable to many points of failure. Our plan had the benefit, then, of overwhelming simplicity. That wasn't making me feel better about it as I trudged up the steepening path to the summit, especially now the snow had stopped. But it was all we'd had time for between getting Noble's call and the deadline he'd imposed.

I felt the skin-twitching feel of an energy working as I left the trees behind. Possibly that was Noble's doing, and maybe it was some kind of spell to detect if I had metal on me. Or something else entirely. We had little idea of his powers. I shivered.

In the distance, above and in front of me, the cabin sat at the top of the trail. The trail was the only approach, going up in front of the cabin. There were steep drops on either side, and the back of the mountain had been pretty much chewed off by a glacier.

Everything around me was covered in at least three feet of fresh snow— more where drifting had piled it up.

To keep the gradient manageable over the last few hundred yards, the trail started to switchback. Snow piled steep and high on the inside of the track. That had forced Noble's snowmobile to take the outer edge of the trail, and I walked on the snow it had compacted. As I got higher, so did the drop I walked alongside.

Alex was somewhere out there, passing from tree shadow to rock like a ghost wolf. We'd counted on him having more cover in the storm, and the first element of our simple plan was already broken.

I could feel him through our Call, though words and distances didn't come through. Of course, that meant Noble could tell he was there as well.

Ursula was on the lower reaches of the mountain. I could sense her faintly.

Gray was climbing the back of the mountain. I couldn't sense him. If I couldn't, did that mean Noble couldn't either? We were going to find out, one way or another.

Neither Noble nor Petersen could be trusted. They'd kill Emily and Alex as soon as they had what they wanted. And if Noble thought he'd outfoxed Petersen, he was blinded by his own arrogance. I estimated we might have about half an hour before the Nagas showed up and it all got messy.

I could see Noble now. The cabin had a flat area in front of it, enough a space to park a couple of snowmobiles. He was standing there on the edge, looking through a telescope at the trail, probably wondering where Alex was.

He was dressed in the type of shabby overalls that the pack used at their fertilizer factories.

I wondered what he'd be thinking. He was a careful planner and he would have factored in the danger Alex and I would pose as we got closer.

It wasn't according to plan, but Noble not being able to see Alex had to have worried him. Maybe that would lead to a false move on his part. All it would take would be one. On either side.

Our plan was all in the timing and the delays. While Noble was out front, he couldn't check what was happening at the back of the mountain. I had to keep him there while Gray got in the back way.

But Gray couldn't signal through the Call, and the TacNet was switched off and stored with the weapons I'd hidden below under the cover of the yew trees around Felix's family cemetery. Even if they couldn't break our encrypted transmissions, the TacNet would have told the Nagas where we were too early. Leaving it behind bought us precious minutes. Instead, we had flares. Very simple communications—too simple for everything that could happen.

With every step I took now, our simple plan seemed more difficult. Without the cover of snow, Alex couldn't sneak in behind me while I diverted Noble. And what if Gray got tired? Took the wrong path up a cliff? What if the Nagas got here too quickly even without tracking our TacNet?

I was closer and closer to Noble with every step. That was the only thing going right for us at the moment.

I was three switchbacks and a hundred feet below him when he called out.

"Who's going to drive poor Emily back down, Farrell?"

He didn't care about that, of course. He just wanted to see if he could figure out why we'd decided to play it this way.

I kept walking, turned the corner. "Alex is here. There's time. We'll talk about how we do it," I said. Eighty feet to go.

"Brought a change of clothes?" he said. "Why do you think you'll need that?"

I eased the backpack straps and kept my head down. Not the change of clothes he'd be expecting, but he wouldn't be hearing about that from me. Instead I replied, "You said you needed to hand me over alive. Just coming prepared."

Sixty feet.

I wondered what kind of weapon he'd have. His best bet would be a shotgun unless he had a lot of range training. If it was just a handgun, we'd find out exactly how quickly I could close that distance. I had a Kevlar vest on and unless he was good or lucky with a handgun, I'd reach him and then he'd be dead. A rifle would be somewhere in between in terms of danger. I might rush him, depending on how competent he looked and how close he let me get first.

The time for that decision wasn't here yet. I walked, concentrating on moving with the least use of energy, keeping him in sight out of the corner of my eyes. I kept my head down—looking as defeated as I dared without overdoing it.

Forty feet.

"Stop there," he said.

Damn. Not close enough.

I was just below the last turn. I stopped and looked up tiredly, my shoulders sagging, sweat drying on my face. I slipped the backpack off as if it were uncomfortable. The less I had to carry when it went down the better.

Where was Gray?

Noble didn't have a weapon in his hands.

Unfortunately, the forty feet left between us was straight up. To get to him, I'd have to run thirty yards along the switchback trail to reach the top and then another thirty yards back to where he was. That would take too much time if he had a weapon down at his feet.

Stalemate. But that was okay for a while. Every moment we spent talking, Gray was getting closer. I hoped.

"You know Petersen's going to double-cross you, don't you?" I said.

"I know he'll try. Leave the backpack there."

I shrugged and started walking again.

Glancing up, I could just see there was a bag on the ground beside him.

A CSI-type body bag.

Suddenly, the wolf was scrabbling inside.

Kill!

No.

I clenched my fists, my lungs laboring to get air. I couldn't lose control now.

Focus.

The wolf faded back, but all that flowed in to replace it was a taste of ashes and despair.

My team was spread out over a mountain that only one of us had ever set foot on before. We had no way to communicate, no way to control the situation. Noble knew the mountain, and all the time we'd been planning, he'd probably been guessing what we'd try. If that was Emily beside him, dead or alive, there was no way either Gray or I could get the drop on him.

If it wasn't, who was it? If Emily was back in the cabin, he couldn't go back in there while I was here. Maybe we had just the sort of stalemate our plan needed.

Or Emily was dead and he had a shotgun and we were screwed already.

If, if, if.

I wouldn't say I'd been a fool to come here like this.

When your options shrink until there are no good choices, it's worse to do nothing.

Do what you can. None of us can do any more.

Thanks, Top.

There was nowhere else to go, nothing else to do, but climb the last steps of the mountain.

The wind was cold on one side of my face and the sun hot on the other.

I couldn't submit to what Noble had planned. Even if that meant Emily and I died. It might be that this was my day to die. Well, then, a fine day it was for it.

The feelings washed through me, leaving a sense of lightness and a purity of purpose.

And a red flare exploded in the sky, fired from down near the ranch.

Ursula.

The Nagas were here already.

Chapter 70

"Your friends have come to join the party, Noble."

There was no time left. I was already sprinting up the last switchback.

I heard the rasp of a zipper.

Maybe I could get him to panic. Maybe I could make him forget about Emily and concentrate on me.

I felt a spike in Alex's emotion through the Call. He sensed my emotions. He was coming.

Noble had to have a weapon in that bag.

I jinked and leaped up the last couple of paces onto the summit's flat space.

Still no weapon pointed at me.

Instead, bizarrely, he had pulled his coveralls back so he was practically naked. His hands were thrust into the bag, gripping Emily's throat and pointing a gun at her head.

"Stop!" he shouted.

Despite knowing it was wrong, I skidded to a halt. I couldn't kill Emily like this. We had lost.

"It's all over, Noble," I said. Anything to distract him. "Petersen will kill you."

"It doesn't matter what you think; I've got you here. You can't fight me. You can't escape me. I'll take what I want and go. Petersen won't find me out on the mountain."

The green flare behind the cabin caught me completely by surprise.

Gray!

But that was the signal that he had Emily. How?

Noble twitched, but all he did was sneer and lower himself into the opening of the body bag. It was obscene.

Without thinking, I was running again. It wasn't Emily in the bag.

The gun dropped from his fingers. It had been nothing but a way to slow me down.

The woman struggled. She was bound and gagged; there was nothing she could do—but as the bag slipped back I saw it was Noble's receptionist. The poor woman who'd been hopelessly in love with him.

And my skin started to burn with the pull of energy.

Faster.

All in the heartbeat it took me to get there, a ball of eye-searing blue light exploded from the bag and I half-tripped as Noble's body distorted in front of me.

I crashed into him, pushing him away from her.

A red flare exploded against the cabin.

Nagas! Right here!

I'd caught Noble off-balance and his wolf fell away, but I was too late for her. As he'd changed, he'd used the energy to tear her body apart and feed his transformation. Her whole front, where they'd touched, was just gone. The sharp edges of her ribs and chest bone stood out starkly. Nothing was left of her abdomen but blood.

We struggled to our feet.

Behind Noble, the cabin had caught fire.

He was huge, his fur mottled with blood and filth from the murder he'd just committed. As he stretched to his full height, his wolf's eyes were level with mine. They blazed—not golden, but red, charged from the woman's dying fear.

And at the same time, I felt him reaching for me with his sick mind. The cold tide washed around me, freezing me in place with its grip.

No.

He needed me to lower my defenses. Tricking me into thinking he was Alex hadn't worked, but fear was doing the job for him even better.

He took one slow step forward.

Fear can paralyze you. Fear can sap the strength from your limbs, and rise up, crackling through you like water abruptly turning to ice, until even your brain stops.

I'd never met anything that scared me like this.

But fear means you're still alive.

Run! I shouted in my own head.

Over that, his bleak, binding monologue hissed through my mind like poison. *There's no way you can escape. It's over. There's no point in running. Give up. It'll stop. Make it shorter.*

Alex was running. He was too far away.

The Call. Take strength.

I managed a shaky step backwards. And fell over the edge toward the trail switchback.

The shock cleared my head, broke the connection with Noble. I had enough time to register what was happening and relax before the deep, soft snow puffed out around me. The forty-foot drop I'd fallen over was more than half snow. The worst was that it tumbled me, so I had to figure out which way was up.

Then I was running.

I couldn't help Gray and Emily. The best I could do was divert Noble.

No. Change! Fight!

It wasn't Tara in my head. That was silent Hana, my wolf.

But I couldn't change now; I had no idea what would happen if I did. When I killed the Naga I'd blanked out completely. Surely that would mean I'd forget about what I had to do here? Would I even know how to change back?

Who do you think got you to change back last time? Hana.

That was Tara speaking.

But I can't trust changing.

He's catching you, was the simple reply to that.

What came from Hana then was a jumbled image rather than words, as if words would take too long.

Noble was huge. I mustn't let him catch me in his jaws. *So obvious.* But the size was a mistake. It made him slow in a fight. It made him clumsy. It wasn't his normal size. He had to adjust for everything. He would tire quickly. Just so long as I kept away from his jaws.

But I've never been a wolf. I'll be even clumsier.

That's why you must let me.

Do it, said Tara. *Trust her.*

I leaped down a section of the switchback.

Noble ran to the end and turned.

He *did* look slow to turn.

But he was frighteningly quick on the straights, and I'd run out of switchback eventually.

Without my really thinking any more about it, my clothes were falling off me. Skin was rippling. A gasp became a howl.

No time.

The world blurred and I fell towards the trail. Hana sizzled through me as if my veins had caught fire. *I* became *we.*

We leaped up, back up the switchback, right past Noble's frustrated, snarling jaws.

Up. Up.

Noble chased, going the long way. We could jump further than him. He was slower going up than he had been coming down. Either he knew we didn't have anywhere else to go, or he was conserving energy.

Could this actually work?

I wasn't blanked out. I wasn't controlling my body, but I was experiencing everything, like some kind of weird fairground ride that you didn't dare fall off.

He came closer. We let him. He lunged and we were a spinning, snarling knot that unraveled and we broke away and jumped again. Up.

He was even slower. He'd not gotten so much as one tooth on me.

But at the top, there was nowhere else to go. The flat space in front of the cabin was about twenty yards across and twelve deep. No space for anything fancy. No way down but the trail. Too long a drop on the sides or the back. Alex too far away. And I had to keep Noble from going around the back and helping the Nagas.

Shots were fired somewhere behind the burning cabin. Shouting. Gray was in trouble. He wasn't armed.

He had to look out for himself. We had to defeat Noble.

Noble stalked us, trying to herd us one way or the other, cut down the options.

We feinted and darted in front of him, but he knew his strengths. He wasn't trying to fight. He was concentrating on getting one good bite, a grip on me and then I'd be facing that cold strength seeping into my head again, shutting everything down.

We got too close. He raked our side with his jaws, drawing blood, only just unable to close on flesh.

Hana! I called.

I couldn't talk to her. I could see the way out of this. A way that Hana as a wolf wouldn't see. A way using my human knowledge and Hana's control of my wolf body.

Images! Tara said.

How to translate years of martial arts and half-remembered physics lessons into pictures?

Hana saw.

Noble thought his size was his overwhelming advantage. He hadn't studied the martial arts. He might know his vulnerabilities in his mind, but he didn't have the feel of those lessons, deep in his body. We did.

Hana dodged as if we were running for the trail. He turned, and we straightened, sprang at him like an arrow. Our jaws fastened on the side of his throat, fangs sinking in.

It was the wrong place. The back of the neck, biting down on the spine, or the front, tearing at the soft arteries; those were killing zones. Not the side. But it hurt him all right.

Noble's wolf screamed and twisted. His sheer bulk allowed him to throw us. And we let him.

We landed, already scurrying backwards to the side of the landing, frightened by his incredible strength and invulnerability. We were cowering. Our tail was between our legs and we were whining with fear.

Noble's eyes shaded to the same red as the fresh blood on his neck, and he charged.

Back. Back.

He was like a tidal wave bearing down on us. He accelerated the short distance between us like a shell from a cannon. He was impossible to escape. He would crash into us and knock us onto our back.

Down!

We couldn't get out the way completely. I had anticipated that.

Roll. Kick!

We didn't have the strength to kick him clear and we weren't small enough for him to pass over without tangling.

Noble flew over the edge, but he'd still hit us in passing and we went with him.

Not the front with the trail and the gentle, twenty-foot fall into the snow.

The side. Straight down.

Chapter 71

A fine day it may have been, but it wasn't my day to die.

I was in a white fog. Was I looking up or down? I didn't think I was dead. I didn't think I was back in restraints and under sedation in the Aurora Center, but it felt a bit like it; nothing seemed to work the right way.

Ah! Still four-legged. Okay, that makes more sense now.

My mind cleared and I could feel Alex's frantic searching through the Call. Unfortunately, all I could communicate was that I was alive. Our Call tingled with his relief and love.

He'd be going up the trail. There wasn't a direct route from there to wherever I was, other than the way I'd taken, and I wasn't going to recommend that.

I worked my way around until my muzzle popped out of the snow.

I was on a ledge with further to fall if I wasn't careful.

I'd hit a bank of snowdrift at about sixty feet, started a small avalanche and been carried down with it.

Noble was bigger and had been traveling faster. He'd fallen further. There was no sign of him, but there was a huge fantail of disturbed snow below me, a much bigger avalanche than I'd caused. He could be anywhere under that.

His real problem was he was so much heavier than me. The old problem of the difference between a cat falling twenty feet and a cow falling the same. Splat. With any luck he'd broken his neck, but snow is tricky to predict. I wasn't going to be happy until I'd seen his dead body, but in the meantime, there was something more urgent.

Emily.

I scrabbled along the ledge, working my way toward the back of the mountain, behind the cabin which was now well ablaze.

Hana and I relaxed. It was easier to let my wolf's instincts feel out a way, sometimes burrowing into a mound, sometimes stepping tentatively out onto the gleaming slope. Left to their own devices, my big paws were sensitive to every nuance of weight and shifting in the snow. Despite a few heart-stopping moments, we quickly got to the edge of the steepest section and then slithered carefully down toward the base.

There were no more shots, but I could hear movements coming from the pine woods ahead.

Alex was above me. I caught a pulse from him as he saw me slinking toward the trees and I could feel him edging out over the lip and starting to work his way down. I could feel the tension in his body, his focus on the feeling through his paws.

The Call was like a sweet shot of brandy, spreading its warmth through my body. We were hunting together.

Another shot. There was a cry and a heavy body thrashed through the brush below.

There were Nagas, out there in the pines below me. They'd come here— *my* territory, my wolf said—and they wanted to harm my friends.

Kill.

I felt the anger rising again, my vision locking down; I felt the strength of the Call flooding into me and began to creep down with more urgency. I needed to taste the intruder's lifeblood.

Kill.

"Amber." A high voice rang out below me. A voice I knew. I had to stop.

She broke away from the pines.

She was scrabbling on the rock, trying to climb back up to the top where she must have seen me before Gray rescued her from the cabin. Something had happened in the dark forest below and she was returning to where she knew she'd be safe. She was looking for me.

Except I wasn't there. And what she was climbing toward wasn't me. It was a wolf.

Stop, I tried to yell. The wolf's throat wasn't made for that sound.

Change. Help, Hana.

Nothing. The wolf was ascendant. It was the utmost I could do to hold still. My body was quivering with a need to kill. I'd drunk too deeply of the Call.

Some noise must have escaped me. Emily stopped looking over her shoulder and instead she looked up the slope.

She froze.

Don't run, Emily, please don't run.

But she did, and that broke the little control I had over the wolf.

Prey! Kill!

It was all I could manage to slow myself down. My wolf was about to launch herself forward just at the moment I was hit by a hard-centered avalanche from behind.

Everything crashed down the slope, tumbling and turning, snow exploding out in all directions until we hit the first of the trees and I bounced off the stiff branches, landing upside down.

All the snow in the tree shook loose and fell on me in one huge, freezing dump.

I thrashed around wildly, trying to get purchase.

The growl from above me stamped down on my chest with an almost physical force.

The wind scoured the snow clear and I was looking up at Alex's bared fangs.

Fate has a way of turning around and handing you your ass when you least expect it, and always in the way you least expect it.

It didn't matter a damn what our positions were elsewhere. As an Athanate, I was House Farrell and Alex was my kin. As a pack, on two legs, I was the alpha. That didn't make any difference here. On four legs, Alex was my alpha. I could barely breathe, he was so dominant.

With all my attention fixed on my lord and master, I barely noticed, but my berserk wolf had evaporated. Control and sense had returned.

That's what the right alpha does.

I peeked up at him.

Some mistake, surely?

No. No mistake. I whined in submission and dropped my eyes.

He took a step back and I rolled upright, keeping my head and tail low to the snow.

The shock of what I'd been about to do as a wolf flooded into me, and immediately, the Call seemed to press down on the feeling and rob it of its strength. There were no words in the Call, but I could sense Alex telling me that it wouldn't happen again now.

And the whole world felt different. Instead of all my energy spilling out and fighting in different directions, I felt calm and focused.

That's what the right alpha does.

In the cover of the trees, about forty yards away, Gray emerged, blood trailing down the side of his face and an MP5 slung around his neck.

He swooped down on a sobbing Emily and picked her up.

"Okay, my girl," he said. "The men are gone. Time for us to go too."

"Wolves," she stammered tearfully, peering around him.

"Friends," he replied.

He looked up at us, his eyes missing nothing. He nodded and then tilted his head back downhill. We understood. There were more Nagas for him to get past down below. We needed to help. Then he turned and dived into the shadows of the pine forest, Emily clinging to his back.

Alex and I wavered. As wolves, we could flank Gray like scouts, but we had no method of warning him about Nagas other than howling. Not a safe option. If we changed back and could get back to the ranch, at least we would have weapons.

Up at the cabin, there was a snowmobile.

We climbed in wolf form. It was steep, but not a technical climb, and both of us felt that four legs were better than two.

Once Gray had disappeared, the forest behind us was silent. As we approached the summit, we heard the noise of gunfire from the trail, a chopped-off scream and more gunfire.

Wrong direction for Gray, too close for Ursula. That meant Noble was alive and fighting Nagas.

As it turned out, we made the summit at the same time he did.

I was shocked all over again at how big he was. He hadn't been badly injured in the fall, but his side was streaked with blood. A bullet wound. There was no difficulty in seeing how he'd responded. His muzzle was slick with blood.

As soon as he saw me, he attacked.

I couldn't push him over the edge; he wouldn't fall for the same trick twice, but we didn't need that. Two wolves are better than one.

Alex and I split and circled, darting aside as he feinted a rush, one way then the other.

Whatever his lack of capability as a fighter, Noble was cunning. He could guess that Alex was more tired than I was. While I had walked up the trail from the ranch, Alex had been forging a path through the snow. When I had fought Noble, Alex had run to help me. However good his stamina, it would all be taking its toll. Noble was probably also thinking that with Alex out of the way, I would be an easier target.

He quit the feints and launched himself at Alex.

They vanished into a snarling, spinning ball of fur and fang. Keeping it like that was Noble's best tactic, because I couldn't interfere without risking getting in Alex's way. I wasn't sure it was due to any judgment on his part though; the slightest hesitation and Alex would be on him.

They kept rolling, each trying to find an opening for a strike against an unprotected throat.

I felt Hana's control leaking back into my limbs. She might have the confidence to attack where I didn't.

And at the edge of my awareness, there was someone running up the trail. I doubt that Alex or Noble heard them. It could only be a Naga.

Time to do something.

I dived forward at the twisting forms. Alex sensed me. He slowed, inviting attack. Noble took the bait. His teeth sank into Alex and for a fraction of a second his body was still and his back was to me. I lunged and closed my jaws around his neck.

It was too early for that fleeting sense of victory I felt. Noble's neck was massively muscled and his whole body reacted to the danger, whipping me around as he tried to dislodge me or get a bite on a limb.

The good part was he had to let go of Alex to do that. Alex came straight back in, missing the throat, but getting his teeth into Noble's face.

Noble outweighed either of us, but not both together. He had to try and end this quickly. He was still more powerful than we were, and he ignored me for a moment to concentrate on slamming Alex against the ground like a rag doll. Alex rolled away, ripping a huge section of Noble's skin and fur off the side of his face as he did.

I just bit harder. There was blood leaking over my muzzle and into my mouth now, and nothing he could do that would make me let go. Other than die.

Noble tried to lift and twist to get his jaws on me.

And the Naga that came over the lip of the trail fired twice.

The rounds were soft-nosed. They went through Noble, deforming as they struck, spreading out and tearing an ever-increasing hole through his abdomen, breaking through his back and punching me in the belly. The metal was so spread out it didn't pierce my skin, but it felt like a horse had just kicked me.

My jaws spasmed and my head jerked.

I heard Alex's howl and another shot.

I felt the break. It was such a subtle thing, a click rather than a crack, as my teeth bore down on Noble's spinal column and suddenly severed it.

The effect was immediate. He lost control of that huge body.

I sensed Noble's mind reaching out with disbelief. The feeling of inhuman nothingness crumbled. Hate and anger poured out like a ruptured dam. Then fear: a massive tide of cold fear sweeping up through his mind as his vision darkened.

I felt the presence of many, but it was just two faces I saw: Melissa and Barbara Green. I wrenched my jaws in the opposite direction, satisfied as the flesh tore. And then I let go, scrabbling to get free from the hulk of his twitching body.

I howled.

A marker. No exultation. No triumph. A crushing sorrow, for all his victims.

It was done; he was dead, at last.

Alex's wolf joined me, leaving the Naga where he'd fallen.

But Alex was wounded. Blood was running down his flanks, wounds from Noble's teeth and a bullet.

Change. Damn it. Change now!

The world wobbled. I slumped forward, human again, clumsy with arms and legs going in the wrong direction.

"Alex," I croaked as I swayed upright. "Change."

He did, and it looked worse on his human form. He knelt exhausted in the packed and bloodied snow.

I spat and wiped the gore from our faces.

"It's all right," he mumbled.

"I'll tell you when it's all right," I replied, and gore or not, I kissed him.

The strongbox heaved, but it remained closed.

The sensations of eukori distracted me, but I concentrated on sensing his body, feeling the injuries. Nothing life-threatening, and I felt as if I was going to float away in relief. There was a lot of damage though. Ribs broken, muscles torn, bleeding inside.

I couldn't fix it all. The bleeding I could stop. I didn't have Bian's abilities, but instinct guided me and veins began to close and heal. I could do nothing for the ribs; they'd have to heal by themselves and until then, they'd be painful. The muscles were somewhere in between—healing, but slowly.

After ten minutes I rocked back onto my heels. We were both shivering.

"Change back," I suggested.

He shook his head. "Not a good idea when you're injured. It takes a lot out of you. More chance to open something that's partway healed."

"Then we're going to have to borrow clothes for you."

Noble's coveralls were still there, and the Naga's snow parka and boots completed a strange ensemble.

While he was dressing, I trotted the short way down the trail where my clothes and backpack had been abandoned.

By the time I got back, Alex was listening to the Nagas' comms system and frowning.

"It's chaos," he said. "I think they had some helicopters due in, but they've been grounded. They still have people on the mountain, but no command structure."

"I've got to get down and help Gray and Ursula. You can't help me there in your state."

I pulled my gear from the backpack and continued dressing while I spoke. We moved to the back of the burning cabin, the chewed-off part of the mountain stretching down below us, full of rocks and edges.

"I'll shift Noble's body down on the skimobile somehow," he said. "We can't leave it up here."

"The pack could always come up and get it."

He nodded, but I could see he was going to be stubborn on this.

"We good?" he asked tentatively.

Are we good that I'm alpha on four legs, he meant. It was freaky how it flipped with our forms, but I guess normal wasn't ever going to apply to us.

"We're better than good." I zipped up and hugged him close. "You saved me."

He tried to quiet me, but I went on.

"I couldn't have lived with myself if I'd killed Emily."

It wasn't just that. I couldn't put it into words yet. It felt right. He would look after me as a wolf. With Diana's help I'd fix my Athanate. It worked. It gave me back the hope that'd leaked out over the last few days.

I wanted nothing more than to feel his arms around me, but the sun was touching the mountaintops. What I had to do was getting more dangerous all the time.

"What we have works, Alex. I can live with weird. We all make sacrifices."

He snorted. "As long as we don't die by it."

"If it's my time, it's still a fine day to die."

He grabbed my face. "Don't go fey on me. You're going to live. We're going to live. Promise me."

Tears froze on my cheeks. I wouldn't make promises I couldn't keep. Instead, I kissed him hard.

"I love you," I said.

Then I turned away, and telling myself this was positively the last time today, I threw myself off the cliff at the rocks below.

Chapter 72

You're not flying, you're falling. Never forget that.

The wind screamed my old Ops 4-10 instructor's words as I braced the batsuit and hurtled down the mountain.

Alex had questioned my reasons for bringing the suit. My answer had been *because sometimes you need to get down a mountain quickly.* There wasn't a quicker way. Base jumpers did it all the time. Of course, they had the advantage of studying the mountain first. I didn't have that luxury.

My team was too spread out, too weak. Ursula was too high up; she'd have Nagas all around her in the forest. Gray was hampered by having to protect Emily. But what the Nagas wouldn't be expecting was someone as well trained as they were coming up behind them. That was my assignment, and I was going to make it count.

If I could get down in time and in one piece.

My options were as stark and balanced as a mathematical equation. I could pop the parachute right now, or keep going, using the batsuit to angle my fall.

With the chute open, I'd still get down quickly and I'd be able to guide myself pretty much anywhere I wanted to go. I'd also be a slow-moving target silhouetted against the darkening sky for any Naga who wanted to shoot.

With the batsuit, they probably wouldn't even notice me, and if they did, they'd never have time to shoot. I'd pop the chute only to slow down at the last possible minute—as the Ops 4-10 slang suggested, use it like a brake.

Fine. Just so long as I could clear the next ridge of pines which was rushing up toward me like a barricade of dark knives. Anything can be lethal if you hit it hard enough. My stomach knotted and I fought to keep myself spread-eagled when what I wanted to do was to tuck up in a ball.

I forgot to breathe and my heart forgot to beat.

I got lucky again. A twitch to the right sent me through the smallest gap in the trees, and still, the slap of a branch against my toes almost sent me wheeling out of the sky.

By the time I'd gotten my heart working right again, I had my first view of the ranch. Still way over the pines.

Coming down on trees? Broken ground? Doesn't matter. Never try and stretch the glide. Pick the least worst place. Concentrate on getting down in one piece.

More good advice from my instructor that I was going to have to ignore; there were Nagas down near the ranch and I wouldn't have a weapon until I retrieved mine from the cemetery.

The instructor was right.

With the sun down behind the mountain now, distances became hard to judge and I got it wrong. The angle wasn't good enough and I should have deployed the chute sooner.

There are a couple of ways I could get to the cemetery, I thought as I crashed through the tops of the last few pines, my chute slowing me just enough.

One of them was to be carried in a pinewood coffin.

When the world stopped tumbling, I was barely six feet off the ground and the chute was wrapped around one of the tallest trees. I'd made it with nothing more than scratches and bruises.

I hit the release and dropped into the snow.

There were Nagas coming to find out what the noise was. The snow had drifted chest high in the cleared area and I had to run in slow motion, wading through it to get to the curving shield of the yew trees.

I could hear their cautious, crunching footsteps in the darkness as I knelt by my cache and dug down. I felt the shape of the bag. My fingers were becoming more and more numb with the cold, till they were clumsy as hooves. I'd forgotten gloves. Stupid. Stupid. And the zipper was frozen as well.

The first one came around the side, about fifty feet from me, pointing a gun in front of him. He couldn't see clearly, and was quite rightly unwilling to make himself a target by shining a flashlight. He could just about see the chute moving in the wind, and that kept his attention.

With my wolf eyes, I could see him easily enough.

I got the zipper open, one link at a time.

A second Naga came around the other side. A third slightly behind him. All of them focused on the chute and the darkness under the pines. They were easing around the edges of the clearing. I had a few seconds before they realized what the chute was, and saw my trail in the snow.

My hands found the cold MP5 and I slid it out quietly, automatically checking the safety and single shot selection. I'd left it with the magazine in and the silencer attached.

Just in time. The first one stopped. He'd seen my tracks and started to swivel toward me.

Tap. Just one shot—no time for the triple hit routine. He was still falling when I fired at the other two. Tap, tap. The one unintentionally shielding the other. Tap.

Both hit. Falling. One screamed, the sound bubbling horribly with blood.

Back to the first. Tap, tap into his body.

Again on the others. Tap, tap.

I waited. No movement and no sound meant nothing yet.

Reaching behind me, I pulled the rest of my gear out of the bag. My harness, the comforting bulk of the HK Mk 23 in a holster, a knife, a couple of grenades and some spare ammunition. The Colonel's TacNet system. Not exactly as much as I wanted going up against an unknown number of Nagas, but as much as I was going to get.

There was still no movement from the Nagas. I took a chance and quickly unzipped the batsuit, dropped it and hurriedly shrugged the harness into place. Then I crept over to the bodies, keeping low to the ground and scanning in every direction.

There was nothing to see, other than darkness in the snow and a few wisps of steam coming off the blood. Nothing to hear but the lament of the wind. And nothing to smell but death.

I couldn't see their faces, to my relief. Even Nagas are people, and I have enough to haunt my nightmares already.

I checked for pulses without success, took their ammunition and hid their weapons beneath a tree.

Then I started running. Gray would be making for the ranch, coming down the mountain in a curve. We'd had enough time on the drive out here to look at a map and get a feel for the layout of the ground and the possible routes down.

I switched the TacNet on now. There was a risk that a base system could get an ID and location on me, but the comms talk suggested the Nagas on the mountain had lost contact with command. I flicked through the channels and found encrypted conversation on one. I tried the standard encryption option that the Naga at the top of the mountain had set on his comms system, and it gave me an entry. They weren't skipping between options. Sloppy work, but I wasn't complaining. And the Nagas didn't have the comms discipline of Ops 4-10. This group was getting seriously twitchy.

"Fox One-Zero-Zero, this is Fox One-Two-Zero. Still no contact Groups Lima and Kilo."

"Shit," someone swore into an open mike.

"Shut up," a voice with authority said. Sounded like a sergeant to me. "Fox One-Zero-Five, update."

Silence.

"Fox One-Zero-Five? Fox One-One-Seven?"

The one who'd sworn spoke again. "They're behind us, Sarge. They're at the ranch."

"Shut up!"

The Naga sergeant was getting rattled. His command circuit had gone silent. Teams on the mountain had disappeared. I assumed that's who Kilo and Lima were.

I had no idea what experience his troops had, but I knew the feeling of being out in the cold and dark, alone against an enemy that seemed more powerful with every passing minute. An open comms policy meant they all knew their promised extraction team wasn't coming. Now they had someone behind them.

Give it up now. Go home.

"Fox One-Zero-Zero, this is Fox One-Three-Zero. I have contact with vehicles turning off Route 85. Eighteen vehicles. That is One-Eight vehicles."

The pack was coming back, but with the state of the road, it could take them anything up to an hour to get here.

Another few seconds of weighing the odds, then I heard the sergeant again.

"Fox One-Three-Zero and Fox One-Two-Zero, Fox teams West and North, clear to proceed to alternate extraction point three. Report passing Fox team East."

"What about us?"

"If you don't can it, Fredricks, I'll fucking plug you myself."

Silence.

The sergeant was staying put at the moment, but he was having trouble controlling his own team, let alone any others. Fox team South would be the nearest to the ranch, on the south side. That'd be where he was. I'd guess that Fox team East was being left in place to cover the route to extraction point three. There was a road out there on the east side and they probably had trucks waiting. It was a retreat, but an orderly one. Much more orderly than I'd like.

I slowed down. I didn't dare run straight into them, and although there'd been nothing on the comms, I'd bet long odds that the sergeant had turned some of his team around to make sure they'd see anyone coming up behind them.

Things were still in my favor. If they'd had their normal mission preparation, I'm sure they'd have included IR scopes, but life had gotten more rushed for the Nagas recently. It was likely that they couldn't see in the dark, but I could.

I spotted their outlying scouts ten minutes after the TacNet went quiet, and I just made it in time—there was a call on the TacNet about movement up the slope. That had to be Gray or Ursula.

I drew a bead on the nearest scout.

Everything seemed to happen at once.

There was gunfire over to my right. Without thinking about it, I used it to mask the quiet sound of shots with my silenced MP5. One down and one missed—the second scout had jerked his head around to see what was happening behind him.

Gray broke cover, fired two more quick shots down at the Nagas and disappeared.

What the hell was that about? A diversion?

Gray and Ursula must have joined forces.

The problem was, the Nagas were alert. No one chased Gray. But the scout I'd missed reported the direction of my incoming fire accurately and I saw movement on my flanks.

If I got surrounded, it was all over. I moved back as quickly as I could without exposing myself, trying to outflank their flankers.

There were more shots from above, but they weren't aimed at me. It couldn't tell if that was Gray firing or the Nagas.

Damn!

What was going on? If Gray was firing, I was sure he didn't have Emily with him. Ursula must have Emily. That meant this had been a diversion for her to get past. Had Gray's appearance done enough? Or had my attack ruined their plan?

This was the old familiar fog of war, and it forced me from the strategic goal of getting Emily safely away, back to the basic tactic of making sure I wasn't captured. What I wouldn't have given for Julie and a couple more like her with me.

I wasn't sure how stretched out the Nagas' line was. Maybe I could get past them. I slipped down a bank and started making my way up to the left.

Almost immediately I stopped and eased into cover. There were the stealthy sounds of someone moving quietly ahead of me. I'd been flanked already. Their line must have been longer than I thought.

I still had the edge. With my wolf eyes, I could see the warmth of their bodies and they couldn't see me. I hoped.

I held my position and felt my concentration flow down into the MP5, along that matte black barrel and out into the cold night. All I needed was a smudge of body heat to cross in front of me and I had one dead Naga.

Then I could hear a second person, a third, a fourth. Little squeaks of snow underfoot. Sighs as their passing brushed snow off the pines. Breathing.

And I could feel the Call.

Not Alex. Ursula.

I took the pressure off the trigger.

Ursula could sense me too, but I couldn't tell her that there were three Nagas closing in on her. She had wolf senses as well, so maybe I didn't need to tell her. I crept sideways, feet coming down softly, toe first, side first, like a cat's paws, soundless.

Where's Emily?

I could see glimpses of the pursuers, ruddy faces and hands seeming to float from tree to tree in the dark, puffs of hot air streaming behind them as they breathed through open mouths, heads turning back and forth, always searching.

Ursula was to my left. Once I got a good look, her size was unmistakable. Her bulky shadow was misshapen—she was carrying Emily. She was moving the quietest, but that meant she was the slowest as well. They were gradually gaining on her.

The trees were thick and her trackers were still spaced out. I couldn't get a shot at more than one at a time and as soon as I did, the flare from my gun would give away my position.

More movement, behind the last Naga. The big blur of several people close together. Too close together; what did they think they were doing?

Too many, though. I had to make them chase me and give Ursula a chance of escape.

As soon as I came to that decision, I put it into action.

I dropped the first Naga. Single shot to the head. Lined up the second.

They were turning. *Not* toward me; to face something behind them.

Shit! Huge! Kodiak bear!

No wonder the Nagas turned that way.

With a roar that seemed to reach down and liquefy the air in my lungs, the bear emerged from the darkness like a shaggy locomotive and struck before the Nagas had even finished swinging around.

The closest Naga was simply tossed aside, with his whole chest caved in.

I hit the other one with a single round as he fired at the bear, and then a massive paw shattered his skull and it was over.

No more Nagas following. The blur I'd seen was the Kodiak.

Even for a Kodiak, he was freaking enormous—a thousand pounds or more. He made a big target and he'd been hit a couple of times in the side, but that hadn't slowed him down.

Would the wounds piss him off?

It was Gray, wasn't it?

He slid to a stop and stretched up on his hind legs to over twice my height, then thumped back down on all fours, spraying snow in all directions.

Freaking hell.

A head that was bigger than my chest swiveled to look at me and his mouth opened.

Yeah, I could fit my head in there, but I wasn't going to.

I really, *really* hoped it was Gray.

I slapped him on the shoulder.

"Go," I said, pointing down to ranch. "Take the lead. I'll make sure no more are following."

I caught a hint of Ursula, still moving through the trees, concentrating on her task and trusting Gray and me to get on with ours. The woman was good. Kodiak-Gray lumbered down to overtake, and they all picked up speed.

Good.

I turned my attention back upslope.

The Naga sergeant had had enough. The TacNet bubbled with terse Fox team South calls as they leapfrogged in alternating groups towards the east rendezvous.

Bug out, boys and girls.

That didn't mean there wasn't someone assigned to come after us, but the forest upslope remained still as I went through my own 'run and pause' routine.

The TacNet buzzed me with an emergency communication tone. Not on the Nagas' frequency, on the frequency the colonel had set for us.

I tuned back in and reset the encryption options.

"Yes," I said shortly, crouching in the lee of a boulder and scanning the silent, black forest above me.

"Amber, it's Naryn. I've come downtown to help if I can. Update me, please."

I grunted a report in staccato sentences between bouts of running and listening for Nagas. He didn't interrupt, didn't ask for clarification of irrelevant details and grasped the urgent problems immediately. That didn't mean I wasn't going to be in trouble for everything that had gone on in the last few days, just that he wouldn't do it tonight.

This Naryn, I could work with.

"Get Ursula to bring Emily to me at once," he said.

"She's been through enough—"

"And this way, she won't remember any of it."

I felt my stomach sink. I'd known there would be a problem. Did it have to end with Emily being damaged?

"I have experience at this. It isn't as bad as you think." Naryn sensed my unwillingness. "Firstly, she's young, and they recover much more quickly and completely than adults. Secondly, her experience today has been extraordinary for her. These memories are so different from others that they're easier to pick out and erase. When I'm finished, she'll vaguely remember a day of backwoods snowboarding with you when she had a fall and banged her head."

"And Werner and Klara?"

"Just a simple blurring. No damage to any of them."

I bit my lip.

"On my Blood, I swear," he said.

I couldn't argue with that. "Okay."

The snowy forest remained quiet.

Enough. The Nagas were gone. I turned and ran as quickly as I could.

Back at the ranch, I hugged a shivering, bewildered Emily. I tried to comfort her while ignoring the guilt I felt. Eventually, Ursula and I got her into the Hill Bitch. I explained to Ursula what needed to be done and handed over the cell to call Naryn.

"I'll look out for her," she said, and drove them off.

It wasn't till she was gone that I wondered what this was going to look like to Felix. Ursula doing what I asked instead of meeting up with Felix's pack. I groaned quietly to myself. Another problem for Alex and me with Felix.

Where was Alex? He should have been down by now.

Gray was still in bear form, heading slowly back up the trail.

Was he too shy to change without his clothes? I smiled to myself. More likely, the wound was best left to start healing before he changed.

I trotted until I drew alongside.

"Thank you, Nick," I said.

The huge head swung around and I got the nerve-racking eyeball-to-eyeball with him, followed by a little huff, steaming in the cold air.

"I owe you, big time." I slapped his shoulder. "Now, I gotta go find Alex. Give me a lift up there on your back, will you?"

The head thumped me in the chest and set me on my butt in the snow.

He turned away and shambled off into the forest.

On my own feet then. It would have been so cool to hitch a ride.

I found Alex about thirty minutes later.

There was no sign of the snowmobile. He was walking very slowly, dragging a travois he'd made from pine saplings and strips of what looked like the snowmobile's seat cover. Noble's corpse was lashed to it.

"Alex! What the hell?" I rushed to take the weight off him. He should have been lying in bed, not dragging a huge wolf corpse down a snowy mountain at night.

"Ran outta gas halfway. This? Gotta do it," he said. "Gotta show the pack. Come on, we'll share."

Chapter 73

An hour later, we had made our painful way down the trail and were within sight of the barn.

The sound of singing drifted across the snow. Half a dozen voices in a haunting *a cappella* tune that I hadn't heard before. Even if I hadn't already been cold, it would have made me shiver.

"For Kyle," Alex said in answer to my unspoken question.

A figure was walking up the trail toward us. It gradually resolved into Duane, Felix's nephew. The shotgun was holstered and slung over his back.

"Give you a hand there," he muttered, and managed to move Alex out of the harness.

"Thanks," I said.

He grunted. "Difficult times. You sure need the help."

We took several steps without saying anything, the squeaking and scratching from pulling the travois in the snow complementing the eerie song from the barn.

"Rogue?" Duane said.

I nodded.

"Heavy bastard."

I wondered what it took to faze Duane.

He didn't speak again until we were right in front of the barn. The singing had stopped and it was quiet. Even the wind had eased off.

"Do you enjoy being Were?" he said, lowering his side. "Enjoy running the mountains?"

Huh?

Before I could think of an answer, the door started to open.

The pack knew we were there, of course. The Call didn't reliably give your location but it was accurate enough for them to know we were right outside. The door rolled back soundlessly, revealing the shadowy depths of the barn lit by hissing brass hurricane lamps hanging from rafters. The wooden floor had been swept clean of straw, and every inch of space was taken by the pack, except for a central aisle.

At the end of the aisle, Felix sat on his canvas camping chair. Ricky and Silas, in wolf form, sat on either side.

We were being greeted as an outsider pack. Felix had felt the new Call.

Alex took the harness back from Duane, and we pulled the travois into the barn. The door closed behind us.

As we dragged our burden the length of the barn I could feel the shock waves ripple through the pack. They could smell the marque. They knew this werewolf belonged to their pack, and yet they'd never seen it before. And they were all there, except for three: Olivia, Ursula and Noble. They knew who it had to be, all their preconceptions about size put aside.

Alex had been right. We needed this as an introduction, to get this confrontation off on the right foot. Or paw, or whatever.

The pack's Call was a tangible thing all around us, yet excluding us. It was like the first time I'd felt it, after chasing the Matlal Were through Commerce. I'd been part of it, then shut out. Now it seemed to be digging deep, tapping into the spirit of this place. Building a wall separating them from us. That wasn't so bad for me, but I felt it cut Alex deeply.

There was nothing to do but to use our own Call, marking us as different and distinct. And our eukori, which was subtle and deeper. I didn't think Felix's pack could feel our eukori and yet, it held echoes of the Call.

Denver is my place as well.

I didn't care if they could feel that attitude from me.

We reached Felix.

"Noble." Felix's one word carried the wound of betrayal for the whole pack. Not just the betrayal of the pack's spirit, but the evil he'd brought in. The pack lived as an entity. They shared the good, but they also had to share the bad. Noble had tainted their marque with his actions, and mixed with their grief over Kyle, the pack's emotions were running high. I tried to tell myself the smell of tinder was purely in my mind.

We had to convince the pack that we were allies, that we could stay in Denver and work together. The pack's will was focused through Felix. He was the key.

Alex and I shifted the weight from our aching shoulders and let the travois thump down where it was. The rogue's huge mouth was open in a dying snarl, pointed at Felix.

We took a couple of steps back.

The Call was like another weight pressing down on me, even heavier than Noble's corpse.

"One threat to the pack replaced with another," Felix said, his eyes going from Noble's body to Alex and me.

"No!" I said. Immediately, I felt Alex's gentle tug through the eukori, calming me down. "We didn't replace this threat, we eliminated it."

"And the soldiers on our land?"

"Dead or gone."

Felix grunted. "In the meantime, you've formed a new pack with Alexander."

"And sent the surviving Matlal Were and the Confederation back up to Wyoming."

"Yes, congratulations." Felix waved it away, dismissing it. "Your new pack is a threat. We do not share territory." He stood abruptly and started to pace. "We've spoken before, Amber, and the options open to us are fewer now."

I caught a glimpse out of the corner of my eye of some of the pack changing. A corner of my mind wondered if they found it easier to be in wolf form when the Call was running so strongly.

"Leave Denver," Felix said, "with our thanks for your efforts. Or stay, and we either fight you, or you make a challenge for leadership. Forming your own pack means you can't join this pack."

The air hummed with the Call. It shimmered in the air like a desert mirage, liquid, changing with every word spoken, every movement made.

We hadn't backed down. We were an alpha pair. If we wanted Denver, why didn't we take it? Felix couldn't stand against both of us if we challenged. The pack accepted that challenges weren't fair fights.

I shuddered and screwed my eyes tight shut, trying to block out the thoughts that the Call was whispering in my head.

"Wait," I said. "Why are we a threat? Why can't we share territory? Are we animals? Is there a shortage of some resource?"

The Call didn't like that.

Too much like a lawyer. It's about feeling, not thinking.

"There's a shortage of one resource, yes," Felix said. "Pack members."

Alex. Olivia. Probably Ursula as far as Felix was concerned.

The silent growl that I felt in my chest built up around me. I tried to ignore it all.

Why was Felix provoking us? Had I misunderstood something he'd said about the Call? He'd told me it was like the combined will of the pack and it could force us in certain directions, but he seemed to be positively pushing for a confrontation. He was deliberately setting the pack on me. What was I missing?

"Olivia wasn't a member of your pack. Alex is my mate. Ursula will make a decision of her own." I paused. "Not directly related to the pack."

Still too much talk.

Whatever he intended, Felix was losing control of them. I could feel the threat from all around. Alex edged closer to me, emphasizing his position.

It felt as if we were balanced on the edge of a blade.

The door opened and closed behind us, the cold wind reaching in.

I was completely focused on Felix, trying to see through the surface at what lay beneath, so I couldn't turn, but my nose told me anyway. David's footsteps clicked on the wooden floor.

The Call flowed over him and dismissed him. One more House Farrell wasn't going to make a difference to the outcome.

"Freaking hell, look at the size of that," David said, brushing past me, ignoring everything that was going on.

A flicker of irritation passed through me before I saw what he was really doing; bringing attention back to something everyone had almost forgotten. He knelt alongside the head and measured Noble's neck with his hands. "Some bite that was, to kill him."

But it was more than that; it was a double diversion. David hadn't ignored anything. He'd been aware of the crisis, probably even before he'd come in. In one simple movement, he'd gotten the pack looking at Noble's corpse and thinking what it'd taken to bring him down. But David was also on his knees right in front of me, and slung over his back was the holster for my BFG, with the handle sticking out the top, inches from my hand.

It was the Variable Choke Tactical Assault Weapon, to give it the official name: the ultimate shotgun, designed to clear whole rooms like this. Deadly against tightly packed enemy. Three of the supercharged rounds in the magazine.

I wondered how often I'd thought David was missing what was really happening and been wrong.

Felix was watching me.

I stretched my hand down and put my hand on David's shoulder, giving him a little pull backwards. I was going to do everything I could to avoid a fight. Defending myself would achieve nothing but weaken the pack. I'd rather die than let the Confederation take this territory, and that's what fighting would do.

Linked through our eukori, Alex hadn't missed the byplay. I felt the same gentle resolution from him.

Given what we'd done, it was still a fine day to die.

"Olivia. Like Kyle," Felix said, as if nothing had interrupted. "Trapped."

The Call tautened again, but with a tinge of sorrow.

"Unless I can do something," I said.

"You can't even change yourself yet. What do you think you could possibly do for Olivia in the short time she has left?"

Felix *knew*. He was bringing attention to it.

"Who do you think killed Noble?" Alex said.

A jolt of surprise ran through the pack. Attention went back to the wounds on Noble's neck. Hopefully no one noticed the gaping holes in his chest.

Felix seemed to be encouraging us to go on.

Why?

Through the eukori, I touched Alex's thoughts. No words, just feelings. Enough.

I'm not body shy at all. Still, shucking my clothes in front of the whole pack did feel a little kinky. It made me feel more vulnerable too, but Alex was right with me.

The pack thought we were preparing for a challenge. I hoped what I was doing was the only way left to avoid it. I hoped it was what Felix intended.

A profound silence fell.

I reached and tangled fingers with Alex. Then I thought of running four-foot through the silent, snowy forest with him; nothing but the sound of our footfalls mixing with our breath and the song of the wind.

It was easier already. I fell forward, limbs twisting, mouth stretching. My paws struck the floor and I pushed up to my full height.

Alex was bigger than before. Being the four-footed alpha, even for such a small pack as ours, worked its strange magic on him.

I would have chuckled, but it came out as a stifled sneeze.

What now?

I scanned the faces watching us. Their faces had taken the strange hard edges and soft glows that came with wolf eyes.

I'd proved I could change. I didn't think that had anything to do with whether I could help Olivia.

The Call crackled through Alex and me, much more vivid now. They were expecting a challenge. Seeing the pair of us, they were expecting Felix to lose.

If we didn't issue the challenge, we were just intruding and liable to be attacked.

Was he forcing us to challenge him? What was he trying to achieve? What did he want? Stability and security for the pack. Surely not at the expense of his own life?

Why not? said Tara. *What were you thinking when David offered the gun? You think Felix loves this territory any less? He'd rather die than let the Confederation in.*

I was so shocked I looked up and caught Felix's eyes.

There was little of the unthinking Call in his look, more of calculation. And hope.

This was worse than the Athanate Assembly. Skylur had been hampered by keeping Panethus in line and avoiding saying anything the Truth Sensors could identify as a lie.

Felix had to manage the whole pack through the Call. But he also had to remain true to the Call; otherwise he'd lose the pack anyway.

If he wasn't resigned to his fate, he was expecting me to understand something, and even more, to communicate it to the whole pack.

I brushed against Alex with eukori, reading him, trying to hold him back.

The Call began to press on us. I felt as if I couldn't get enough air in my lungs.

Challenge!

If I didn't get it, Felix *wanted* us to challenge him and take over. He'd put the pack ahead of his life. He'd put his life in my hands.

Noble talking: *The Were are all about spirit. About heart and feeling and emotion. They are enthused. The word means filled with a sense of the divine.*

I had moments to get it right, or Alex would challenge and I'd back him.

Was I enthused?

The Were had been a problem for me, threatening to drive my Athanate rogue, or threatening to go rogue because of my Athanate. I'd used it. The ability to change. Cool, huh? And Felix had been needling me the whole time. I'd been accidentally infused. Not my fault. Why couldn't they just accept it?

Wrong. Wrong. Wrong. The problem wasn't with Felix or the pack. The problem was in me. I was giving all the wrong signals. The things I'd suggested to the pack might work, but not while I was broadcasting a rejection of being Were.

A Were has to be whole-hearted, or be false.

Noble had managed to fake it. They wouldn't accept another fake.

What had Duane said? *Do you enjoy being Were? Running the mountain?*

Were belonged. I could feel the pack's roots in this land.

Did I belong like that?

I felt Alex tensing, readying himself. Felix had stopped in front of us. Committed. Waiting.

I thought about Bitter Hooks, wanting to run through the sacred woods by the light of the moon. I thought about the homesickness for Denver when I'd been away all over the world. The longing for the mountains, for home.

My feelings today. My love for this strange mountain. The forests above us that I'd flown over and fought in.

Our determination to keep the Confederation out. To expel the intruders.

And very quietly, the most profound sense of place unfolded inside me.

I thought of running with Alex, a whole day, a whole night, nothing but the vast wilderness around us, no tomorrows or yesterdays. Running for the joy of it.

Alex's love for the land. His eagerness to dig into its history and peoples.

Our shared grief for Hope, buried at Bitter Hooks.

All our feelings. All our joys. All our sorrows.

We belong here, we said.

We offered ourselves up to the Call, letting it shine through us like a searchlight.

It changed us, and we changed it.

Chapter 74

The three of us stumbled from the barn into the freezing night, blinded a bit in the eyes and a lot in the head.

The pack stayed behind.

Felix hadn't suddenly changed his mind about everything. The pack accepted that we were different and in Denver. We supported Felix. His dominance had grown from it. The pack liked that. They'd tasted our emotions, our love for the territory. And they respected that.

Exactly what that made us and how the relationship would develop, Felix had left for contemplation, as Ricky would have said.

He had invited us to return and stay at Coykuti. I found myself looking forward to it.

It was like my dad had once said to me. *Break bread over a disagreement— lots of times, if you have to. There's not many arguments that don't wear down with use.*

It was enough for me, for now, and more than enough for Alex.

For all the bravado and projecting that we were more than a match for Felix, changing twice had re-opened Alex's injuries. He was still too proud to allow David to help, but I propped him up under the guise of walking with my arm around him.

David had parked the Hill Bitch close, thank the stars.

Duane was standing next to it.

As we came up, he kicked one of the oversized tires. "I see you listened," he drawled. Whether he was talking about tires or how to communicate with the pack, who knew?

"Yeah. G'night, Duane."

"G'night." He wandered back toward the barn, whistling an old tune.

David updated me while I got Alex comfortable in the back.

He'd gotten back from Fort Collins as soon as the roads opened. He'd passed by Manassah and the Kwan to check everything.

A small group of Nagas had attacked the Kwan. None had survived.

The FBI had grounded the helicopters that were intended to come out and airlift the Nagas on the mountain.

Petersen and the rest of his cronies in command had fled the country.

David had joined Ursula, Emily and Naryn and they'd swapped cars to allow him to come back out here while Emily was taken home.

I got in with Alex and worked some more Athanate healing on him. Nothing to do with enjoying it at all. The strongbox rattled but subsided. Even if I had to ask Kaothos to come over and sit on that damned strongbox, I was going to find a way to comfort my kin.

"I can understand that you didn't want the gun," David said, interrupting me. "But you've got a list of all the pack members. You could have used that to force them to make you a concession."

"I could, I guess," I said. "Not the best way to start a relationship, though. Besides, I gave Felix my oath that I wouldn't use it except for the pack's benefit. He knows I wouldn't have gone through with any threat."

"The pack doesn't, though. I got the feeling he was kinda playing it to achieve a result."

"Hmm."

There was no doubt about it. Felix had spent a long time running this pack, which was exactly the reason he needed to be the one to keep running it. In that time, he'd probably learned all there was to working with the Call for the good of the pack. I doubted he'd planned it from the start, but I'd definitely been maneuvered at that meeting, and skillfully, too.

And if Felix was doing that to me without me being aware of it, what about Skylur? He was even older: more canny, more subtle, and much longer at the job.

Was I just a pawn between them?

What if they'd conspired to use me to set up an alliance between the pack and Altau? Here was me thinking it was my idea, and in fact they'd manipulated me into it.

No. I shuddered. Enough paranoia. Felix had put his life on the line, betting it would go the way it did.

"After I drop you off, I've got to collect Jen and the others at DIA." David interrupted my thoughts. "Where do you want to go?"

"Manassah," I said.

Alex stirred.

"My home," he said.

"No." I rested my hand on him. "We're going back to Manassah. There, you will rest in bed according to the instructions of your physician. That's me." I rubbed my hand lightly over his chest and kissed his forehead. "Jen will be coming back, and you are going to be looked after by both of us. Me *and* Jen."

He snorted, wincing as it hurt his ribs. "Can't you just find me another mutant Were monster to fight instead?"

Humor. Good. That was a start. I could work with that.

In fact, I'd probably need lots of it for the job. My kin were a problem, but what was the old joke? Ah, yes. *The sort of problem I like wrestling with.*

www.ingramcontent.com/pod-product-compliance
Lightning Source LLC
Chambersburg PA
CBHW030847030726
47495CB00005B/1417